the book of elsewhere

the book of elsewhere

a novel

Keanu Reeves
China Miéville

NEW YORK

Published in the United States by Del Rey, an imprint of Random House, a division of Penguin Random House LLC, New York.

DEL REY and the CIRCLE colophon are registered trademarks of Penguin Random House LLC.

This novel is based on the comic book series BRZRKR, published by BOOM! Studios.

LIBRARY OF CONGRESS CATALOGING-IN-PUBLICATION DATA
Names: Reeves, Keanu, author. | Miéville, China, author.
Title: The book of elsewhere : a novel / Keanu Reeves, China Miéville.
Description: First edition. | New York : Del Rey, 2024.
Identifiers: LCCN 2024013268 (print) | LCCN 2024013269 (ebook) |
    ISBN 9780593446591 (hardcover ; acid-free paper) |
    ISBN 9780593972434 (international ; acid-free paper) |
    ISBN 9780593875100 (deluxe) | ISBN 9780593446614 (ebook)
Subjects: LCGFT: Epic fiction. | Science fiction. | Fantasy fiction. | Novels.
Classification: LCC PS3618.E44545 B66 2024 (print) |
    LCC PS3618.E44545 (ebook) | DDC 813/.6—dc23/eng/20240325
    LC record available at https://lccn.loc.gov/2024013268
    LC ebook record available at https://lccn.loc.gov/2024013269

Printed in the United States of America on acid-free paper

randomhousebooks.com

1st Printing

First Edition

Illustrations by Sister Hyde
Endpaper illustrations (deluxe edition) by Daniel Mora Chaves
Book design by Elizabeth Rendfleisch

TO OUR MOTHERS,

for life, for storytelling . . . for love

And if the earthly no longer knows your name,
whisper to the silent earth: I'm flowing.
To the flashing water say: I am.

—Rainer Maria Rilke (Translated by Stephen Mitchell)

the book of elsewhere

PROLOGUE

A ROOM, FULL OF VIOLENCE TO COME. THEN WITH THE NASTY white light of LEDs. Then a man came in and sat between the metal lockers. He took a machine from his pack and ran protocols on it. Alone awhile, he stared at its screen. His comrades followed him in at last.

The man kept on with his preparations. All the other soldiers had their own rituals.

Two laughed together at dirty jokes. Two more in quiet focused synchrony checked their weapons. Another, shirtless, brisk, dropped and clap-push-upped at his comrades' feet. The leader of the night's enterprise came. He examined a map with such close attention it was as if he had found it in a tomb. The first soldier continued running diagnostics on his scanner.

Someone entered ready already, bulked up in an insignia-less khaki jacket zipped up to his chin as if it were cold. No one paid him attention. But as he cast his eyes around the room they caught those of the man with the scanner and the two nodded at each other.

The door sounded, a final time. This time everyone looked up at who stood at the threshold.

A tall lean figure in unmarked dark clothes, looking at them from below a long fringe of black hair. He stood still in silhouette.

Alone among his comrades, the man with the scanner stole a glance at one of those who had been preparing his weapon, while that man, in turn, regarded the new arrival, as did all the others.

The dark-haired man entered and that stillness broke and everyone went back to how it had been. The first man raised his scanner again, checking on its workings, took in the whole room in its scrying screen. He let it linger for another moment over he at whom he'd sneaked a look, switching his machine's registers, converting the soldiers into a landscape of colored contours.

In the corner the newcomer stood head down and alone. Someone approached him.

The man with the scanner frowned. It was not the unique vortex of darkness on the screen that made him hesitate: he had seen the dark-haired man so manifest many times before. It was the anomaly of he who approached him—the shorter soldier with his jacket done up tight. That jacket was white and opaque on the screen, as clothes should not be. It glowed. It was shielded.

"Hey," the deployer of the scanner said at what he saw on-screen. "Ulafson?" He watched as the soldier in the jacket tentatively approached the Unit's asset.

He was too far away to hear. He scrolled to an audio-capture setting to read the scanner's AI approximation of what it discerned from lip motions and the faint fringes of sound waves, but it could not get a clear reading.

The tall man turned to look at Ulafson approaching him and whispered as if beseeching. Ulafson held out his arms and came in fast, suddenly. His target regarded him without emotion. In came the would-be embracer, mouthing something, looking as if he was crying, and the man with the scanner said, "Hey!" again, loud enough now that everyone turned, and they all shouted too, and they saw the soldier in the done-up jacket pull a pistol from its pocket, and he was sobbing, you could see it now, and he aimed his weapon not at the figure toward whom he stumbled but out at the room, at everyone who now watched.

"Stay back!" he shouted.

The tall man with black hair reached out with his palm flat against the oncomer's chest, blocked his path. He did not punch, did not knock him down, just stopped him. The sad-faced target did not speak or move in any other way, only held the shorter man at arm's length as he strained to close the last distance.

The jacketed man shoved and grunted as the other held him off, and with his free hand unzipped his coat and reached into some inside pocket and there came a click and a glint of metal.

"Weapon!" someone shouted, as if he were not already holding a weapon, aiming it at them, at those alongside whom he'd killed and almost died. "Ulafson, no!" came another voice.

Gunshots. Very loud. Ulafson spasmed as the soldier with the rifle, at whom his comrade had glanced, braced, firing short bursts, face aghast, sending fire into the upper chest and thighs, avoiding whatever it was for which he reached, and Ulafson cried out under the onslaught and dropped his pistol but stayed standing, somehow, still shoving, fumbling, as bullets tore through and into his own target, who kept his face impassive as blood bloomed from him.

But he twitched, and his arm slipped. Those very bullets that were killing the jacketed man pushed him past his quarry's blocking arm at last, right up close, into a clinch. With a last breath of triumph he pushed a hidden trigger.

The room filled again, with smoke and metal and noise and fire.

THE FIRST MAN WHO HAD ENTERED THE ROOM WAS NOT THE VERY LAST OUT, but he stayed through the tough bloody business of the cleanup.

He had been a good distance from the blast zone, half-shielded by those whose remains he watched being scooped, tagged, collected with what shreds of respect could be afforded spatters. He had recited their names in his head. He did not know how many yet alive would not wake up. How many, like him, would be back in the field after a diligent pause. How many had trudged past him to wash their friends from themselves.

A hand on his shoulder. That comrade who had fired first.

"Coming?"

"I'll follow you," he said.

At the far end of the chamber stood the team leader, his map forgotten, his face calm under blood. He lit a cigar, adding its smoke to the stink of gunpowder and herbs.

Sitting on the bench, at the epicenter of the scorched star of red and black, was the dark-haired man the immolator had tried to take with him.

Above his lips his face looked serene and almost clean, shielded as it had been by his chin, which was now a ruin, jags of jawbone dripping gore and skin. He sat with his elbows on his thighs. The watcher glimpsed spine through the burned cave where the man's chest had been. Saw the motion of innards, like fish troubled by light.

He swiveled his scanner slightly, keeping his hand low, taking in the two. It was still on its audio-capture setting.

When the team leader spoke, words crossed the scanner's screen.

—You OK, son?

The seated man did not look up. He sighed out blood and moved that ragged mouth.

—Tired / Diet / [?] the watcher read.

—Jesus what a mess, came the other's words. —What was he fucking thinking?

His interlocutor shrugged. He reached under the overhang of his own torso meat and pulled something out of himself. Held it up.

—? Class / Glass / ?, the machine said he said.

—Yeah, the other said. —He was wrapped in bottles. Techs'll figure out what was in them.

—Four Thieves Vinegar, the machine had the ruined lips respond. —And holy water. Rock salt / sold [?] and the

nails are from horseshoes. And you can smell it. Sage.
He set off burning sage.

—What do you mean? How do you know?

—I know what salt and vinegar feel like in a wound.
Ulafson bagged / packed? the bomb full of charms. And,
Keever, that's not all.

The ruined, dark-haired figure passed over a tiny scrap of scorched
and bloody paper.

—That was under my ribs.

—I can't read it.

—It's a name.

He gestured around the room and continued.

— Most / nosed? went up but there are scraps. Names.
The names of the Unit's dead. The ones who got too
close.

The two men looked at each other awhile.

—I'm so tired, the seated man said. His scorched heart dripped.
—Of this. He gestured at the room. At himself. At last he looked up
and made an abrupt bubbling sound.

The older man said, "Are you laughing?" He said it loud enough
that the watcher did not need to read the words.

—It's the cigar, the other said, as the watcher looked back at
the screen. —Déjà vu.

The Doctor's Story

I DO NOT HAVE LONG. THESE WILL BE AMONG THE LAST WORDS I will write. This knowledge brings me sorrow. Not so much for my end: I am old enough. But for my pitiable state. When even a devoted dog, a creature able to love without the complications that color human affections, turns her face from me in distaste, disconsolation is natural. I know that what Lun reacts to is the smell of the medication for my jaw, but that is scant comfort. Her animadversion arouses in me shame, for all I might strive to disavow it, a sense that I am a transgressor, an abandoner, to provoke such reaction in her.

Sharper still than that immediate grief, of course, are my concerns for those of my family who have not—yet, I hope—been able to leave their homes. I cannot conceive of the darkness that engulfs Austria, and likely all Europe, being forced into retreat with alacrity.

The loci of my pain are not unlinked in my mind's obscure byways. Lun's inability to face me brought to me the visage of Dolf, among my sisters, averting her own gaze.

Pain will be with me until I take my final leave.

I do not know whom I hope shall find this note. Perhaps I shall consign it to the fire. But after nearly twenty years, I will finally commit these memories to paper. I have always used writing to learn what it is that I think. And I find myself disinclined to leave these mysteries unexamined. I would like to know what I think about this.

With death so close to me, and all about, how could I, who have found such import in the return of that which was buried, do other than revisit this particular visitation from my past?

My ruminations on Thanatos derive above all from the testimonials of those returned from the Great War. So many of their dreams were direct relivings of horrors. If the unconscious is above all driven to avoid unpleasure, whence came such repeated goings-back to agonies? My encounters with those wretches astonished me. But data are rarely adequate to change one's ideas. What is needed is a shock, a crisis all one's own.

I had a patient.

We met only three times. These were long sessions. He was a tall and dark and well-built man of middle years. He wore an expensive suit and met my eye and shook my hand firmly. I thought him a soldier. I thought him one of those returnees, doing an excellent job of covering recurrent nightmares.

He said to me he wished to understand himself.

I remember the first day very acutely. I remember sitting in the gray light of the morning, to one side of him as he lay on the couch, a notebook before me, listening as he spoke in his gentle, urgent voice, telling me a story of his life.

His first words in the session—I have my notes still, though I will destroy them soon—underlined my suspicions about what assailed him.

"I kill and kill and kill again," he said. "And the truth is, I would like to rest or, and, to do something other, other than kill that is, or at least to have the choice so to do, but no, the killing always comes back and overtakes me. And sometimes, not frequently but many times over the course of my life, I die. And it hurts. And it is a bloody business. And I feel every blow. Every cut through flesh. I feel the scorch and blast of every bomb.

"And then I come back.

"I return, and I kill and kill and kill again, and eventually I die again, and the whole merry-go-round continues. So please tell me, Herr Doktor," he said to me, "what sort of man am I?"

Now, I believed him to be describing one of those charnel dreams of which I'd heard so many. I understood him to be asking me, as I was then asking, why it was to such carnage that the unconscious returned. But that man I will not name raised himself up and turned his head to look directly at me, in a breach of the protocol that I en-courage, and I could not break his gaze. And he brought the first moment of that two-pronged Damascene shock that shattered all my paradigms.

"I come back," he said again, and in the calm timbre with which he made that ghastly claim, I knew that my earlier theories were inade-quate to deal with such existential and everyday horrors.

I still thought then that what he entrusted to me was an almost fabular truth. As indeed, among other things, it was.

But I saw that man see into me, see what I was thinking. He shook his head. And—kindly, as if mindful of my growing horror, and though I had not said a word—he said, "No, Herr Doktor. No. Or not only that. Everything means something else, it is true, but sometimes it also means precisely itself. Please listen to me. I am here to ask you, Why? What am I?"

He would not let me look away. And here came the second prong. I knew what he was going to say, and I knew the truth of it. I knew then that as well as symbolic, his declaration was literal. And I knew that I would not be the same man after that day. That I was haunted.

"I kill," he said to me, slow and implacable. "I die," he said. "I come back."

SIGNS OF LIFE

THE BUILDINGS LOWER TO EITHER SIDE OF THE WIDE AVENUE out from the center of the city, as if the sky is pressing down on the stubby towers and dusty light-bleached displays of cheap cakes and party supplies, rooms of repurposed furniture, the offices of photocopier servicers and failing notaries. A man—let's call him a man—walked this route. He considered that predatory sky. He did not shake his head—in this epoch he abjured most extraneous motions—but he blinked quickly, and if you had known him well you might have recognized in that a sign that his own fancies intrigued him.

He was a tall and solid man, and had those he passed observed him, most would have considered him white. He wore a gray bomber jacket and black jeans, and his dark hair gusted around his beard and downcast face. Far behind him: the mirror glass of banks and finance and rentier towers, façades of blocky white and off-white stone in vulgar mummery of some imagined Greece, faux obsidian, hotels named, sans serif, for characters from local fables unloved by dissidents.

By small parks the thoroughfare narrowed, overwatched by apartment buildings called graystones in the local tongue, for the brownstones of New York they faintly resembled. The sun was cool and very bright behind clouds, so the pedestrians that passed the traveler were announced or followed by long vague shadows. People sat on stoops by bodegas and bickered and played dice, ignored him. A priest smoked a sagging cigarette at the door to a corrugated-iron church. He nodded a wary greeting, to which the man responded in kind. Two boys sifting through metal trash at the gates of a reclamation yard paused at his approach. The man did not look at them and they whispered, their observations drowned out by the complaints of a car being crushed.

Boys, leave that man be. That man does not kill children anymore, when he can avoid doing so, but still, leave him alone.

The boys were shrewd, like the feral dogs that watched the man, and did not come close.

INTO THE CITY'S OUTERMOST KILOMETERS. WAREHOUSES AND HOUSING

projects, vacant lots used as car parks and meeting points for petty commerce. Through gaps in walls the man could see the dry grass-land of the country. He stood below a little figure in red LED swaying from the traffic light, absurd at an intersection between nothing and nothing. Hearing a siren, he waited at the curb. It was an ambulance, growing more distant, not the police.

When the green figure appeared the man crossed and went by an alley to a yard with sprawling two- and three-story buildings on all sides, graffitied and shored up by trash. Here was a wheelless and dust-coated Dacia underfringed by weeds and, at the other end of the space, by a closed garage door, the remains of a second, burned-out car.

He scanned the windows. He walked without hurrying to the ruin. It had rained hard the night before last but the stink of carbon and burned plastic was still strong. He took a key from a pocket, unlocked the padlock, and opened the metal door enough to enter, closed it behind himself, and bolted it from the inside.

A machine shop filled the ground floor. Band saws, hydraulic presses, a lathe surrounded by gleaming coiled flecks. A finger of gray light picked him out from high overhead, where dirty glass had been punched through by a bullet. The floor was a foul sastrugi of oil and dust, the clots a drabber black that he knew was blood. You would need specialized expertise to understand that these smears had been shaped deliberately, to obscure the story the spoor might tell. He had that knowledge, and he crossed to the tall cabinet of tools in the darkest part of the room. He pulled it away from the wall, uncovering a door. That, too, he unlocked. Behind it was a hidden ladder. He descended.

His feet touched down in blackness and he turned on his flashlight. The ceiling of a tunnel arched a handspan above his head, bare bulbs hanging at eye height, so you'd have to avert your eyes from their glare were every one not shot out.

He listened. Drips, faint syncopation. The whispers of settling earth.

The man walked, ducking the bulb glass. He turned with the hallway, left through a low threshold into a tiny chamber. He brought his flashlight up in an arc that made the cold mottles of the wall shine. His beam found and followed a path bullets had taken, holes stamped into the concrete underscored by dark sprays of blood across workbenches, the ruins of laptops, the bodies of three men fallen across each other in strange exactitude, their limbs fanned out like those of dancers posing.

He smelled causticity under the rot. With his booted right foot he turned over the topmost of the dead and did not stir to see the melted mess where once had been a face, teeth and nose bone and the ridges of the skull protruding from a crust where flesh had bubbled. He met the eyeless gaze.

"So," he said. His voice was gentle. He spoke not to the carcass but to the room itself. "What do you say?"

The room withheld. He had known it would. He put his fingers on the wreckage of the body but what secrets it had were not for him.

Back to the tunnel. A second chamber, empty weapons racks. He whispered to them too. A square room, very tall, faint light down from a hole like a drain above, all the way up into the day, the sky beyond a grill. He let the edges of light come down on him as if he were Bastet in her Luxor temple.

Overturned chairs, empty sockets, monitors on the walls, in the center of each a single shot. No computers left behind. Another, larger chamber. Double bunks: sleeping for ten people. Tins on shelves. A fridge, a microwave where two walls met, in the opposite corner a toilet and a shower nozzle over a drain. A rail around the showerhead leaned down floorward toward where a plastic curtain lay. A last door in the farthest wall of the room, lying aslant, torn from its hinges, on a slope of fallen dirt. Darkness beyond it, clotted with rubble.

The room had been made like a temple with an offering at its center, a head-height ziggurat of dead. Six men, three women. The man knew that number already; you could not tell from this crude architecture, a cone of limbs and dark clothes and the remains of faces tangled in the passionless orgy of a graveless mass grave. The dead's shadows crawled away from his light. Not even the posthumous recalcitrance, angular elbow or jutting knee, remained to this coagulation, softened in its outlines as it was by secondary flaccidity and gravity, its edges blurred by that corrosive disguiser of particularities. Amid set slime of flesh and belts and bergens, bone points and the stubs of broken weapons protruded like karst landscape.

The man sat at the table.

"What do you say?" he said. The room said nothing. "It would be nice to understand," he said. "At least."

He placed the flashlight so it illuminated the dead. He leaned on his elbows and clasped his hands. When he spoke again, if you had heard him you would not have known what it was he said, though you might have discerned the code shift, a slip from living to long-dead language, and you might have made out that every phrase he spoke was another question.

...

HOURS.

Sometimes he turned off his flashlight and sat in the company of the dark. Like the void before and under and after everything. Twice he circumnavigated the room, stepping through blood and spent casings and such. He stood at the entrance to that blocked-off tunnel and considered it awhile. He looked at each sleeping space but he did not lie down or feel under pillows for diaries or love letters. He knew that such searching had been done. He waited and whatever he hoped for did not come.

The man knew it was night when he heard footsteps from the tunnel.

He did not turn. He rested his flashlight on its base so the low ceiling glowed and he was underlit. The steps came right behind him, and stopped.

A voice came from the threshold.

"Hey, B."

"Hello, Keever," the man said.

The newcomer came to stand before him. A dense, muscular man, in nondescript clothes. He had close-cropped hair and a deeply lined dark face.

"Communing again?" Keever said.

"Your verb," said the man, "not mine."

"What's yours?"

B shook his head. "I don't have a verb," he said. "I can give you a noun. Not an English one. Toska."

"Sadness?" Keever said. "You're sad? That's what all this is about?"

"I didn't know you knew Russian," B said. "Anyway, I said toska: 'sadness' doesn't really get it."

Keever sat. His eyes went to the broken door and the crammed ruin and earth beyond. He looked then at the pile of dead.

"You want to talk about it, son?" Keever said. "It's not news to me that you've been blue. Don't tell me no you haven't. Ever since Ulafson."

B did not look up.

"Hey," Keever said. He pointed at the ragged hem of a hoodie amid the knoll. An unlikely orange, a commemorative garment for some pop group's tour. "I remember that. That fucker took a pop at me. That was the head honcho, wasn't it?"

"Blue,'" B said. "Huh. I'm not exactly sad. I think…curious is closer to it. I'm just…" He shook his head. "I'm just trying to hear whatever's there for me to hear."

"Are you even sure there's a message?" Keever said.

"No. How did you find me, Keever?"

"B. Come on. This is, what, the third time? You're not as mysterious as you think."

"I never said I was mysterious."

Keever glanced again at that discolored hoodie. B watched him and knew he was bringing to mind the meat smack of bullets, a pull, a headbutt, B's own.

"So here you are," said B.

Keever looked at him. At B's forehead, which had quite exploded the target's skull.

B and Keever were very used to silence.

Keever sat awhile in the cold silver of the flashlight. B took in the configurations of death with the exactitude of a scholar.

"What does it say to you?" Keever said at last.

B stared into the blackness beyond that last doorway, there under the earth.

"That's a good question," he said. "That's close, Keever. But that's not quite it." He gestured into the dark. "It's not that I can read it. If what we leave behind is a text, when we do what we do, it's not in any language I can read."

"And you can read them all."

"It's not even that I feel anything in particular," B said. "But I do feel like I ought to."

"You can't keep doing this, son," Keever said. "You know the score. Once we've done a sweep, whether it's cleared out or not, it's out of bounds. In, out, no trace. No ID, no flag marks, wiped off the databases, no fingerprints, spray the enzyme around, no faces . . ." He gestured at the cadaver pile. "Us or them. Now, what if someone clocks a dude like you wandering around? We can't risk you being seen."

"Or you," B said. "You're here, aren't you?"

"You didn't leave me any choice. I'm only here to wag my finger at you."

B stood and left the circle of light.

"Keever," he said, "what's the percentage in the Unit giving me orders?" He did not sound angry. "They know I'm not going to obey them unless I want to. In which case I'm not obeying, am I, and they're not orders. They know—you know—I don't care about what they care about. This is an arrangement of convenience and that's OK. But I don't understand why, given all that, they do this charade. Issuing 'orders.' Why they make you go through these motions. Telling me off."

Keever shrugged. "Hell if I know," he said.

"They'd rather have rules I don't care about," B said, "and that I break, than not have them at all. Insubordination's a lesser evil than independence, I guess."

"Like I say," Keever said. "I don't know. They say to me, 'Go tell B not to do that again,' and, unlike you, I do what I'm told. So here I am. Orders obeyed."

"And now what?" B said.

Keever pursed his lips.

"I don't know," he said. "I thought maybe you could use some company."

B pursed his lips too.

"I don't know if I can," he said. "Use it."

"Well," Keever said. "Like I say, here I am, wagging my finger." He did so. "I'll go report that Subject Unute declined to follow protocols again."

"You do that."

"Be cool," Keever said. He rose and slapped B gently on the

shoulder. B paid him no great attention. Only listened as Keever re-ceded. Alone, B placed his hand over the flashlight's bulb, and the room grew dark and his hand glowed.

He turned when he heard footsteps again, scant minutes thereaf-ter, moving much more quickly than before. He was facing the en-trance when Keever came back in.

"Message," Keever said. "Came through when I got aboveground."

"What is it?" B said.

Keever gestured at that last blocked-off doorway. The dark and the rubble.

"Base is getting . . ." He frowned. "They say they're getting a read. From one of Thakka's TTE scanners."

"What?"

"It's got to be a glitch," Keever said. "It's been cold since . . . you know. But they know I'm here and they know you're here . . ."

"And what are the odds of that?" B said.

". . . and they want us to check it."

"What exactly do they say they're getting?"

"Look, you know it's a basic signal, and it's pretty scrambled even when it's working . . ."

"What are they getting?"

Keever blinked. "Signs of life."

For a moment, B held his stare. Then he was at the doorway before Keever even saw him move. Crouched on the fallen door and thrust-ing his hands across the threshold and he was pulling and pushing at the ruined supports beyond and yanking the stone-flecked collapsed earth of the blocked-off tunnel and shoving his arms into it, in an un-settling parody of surgery.

"B, slow down," Keever said. "Look, you weren't . . . You were in your zone when it happened, but I'm telling you I saw it, it wasn't just the collapse. I saw . . ." He hesitated. "I saw Thakka check out. Him and Grayson both. They were gone. And the signal went out. That was when . . ."

Then, that was when. That had been when Keever, seeing those losses, had sent the grenade underarm right through B's braced legs, as B, dripping, broken rifle in one hand, broken rifleman in the other, breathing fast like a bull, had stood, he learned, with the darkness of the tunnel and Grayson's and Thakka's bodies beyond him. Keever's grenade had come down, bouncing toward the cell leader at the farthest end of that narrow exit tunnel. Last chance to get him. Making the tunnel a tomb.

"They were dead," Keever said. "Otherwise I would never. Whatever this read is that base is getting now, they were both dead. That's why I brought everything down."

Still, B dug. They both knew that those who gave Keever orders would have told him to collapse the tunnel on living comrades if it was necessary. From the tangle and the morass, he dragged a wooden erstwhile support and braced himself under weight that no other person could have lifted and the dust of it gusted around him. He let it fall.

"B, it's not stable . . ."

"Then get out."

Keever hesitated. Then he too reached for the metal and wood interlocked like spillikins beyond the threshold. He pulled and threw behind him what he dislodged.

"Easy," Keever said. But B shoved farther into the snarl of matter packing the tunnel and yanked and threw behind him back into the chamber handfuls of dirt and bricks and half bricks blackened with blood from his own hands, which he ignored. He burrowed without words and Keever dug too and minutes passed and the men did not slow though Keever's breath came ever louder. B tunneled and Keever did what he could to prop up the way B made. Keever paused at a crepitus of stone as pebbles and rebar came pattering down about him.

"Goddamnit, B. Some of us can die, you know."

Keever hunched and went crawling blindly into the dust and

gasped because when he tumbled forward, landing on all fours, he was beyond the blockade, crouched in the shadows and the spectral light of a glow stick in the tunnel beyond. Where stood B. Who gestured.

At the farthest limits of the phosphor glow, Keever saw a huddled dead man. The target, broken apart. The leader of this group of declared enemies, where they had killed him.

Keever's gaze came back along this last tunnel, over the roughened rubble crater and the scorch of his grenade, to another dead man, lying on his stomach. Grayson, where a bullet had hit his neck. Keever remembered that abrupt vision in muzzle flash. Grayson's arms and legs in a forever dive into death. Shadows and mold upon his skin, now.

There, a third figure.

Thakka. Slumped against a tunnel wall, his legs crumpled and his back against the concrete, his face twisted to face them, a hole cracking open one side of his head, his mouth bloodied and wide open, his eyes bloodied and wide open and looking at B and Keever.

His eyes moved. His lips moving.

Thakka blinked. Two days before, Keever had seen Thakka die. So, then he'd entombed the man's body with a grenade blast. Now Thakka's mouth formed words.

KEEVER HEARD HIS OWN CURSE.

He was by Thakka's side, he crouched by him, staring into those too-wide eyes.

"Thakka," he said. "Thakka, Thakka, man, Thakka. You hear me?"

B stood behind him, watching, poised as if to inflict violence. Keever held Thakka's head, trying not to touch the cavern in the man's flesh. He muttered to Thakka, meeting his eyes, had his hand on Thakka's neck, feeling a strong and lurching pulse. Thakka's skin was cold but you could feel the warmth of life within him, too, tremulous, tentative.

"My God, Thakka."

Thakka's lips kept moving but Keever heard nothing. It was only Thakka's lips and eyes that moved. His rifle lay across his lap.

"Look at me," Keever said.

Thakka looked. His eyes flitted so fast that Keever did not know if the man understood. His own stare went from Thakka's pupils to that off-center hole that changed the contours of his head, mesmerized Keever with the deeps of blood- and skull-rimmed hole.

"Hey!" Keever called. "B!"

B knelt, not looking at Keever or Thakka, putting his fingers into the dirt, bringing his face right down, centimeters over the floor, pulling another glow stick from his belt and breaking it and placing it close to his own eyes.

"What . . . ?" Keever said, but Thakka was gasping and you could hear now that it was not random exhalations, that these were words. He put his ear close to the dry lips.

" . . . came and said so," Thakka whispered. "Rooting right around. Right around. I had a dog so I knew."

"OK, Thakka," Keever said. "OK, son. Just sit tight." He felt in the stiff remnants of the man's uniform for the body scanner that had sent its plaintive, impossible little signal through the earth. "B," he called again.

But B had gone to the farthest part of the darkness, beyond the main enemy's remains, right to where the tunnel ended. He held on to stubs of metal in the wall, the same color as the darkness out of which they rose.

"Please, B," Keever said.

"What day is it?" Thakka said. Louder now. A calm midwestern voice. "Keever," he said. "It's cold, no? They don't care about you. No disrespect. They don't care about me, either."

B returned. Squatted down a ways away. "Thakka," he said. "What happened?"

"Oh," Thakka said. He grimaced and twitched at the sight of B and twisted his face away from him and it was a horrid thing to see, that expression on his face.

"What happened, Thakka?" B said.

Thakka licked his lips and shook his head. He kept his eyes on B and whined and whispered too low for B to hear. Keever lowered his ear to Thakka's mouth again.

"I have a dog," Thakka whispered. "My dog came by." A soundless chuckle. "Good boy. There are always questions," he whispered. "But no name no rank no number, right? Need to know."

Thakka's eyes were still on B and they grew wider than they should have been able to. The noise he made could have been from a crushed or punctured lung, or it could have been fear.

water

Y OU HAVE BEEN WALKING FOR A LONG TIME. YOU HAVE BEEN WALK-
ing for no time at all. Something and its opposite can both be true.

When you told Kaisheen that you had a journey to make she was
sorrowful and angry and she asked you not to go. Her child was only just
born and his eyes and mouth and the set of his expressions were still
imprecise as clay and Kaisheen said she did not know which of her husbands was the sperm giver, but the baby breathed and you knew it could
not be you. She said it might be (you did not explain why she was wrong)
and that would bring responsibilities, and she said it would be wrong to
deprive him of a parent. She said she did not want to be without you.

More than once you have tried cruelty and will surely do so again,
but for more than four hundred seasons you've been experimenting with
dispassion, and you calmly walked away from her pain.

If that boy still lives he is an old man, and perhaps his stories are of a
boy one of whose fathers left him. If he lives, almost the whole of his life
but for those first few days you have been on this journey.

Once you spent three lifetimes sitting without moving on a stone
chair halfway up a mountain, to see what would happen. Nothing happened.

This time you came south without urgency through vivid varied landscapes, avoiding small settlements, tracking through dense wetlands as humid as if the world itself were sweating, past frozen rivers, readying themselves to flow one day, to disappear, leaving stone behind.

Years ago you reached the shoreline and you knew that the place called Suhal was across the shallow sea. You sought and found the people of the estuary. They have strong jawlines, and they consider for a long time before they speak. They considered for a long time before they agreed to take you on their canoes, into the archipelago.

They declined your offers to row, according to norms of hospitality, so instead you were like a carved watcher at the front of a long vessel. Once, the second youngest of the crew fell overboard in a storm and you followed him in and brought him back up through the dark. Once, when the waves stilled against nature, the back of a great green beast surfaced an oar's length away and up reared a head both serpentine and crustaceous, mandibles tapping in hunger, and while the crew screamed and begged their dead for help and called the animal the name of whatever evil ocean deity they considered it, you stood on the yawing deck screaming too, but with relief, because it had been days since you had unclenched, released the cold fire that always grew within you, as you knew you must, and you let it out, and you saw through a haze of blue-white-blue that spread across your eyes, and you jumped from the canoe with your obsidian out and gouged the startled leviathan and you (must have) fought it and its teeth (must have) pierced you to give you that diminishing wound in your flank and the two of you (must have) turned the churning waves red and you (must have) killed it and cut out its tongue and let its body sink to be eaten by the tiniest creatures and you came back to the boat your ragefugue ebbing as you crawled slippery aboard again and the crew called you godkiller and thanked you and shunned you too and what you felt for them was compassion and you pretended that the drug they added to your meat at the next island was efficacious and you pretended not to wake, listened to them rouse themselves and gather their tools and charms and creep soundlessly, as they imagined, back to their boat, and you did not move while you heard their oars over the light waves.

Now you sit up, alone, in the bright and ruthless sun, when they are long out of sight. They have left you food and gourds of water.

Companionless, boatless, you walk again.

You slip down scree and you pack your clothes with as many stones as they will take.

You walk laden. Out of the low remnants of the trees, out from under the curiosity of bright birds, into the shallows, your feet cut by clamshells and wrapped as if in response by the gentle warmth of weeds. Into the surf. To the depth of your waist, your chest, your shoulders. Your neck. Your beard, your clamped-shut lips.

You take a long deep breath before the next step down onto this coral road between islands. The warm brine closes over your head and you stare through it into the sun and the sun stares at you and you tell yourself the stories of your life as down you go.

No you are not the oldest thing that has ever lived, of that you are confident. On some far-off continent there must be proliferating aspen trees all sharing one complex of roots, born perhaps the day before you were. There must be miles-long seagrass meadows all arisen from one ur-clot, ancient many lifetimes before you opened your eyes. But if there are in the world more older living things than you that you could count on both hands, you would be astounded. And it is close to a thousand years since you were last surprised.

Your mother said to you, You are a gift. You were a gift. She said, You have a gift.

She told you these things when you were young, though grown too quickly into a man's body and face. When she told you, you loved her, as you love her still, if you can love the dead, but then you loved her with a wordless and unquestioning fervor and without the subtleties of age or the suspicions that the world instills and she was, you know now, able to mask her own concerns and unhappinesses with some facility and you perfectly recall her saying I love you back. You can hear again the cadence of her pride. It was only several lifetimes after she died that, bringing to mind her face, you understood the emotion you recollected in her. That she was proud, but she was sorrowful for you, too. She admired you and she worried over how you were being admired, for what it would do to you. If she believed you gifted by gods, a gift to her and to her people, had she no less also thought you cursed? Her love for you: what did it do?

You have been descending long enough on this incline hauling your slate ballast that the churning plane where sea meets sky is as far above you as an oak tree's canopy is above a woman on a forest path. You watch the dappling of the sunlight with the sting and haze of submarine vision.

First, she said, there was Nothing. All at rest. Then came Something, to shake the Nothing out of its peace. Out of Something came Things in proliferation, noise and edges and motion, darkness and light and gloaming, rocks and stars and water and fire and cold. Out of them came muck and slime. Out of that came darting specks. Out of them after a while came trees and birds and us.

Here, now, they come, the press and pain in your chest, the surge of your blood, the drumbeats of your heart.

You spent seven years once with a steppes culture long since fallen. You submerged yourself in their sacred pools. For longer and longer every day. Such techniques stay with you, as do all your memories. You can hold your breath for minutes yet. It will not be pleasant, but you can.

You clench the muscles of your belly and put out a hand to lean against the up-dangling slippery trunk of a great kelp and the matter of your path eddies and billows, here it is, and is this an eel to ask what you are? Are these moving bruises in your eyes observant fish come to question? You nod at the visions politely, descend into darker, more pressing water.

We were nomads, your mother said to you. We found a valley. We settled there. We were not warriors. Four times every year horsemen came, an aggregate band, our neighbors, a temporary coalition of predation, with their weapons out, to take our food, our families, for slaves and spouses and games.

Passing under a coral arch, in your mind, kindly enough, you whisper, Mother, do you know how many stories start like that?

A stonefish watches you tell her memory that in the epochs that followed her death, people forgot how to ride horses, and the horses went wild again, and then people learned again, and then forgot again.

We were plucked like fruit and we bled, your mother said to you, and who needs a weapon more than those who are not born to war? She said, We needed a tool. So I asked the gods.

What happened? you asked her. Her little man, sat by her (too big for her lap already), eyes open wide. How did you ask them?

I made a drink, she said, to make me dream. Some plants are pathways, you know that, little Unute, like some flesh is a pathway.

Unute is your name, she said. Unute was what the drink said through me that night.

What did you do? you asked.

Aren't I telling you? she said. Only listen, Unute. The brew opened the doors of the storm and I went to a blue place, to where the storm lives, or the storm came through or we met on the threshold, and I fucked the lightning, and the next day my tummy was big, and we called you the Impatient Boy. Two moons later out you came.

So my father is not my father? you said.

Hush, silly, she said. Your father is your father, he's your dayfather, and the blue lightning is your nightfather. Don't interrupt a story, Unute, or the flowers won't grow. Fire didn't frighten you and you didn't shout with pain when you played with burning sticks. Three moons after the fire you killed a wolf that came for scraps, you killed it with your teeth and your little hands. A season after that you played with young men fighting with the axeclubs we had copied from the raiders and I still don't know if yours was a game or a true conflict, only that the war in you saw the war in them as it had seen the snarl in the wolf, and out your own war came.

You said you hadn't meant to and your father gave the dead boy's parents rights of chanting for the bloodsorry and they hated you thereafter for their son, but they said you were the weapon, and we called their dead boy the whetstone that had sharpened you.

The water through which you walk is not lightless. You know you'd have to go much farther for that, you know that the spears of the sun extend deep into the sea, but it is cold and it is dim where you are and the animals that watch you have the furtiveness of shadow dwellers. And still the way goes down and enough minutes have passed that your head hurts and the water presses in.

Unute, keep going.

And the best spearman in the band taught you, your mother said to you. And your wounds healed months' worth of healing in days, little weapon. And when your eyes began to shine the color of your father's eyes, glow as blue as your nightfather lightning, we put you in the pit with great animals we had trapped. They thought we gave them to you, did not know that we were giving them to you. You danced your war and took apart the bears and *Smilodons* and the monsters of the foothills, and if in those dream spasms, in the warpings that overcame you so you'd cry out and become a beast, if occasionally you broke apart your teachers or pulled the limbs from your playmates so they bled out in shock or if you caved in the chests of our people, well, everyone knew not to get too close to Unute the weapon in his transports. Everyone knew to run and hide when your eyes shone with the shocklight. You were not a bad boy but a dangerous thing and you were always sorry and they were careless.

She said, And then the raiders came back.

You trudge along a gorge of vaulting coral overhangs and each moment your chest burns of not-breathing. Your mother always sang this part of the story and you sing it now into the water, opening your mouth for the watching morays. She sang, you sing:

Listen!
These horsemen

ochre warnings on their faces
laughed at warlessness offered
rode to where the mountains watched
to where the nightfather lightning spilled seed
to the weaponboy.

Unute of the eyes!
clubaxe-edge, child, spearpoint, in conclave.

In he went dancing
through the horses
through their riders.

This is his fugue.
War-rage!   Hamask!
Spasm of the warp!
Frenzy!   Fury!

Unute took a bloodroad
Unute walked the bones
He was filled with arrows and he did not cease
He was the cleaving edge
He was the play of terror
He was the ender of things.

We loved you, your mother said. After you were done with them we swaddled you. You were still a baby. We wrapped you and we cleaned the dead from you and said to you thank you and told you that we loved you.

Every step is pain. When you strode into the surf you hoped the decline would be met and matched by an incline beyond, that you would ascend again after a time of walking, your head and heart and lungs in torments, that was your wager, that there was a crag in the reef that came close enough to the surface that your head would come up and out into the air before your lungs failed, that by a sequence of such up-down travels you would make your way, and if the war energies came up in you on this walk, the inverted hunger, the necessity of destruction in the chill shine of your eyes, that you would slake them on sharks and coral towers, and carry on again beyond the eddying blood in your trembling recovery up and down toward the southern continents. That that would be the way of it.

You long ago identified in yourself, no matter what evidence you amass that the thought is folly, a sense of toldness. That certain things must be, to make the shape of life a story. You have seen such a hankering in most of the people you've known. It is because you share that dangerous inclination that you hesitate to say you are not human.

It is wrong many more times than it is right.

This way goes only deeper, into the darkest part of the sea. And you are slowing, and your fingers are too numb to remove the stones from your clothes.

The story in you accelerates. Not in your mother's voice, now. One you tell yourself, from memories and investigations, from hints and conclusions.

Here you are, in a widening place, where—Look!—the blue darkens and there is nothing beyond a coral wall, you are at a cliff edge and there is nothing but the blackest water beyond. You stumble. And hazy as your mind grows the story you tell yourself goes faster and faster because you are not at the end of it yet and because you do not have long left. Quickly then.

There were always more tribes to fear, to be stopped, which had to be stopped before they started, they said, your band and your dayfather said, and your mother too until she stopped saying it. They bade you raise your war-rage against fisherfolk and mountain dwellers and edifices in the snow, whose spires have long been pounded into dust, but which were when you crested the path between peaks the greatest city that ever was.

You went in

cut the king apart cut the guards apart walked the boneroad left the bloody hall descended the great stairs cut through every person in the city sat atop a pyramid of the dead. You saw

lightning come down in the distance, red this time, and your father saw and cursed your mother and you saw him in the valley and he took something from her and threw something into the pit where once you'd torn bears apart and he shouted at your mother when she said she was fearful for you and wanted your pain to end, you didn't know what she meant because you did not know that what you felt was not just what it was to be alive. You would ask her more you decided and you followed your dayfather but in a gorge ten thousand arrows met you and you hamasked, shifted into the blue-glowing-glaring-eyed version of yourself and performed your urgent bloody changes on the attackers and on those among your own band who did not heed the strictures about keeping distance and you heard your father shout and you knew it was a trap and a distraction and you came back to yourself enough to follow him, to outrun the last of the horses back to your own settlement and you

found your father crouched over your mother, she was dead, at invaders' hands, and you felt like a desert and you told him this was his desert and you walked away and they came and killed him too and you walked on to where at a meeting place of stone an army of all the tribes through which you'd walked your road waited.

You did not lift your hands against them, when they came for you and raised their weapons.

At the edge of the undersea, here you are, crawling like a thirsty person in a desert, toward dark into which you stare as if it is an eye, and this is the last of it, you cannot stand, the stones keep you down, and the darkness rises before you from the canyons at the bottom of the world, and comes in from your edges, and descends more powerfully now than the light of the sun, pouring down from the dark of space into the sea to enshroud you, and the only word for this is agony, and you lie down you don't know if supine or prone but sightless and this is the last of it.

You remember your enemies' blades coming down, thousands of years ago. You cannot stop yourself inhaling the terrible water of the sea.

The pain in your lungs does not cease. Drowning was always the worst way to die.

You die.

and then comes pushing

a push and bursting free

of a shell, amid thick and clouded sediment of meat and blood, and here you are, thinking again, naked and raw, salt stinging your new flesh and washing you clean, and here you are denied that first painful and lovely breath with which you have greeted your hatchings in the air, and you make out the cavern of the ovum out of which you have come, that has grown from the weird fertility of your drowned body, clogged there, wedged on the undersea clifftop, just as you came out of your first egg in that sunbaked stone place where you were first pulled and cut apart, and out of every one of the eggs since, when you have chosen or been forced to the limits of even your recalcitrant body, born anew naked as on your first birth, so you have no stones nor any pockets for them now, and even without air within you you are buoyant and you let yourself rise to know which way is up. That is the direction in which you kick.

And you breach the surface, and at last you take that first breath.

NEW DARK

B, WHOM KEEVER CALLED "SON," STOLE A CAR AND DROVE fast and for a long time through ugly foothills to the coast. He bought supplies. He threw his burner phone into the water.

Took smaller roads, through bowed-down sprawls of malls and concrete dormitory-style housing, not small towns but small-feeling, out of the way, redolent with the parochialism of a depressed zone. He abandoned his vehicle in scrub and entered an area of strong chemical smells and puddles glinting with the pretty toxins of runoff.

He found a place as good as any. The top floor of a deserted office block. He stood at the window and counted passersby and vehicles at the intersection below, and he counted the lights that went on when the day ended, in workshops and grocery stores. If he shot it would be heard, but his first night there he heard three shots himself, less than a kilometer away, and no screams or sirens followed.

He found a usable chair and wiped clean what had been a boss's desk. He pulled it over to face the glass-door entrance of the last room of the corridor. On it, B placed a SIG Sauer P320 chambered with a ten-round .45 ACP magazine, a Daewoo K5 full of 9mms, a KA-BAR Becker BK22 and a G.I. Tanto, both unsheathed, an extended S&W

baton. He arranged them in a neat line. He considered how people now enjoyed such names of weapons, as if gun knife knife stick was not enough, was not as true.

You will only perceive your tools when they are broken, he remembered.

He stopped moving so fast, at last. He breathed out and sat back. He looked down. He shook his head, hard, as he would not have were he not alone, as if he was refusing to respond to a question, from an observer, from within himself. As if he would not answer, or ask, What am I doing?

For two days he sat behind his arms amid the dust. He waited and watched the corridor and was watched in turn by the sun-bleached eyes of a pinup declaring a summer month of a year long gone.

On the third day he leaned forward, the first time he had moved since his arrival.

It was a little before sundown, and through the hallway before him slanted a block of thick light. The motes within were shuddering. Below the stochastic whispers of the building's slow collapse he discerned a more regular rhythm.

He tap-tapped the tip of the index finger of his right hand with his thumb, feeling the contours of a callus.

What were the rules? he wondered, as he did every few years. What was the threshold of size or seriousness of injury that would prompt the energies of his odd body to reknit, to eradicate signs of wear and trauma? Why did some small scars remain, others smooth out? He could not have said why this tiny nub of skin he felt should stay impacted, though he did not quibble with the decision (as it were) of the celestial tribunal or alien overlords or planar overseer or evolutionary quirk or storms of mindless chance or his own remorseless, what, divinity? He could not remember the source of the nub on his fingertip, so either it had originated in his between-lives yolk state or it had arisen during a fight fugue. Or he had simply not noticed. No matter.

He listened.

Perhaps once every two or three centuries, the man would make a gesture as if for an imagined audience, a moment of flamboyance to contrast with the usual thrift of his habitus. He never knew he would do so before he did, as now, as he watched himself reach out, beckon.

"Come," he heard himself say.

What was coming came.

It came slowly. It made him wait, whether out of the thoroughness of the hunt or in its own counterperformance, its own sense of drama.

For two, three hours, B sensed, then felt, then heard the unique irregularity of sentient life, a searcher searching. The sun was all gone and gloom filled the passageway from the farthest end, where the doors to dead elevators stood closed and reflective. Now here, came a slowing approach, the huff-huff of horny hard feet on the scuffed corporate carpet, a stepping closer, an incoming, a meeting about to be, a re-meeting.

B could not see into the dark where the stairwell met the hallway. But he could make out shifts of that blackness, the arrival into its absence of a new dark, which watched him, paused for one luxurious moment before it kept on coming.

"Oh," he said. His voice was all sorrowful in the corridor.

"I shouldn't have expected that to work," he said. "But I am disappointed. I am sorry you're here.

"Hello," he said. "Again."

SHE KNEW THAT WHEN HE STOOD BEFORE HER KEEVER WAS "AT EASE," BUT to Diana, the stand-up-straight legs-apart arms-behind-back attention read tense, and it made her tense, too, to be the focus of such puckered-up respect. It made her colleagues seem prim.

Diana Ahuja had dutifully read Sontag; she had a Tom of Finland coffee-table book; she'd shaken her stuff to the Village People now and then: it was hardly a revelation to her that the machismo of the military was camp. Every two months, when she stood in the range for the obligatory certification check, the clench-assed enthusiastic shooting stances of the soldiers around her put her in mind of a dance troupe. What had been more of a surprise to her, at the start of this stage of her career, was what fusspots they were. Not that Diana was a slob. She'd fight for a woman's right to be unkempt, of course, whoever that woman was, but mindful of the gazes upon her, not being white, as well as, honestly, enjoying the play of femming up a bit, slovenliness was not her own style. Still, she liked to think herself more soignée than spruce. Just one of the—Let me count the ways, she thought—reasons that her military affiliation still felt so counterintuitive.

But you had to go where the resources were. If you were a cephalopod scientist, it would be DARPA that would offer you the lab you'd never thought you could have. Want to understand the chromatophores that grant your beloved cuttlefish the miracle of their camouflage? Go right ahead. Just make your peace with the fact that your research will end up in self-mottling DPM, or ignore it.

In the same way, if you want to study Unute, when you come to understand that he of whom you'd learned through careful reading in obscurities, whom you'd believed a myth, was real, that he still walked, who else would pay your way but those who hanker for immortal warriors? It was always going to be secretive military minds that would enable her to do what she pined to do: to reach for, to parse, to understand him. And not only him but, even more, the source of him. That mystery. That which had made him, which could do, grant, who knew what else?

So now she had her designated rank, and tough folks like Keever saluted her.

"I know you gave your report," Diana said to Keever. "You know I've read it more than once. And I'm genuinely sorry to ask you to repeat yourself after all this time. You understand that this isn't anything against anyone involved." She scanned the names on the report on her desk, those who'd already heard his speech. Sanders, Jacobson, Lear; fine techs with exemplary records. Beech, impatient but too smart to let her mask slip. Shur and Kneen, of the psych and stats departments respectively, the former newish but already making an impact, the latter adequately respected, more mascot than colleague, source of little wisdom. "I'm not suggesting they wouldn't understand the importance of anything you said," Diana said. "I'm saying that sometimes you need to hear it yourself—I need to hear it myself—to put it together. Sometimes I have to follow my nose."

"Ma'am."

"I'm obviously concerned that we can't get hold of Unute."

"He's done this before, ma'am."

"Not for this long and not this abruptly. I need to bring him in. There's too much to keep tabs on. And apart from anything else, Keever, he's off his meds."

"His what now?"

"Some protocols I've got him on. By choice, let me be clear. His choice."

"For what, ma'am?"

"For me to do my job. They help him reach certain states. It's not the end of the world if he misses a few days, but this long could set us back. Maybe to find him I have to figure out what spooked him."

"Spooked?"

"Yeah, it's not the verb I'd usually go for, either. I just... after this business with Thakka, everything's been happening so fast."

"With respect, ma'am, I disagree. This..." He gestured. "Him going AWOL. This had been building for some time. I'm on record as having warned about his mood for a while now. That said... I understand what you're saying, and it is maybe more acute. He seemed pretty het up that day."

Diana nodded. "I'm sorry," she said at last, "but we're going to go over everything again. When Unute found the tracks, in the tunnel, did he seem surprised?"

"I mean, ma'am, sometimes it's hard to, uh..."

"He's not always the most expressive, is he?"

"That he is not, ma'am. Until he is."

They watched each other for a while.

"I may not be a field agent," Diana said, "but I'm not a fool. I know you know him better than anyone else here."

"That's not saying much."

"It's not nothing, either," she said. "And you are right. We both know that he's been . . ." Diana considered.

"Moody," Keever said.

"Troubled," she said. "Something's been up with him for a while now."

"Yeah. For eighty thousand years."

"Perhaps. But come on. No one's saying that he's ever been without his hidden depths. He's hardly the life of the party at the best of times. Even when he's comparatively chatty. But you said it yourself: something's been up with him recently."

"Since Ulafson," Keever said. "You need me to say it?"

They stood in silence. Diana inclined her head.

"That was a shock," she said. "To all of us."

"Maybe," Keever said. She looked at him sharply. "I don't know. I mean, yeah, it obviously had an impact on him. And at the time, B— Unute—he didn't seem shocked. He just stood there. As if he'd known it would happen. Or as if it had happened before."

"Yes," Diana said. "I saw the footage."

"He liked him, B did," Keever said. "Ulafson. I feel like whatever's going on with him now started then."

"Yes," she said. Cautiously, though. The days after the attack were vivid in her mind, the cleanup of the carnage in the changing room, the wiping of the blood and matter from the walls and lockers. The minute investigations into the remains of Ulafson and those scraps of his zip-up jacket too tenacious to have burned into nothing. And she recalled, too, the days thereafter. When Sunderland transferred out of the Unit, and Chapman out of the forces altogether. Unute had said nothing. Had displayed no particular emotion, she'd thought. And now, but now, remembering his intensive quiet contemplation, as Keever spoke, it felt to her that what she had marked then was that he was showing no *new* emotion. Only an intensification of a rising melancholy she'd already discerned. Remembering them now, Diana recalled his silences then as pregnant.

"I think it started before," she said finally. "Ulafson heightened something. He used to go off on his own and revisit mission sites from time to time before Ulafson—he's just been doing it a lot more since."

"When he found those tracks down there," Keever said, "in the tunnel, past Thakka, it wasn't like B was trying to figure out what he was looking at. It wasn't like he was trying to figure anything out. He didn't seem surprised. But he did seem urgent. I kept saying, 'What is it? What is it?' And I think I said that because some part of me could tell he knew what it was he was seeing."

"But he didn't answer?"

Keever shook his head. "He kept going into the dark. The whole place was unstable—every time you moved, more came down. I was calling to him. I couldn't see him. And then the whole end of the tunnel collapsed behind him. I had to call for a wipe team and a medevac before I could get up. That's when I let them take Thakka. I went looking for B."

"But he was still down there and there was no way through, you said."

"He had not."

"And he hadn't come past you."

"He had not."

"So you left and went looking? Against orders?"

"Yes ma'am," Keever said. Not a flinch. "I was concerned. I went out the way I came, and I established a perimeter and tracked, and after a few minutes I found him, too. He was at the edge of a road a little way past the building. The same one he came in on. 'How'd you get out?' I said. 'You didn't come back past me.' He didn't say anything. He was standing there with his face up, like he was sniffing the air. He just pointed into the dust. 'It came this way,' he said." Keever shrugged. "I couldn't see a damn thing."

"It?" Diana said.

"That's what I said. 'The animal,' he said, 'that made those tracks.'

Well, we took some shots of where he was pointing—you saw them. Like I say, I couldn't make out anything. The team was already out in local cop uniforms, securing the area, so I liaised with them and got the scene ready for Tacoma. I told B to stay where he was."

"And he didn't obey you," she said.

Keever's mouth twisted.

"It's funny you should say that. Him and me were talking about that just before we found Thakka. No ma'am, he did not. When've you ever known him to obey any of us? He's never obeyed any instructions. You know it, I know it, he knows it, and they know it all the way to the top. He just does what he wants to and the brass finds ways of wanting the same things so they can issue an order to his back and get to say he did what they told him."

"So what happened?"

"I said, 'Stay right there,' and he just looked at me and I knew he was about to hit the road. 'Come on,' I said. 'I have to go,' he said. And he did. By the time you got there—"

"Which was what, four, five hours after?" Diana said.

"Right. By the time you guys got there, B was long gone."

"And you don't know where he is?"

"I do not."

"What," Diana said carefully, "is your opinion? None of us know anything, OK, but what do you think he's doing?"

She could see Keever considering whether to say to her what he was thinking.

"I don't know," he said at last. "And I don't think he does either. Or . . . there was a look in his eye. Makes me think maybe he just doesn't think he does. Or he does but he doesn't want to. May I ask a question?"

"Please."

"What did you find out? About Thakka?"

Diana looked up at the ugly fluorescent lights. She tried to recall the protocols of what and how much she was supposed to tell or be allowed to tell whom, of what rank, and then exactly what rank Keever was and what additional information about that was included on his personnel sheet, and she tried to fathom what advantage any insight she might give him, licit or otherwise, might grant him, in what internal games and micropolitics of the base he was engaged in, and she sighed because she hated and was bad at such calculations. Which was why she went, as she was doubtless supposed not to, by gut. By trust. She trusted Keever.

He might have intuited all that; he, the more expert player of the opaque games, might be relying on that trust in him. It was a maze of mirrors, as Angleton had said. And he hadn't even known about B.

"We found out nothing," she said. She glanced at the door to her office, to indicate to Keever that this was between them. "Officially? There was a fault in his scanners. Officially he was alive and unconscious down there the whole time, and the signal sent the wrong message, that he'd been neutralized, and we didn't know that until the connection reestablished. By which time it was too late to stabilize him."

She could see him considering how to say what he wanted to say.

"Bullshit, ma'am" was what he went with, coldly. "With respect. I felt him. He was getting warmer when I put my hands on him, but he'd been cold. I mean cold cold . . ."

"I know. Officially, I said."

"What happened . . . he'd stopped being dead is what happened."

Now it was Keever who was close to whispering.

"I believe you," she said. "What can I tell you? Investigations are ongoing."

"It makes no sense," Keever said.

"I agree." She tilted her head. "Though it's maybe a little late to start worrying about that in this unit."

"No, that's my point," he said. "I mean, you say that's the official theory. But you obviously don't buy it. And I bet no one does. So who's coming up with it?"

Diana pointed straight up.

"But why?" Keever said. "For whom? Whoever's cooking this up must be doing it so as not to look... what, foolish? Credulous? Woo-woo? But like you say, this unit's entire raison d'être is to work with a warrior who won't die. Who a decent proportion of the few people in the world who know about him think is the devil or the son of death, or the fucking manifestation of entropy itself. And with respect, and without knowing what you've got going on in all your folders, I've never heard you or any of your colleagues offer any better explana-tions. So why, now, is believability the issue? Aren't they kind of shut-ting the barn door after the horse has bolted?"

Diana smiled without pleasure.

"Bolted, galloped away, yes, AWOL," she said. "We await word from the horse, wherever he is, whatever he's doing, whenever he feels like checking in. I hear you, Keever. I do." She took out her read-ing glasses and cleaned them and put them away. "I agree. What about Stonier?"

"Ma'am, what about him?"

"How did he get to be part of the medevac squad?"

This time Keever hesitated.

"Due respect, ma'am, I was, as you know, hundreds of klicks away waiting for you when y'all put that team together..."

"You know I had nothing to do with it."

"I mean the office. The Unit, this place. I was in the field. How would I have anything to do with it?"

"I thought maybe Stonier had gotten through to you. Made a re-quest..."

"If he had," Keever said, "I'd have told him no way. I'd've told him to stand down."

"So it was just coincidence that he was deployed? On that mis-sion?"

"No," Keever said. "That's not what I'm saying. You know as well as I do how rumors spread. We talk a good talk but we're as leaky a ship as most other organizations, at least internally. When we called through word to base, it must have gotten out pretty quickly that Thakka was alive. And I think Stonier just put in a word with whoever was in charge. Or maybe he just . . ." He shrugged. "Maybe he just suited up and got on the plane with you guys."

"Why?" Diana said.

"Are you serious?" Keever said. "Wouldn't you?"

Diana closed her eyes.

She had not paid attention to the squad before her in the chopper. She had been in the third wave into the shaft, after the armed point had shouted, "Clear" and the science team had started their setup. She had come past the deadpile, vivid, by then, under floodlights. She had clambered over the rubble fringe in the chamber thronging with techs, into the stub of tunnel.

The air had been astringent as the bioengineers had poured on their unguents to see through the damage their own reagent had wrought. Every one of the dead, on both sides, all of whom had been identified by the initial strike team, now had to be identified a second time. Because what had happened since should not be possible. So every variable had to be reexamined.

Diana had set to with her own scanners, hunting eccentric energy fields. She had come forward, staring, and there, in Keever's arms, while a medic leaned over and intubated and fussed with him, was Thakka. He twitched and blinked. He paddled his arms as if he were in water. One of his hands was clasped shut. He looked up at her or through her and whispered words she could not make out.

She was not able to stop looking at the hole in him, long since dry, the hollow bone chamber and the slop of brain and burn that should not possibly have allowed him to live. She came close. She touched Thakka's flesh. She gestured silently and Keever moved aside, and Diana watched the medic inject adrenaline and more into Thakka's collapsing veins. Her fingers slick with his sweat, the woman peeled parts of his ragged stinking uniform from him. Itemized his injuries while he whispered without sense.

Diana hunkered so that Thakka was in her shadow, beyond the

reach of the temporary lights, and yes, his movements had grown slowly ever more sluggish. She reached down to put her palm to his forehead and his skin grew cooler while she held it and while the medic began to shout at him to stay with them, to stay with them, and there in the sunken tunnel in the dark Thakka looked at each of them in turn with the calm of one on a journey. He blinked as slowly as anyone Diana had ever seen.

She had always been good at losing herself in work. Entering flowstate.

What pulled her violently out of it was a cry.

Standing framed within the ripped-up doorway, backlit by the LEDs, was a man. Diana thought he was staring at her. His silhouette was so dark, his sound, his whine, so dreadful that for an instant she saw him as some psychopomp come to escort Thakka's soul to the drab ashy place beyond. Would that be so much stranger than the work she daily did? But Keever strode toward the newcomer with his arms up, and she saw the man stumble forward and she recognized him then, one of the poised and muscled specialists, now folding as if he would fall, then rising again and holding himself up, making no more noise, staring at Thakka.

There is unique pathos to the grief of the stoic.

Stonier, that was his name. He shoved past Keever and went down to his knees. He pushed Diana's hands and the doctor's hands away and gripped Thakka. And Thakka looked up at him with a last brightness in his eyes. Perhaps recognized him. Stonier whispered. Diana could not make it out. It was not for her.

"Why are you here?" Keever said. "Get out of here, son—we've got him now. You get back out of here, now, go on now."

Stonier stayed, staring, holding on, while Thakka moved more and more slowly, and closed his eyes again.

No one interfered. The medic's motions slowed. Stonier spoke into Thakka's ear. Patted him. Thakka's fingers twitched, and his hands, one open one closed, reached for Stonier, and Stonier fumbled abruptly and needily to grip them.

"That's enough," Diana heard herself say at that sight. "I need you to . . ."

But that was all. She did nothing while Stonier's hands crawled over the man on his way.

Only when Thakka had died again, a second and last time, had Keever pulled Stonier up and pushed him out.

"Wouldn't you?" Keever said again to her, now. "If someone you loved was gone and then you heard that he was alive after all? Wouldn't you come see?"

"Where is he?" she said. "Has he been discharged?"

"Stonier? What, for disobeying orders?" Keever said. "Just for being there? No ma'am. This isn't the old days. Stonier's a good soldier. And especially in an outfit like ours, there's such a thing as discretion when it comes to insubordination. Special Forces rules. He's being offered compassionate leave. He won't take it, of course. He's with Shur right now."

Diana turned her head toward the main entrance to the base. The whole place—and every operation they carried out—was deniable and denied, of course, but the bureaucratic mania for subdivision inhered no less in the Most Secret realms than in those more public. Thus Dr. Shur's was among the first of the offices a visitor to Zone 1, the least restricted area, might encounter.

"Counseling," Keever said quietly, "is definitely not optional anymore."

"I can imagine what you think of that," Diana said.

Keever looked at her full-on.

"Maybe you should get over yourself," he said at last. "Ma'am. You think you've got my number?" he said quietly. "I'm a soldier, so I think counseling's for pussy snowflakes? You're damn right I'm a soldier, and what I want is for my people to be the best, and this isn't the 1980s. You ever read Karl Marlantes? What do you know about the history of military psychiatry? You think I don't believe in trauma? You think I think sadness is for the weak or some shit? You think I don't care about my people? You weren't looking at him."

"I was looking right at him—"

"Not Thakka. Stonier. I was watching him. Saw his eyes. Saw him fumbling around, gripping something tight. I guarantee you it was something Thakka gave him, in the last moments, and I bet you he's holding on to it like a life preserver. I want him to be OK whether he sticks it out here or not, and if he does, I want him to be the best fighting man he can be, and that does not mean pretending he's impregnable. Where do you think the idea for hiring Shur even came from?"

Diana stared.

"Yeah," Keever said. "I don't get to sign off on that kind of shit, obviously, I'm just a grunt, but it was me who put in the request. After Ulafson. It's because of me she's here at all."

"You surprise me."

Keever sighed. "I'm old-school, sure. I'm the bottle-it-up generation. And do I think some of the ways people talk these days are kind of goofy? Sure. I'm used to a different kind of trigger, and a different kind of warning. But only an idiot thinks the ways they were trained are automatically the best. It was me who put in the request, and it was me who helped select from the applicants. Yes, having Shur on the staff looks good for funding. But also, she's been helpful. She's good at her job."

"How would you know?" Diana said.

"How do you think?" Keever said. She stared at him again, in an extended silence. "Think I'm above talking to her? New tricks may not come easy, but I can be a dogged old dog. She's good at getting you talking," he said. "Gives you strategies. Ways to keep going even when things are . . ."

Diana glanced again in the direction of the counselor's office. "Poor man," she whispered.

"Yeah," Keever said. "Poor Stonier."

She did not correct him but he looked down as if she had.

"Poor Thakka," he said. "And poor Stonier." He surprised her again, then, with the gentleness of his voice and with what he said: "I was at their wedding."

. . .

"DID YOU HAVE THOUGHTS OF SUICIDE TODAY?"

Diana remembered when she'd last asked B that. Not even long ago. After a particularly intense mission, replayed in the glowing lights of B's readouts, of his various bodily and mental responses, in a strange and fabulous display. New synapses, new thoughts. The question had been a provocation. It always was.

"I told you," he had said. "I don't want to die. What I want is mortality, and that's not the same thing."

Diana leaned over Thakka's body on the mortuary slab and read the pathology reports. She cross-referenced them with reports from the field agents who had been there with him when he had gone down, who had seen it all. Trained specialists, instilled with muscle memory to militate against panic and the excitable solecisms of untrained witnesses. Only two had had line of sight at the moment of his death. The first time. The first death.

They reported the slamming impact into Thakka's head, the spray of bone shards, blood and skin, the howl cut off, the collapse. What had clearly been his demise.

She sat by the body.

Once, Unute, B, had told Diana of a mother lode of his own body, bodies, bones.

"I was kidnapped, so to speak," he had said. "I mean, that's happened a few times. This time, though, it was different. My kidnapper just kept on killing me. Research, I guess."

"Who were they?" she had said. "And how the hell did they do it? When was this?"

"A long time ago. Yeah, you'd be surprised: people find ways to do pretty much anything. And—" He had pursed his lips. "I was never exactly sure who they were. I don't know if they were, either. One of the sects. What I do know is they hated me. Thought I was the end of the world, so they had to finish me. The end, as in, the way they talked, going back to what it was before: nothing. Like I was saying life was a mistake. I guess they thought I was the beginning, too. What there was before. In any case, it's not easy to kill me once, let alone again and again. You have to give them that."

"Didn't you just egg somewhere else?" she had said. "When you died?"

"I couldn't always do that. For a long time that only happened right there where I died. So, that time, I kept coming back right there. Into a growing mess of my old dead selves."

"What?" she had said. You never knew, with him, when you'd learn some impossibly extraordinary new thing. "You only used to rehatch where you fell?"

"Yeah," he had said. "You didn't know that? I thought Caldwell knew."

"Where was this? This kidnapping?"

"I don't know."

"You remember everything!"

"I never knew. I didn't keep track of where I was going."

Later Diana had played Caldwell the recording of that conversation.

"Did you?" she had asked Caldwell. "Know? That the distance-hatchings weren't always possible?"

"I did not," he had said. He'd steepled his fingers. He was mannered, she thought, even in his excitement. His voice had been terse: "I don't know why B would think I already knew that. But that fact makes a certain sense of some findings." He had scrawled notes. "The way some machines seem to crop up all across great distances. This is important."

When he had finished writing, he had gestured at her screen, the waveform of the conversation she was playing, with his pen. "He likes you," he had said.

Stephen Caldwell, head of Belief Systems and Ancient Technology Migration, was technically below Diana in rank, but neither of them stood on ceremony.

"What would that even mean for something like him?" she had said. "But yes. I think he does."

"You've only been working with him, what, a year? And you've got better results than any of your predecessors. The protocols you've got him on . . . I've never known him so . . . introspective. Talkative. Does he still want to die?"

"He doesn't," she had said. "He never did."

"Yes yes, I'm familiar with his line," Caldwell had said. "So he says. And I always like hearing you explain it."

I like hearing him explain it, she had not said.

Now, by Thakka's body, Diana heard the hiss of doors, a distant commotion. She knew before she looked up that B, Unute, had returned.

HE APPROACHED HER DOWN THE CORRIDOR IN HIS DARK CLOTHES, GUARDS

and Caldwell in his wake. She waited. Through the window she saw B walk with long and easy strides even though he was weighed down, carrying across his shoulders something big and swaying and sagging with the horrid indignity of flesh, something that dripped and smeared him, left him red. With one hip, he pushed open the door to where she stood. The noise of his entourage came in with him.

B stopped by a gurney. He nodded at her in greeting.

"Where have you been?" she said. "You're behind on the protocols, I've been, we've been—you can't just, it's been too long, where have you been?"

She could not make out what his burden was. He hefted it, lifted it straight up above his head. It lolled and dripped in his hands and she gasped because she thought that it was a corpse, the horribly truncated body of a man, and she knew what he would do and she swore and stepped quickly backward.

He threw it down. The heavy thing hit the stainless steel table with wet percussion, spattered the front of Diana's white coat. It lay at the center of a new red star.

Diana saw twisted backbent hind legs. Hooves. She smelled musk.

She sought and did not find a head, a human face, only a carnage of meat and bone and protruding vertebrae.

"Put this in a containment lab, please," Unute said without a glance at the team behind him. None of them moved. He wiped his hand across his face, smearing blood.

Diana looked at Caldwell and he at her. She gestured at the table.

"What is this?" she said at last.

"I need to clean up," B said. "And I need to think. I'll tell you everything I can as soon as I can. I'll buzz you. Something's happened."

He left the chamber. After a moment, the tech team brought out swabs and sponges and bleach and set to work.

"WELL?" CALDWELL SAID TO DIANA.

He held up his fingers in his arch way. This thin, ageless white man, all suits and bow ties and glasses in outdated styles, all clipped beard and accent. An archaeologist, formally, but, as with all the scholars in the Unute project, that undersold the variety of his expertise and interests. When Diana had first met him, she had hoped that she and he would become friends as well as collaborators in projects Top and NPU (Ne Plus Ultra) Secret. That one day she might tease him about his spidery manner.

Was there ever anything so excruciating as an office induction?

Of course she had been invited to apply because she knew a little, had understood enough to put out specific and necessary feelers, sought work on the strength of what she had put together through her own stumbling researches, her (count them) three PhDs. What she'd ascertained through the cross-referencing of avant-garde physics, historical anomalies, and the holy texts of derided cults. The rumors she had not mentioned to the Nobel committee when she'd declined their offer. Thus it was that by the time Diana had entered the meeting room in the wood-shrouded base a good ways outside of Tacoma, Washington, un- or mismarked on maps, one of a handful of newbies there to spend the morning sitting through presentations on military and civilian ranking, fire prevention, lab safety, workplace-harassment protocols, and the Unit softball league, she, like everyone present, was already clear-minded about how the department they were there to build was dedicated to the collaboration with; study, decoding, and keeping secret of; questioning and protecting (laughable as that was) of; and performing necessary wetwork with an eighty-thousand-year-old warrior who would not die.

Thereafter would come to her the fundamental rewritings of history and prehistory occasioned by her new subject. A sine wave, a rise and fall of antique and quite occulted civilizations. The impossible new science they were all there to advance, that field that shaded from morphology to speculative biology to quantum physics to fulminology; thence to mythography and ontology; sometimes even fucking theology. They never gave an official name to this spread, but Diana knew she was not the only person at the base to consider herself a Unutologist.

Not many would accept a job offer accompanied by the warning she had been given: that it would put her life in permanent danger and that she would never be able to speak of her work to anyone she loved. You don't get recruited to such a field solely on scholarly promise, no matter how great it is. There had to be more to her, she knew, to pique the interest of those she'd never met, making the decisions.

Caldwell had been in the room during her orientation. That was when she had caught his eye, and when she had briefly hoped he would turn out to be teasable.

"Why do you suppose he's making us wait?" he said now. "What do you think's behind that unexpected gift?"

They were silent for a while. Diana glanced around.

"Any progress?" she said. "Whatever's going on, we can't assume it'll change things. We have to keep on . . ."

"Keep on keeping on, yes," Caldwell said. "I'll let you know if I have anything of interest to report, Diana. As you're aware."

"So you say," she said. "I saw reports of more parings to be retrieved. Is that right?"

"I'm pursuing. The rumor I was most interested in turned out to be a dead end. I got my hopes up a bit: it sounded like this might be connected to the mythical mother lode. But it's not real."

"How do you know?"

"Have you ever known him to have any illnesses? Skin conditions?"

"Of course not."

"Quite. So when it turns out that what's being hidden is described as his wart . . . you know you're being led up the garden path." They both smiled without humor. "So back to the drawing board. While he puts on whatever show it is he's currently putting on."

"I mean," she said, "we're all putting on a show. This time, though, he does seem perturbed. Perhaps he's in shock."

"Unute? Do you think so?"

"No," she said. "I don't. What I mean is . . . He said he had to think: maybe he's surprised by something."

"Again, let me say: really?"

"He can be surprised," Diana said. "Once in a long while. He told me so. I didn't think I'd see it in my lifetime. But sometimes you get lucky."

"Or unlucky."

"Or both," Diana said. "It's always both."

A TURN FROM SOUTH TWENTY-FIRST STREET ONTO COURT EAST. A MAN came; he was craggy and tall and pale and tense and muscular and his jaw was clenched and he was not looking at anything. Jeff Stonier walked an alley between main streets. He had always liked the big skies over Tacoma.

So had Arman. So how could he look up now into the cloud-flecked blue arc and not feel cheated? And like he was cheating?

Stonier kept his eyes ahead then. He was taking a long way. Steeling himself. He knew he was daring himself.

"I'm a city boy," Arman Thakka had said to him. Their first conversation.

They'd been sitting next to each other in a battered old Huey screaming over the Gambian trees low enough that if you'd reached out you could have snatched a leaf from the baobabs. Unute had been sitting opposite them, forearms on his thighs, looking down at his own booted feet, in that pose he had, as if he was too sad even to raise his head. Stonier had been watching him through his goggles, not saying anything, holding tightly on to his weapon. Tense not because of the contact incoming but because this had been it. His first engagement as part of the Unit about which he'd heard hints for three years, which for two he'd tried to work out how to apply to join, before spending a further year taking the entrance course. A pass, at last, followed by two and a half months of induction. During which the most important order given to his cohort, they had been told, repeatedly, was "Get over it." "It" being many things: disbelief; the desire for clarification that would never come; any sense of how such clear impossibilities as they would serve could be; the awe at their new comrade.

That comrade would not issue orders. He was not a superior. Nor was he safe to be around, to get too close to. Has everybody got that? He was the country's greatest asset and its worst threat. He was the Unit's purpose.

The "It" they should get over, Stonier understood, was the desire to understand.

"You may hear him called B, but to you he's Unute," Keever had said.

Stonier remembered the videos they had shown him. Snatched and flailing viewpoints of turning shoulder cams. Unute sidestepping an oncoming jeep, punching its side, breaking it apart. Unute, a speck, jumping, kicking through the cockpit glass of a helicopter in flight. Unute against a tank, yanking a driver out through a porthole much too small for his body, howling like an animal. Unute against a mortar, a mine, still standing amid the rain of himself, unleashing the hell given him. Unute against a torrent of soldiers. Against Unit personnel, too, who did not keep their distance when his eyes sparked cold blue.

Now here Stonier was sitting, opposite this thing, this avatar of war.

And the guy next to Stonier, an old-timer whose fourth mission this was, Stonier remembered, had suddenly leaned in and indicated for Stonier to switch to a private channel. When he had done so and braced himself, ready for whatever supersecret intel was incoming, what Thakka had said to Stonier was "I'm a city boy. Chicago. You're local, right?"

Stonier had stared at him.

"I can't take any place seriously that's under a mill," Thakka had said. "No offense, but Tacoma's a village as far as I'm concerned."

Keever's voice had cut through on the main channel, telling them that it was time.

And when, twenty-six minutes later, they had climbed back into the aircraft, gasping and slick and clutching new burns, wet with viscous blood and oil, hauling between them a comrade named Dansen who would live but would not walk again, staring up at Unute, who waited for them in the chopper holding the ruined pulp of their main target's head and staring at it as his breathing slowed and the blue faded as the unease of the air and the world around him died slowly down, when they fell back into their places and buckled their restraints and rehydrated as the bird dusted off amid a reversed rain of bullets from below, Stonier had heard the click of that private channel opening again and Thakka's voice came back, exhausted now but not much less cheerful.

"I don't mean to be a dick about it" was what Arman Thakka had said. "Tacoma, I mean. It's just I heard you were local so I figured you might be the guy to ask what are the best places to go."

Stonier had taken him to Lucky Silver Tavern.

"What do you do to wind down?" Thakka had said.

"I dunno." Stonier had said. "Video games sometimes? You play?"

"I do puzzles."

"The fuck?"

"Yeah." That sleek and languid smile! "Oh, do your worst, tell me how lame that is—I'm way past shame." Arman had shrugged. "I lurve puzzles."

"And you such a wild guy," Stonier had said.

"Well, maybe that's it," Thakka had said. "An outlet for all my anal tendencies."

Stonier had blushed and laughed.

They'd had breakfast at Marcia's Silver Spoon Cafe. All this silver. "I'm Hillside," Stonier had said. "It used to be the bad part of town."

"What's the bad part of town now?"

"There isn't one."

"There's always a bad part of town," Thakka had said.

More than once he had told Stonier that he wanted to see where he had grown up. But Stonier wouldn't take him to Hillside, and even though Arman had made a joke of it, Stonier knew it had saddened him, which had saddened Stonier in turn, because he was never sure of the source of his own resistance.

"It's not the same anymore," he had said. "It's all gentrifying now."

"Where's not?" Thakka had said. "So why don't you show me around and tell me what's not there anymore?"

Sure, Stonier had said. But he had not.

Hey! he thought now. Better late than never, he thought, sending it out to wherever Arman might be. Because here Stonier was, walking at last between the flat gray rear wall of a warehouse to his east, an ugly deserted office building to the west, here in Hillside.

A chain-link fence bowed toward him where one post had snapped, swaying with gravity and the wind. Better late than never, Arman, Stonier said soundlessly, and he knew then that that was not always true.

He was alone on the narrow backstreet. These façades were not meant to be seen. Here there was no impetus to scrape old graffiti from walls nor to employ a nose-pierced kid on a design course to replace them with their own wry riffs on Obey Giant or some googly-eyed post-Haring Merrie Melodies animals or their caricatures of Trump or some other folk devil. So it was that Stonier walked amid cruder Mene Mene Tekel Upharsins. Numbered, numbered, weighed, divided, they read Fuck you and they read Cocksucker and they were images of jizzing pricks and someone's dog had taken a shit and it lay below those sigils like a bad offering, and Stonier was alone on the street in Hillside, and late was not always better than never.

THEY FOUND UNUTE FINALLY, SHOWERED AND BANDAGED AND CHANGED, AT the shock-glass window to the reinforced lab wherein was the dead thing he'd brought. He looked in through the wire-strengthened window at white-robed scientists checking spectrographs and gauss meters, tracing the outlines of the Kirlian glow around the bleeding meat. Caldwell held up a printout of preliminary results.

"They're OK," B said as Caldwell and Diana approached. "They probably have a few hours at least."

Within the harshly lit room, one woman had her masked face almost entirely within the opened-up cavern of flesh, rooting like a haruspex. Caldwell held up a printout of preliminary results.

"A pig," he said. "You brought us a pig, Unute. Hungry? Are you angling for a luau? Is it time," he said, "for a pig pickin'?" Caldwell exaggerated his fusty accent for those last words. So you can mock yourself, Diana thought. You just don't want anyone else doing it.

"What it is," B said, turning to them, "is a babirusa."

"A what?" Diana said.

"A deer-pig," Unute said. "A babirusa. You can't tell now—" He gestured at the glass. "Because of what I did. Come with me."

The room he led them to was at the end of a long corridor, behind more than one lock, on the highest floor of the building. It was at a corner edge of the overhang of steel and glass, so its long wall of window was not vertical but slanted in on its descent. A big desk was at the center of the chamber. The walls were cold gray, unbroken by anything but one large world map. The Peters projection, its long

Africa drawing Diana's eye. Six chairs waited against the walls of the room.

"I didn't see any cameras in this wing," Diana said.

B nodded. "One of my conditions." He stood with the tips of his boots almost against the window glass and looked down into the dark of the forest. "Helipad's pretty close," he said. "They thought it would be useful if they wanted me to move quickly."

"What is this place?" Diana said.

"My office," B said. He turned. Gestured for them to sit, sat himself.

"You have an office?" Diana said.

"I believe I'd heard that," Caldwell said, bringing one of the chairs in front of the desk. "I may even have seen it marked on charts."

"You might have heard it but you've definitely not seen it marked," B said. "And I don't use it much. But when I started working with you . . ." He gestured around himself at the building, then pointed two-fingered at Diana and Caldwell. "When I started working here they offered me one. Kind of insisted. Once in a while it's good to know it's here."

"Nice view," Diana said.

He pointed at the ceiling. "Storage space. For I don't know what. But, you know, it's a nice gesture." He pointed at the door. "A little privacy. Tucked out of the way."

He clasped his hands on the desk. Diana had never seen him so like a teacher. She lowered herself into a seat considerably more comfortable than her own.

"Are these Eames chairs?" she said.

"Yeah," Unute said. "They're 117s. I like the armrests. I always found Aerons overrated."

Part of her wanted to bray with laughter and never stop. At this man liking one chair more than another. She felt such giddiness whenever Unute expressed any preference, for anything. "I like that stuff," he had said to her once when he'd entered the kitchenette as she was heating up a pan of popcorn, and she remembered the tide of hysterics she had had to batten down as he'd waited for her to tear open the foil. What could you do but cackle at the lunacy of the fact that one who had, eons ago, crossed humanless continents on land bridges long sunk, who had stabbed mammoths to death with their own tusks, who had been ancient when Gilgamesh was young preferred Jiffy Pop to Orville Redenbacher's popcorn? Or Betty Crocker to the Baker's Dozen? Or Eames to Herman Miller, or Franklin-Christoph pens to Montblanc, or pizza to noodles or anything to anything at all?

What could any of it matter to one such as him?

Everything mattered, though, was what she had begun to understand.

B had told her he liked Etta James and Laphroaig, though he could dance and had danced to the screams of dying dire wolves. And though he could drink and had drunk piss and blood and stagnant mud. He could sit on jagged flint in a sleet-racked chasm if he had to. He had done. But why would he not care for certain chairs over others?

She might as well turn her surprise on its head. Why would he not have clear opinions about everything that had ever existed?

Diana watched him now considering how best to say what he had to say. She could not remember the last time she had seen him so hesitant. He tapped his thumb and right forefinger together in some ancient rhythm. He did not speak.

"Where did you disappear to, Unute?" Caldwell said.

"I went hunting."

"And you brought us a dead pig," Diana said.

"That's what I want to explain," he said. "The babirusa. I hunted by sitting still."

He sat awhile in silence again.

Diana felt Caldwell's hand on her arm, quietly getting her attention. He held out his phone. She looked at what he had called up on the internal net: an image of babirusas. Dense, strangely sleek swine, something of the hippo to the lines of their backs and necks. Most dramatic were their teeth. From each (each male: she saw the search term) two great pairs of ivory tusks arced up and back in curves toward the animal's head. The foremost pair protruded from its lower lips, with a sweep exaggerated and dramatic enough. But the rearmost jutted right out of the skin of the beast's snout itself, crisscrossing sometimes, in an extraordinary curl toward its own forehead.

"And why did you go hunting?" Caldwell said.

Unute glanced up, at that. There was to his look, under that usual melancholy inscrutability, a ghost, something very faintly defiant. It brought to Diana's mind what Keever had said about B's insight into himself. For a moment, Diana's fingers went to her lips. B looked to her, in that instant, like a child trying not to hope.

"Very few things that happen," B said at last, "that happen to me, haven't happened before, one way or another. That includes weirder stuff than you've ever seen. 'Magic.'" He made air quotes. "I've ..." He considered. "I've shot animals out of the sky that you and your bosses would call something like ASUs, Aerial Saurian Unidentifieds, just so you could avoid using the word 'dragons.' But let's talk about people. You know you're not the first people to study me."

"There've always been cults," Caldwell managed to say. Diana thought she saw great lizards behind his eyes.

"I'm not talking about them, I'm talking about scientists. Not a great distinction, admittedly. Anyway, I've been probed and examined over a long time. You're not the first with a secret unit, either."

"A you-shaped unit," Diana said.

"You mentioned Henry Cavendish, once ..." Caldwell said.

"And Mary Somerville," Unute said. "And Abbas ibn Firnas, and Wang Yangming and Mahendra Sūri and Maria al-Qibtiyya, names you probably know. I could go on. But also Kai Monch Gerin, whom I know you haven't heard of. And Agrista the Bat-Eared, and Cyunrod Kiss. There've been folks with institutes as impressive as yours, in their own ways. All their research is dust now. No one will ever know about it if I don't tell anyone." In his affectless voice Diana felt such weariness. "I've told you that the usual story is bullshit. That it goes: Paleolithic ignorance, then"—he clapped his hands—"Neolithic

Revolution! Then you give it a few more thousands of years and—poof!—you've got writing. And now finally the party begins." He shook his head. "I've told you. It went up and down a ton of times. You get a fire or pyroclastic flow or meteor strike or me or whatever, and the slate's wiped, and there are always reasons you can't find evidence. People rode horses when I was born. The first time I learned to read was seventy-seven thousand years ago. Then shit happens, and that gets lost. Later it starts again. Same with agriculture. Same with math. Same with astronomy. Animal husbandry. City planning. You get the picture."

Diana could see the hunger in Caldwell's eyes and knew that her own must be glowing similarly. There was always too much. You meet an informant with a perfect memory, nearly twenty times older than the oldest pyramid, and who, for reasons of exhaustion and mutual benefit and frustration and whatever, is willing to tell you most of what you want to know. Well, you think, you have the answers to everything right here. But how do you even know where to start? How do you know what questions to spend your time on, when every sliver of information, every history-shattering revelation he drops over vending-machine coffee or idly while you draw his blood, throws up its own infinite library of further questions?

So, yes, no, he did not need to go on. Though they fell on it when he did.

Caldwell and Diana knew of a few of these lost civilizations he'd mentioned. They'd eagerly imbibe whatever details he'd drop, beg for more, which he might indulge, might not. The Draboon Imperium. The Calabash Queendom. The Commonwealth of the Palms. Atlantis and Mu and Hyperborea, sure. Diana and Caldwell had heard a little about their spires and libraries, their synchemical sciences, their flying machines.

And of course, though she doubted it, or thought she did, and wanted to, it being in the nature of these insights that she could never find a scintilla of evidence, Diana could never be cast-iron certain that B wasn't just fucking with them.

"What's your point?" Caldwell said. That might have made her laugh, in a certain mood. What's your point, man, blathering on about the splendor of lost worlds?

"Like I always say," B said. "Nothing that's happened hasn't happened before. Let me tell you a story. I was on a plateau." He spoke softly. "Overlooking a valley. A river cutting through the rainforest."

"Where?" Caldwell said.

B did something, some flick of his fingers. Diana heard an abrupt soft thwack and the map shuddered and a pencil clattered to the floor. She saw a puncture and a pencil mark on an archipelago.

"It wasn't Indonesia then," B said.

"When's 'then'?" Diana said.

"Seventeen thousand years before any humans were there. Forest. A valley. Swampland. I was watching. No one else would come for a few thousand years. But I wasn't alone if you count animals, and I did. I watched them come and go. Then one year, these babirusas moved in.

"It was a good place," he said. "Fertile, safe. So they stuck around. They got used to me. I swam in the river and I gave the piglets names. Now, there were tigers in that part of the world then. A century and a half after the babirusas got there, some tigers found them. Had quite the feast. I didn't intervene."

He looked thoughtful. Diana did not ask him why he had held back.

"But then the tigers moved on," B said. "And eventually the pigs that had stayed hidden came out, and life started again. And it was good again, after a while. Until a pack of *Megacyons*—they're gone now, kind of dogs—showed up. The whole thing happens again. I still stayed out of it. After a few hundred times you end up swearing you'll never intervene in anything again, and I was trying to stick to that. Lucky for you I changed my mind later, but that's not the point. I felt sorry for these babirusas. I liked them. But this was one of those Prime Directive, stay-out-of-it times, so I was just watching. So. A few years after the dog pack, when the pigs have settled down yet again, you want to guess what found the valley next?"

Neither Diana nor Caldwell spoke.

"Another group of babirusas," B said. "Tougher than my guys. Like I said, this was a good spot. And let me tell you, a babirusa fight is something to see." He bared his teeth as if they were tusks.

"Now," Unute said, slowly and quietly, looking down at the table. "I'm going to tell you what I saw when the intruders had stripped the place, and the original pack, who'd managed to get away, crept back, yet again.

"One of them, one of 'my' pigs, was a dominant adult female. I'd seen her before. I don't know how she'd survived, but there she was, standing on her own. She was bloodied and limping and cut up, looking at her reflection in the swamp water. Her litter was all dead. She just stood still. Sometimes one or another of the females, even some of the younger males, went over to her and nuzzled her, like they wanted comfort, or to comfort her, or like they were asking her questions. She didn't respond."

Diana held her hand to her mouth again. She sat slowly up.

"In the end," B said, "as the night came down, she limped off suddenly through the mud, into the rainforest. I followed her. She didn't see. She started rooting around. She must have been starving, because the intruders had stripped most of the best stuff from that area, but I saw her ignore some tubers and grasses that I knew she'd eaten before. She was after something more specific. She found it, too. A particular mushroom. She plucked it, really gentle, with her lips, carried it in her mouth, and put it down by this one bush. Which she started stripping the leaves from. Laying them on the mushroom. Then she went looking for a flower, one specific flower out of all the flowers in the woods. She brought that too. On this goes. When she'd finished putting this exact concoction together, that was what she ate, at last. And then she lay down, and after a while she began to moan."

Diana stood. Stared at B. He stared back at her.

"Later that night," he said, his voice level, "I climbed the ridge. There was a weird feeling in the air. I was tense. I thought there'd be a storm. It wasn't a storm. But I saw something."

"No," Diana said. "No." She could see that Caldwell did not understand.

"Not a storm," B said, "no rain, no wind. But while I was standing there watching the sky, it seemed to tense, and suddenly a bolt of cold bright blue lightning came out of the sky. Right past me. Right down into the valley.

"I saw it crack right down, in one massive jag, right down like a spear. Right into one of the babirusas. Right into one of those pigs."

Diana crossed to the door. Caldwell called her name but she did not wait. She went into the corridor and began to run back the way she had come, hearing her name again and Caldwell's footsteps and after him B's steady tread, but she was finding her way back as fast as she could, opening doors with the pass on her lanyard, down, into brighter, more familiar passageways, down, into lower zones, past toobright laboratories, down to the secure wing. To the reinforced lab where they had taken the ruined babirusa body.

A mass of staff stood outside it, leaning in at the viewing window to the inner room. Diana pushed in to join them at the glass.

On the table, where they had strapped the lolling corpse, that ruined pig matter had recongealed, broken down, bubbled across the table, re-formed, risen, taken on new dimensions, a distinct new form. There it waited in a big ovoid shape, leathery, upright, glued to the surface with the remains of its own flesh.

A great egg.

An egg exactly such as that out of which would emerge Unute, on those rare moments in history when his body gave out.

The Servant's Story

MERCY, AS YOU ASK ME SO NICE, THEN I SHALL TELL YOU A LITTLE of my story. But you must know that it has never been my story. Not truly.

I do not have my letters but I have sat many times with those as do, content enough while they communed in silent conversation with the book upon their lap or bent over the table, quill in hand, making their own marks, and not being without curiosity I've regarded their endeavors. All of which is to say I know the period, that little watching eye. And I know the comma, which to me has always looked like a beckoning finger. What word is that? I asked once, of one such curling little inkworm. Asked it of he of whom I'll tell you.

No word, said he. It is a pause. As if for breath.

Was not that prettily put?

Let me vouchsafe you a secret that my life has taught me. All of us may believe, or wish to, that our lives are tales that demand words aplenty for the telling. This is foolish and wicked pride: the age of prophets, of tales worth telling, is over.

Or over in the main part. There is one such who walks still. His stories demand a tome. Yes, he of whom you ask.

Thank you for your hand upon my brow. Cold as you are.

I am not the first you've asked, I warrant, for such tales. When I was very young I swore not to speak of him to others. To tell none of what I learned or saw in his company.

Now, an oath is a thing. And all things are worthy of respect, by virtue of their being things, their being at all, because, being, they are made not only by those who swear them but by our Lord, as I might once have said. An oath should be neither made nor broken lightly. And—I do not say but—this kindness you do me with your presence, this water you bring me, your touch, for all that I'll thank you not to lay your cold hand upon me again, all make me desirous to answer your questions.

Tell me, who was it let you in?

No matter.

He did not ask me for the oath, that man. It was to me that I made it.

It was to me that I made my promise, and regard me now, old and tired, lying here amid estuary sounds and bedpan smells. Pray you do not think I speak with rancor. The I who made that promise, and the me to whom I made it, were both young and eager and foolish. This me here, to whom you speak, is less foolish, in the smallest part, and thus is not the same person. Both promiser and promised-to are gone now, and with them, I wot, the oath itself.

He never asked me for secrecy. He never asked me for anything.

The first time he said more to me than Yes or No or Tea or Get out of my way, in tones of infinite distraction, he told me a story of pigs upon an island, lightning in strange colors, a young pig grown un-natural strong. He lost himself in his telling, as if through repeating it the story gifted him some calm or insight. I knew by the up-down rhythms of his words that he had spoken them aloud before, but that it was the first time for a long time.

His house was large and splendid enough and cold and isolated on the moors and he told me the story of the pig in a first-floor room, a study that for all my weeks of service for him I had ne'er yet seen. As if since my arrival the corridors folded themselves up, all mischief, behind my back and bucket. He did not light the fire within the grate and yet he did not shiver as did I. He was accompanied in his telling—in a manner ill-suited—by the scrape of viol and the wail of hoboy played by roustabouts below, where his guests were at their pleasures. It was from the dangers whereof he had delivered me.

You are a patient guest.

Your skin is lineless and nesh, but is that antiquity behind your eyes?

You deserve a better teller than I of such matters. I, though, am all that is available, to either of us. So then.

My master had repaired thence to that house some years since, acquired it with a fortune gained, according to whispers, by illicit means. With such rumors followed others, of debauchery, such as loose-tongued fools all these years on enjoy speaking of Dashwood's or the Order of the Second Circle.

Among the countless of my faults was never the love of wicked-ness, and it was not on account of but despite such stories that at last I journeyed to that place and said I was hardworking and asked if there was a position. My parents and sister had died, and I, not wel-come in the village of my birth, was hungry unto death.

He it was who let me in and heard my plea. I had hoped to forge some bonds among the other staff but that was not to be. They were not many, and they seemed no more indifferent to my ambiguities than had been my erstwhile neighbors. Though such qualities never troubled my master then or ever.

I and all the others of the house had been given to ready for a party. When the carriages arrived I knew not the visages of those within but from the whispers of the household did I learn that this was Sir Thus and this Lady So and this Dowager Et and that Lord Cetera, and so on in such manner. And before the clock struck twelve the scandals I had heard were outshone in license by what I witnessed from these my betters. I'll not tarry with the sins I saw. I would have you know, however, that even then, before he told me tales of animal courage and tragedy, upon my master's face as he engaged without restraint in the carnality and blasphemy of that night, I saw, alone among the revelers, not eagerness but infinite patience. And a question.

The question? The question that I saw was, Shall this be what it is, to be?

As I lie here and speak, for all your care and patience with me, your mien suggests again that aspects of this story are familiar to you.

As I crossed a room with possets, a brash young lordling took ahold of my breast and began to laugh at what he felt and I begged him to let me go and a woman still resplendent in a tiara and nothing else joined him in his investigations and those about them laughed eagerly enough. My master watched and I saw that cool distance in his gaze and wondered if I must submit to those unasked-for attentions, as did, I saw, others of the staff, with resistance of various degrees.

I was a curio to them who felt me and took my clothes, as I have often been, with the chimerical cunny-pizzle at my thighs.

So. I tottered and hoped that the goblets I would spill might smite them but the tray was caught. By my master. Whom but a moment before had been all the way across the chamber.

He said, Let this one be, and held me up.

She and he who had hold of me berated him and lamented the quality of his hospitality, at first in jest, then with a harsher tone, and the lady grasped my hair and made to pull me from his hands.

I watched only my master. I cannot give a name to the emotions I saw upon his face. I have come to believe that what I witnessed in that instant in his dark eyes was a yearning not to have a care. Chased, from a deep place within, to his own anguish, by that very care he did not welcome.

He slapped the woman's face and she screamed at him and none spoke until he laughed with gusto though I saw only melancholy in his eyes, and most of his guests, relieved like children granted permission, started up again their own glee and cachination, though the pair who had toyed with me did not.

Faze cuh too voodray, my master bellowed as he took me thence. We left to the sound of the boisterous obedience of the sots and reprobates. He took me to the room above. There it was that, not seeming to know whereof he did it, he told me of the pigs.

I pray you forgive me. Kind as you are you cannot hide your impatience. I shall be as quick as I am able with the rest of the tale. My time in this vale will soon be done. Even if yours, perhaps, it comes to me to think, will not. You have the look of one who has traveled long. I feel as if I speak to a deeper watcher behind your eyes.

He spoke to me, my master, with a manner of gloomy abstraction and I told him thank you for delivering me and he shook his head. I asked him why he had come to my aid, not saying that grateful as I was, even as we waited there, a maid, a cook, and a stable boy were subject to the appetites of his visitors below, and they had not seemed to me glad of such attentions, yet had their plights not troubled him to action.

He said, Bromach enjoins us to protect those who need protecting.

I did not understand and I said nothing.

He sat with me the rest of that night, until the guests were gone. I recalled the expressions of those he had interrupted when he'd pulled me from them and I knew this was not the last I would see of them.

At week's end I told him of the figures I had glimpsed in the thickets and sedge, watching the house. He did not tell me to clear my head of fancies but nodded with more sorrow and told me we would see what we would see.

The night was dark and I awoke to a warning owl. I rose from my bed and heard the steps of infiltrators, their careful creep howbeit. I looked out when they were past my room and saw the woman and the man from the gathering and two men with them who skulked with greater expertise, and I believed them footpads enticed to this folly with the others' coin. I could not fathom how they had missed my room, but then it came to me that it was not me they sought, that the enticements of my strange flesh were as nothing to the exigencies of revenge for the slight that they perceived in having had that flesh denied them.

I followed them as close as I durst in the dark passages. I was in agonies about how to warn my master. They knew the way to his bedchamber. I prepared myself to call out, whatever it brought down upon me, at the touch of the first man on the handle of the door. My heart sounded in me like the drums in Hell as we approached but even as I drew breath, that door opened.

Without light I only heard a quick and sudden rush. Three gasps, one two three. The first instant of a scream instantly snuffed, a gush and dripping. I could not see. For that I thank the Lord Jesus.

Something pulled me into the room. My master's hand, I knew it. I felt his finger upon my lips and heard his whisper: Stay silent, whatsoever you see. I prepared, but even so when he struck his flint and lit the candle, I could not but let out a sound like a tormented soul at the sight of all that red, at the last and endless stares of those who had come for him.

My master bade me hush.

I was able to obey him, until I turned and I saw him in turn. At that sight did I cry out again.

A bodkin in his neck shuddered with his breaths and whispers. From the place wherein it stuck him blood gushed as did water from the rocks of Massah and Meribah. He saw where I stared, pulled the dagger thence. Out came more gore.

He said, It will close. He placed his bloody finger on my own lips and shushed me once more.

And I was quiet, for him.

When the blood had stopped, he said to me, Now I will have to move on.

It was not an invitation, but nor was it not. I said to him I would come.

That man was not my master after that night. I do not know what he was to me, but I believe and hope I know what I might have been to him.

He warned me. So I knew he would not change, as did I, with the passing of the decades. His knees did not grow stiff. No silver threads tangled in the obsidian of his hair.

For years thereafter, I awaited what I knew would come. He had warned me at the start.

I will not love you, he said to me. I cannot. But I am not indifferent. There are epochs when I can sit alongside those who matter something to me while they wither and while they die. And there are those eons wherein I do not have the strength for such things. I tell you now, he said when I was still in the spring of my life, that this era is of the latter kind. To have seen so much, so many endings, should inure mine eyes, you might think, and so it is. But here is a secret: always, also, below that, the contrary is also true. The more is seen the more each sight strikes and can sting. Doubly so when I, unseeing, wreak, then see what I have wrought thereafter. I will not ask you to walk with me, and if you do, know that one day when the years anchor you too visibly to death, of which for all that it surrounds me I have no taste to witness a glim more than I must, you will awake and I will be gone. I tell you this, and I tell you that I would not walk with any who made me such a promise, and if I do not urge you to turn from me it is but because I will not urge anyone to do anything. Should you go your own way I will not blame you, and will celebrate that you have abjured the certainty of abandonment. If this is to be the case, you should head away from me. He pointed.

You should head yonder. My way is this way. He reversed the direction of his finger.

You know which way I took.

We traveled together a long time. He showed me many things.

We were rich, we were penniless, we were of moderate means, then rich again, and poor at last. He was violent, never with me, and he was gentle. We were holy and profane.

I could have wished a better place than this to see out these my days. But they are fools who plan and worse fools who hoard their money for any such vain plans and I do not regret how I have lived. Alongside him.

But you are not here for these stories. I have the right of it, do I not?

Thank you again for the water, for unexpected company at my end.

Years after I had joined him—and this was years ago—I gathered the courage to ask him who was Bromach. Bromach, whom he had told me at the start had required that I be protected. Bromach, because of whom I had been saved, Bromach who would only abide so much. Bromach of whom he had never spoken again. I asked him then because though I was not old, I was not young anymore, and I did not know how much time I had left with him.

He smiled at my question. That was a rare occurrence.

Bromach was a god, he said.

What god? Of what?

Of whatever I want, he told me. And his name is Bromach and Aspad and Tremelinkid and Bo and he is a she and a he and both and neither, four-corners style, cat you scotty—(I knew not and know not what he meant by this)—and they are a they, a lion an eagle a woman a camel a man, the god of kindness, vengeance, bitterness, sorrow, lack of interest. Sometimes, he said, I invent my own gods to worship. That is the lot of the kin of gods. We will not be worshipped in our part, and no one should worship their own parents, and we will not, cannot parent as did they. We are, I am, too full of power. You might call that the fault of human flesh, too weak for my emissions. Consider my puissance too much if you will, but my power leaves me barren. Without worshippers or wains, we, I (quoth he), for all others who have announced themselves of like stock have lied or erred, and I am alone, must create my own passions of life and its beyond. Sometimes including gods to obey, for a while.

He was gay and sorrowful in one moment, so I kissed him.

When I awoke—this was years thereafter—and he was gone, I was not angry. He had warned me. I was not angry that he left me penniless at my end. I believe in my heart he would have bequeathed it had we any money left, but he had never promised that.

Only he, among all who walk the earth, has a story worth writing down. This I said, and thus have I long believed. But as I lie here and feel the end approach—I have no fear of it—I am proud of what mark I believe I am in that, in the book of the world.

The great, great run of us, in the tales told by winds and mountains and trees and cities and the sea and Leviathan and the abyss and by him, my erstwhile master then companion, of whom we spoke, are full stops. We are what happens in the infinitely small instances between one moment worthy of remark and another. We are specks. Milliards of us contained within each such tiny beady ink eye.

But I believe, and I hope it is not the arrogance of love that befuddles me because I do not say I loved him and I know he never loved me, but I believe that were he ever to speak of me, if he were to write the great book of his own life, when it came to the few years I was at his side, that he, for the curl of a moment, as if raising a finger, would pause as if for breath.

That I am one of the elect, privileged forever to be a comma.

One more sip? Thank you.

If I could, I would tell you, but I do not know his whereabouts. It is that, is it not, for which you have come? You are a seeker, are you not?

Oh! It is not him you pursue? You have prevailed and would pre-
vail upon others to find him, those who knew and know not that that
was and is their lot, their destiny and duty? They will not heed you?
Have failed to do as you have urged?

And the pig?

After all your patience, you are here not for my story nor even his,
but for that story he told me, of the pig? Mercy. You seek the pig?

Quick then. The Angel of Death comes closer.

And here on the shores of the last sea, my inner eyes are clear, and
behind that skull-faced doomsman of the Lord is, yes, something
colder, colder and older than that ender of ways and anything, and it
watches, that stirlessness, a vorago thowless and silent, from and of
darkness, like that in the center of eyes.

Look at me.

What is it you would know?

CHILD'S POSE

THE BIG WINDOWS IN DR. SHUR'S OFFICE FACED INTO THE darkness of the forest. She was standing by them as Stonier came in, meeting the fascinated stare of a deer. The animal shied at Stonier's entrance and bounded into the trees.

Shur sat in the armchair by her desk and gestured Stonier into the chair facing it.

She was as old as his mother, and watching him with a not dissimilar concerned gaze. He was experienced enough to know how many "unlikely" figures, according to clichés, excelled in the military. He himself was, he knew, one such, according to certain conventions. Still, he found it hard to imagine this gentle smiling white woman in floral prints barking orders or snapping to attention in response thereto.

"Did you meet with Caldwell yet?" she said at last.

"I'm seeing him today. Got another message about whatever this project is. He said he wants me because of my experience." He shrugged. "Said I'd hear him out. Maybe he's trying to take my mind off things. I wouldn't have had him down as giving a shit. He said—"

Shur held up one hand. "Remember what I said? I'm not going to ask you to break confidences. I don't want to know any details. When we discussed it before, you said it made you uneasy. That tells me something about the place Caldwell has in your head, and that you've told me he had in your husband's head. And I know you don't know why, but that's OK. It's good to see you trust your instincts. I'm sensing pride in you. And that's good too. I think you feel pressure to do as he suggests, but that you're resisting it, using the techniques we've discussed. You work in a dramatic and, often, unfortunately, pretty negative world. So it's even more important that you learn to work in positive ways. To focus on positive things. Especially given your loss."

"It's hard," Stonier said. "He was gone." Shur waited. "I was really trying. I missed him but I was trying. Even if I was numb. And then all of a sudden . . . he wasn't dead? But then . . . now he is? After all? What am I supposed to do with that? You get why it's a bit hard to hear you talk about positivity."

"When I say 'positive,' I don't mean for you to deny pain. That's, well, denial. Everyone we love is a vector. And the winding down of that is agony. And for reasons we don't understand, you've had to face it twice. And I'm so sorry for that. It's more than anyone should have to deal with. But you do, and how you do matters." She sat back. "Have you looked into any of those groups I listed for you?" she said.

"Not yet."

"I'm not going to rush you. But I will say, again, that I think they could be good for you. Not everyone loves or loved their spouse like you do. He carried the token you gave him." Stonier started at that. He touched his jacket, above an inside pocket. "You told me."

"Not exactly," he said. "What I gave him was a lot of shit about his stupid hobbies." He smiled. "Which he then got me into too."

"Are you ready to share what it was?"

"Nah," he said. "It's embarrassing. Like reading out a love poem. The first time we played his games together, he took what I was holding and he kissed it, and kept it. And then I got it back," he whispered. "He was holding it, in the tunnel . . ."

"And now you have it back. This connection, this is why, in my opinion, you—*you* you, not just anyone—you'd benefit from being part of a community. You're experiencing a very particular coagulation of love, loss, and anger. Be proud of yourself. For a lot of reasons. Like, you think that Dr. Caldwell sees that in you too, and wants it for whatever he's doing, and you're standing up for yourself. Everyone has their own agenda. That's OK. Agendas are OK. But you want to do something positive with your love, maybe with your anger, too. That's why I gave you that list."

"That list?" He almost shouted that. "Volleyball? Rock climbing?"

"What is it that makes you so angry about it?" Shur said.

"You want me to take up painting? Knitting? The fucking Life Project? What even is that? I'm not some goddamn flake—"

"Has anyone in your family ever suffered from Alzheimer's?" Her question closed his mouth. "One of the ways you can calm people with Alzheimer's is to give them a doll. You tell them to look after it. It can help."

"You think I'm losing my mind."

"Not at all. The dolls don't just work on people far gone. One of the most powerful things I ever saw was an interview with a patient, not too far into the disease. He had perfect insight. He held up the doll and he said, 'Don't get me wrong. I know it's not real. I don't know why it helps me to look after it. But it does.' And he smiled."

Stonier stared. "What's your point?" he said.

"You say you know that knitting and rock climbing are wastes of time. And primal scream or rebirth therapy or, sure, the Life Project, are"—she made quote motions—"'flaky,' and 'stupid,' and 'pretend.' That only people fooled by them could benefit. And you think because I'm suggesting them, I think you're a fool, and maybe I'm a fool too. But I'm not asking you to buy into anything. I'm saying I think that there's a chance—a chance—that they could help you even though you 'know' . . . " She shrugged. "How they sound."

He licked his lips. "The Life Project?" he said warily.

"Dr. Alam's Life Project," she said, mockingly grand, then slipped back to her usual voice. "Yes. A positivity center, yes, stupid, I know, I get it. The fight against despair. OK, roll your eyes. What if you tried it anyway? Skepticism and all?"

He said, "I'll think about it."

"I know. I think you've been thinking about it since I suggested it."

He looked into the shadowed darkness where the deer had run. An owl, he saw, watched him from that gloom now.

THE HIGHER THE SECURITY PROTOCOLS OF A LAB, THE MORE STEPPED SEATS

in a semicircle there were in the viewing rooms, ranged around the wire-threaded glass, looking in. But everyone must sleep. And, too, was there not that certain politesse in the Unit, the granting of sufficient solitude to he for whom they were all there? Was that not what the small hours were for? So Unute was alone in the back row of the largest amphitheater. He stared into the white-lit chamber, all trays and blades and paraphernalia in locked cabinets. In the center was the gurney. Atop it, congealing out of fleshy matter in swirls like candlemelt, an egg-pod. More than a meter high. Veinlike protrusions mapped its surface. It was the color of an island hog.

When Unute, B, turned his head at last, he saw through the door pane into the corridor beyond. Made out a dim figure, standing still, backlit by the hallway fluorescents. Someone had come to press their face at the window of the viewing room, into which their own pass did not grant access, perhaps. They cupped their face to blank out reflection. A man in a child's pose.

B and the observer regarded each other. Had the man made out the words B was muttering without sound when he stared at the egg? Had he read from those lips, Come on, please?

When a guard paused, B noted how gently she put a hand upon the watcher's shoulder, so that he stepped back and the light illuminated him, and B knew him. Stonier.

B watched him go. Considered grief, the shape of this mourning of this man of this age in this late imperial market epoch, and beneath such distinctions the emotion's unchanged foundation. The sorrow B had seen in Ulafson. Had witnessed a near infinity of times.

He did not look up when the door opened, nor when Diana sidled along the rows and sat in the next but one chair to him.

"What do you have?" B said to her.

"Not much." She handed him a dossier. "That's the report on Thakka. I've never seen the meds so bewildered. And remember, I've seen them work on you. At least when you're injured you have the decency to heal, even if impossibly quickly. And if it's ever enough to kill you . . ." She gestured at the pod. "Thakka . . . he didn't heal. He had a fucking hole in him, and he still came back to say hi."

"Anything on the babirusa?" B said.

"Before the egg? No. It was pig meat. They went over it a ton of times with a gauss field, and the whole lab's a Faraday cage. It's clean. No tags."

"It would never let anyone chip it, anyway," B said. "I don't think." He sounded not quite certain.

She stared at the pod. "How is it?" she said. "Pushing out of something like that?"

"I can only tell you what it's like just afterward," he said. "On the outside."

"It must be an effort," she said. "It's tough, that stuff. You must be born—reborn—straining."

Diana had seen photographs of two of the chrysalises from which Unute had emerged, after injury catastrophic enough to temporarily end even his unfathomable body. One image had been sepia, of the object alone: in the other, two women and a man in Damascene fashions of a century's vintage stood stiffly alongside the ovoid shape, in the corner of a garden. That picture had been colored, carefully, by hand. The egg before her was darker, bloodier-colored, than in that image.

She said, "I can't believe that things . . . that time . . . What's the word? That it echoes."

B gestured for her to clarify.

"That eventually after you," she said, "thousands of years later, the same story would recur. Like with your mother. Your band. Peaceful settlement, invasion, cruelty, desperation. Narcotic, ecstasy. Appeal. To something. Some power. Some source." Her face was hungry. "Glowing, electric-blue intervention. And then a weapon's born. A weapon that won't die. And, after that, revenge."

"Diana," he said. "You're one in a long line of smart people I've known who are capable of missing obvious things. 'Eventually'? You can't imagine how many times I've seen, you name it, squirrels on a good tree get pushed out by other animals. Badgers. Mink. Frogs. How many times I've seen one of them look like it was pleading with the sky. How often I've watched a shoal of fish in a nice rock pool get pushed out, eaten, chased away. Seen one of the displaced ones eat some weird algae and stare up as if into . . ." He shook his head. "Heaven. Waiting for lightning." He shrugged. "Stare up at me."

"What?" Diana managed to whisper.

"Deer. Bears. Iguanas. Termites. Bats. Chimps. Dodoes. I've watched a snail petition its gods. Against other snails. People, too. I remember a young *erectus* woman chewing nasty-looking leaves after a raid by tougher *erecti*. I saw the same sort of thing twice with Neanderthal families, six thousand years apart. Not because of other Neanderthals, by the way: *sapiens* was always more trouble. That's a cliché but it's true. I saw a *floresiensis* woman try it after a particularly brutal raid. Maybe if she'd picked a different drug it might have worked. In which case, maybe it would have been her species that made it through. And my mother wasn't the only *sapiens* to give it a go," he said. "You have no idea how many times I've seen it tried. This little cycle, what gave rise to me. It's the most common story in the world."

"There's more of you . . . ?"

"No," he said. "You're right that this was something special." He nodded at the glass. "I've seen a whole lot of prayers unanswered. This is the only time I ever saw the lightning come in response. The exact combination of drugs and temperature and genetics and stress that worked for my mom? Worked for his, too."

"What was that blue lightning?" she said at last.

"I don't know what it was," he said. "You know that. I'm past that, I'm here for help in how to be. You're the one who still thinks you can figure out whats and whys. You'll be disappointed. Anyway, this is the only other time I know of when it worked. The first time as tragedy. Then as farce." He smiled. "You know, Karl was always much funnier than most people make him out to be."

"This pig . . ." Diana whispered. "This is farce. The repetition of you, the original tragedy."

"What I said," B said, "is that's the only other time I saw it. Doesn't follow it never struck before. Why would I assume I'm the first time it worked? Maybe him and me are both farces."

Diana heard his words as if he were a long way away. She shook her head as if to clear her ears, as if her shock were water.

"You'll be getting a data dump soon," he said. "From what's in there. Maybe it'll get you further along your way. Closer to your cloned supersoldiers."

Diana said nothing.

"Butter wouldn't melt," he said. "I've told you, I don't care. I want what I want, and you, plural, want what you want. By all means: take your samples of me, do your work. Extract what you can, put it into your people. Make your unkillable killers if you can. Just give me what I want."

"What I've always wanted," she said finally, "is to understand."

"Understanding's overrated," he said. "Look at you. So demure."

That was his adjective for her during such little exchanges, and she hated it because it did not feel inaccurate. Refusing to engage with his provocations about supersoldiers and genetic splicing, she felt coy. She was obeying protocols, neither confirming nor denying, even to him. Maybe he could hear heartbeats, despite having denied it. Eighty thousand years of data would make him a more efficient lie detector than any junk-science polygraph.

"Which is why we don't lie to him," Caldwell had told her. "We won't risk the bad blood."

"But the Eutychus Program is Neeby," she had said. NEBE—Not Even B's Ears. "If I can't deny it, what do I do?"

"When he talks about it—and he will—say nothing."

"That'll fool him?"

"Of course not. But you won't have *lied*."

"Omission is lying."

"Take that up with a philosopher," Caldwell had said. "Or a priest."

"I don't care what you do with what you learn, if you help me," B said now. "Do you think you're the first people to think of using whatever this is?" He hit his own chest, three times, hard. "I've said you're not the first, the second, nor thousandth. These pills you give me—force-tracking this, field-dampening that—they're just the herbs and salts others have tried. Those carbon-peapod quantum-latticework ziplock restraints you're trying to build? Diana, your face. I can access the manifests, you know, and my physics isn't up to yours but it'll do. You have my blessing. I know what you're doing, and I'll even let you test them on me. You're not the first people to make progress in that area, either. The last woman who did was a witch, thirteen hundred years ago. I helped her too. Let her try her ropes. She called me a wolf, and she called them Fenrir's bonds. I broke out of them, but it wasn't easy."

What do you want, B? Diana couldn't stop herself from recalling the first time she'd asked. To die?

He'd said, You're not listening. You think you're pretty cynical. But this isn't a fairy story for you to be revisionist about. You don't get to disabuse me, I don't think I'm "the Boy Who Learned What Fear Was." I know this isn't "Koschei the Deathless." What I want isn't a moral. I don't want to die. But I do want to be able to.

Death not as destination but as horizon. Not death up close. His desire not for the end but to continue not-ending in a quite new way. In the shadow of life's culminating end. And if that was what he craved, wasn't that, though he hadn't said this to her either, to suggest that he was not, now, living? What could it be, to exist with the banality of endlessness?

Perhaps he'd seen that epiphany in her. He had smiled a little at her silence. Had added, with winning ruefulness, "I admit I'm not one hundred percent sure that 'Koschei the Deathless' wasn't based on me."

Thenceforth the collaborations. The quantum scatter tracking, existential analysis plus electron microscopy plus stress-response evaluation plus ultrawave detection plus meditation plus biophysics closer to dissident philosophy than mainstream science. Paid for by him with his interventions in the field, her work designed (for her) to understand, to seek and tap his wellspring, and, for him, to strip away his recalcitrant deathlessness. To give him life worthy of the word.

He doesn't want to die. He wants to live.

"I saw it born," he said now, looking at the pod. "The first time. I'd only died a few times then and always hatched right there where I'd fallen. When I was young, I hurt my mother. I remember I bit her when I fed."

"So you even remember babyhood," Diana said. "It's only the berserk that you forget."

"I don't forget," he said. "During the riastrid"—he used the old Irish word—"I'm not conscious enough to be aware in the first place. But listen. Unlike mine, that little pig's mom didn't stand a chance when it came out." He looked down. "I'm glad you haven't asked me its name," he said. "I never gave it one. That's a lie: I've given it many over the years, but none stuck."

"If you've seen so many attempts at a . . . protective invocation," Diana said, "why did this one work?"

He shrugged. "I realize," he said, after a pause, "I may be a pain for your bosses. The ones you've never met. In smoke-filled rooms. Maybe they're not smoke-filled these days. I mean, I'm playing nice. You get your blood and skin. But I know it would be easier for them if I didn't have opinions. If I were an animal, say. It wouldn't be crazy for them to think it would be simpler than dealing with me. They'll be pressuring you to switch your efforts. Build your resources out of that. Go to war behind immortal pigs on tight leashes. Now, I've had to deal with that thing, and with the Cult of the Tusk and the other kooks who've worshipped it, and all I can say is good luck. Why did this one work? How did it manage to be born?" B stared into the cold glow like a scryer into a dark glass. His stare had to it intensity, sorrow such as Diana had not seen in him before. "I've asked myself the same question. And I don't know.

"It's funny: no one knows what they do with those tusks. They aren't any use to dig with. 'Explorers' said they used them against each other during the mating season. The locals called bullshit, rightly so. Now the argument's that they're for display. Which is a way of saying you have no idea. And all the while those tusks just keep on growing. They have to grind them down, gnaw on things, scrape them, their whole lives. Imagine if they didn't."

"Why didn't you tell us about this thing before?" Diana said.

"When you say things like that," B said, "you remind me how young you are. I get that this pig is a revelation to you, and it's important to me, too. But I didn't tell you about it because I wasn't thinking about it. Because it was a while since I'd seen it." He shrugged. "I get that you might make connections quickly. 'That reminds me of this.' 'That's because you have so few memories in such tiny storehouses. But do you understand how much stuff is in my head? I don't forget things, but that's not the same as having it all to hand or knowing what's useful. How am I supposed to know which of the things that have happened to me matter? Let alone to you? I didn't tell you about the pig like I didn't tell you…" B looked straight up for inspiration. "That a herd of *Glyptodons* survived in Burgundy until the 400s A.D. Like I didn't tell you how many nemeses I've had, or how many of them just…" He made a puff-of-smoke motion. "Just disappeared one day. Mid-fight, even, once. Like I didn't tell you that Sargis was a woman and Shamiram was a man, not the other way around. That there've been cultists who hated me as well as those who worshipped me, followers of life itself who've tried to kill me. That the first scuba gear was invented eighteen thousand years ago. Like I didn't tell you that I've seen inanimate objects come to life. Shall I go on?"

Diana strove to itemize everything he said. A human with a perfect memory isn't human. The thought came to her, but it didn't feel like hers.

"Go on," he said gently. "Write it all down. I'm saying those aren't secrets. It doesn't always occur to me what to tell you because there's so much you don't know, I don't know where to start. So. Yes: there's a babirusa that was born when a she-beast fucked lightning. Like I was."

Was this B or Unute speaking? Diana wondered.

"How did you find it?" she said. "To bring it here."

There was the question that everyone had seemed too shy to ask.

"I didn't," he said. "It found me. Like it always does."

"How? Why?"

"I'll ask it if it gets back," he said. "I hope I can't. I always do. Maybe it'll tell me one day."

"You say it always finds you. That means you always find it, too." She couldn't have said his eyes widened, but he did blink quickly. What are you looking for? she nearly said. But she saw him then like an animal, ready to run, easy—strange to think it—to spook. And she did not ask her question.

"What," Diana said slowly, at last, instead, "does all this have to do with Thakka? Doesn't it seem a stretch that this pig just happens to arrive as this thing with Thakka happens?"

"Did Caldwell ask you to ask me that?" B said.

"What?"

"If this is what you're wondering, Caldwell is too. And the two of you decided that you're more persuasive than him? Good call."

"Unute." She let a little brittleness into her voice. "We know we'll never be able to persuade you to do anything you don't want to. Is it obvious that you spar with Caldwell, sometimes, and seem to prefer my company? Sure. Will we ignore that? No. Does that mean we're playing games? No. We wouldn't be so stupid. If you're trying to trip me up, you should know I couldn't be more off-balance to start with. My job is to deal with an immortal, impossibly strong, fugue-state-suffering harbinger of death . . ."

"OK," he said. "The truth is, it always gets to me, when the babirusa comes. As you can tell. What does this have to do with Thakka? If anything? I don't know. It's a long time since I've seen anything new, and this is new. Thakka was dead. Then alive again. And I found tracks: the babirusa had been there, after the mission. It's not the first time that the pig's been on my trail. But I've never seen anyone come back from the dead when he visits before."

"It's only usually the pig that comes back," Diana said. "And you."

DIANA CALLED UP FAMILIAR FOOTAGE. PREPARATIONS IN THE LOCKER ROOM.

The washed-out color of the digital footage, fizzing soundtrack. Specialists strapping on gear. Thakka and Chapman checking weapons. Stonier setting scanner calibrations. Miller and Cohn laughing at some scatological joke. Grayson exercising—just like him to do that in the middle of the room. Keever checking the map. Ulafson walking over to Unute off in the left-hand corner of the screen. Ulafson reaching into the pocket of his tightly done-up jacket—you had to know where to look on the crowded screen to notice his movement—trying to come closer. Unute holding him back, his arm suddenly up and unyielding. Until the shove of bullets pushing them into a bloody hug.

The screen going white, then black, as the RKG-3 exploded.

Diana remembered the odor in the room itself, just after. Walking through the strong smell of scorch and chemicals, vinegar and salvia, the shreds of bottles and amulets and trinkets and the names of the Uniteers dead to particular circumstances, a shrapnel of apotropaic gewgaws and mementos and holy nonsense, as if such hedge charms could do what heavy ordnance could not, as if they had not been deployed by Unute's enemies many thousands of times.

Diana shook her head to clear it of these memories. She slept for three and a half hours. When she woke she went to Caldwell's office. She knocked and waited and opened the door onto Caldwell speaking into a dictaphone. Something about Akkadian and cuneiform. He met her gaze while he finished his sentence. His eyes were wide and red-rimmed.

"It's bad form to come in before you're invited," he said to her.

"It's bad form not to answer a knock on the door," she said. "You saw my email? What B's been saying?"

"I did," he said.

"He's more or less telling us he knows all the secrets of the world and he'll tell us any of them but we have to ask the right question. Which means we have to ask every question that exists."

Caldwell pulled up her message again. "*Glyptodons*," he said. "Inanimate objects?"

"Magnetism, particle fields, maybe. He's said enough times that our chronology of science is wrong—maybe someone got there before us."

Diana followed Caldwell's agitated gaze to his shelves, his folders and files, his bound volumes. A concordance of ancient technology. Carefully, she said, "None of this means your model is wrong."

She'd seen the color-coded graphs he had worked on for years. Graphics of the historic spread of tools, as traced by cutting-edge archaeology and insights gleaned from Unute himself. The memetic viraling, from polity to ancient polity, of shard-edged flint blades, amphorae and the rolling modular seals pressing monstrous images into the clay that closed them, of mechanisms like that of the Antikythera device, of wheels and bronze and iron.

Where you go, technology follows, Caldwell had told Unute. Who had, Diana remembered, inclined his head, with faint interest.

"How does it not?" Caldwell said to her now. "I've spent a lifetime building up a theory that he's a vector for innovation, not that he meets it on its way. If he's bumping up against sciences like that, way beyond anything in the standard model or the secret standard model, then he's not a vanguard. Whether he knows it or not, it's more likely he's chasing something."

"Does it have to be either/or?" Diana said.

Caldwell tapped his lips with the tip of his finger. "Self-organizing," he said quietly. "Animate inanimates would mean the opposite of winding down. Increasing in complexity, decreasing in chaos. A heroic stand against thermodynamics." He shook his head and said, more clearly, "And he still says he doesn't know what to make of Thakka?"

"No. And I believe him. I get the impression he's waiting for us to come up with something on that front."

"Thakka's body's on ice," Caldwell said. "I have one or two ideas I'm going to pursue with it. Usual drill: we've let the new school have its go, so I'll give it a try old-school."

"Goetic magic? The *Abramelin*?" She kept her voice neutral.

"Some stuff from the *Schemhamphorash*, I think, and *Le Dragon Rouge*. I know, it's a long shot."

"I'm never sure," Diana said, "whether you'd prefer it if old grimoires would or wouldn't work better than nano-scattering abneutron field progression."

"Neither am I," Caldwell said. "I still wonder if there's something we're not picking up about Thakka specifically. What if this isn't something that *happened* to him but something that happened to *him*?"

"We just can't find anything in particular about him."

"There's looking and looking, isn't there? I'll let you know if I have any luck. What about you?"

"There's something in the way B talks about Babe," Diana began. Caldwell raised an eyebrow. "It's a pig," she said, "and I refuse to say Bah-bee-roo-sa every single time. I've never heard him talk about anything like he talked about that animal. I'm wondering about . . . well, pigs. I've been chasing symbols, undercurrents."

"Interesting," Caldwell said. "A rich seam. The Gadarene swine. Long pig." He counted slowly on his fingers. "Twrch Trwyth. Circe's propensity for choerosmorphism. I suppose you could call this the porcine uncanny. Do you know William Hope Hodgson? He wrote an outstanding exemplar of the tradition."

Diana made sure he saw her looking skeptical. "I'll tell you what turns up," she said.

There came another knock. This time Caldwell called, "Come in" smartly enough.

Stonier entered. He stood to a sort of suspicious attention.

"You wanted to see me again, sir?" he said.

"Yes," Caldwell said. To Diana, he said quietly, "As mentioned, I'm pursuing an avenue of investigation."

"I'm sure," she said. Something passed between her eyes and his. "Keep me informed." She slipped out, closing the door behind herself.

CALDWELL GESTURED TO A CHAIR.

"I prefer to stand, sir," Stonier said.

"As you like." Caldwell touched his fingertips together. "Thank you for coming. How are you?"

"Sir."

What was this emotion on Stonier's face? It was not quite dislike. Not quite distrust. It was not disdain. It was dismal and disquieted and dysregulated and disciplined and distant.

"This unit is no stranger to such tragic losses." Caldwell spoke carefully. "And there's something uniquely painful about the particular friendly-fire incidents we suffer."

Stonier looked right at him.

"I'd like to ask you some questions about Thakka."

"I don't have anything to say that's not in the report," Stonier said.

Only an inner core of techs and high-ranking researchers knew that the official story, the one Stonier had been given, that Thakka had lingered, reading as dead on a fritzy scanner, was obfuscatory. Yes, Stonier had seen his husband's head, that second time in the tunnel, and might have asked himself how he could have held on with such injuries, but it had been a desperate moment, and perhaps he doubted his memories.

"You met Thakka on duty here, I understand," Caldwell said. "I know how competitive it is to get into this unit. We're all fortunate to work in this remarkable field. And we all know that Unute, who has, let's not forget, also saved a great many of your comrades, can't be held responsible for his actions in his charged state. You've expressed your reservations about taking part in my work, and I could simply order your participation, but it's important to me that this is voluntary. I want to talk to you because no one knew Thakka like you. I want to see if we can piece anything together about him that we've missed. I'm pursuing this to see if there are ways we might minimize the danger from having—excuse me, that's not the right formulation—from choosing to work with Unute. I'd welcome your help. For all our sakes."

The silence stretched out. Caldwell took a deep breath and slapped his hands down upon his desk.

"We are, as I say, fortunate in this work. You could say blessed." Now he looked up and met Stonier's eyes. "You could say, 'Bless us.'"

Caldwell made sure not to change his expression. Internally, he relaxed into relief and disappointment. Sign offered, but countersign not forthcoming. This was verification. This interaction was not to be a liaison of any occulted elect.

"So," Caldwell said, his voice careful. "Might it interest you to develop such protocols?"

"We all always knew it wasn't safe to work alongside Unute," Stonier said.

Caldwell knew to what species of my-country-right-or-wrong pop stoicism he was about to be subjected. He was surprised. For all that Stonier was hard to read—nomen est omen—Caldwell would have thought the pain he discerned in the man would preclude such bromides. This was in part what had made him wonder if he saw in Stonier a confederate in his nameless sect, fellow hierophant of clandestine

NOTHING CROSSED STONIER'S FACE.

knowledge. To risk finding out, with a calculation that, even if it turned out not to be true—as was the case—the work Caldwell presented would appeal to a man a hair away from breaking things with rage and loss.

But Stonier kept his eyes on the middle distance, and explained that They Had All Known the Risks, that There Was No Greater Honor, and so on. And Caldwell had to hear it all out. He waited through Thakka Died Doing His Job, and more such.

"As I said," Stonier said, "there's nothing I can tell you. If you'll excuse me, sir, I have another appointment."

"With Shur?" Caldwell said. "I was aware that a course of sessions is obligatory under certain circumstances. Which is rather to the point of what I've been saying—that we've been having more of those circumstances than we might like. Perhaps that's why these sessions are no longer outsourced."

You could see the logic of it, Caldwell supposed. He knew that the more serious officers were less likely to sneer than did armchair specialists. If you insisted that trauma such as inevitably impacted those in the Unit be addressed by an expert, then in-house would be better. A soldier perhaps needed to describe to a professional interlocutor not violence in its vague enormity but the exact and particular bloodiness of seeing the man alongside whom they worked at killing, eighty thousand years old and who could not die, entering a blank- and glowing-eyed state and shoving the head of an enemy right into the gun turret of a tank or ripping his own comrade's ribs out through his back. Leaving a man whom everyone had believed dead but who had been alive, in a cavern beyond a doorway, crooning to no one, begging for help, dying of thirst and a terrible wound.

"Of course," Caldwell said. The man was hopeless. "I'm sure that's invaluable."

When Stonier answered, Caldwell realized that his own tone had perhaps not been so open-minded as he'd intended.

"It is" was what Stonier said, and it was a challenge. "It really is."

Caldwell was not ashamed. But he was interested. "I'm glad to hear it," he said. He had no idea if he was lying, patronizing the man, or telling the truth.

KEEVER ENTERED WHILE UNUTE WATCHED THE CLEANING CREW, IN PROTEC-

tive gear, waddle across the lab in the glow from the oscilloscopes, then begin scrubbing in the shadow of the pod.

"I didn't think you'd have the clearance to get in here, Jim," B said. Keever held up the lanyard he wore. Showed B the photo of a Dr. Kim from Section 3. "There's always someone who owes you a favor," he said.

"Nawa hamkke hae, Kim baksa," B said.

"Jeongmal gamsahabnida," Keever said, and sat. B gestured at the backpack Keever had set down.

"Going somewhere?"

"For a couple days," Keever hesitated. "I got a call from Joanie. Miller's wife? I don't know if . . ."

"Sure," B said. "I remember Miller."

"I didn't think you'd forget, I'm just never sure which names you know. Joanie called me. She's not doing well. She said she needed to talk to me, wouldn't do it on the phone. I think she needs to . . . to vent. I have a responsibility."

After a silence, B said, "What have you heard?" He nodded at the window. "About what's in there?"

"That it's an old friend of yours," Keever said. "That's all. What are you doing here, B? I've never seen you like this."

"You're not the only one with a responsibility."

"To do what?"

"To be a familiar face."

They were quiet for a while.

"For a long time," B said at last, "I've kept a diary."

"Are You There God?" Keever said. "It's Me, Berserker."

"Not exactly. A record of my deaths."

"That's some macabre shit," Keever said.

"Only the ones when I hatch again somewhere else," B said thoughtfully. "I've always thought that those are the ones that really matter."

"With your memory," Keever said. "What's the point . . . ?"

"It's not about remembering. Mathematicians remember formulas but they still do their working out on a blackboard."

"And did you?" Keever said. "Work it out?"

"No. That's the problem. Sometimes at the point of ending, I kind of know I'm going to hatch in another place. Sometimes I can almost figure out where it's going to be. Or even decide, it feels like. But never quite. Maybe I've been doing it wrong."

"Dying?"

"Sure. And thinking about it. I was looking at the details of what happened to me, to try to figure out patterns. But what if that's not the most important aspect? What about what happens to everyone else? Maybe I shouldn't have been keeping a list of my deaths, but the ones I cause. Maybe that's where the pattern is."

Keever said nothing.

"And whatever it is that's going on with me—it being everything—it's maybe especially about what I do when I'm in fugue," B said. "The deaths. And especially especially the ones that I didn't mean to do. That I'd undo if I could. Maybe they're the key. And I can think about them but the truth is, I don't like to. Maybe I should, though. You and me," B said. "We've never really talked about what I am."

"I don't care what you are."

"That's good of you. But the world does. I never liked the idea that I was a demigod. It's been the most popular theory, and if it's true, the questions wouldn't be about what happens to me or how I feel about it, but what I do to the universe. Do I bring good or bad? Life or, you know, not life?"

"None of it was your fault, son," Keever said. "Nobody blames you."

"Everybody blames me," B said calmly. "Ulafson blamed me. How many comrades had he seen me kill?"

"Well, he was wrong. I know you heard about Shur, that we got her in when you were pig hunting. That's why we hired her. To keep people's heads together. To stop them from being wrong about you."

"What if she's here to stop people from being right about me?"

B was tired. Of the metaphysics of murder. Of being such a metaphysic, perhaps. A memory came to him, blurred, dark rooms, the hidden bunkers, he, in the rising riastrid glory, fists, the gun, that wet burrow of bullets into his self, and rip bite shoot gouge, and stay back, comrades, stay back, investigators of and companions to this immortal flesh, because here he was on a mission and bang cut slice and here came luminous darkness chasing the lightning at the edges of his vision, and in the last instants before the light effaced him, here came Thakka, be careful, Thakka, you are too close, and—

"Thakka knew the risks," Keever said. "I'm sorry, but it was his mistake."

B said, "Stonier blames me. I blame me."

"B," Keever began.

But B's face changed. He rose. From beyond the glass, shouts were audible.

"Get . . . out . . ." he said, moving his lips with exaggerated motions. He semaphored his hands, strained to get the attention of the cleaners within, pointing at the gurney.

The egg was vibrating.

"Get . . . out."

One of the women saw him waving and grabbed her colleagues and tried to drag them back and B jumped over the seats before him to land hands down by the window. He rapped hard on the glass. From the corridor came a commotion. The door to the viewing room banged open and Caldwell and Diana ran in, summoned by alarms. The cleaners scrambled for the lab exit.

B, Unute, the berserker, the deathless, stood like one visiting an imprisoned lover, hand on glass, by where the flesh pod shook.

"Christ, Jim," he said. "Poor thing. I really hoped maybe this time was different, maybe the egg wouldn't come, or when it did that it was rotten. Or a shroud. I tried, I really tried."

The skin of the egg stretched up. A point. It peaked, pushed out from within, straining into a spike. The membrane abruptly ripped. A bone blade burst up and out and through. A gush of cream- and rust-colored slime sopped out and across the gurney and onto the floor to mix with soapy water.

"I tried," B said again, with terrible sadness. "I knew it wouldn't work," he said, "it's not like I haven't done it before, but I've done everything before, and I still tried."

Stiff legs, quivering hooves drummed up spray, and a twisting heavy thing vibrated and kicked and came out, steaming, raw. Staring. A slick and slickly muscled pig, stumbling, standing, swaying.

It was red-skinned. No, Keever saw, it did not have a skin, not yet, would soon grow that last part of this iteration, and its two new eyes rolled, no lids yet to protect them. Four tusks, each sharp and tightly curved and white and as long as a forearm, dripping with slop.

The babirusa wheezed. It peered around.

"I took its head completely apart," B said. "I didn't leave anything. I really tried."

The huge skinless pig turned to face him.

It launched itself at the window. You could hear it now, you could hear the scream like a tormented child, a screech of eons' worth of rage.

The babirusa reared on its hind legs and hammered with its two front hooves hard enough to make glass designed to withstand an M16 shot shake. It slammed its tusks against the barrier, smearing it with its own rebirth matter, screaming and staring at B and screaming and screaming and screaming to get at him.

"I tried to kill it for a last time," he said. "I tried to let it stay dead."

tooth

THE TUSK OF A DEER-PIG IS NOT THE BEST WEAPON. ITS TIP IS SHARP enough but it is no wicked mako jag. It may pierce but it cannot slice well. What it gains in ostentation, the spiral curve for which a tusk strains loses in efficiencies of death. All this you know. If you were to design a tool for killing it would not be a pig. This you know.

The pig stares. It is watching you and you are naked in the heat and in the deepest parts of its melancholy eyes you see the spit and glint of glow, blue lightning light.

The pig's muscles are tight and ready. You stand on opposite sides of a wide stretch of gray flint between rock striae. You came here through a desert.

You came here once before, centuries ago. You made this a testing place and in it you let yourself die of thirst. To wake again, pushing out of the egg grown from your own dead flesh, discovering yourself hydrated once more.

If you were tasked to make a weapon you would not make a person, either, not even one admixed with the strength of the storm as you are: your hands have no talons, you have no tail to keep you steady, you have no shell, no venom to spit. But you are the world's weapon, and if the world can do its killing with so poor an instrument as you why would it not do so too with a snag-toothed galloper like this?

The pig has let its tusks grow very long this time and they are not so back-curved as before. The image comes to you of the animal standing for weeks at a tree, bracing itself, bracing its teeth, pulling, to shape them against their inclinations into these batons.

You hold up your hands, palms out.

—Pig, you shout. —Little brother.

The animal screams.

—Pig brother, you shout. —Once there was a grub called Anger. It crawled in the water and ate the bowels of fish and it hated them. It smeared itself with itself. It made a pupa with its spit and slept inside and when it came out it was a dragonfly that shone and its name was Gladness. It flew away.

The pig watches you.

That story was told to you by a spirit spitter of the Fern Clan. They were squat people with broad faces and backward-sloping skulls, but they welcomed you as if you did not have the physiology and physiognomy of people given to killing them. Their dragonfly and fly and moth stories calmed you and so you tell this one to the pig that has found you.

The pig stamps, you hear the crack of its hooves. Little brother, you think, you're a creature of the river shore, this hot stone must hurt, but you have to be done talking now even in your own head, because here the deer-pig comes, running, head down, the spearpoints of its teeth pointed at you.

You sing to it as it comes. A song of mourning.

—I'm sorry little brother, you shout. —You hurt her coming out. She would have died anyway. All I did was ease her way.

You slide sideways at the right instant and turn as the pig snorts its frustration and comes ungainly to a stop when it can and turns to watch you with its sad little eyes. Runs at you again, as the sweat runs down you.

Again. You let your attention go and look up at the birds, seeking always the watching bird superior of which you dream. You listen to the drum of the pig's feet and now for your third evasion you jump straight up and let it pass beneath you. But it stops with perfect abruptness below you, teeth like trap-bottom spikes.

—Clever.

You come down and into your thigh one of the waiting tusks goes, look at all that blood, feel the rip of muscle, no matter how many times you've been torn apart you are not indifferent to pain. Listen to the triumphant shout of the pig, at the edge of its fugue, the slip that you know so well from chronology into a timelessness of carnage, and if you can hear in the piggy call that sadness of the void that you know will not be filled even by such successful violence, well, there is nothing you can do now to stop this dance.

And, here, rising in you in echo, what is this but your own counter-trance?

Blue-white lightning across your vision. You hear your own scream. You feel the snap and judder of burning bright arcs and in and back you go behind your eyes, looking out of them as through a gap between leaves in a canopy overhead, and you are deep, deep, and it has been days since you have released this and

let it

out

of the darkening sky, and when you come back, standing against stone, what you see is sunset, and you have your body again, your eyes with which to see the dusk, skin to feel the cooling, and what you are thinking of is the pig's mother's death.

Breathe deep, Unute.

Your left leg, gored, is broken in two places. A bloody bone spur protrudes. You can touch your molars with your hand through a hole in your throbbing cheek. Thud thud in your head.

Now look across the stone.

The pig as-if stares at you with the holes where you took its eyes. It lies quite still amid its entrails.

—Little brother, you say. —Go to sleep.

Let your leg reknit.

Lift the carcass onto your shoulders and walk hours into the dried-up remains of flora by a knoll. Strip the twigs of thorns. Make fire. You lift the body of the deer-pig, heft it as high as you can, to drop it in the heat.

And as you glance up at the dripping dead belly, you see ink. A sigil.

You bring the thing down slowly. Look closely at a circle, half the size of your palm. Four lines ajut from it, two curling to either side. You wipe it and it does not smear. This is a tattoo.

This is not a thing you have ever seen before on this beast.

You grip the largest of its tusks and wrench, snap it, splintering it off. Take it to the deer-pig's underside, and score it with that blade of brokenness. Bloodily you cut the tattoo from the creature's skin and wipe it clean. Lay it near the fire to dry.

Only then do you give the pig to the flames.

You do not sleep. Give it the respect of watching it burn.

All through the next day. Push your hands into the ash and coals at last, and there is a sting to it, but you touched fire when you were a month old and did not flinch. Now you bring handfuls of the ashes and from outcrops and the edges of gorges you let the wind take them.

Look at your hands. You remember the feeling of the crack deep within the pig's mother's neck, the cessation of her keens.

Your brother had full-grown tusks when it was two months old. When it was three months old, it used them to defend its band. A great snake reared up from the swamp wherein its siblings and cousins snuffled and rolled, a tongue the size of Unute's hand tasting the warm air while the pigs screeched. Alone among the herd the piglet child of the lightning ran not from but toward it, sank its teeth within its neck, thrashed and kicked and ripped.

You followed it. For years. Staying beyond the bounds of pig society while it huffed and fought and screamed with that vatic violence, shredded through predators and invading pigs and those pigs from its own band that did not get away from it far enough when it was in that glow. Your task, all those years, was to watch. You followed it throughout its first life.

The first time it died it was because it misjudged momentum and flailed on a cliff above a harsh landscape, and you ran for it, broke your own injunction to keep distant, reached out to grab, but it was too far from you and you saw it fall and felt the air pulse and saw the explosion of blue lightning when it shattered on the earth. You stood over the remains and not knowing if that was the last of it you wept. But over the hours you saw the gobs and gobbets of its ruins smear together and grow like tallow running in reverse. To make a chrysalis. That made you weep in a different mood.

When it kicked out of its egg and stared, dripping, with its newly reconfigured eyes and an expression of shock, you greeted it. You had been waiting and you held your arms out.

But the deer-pig regarded you only with wariness. It would not walk with you.

You followed it throughout its second and third and fourth lives, too, and much of its fifth, and good proportions of the eleven that came after, and then, even after you were certain that you could not learn anything about yourself from any of the lives or killings of this berserker pig, you could banish neither curiosity nor fraternity. You sought and found it again, sometimes, in the years thereafter. Tasted ozone in the air when the animal entered its murderous raptures.

The second time it died it had chased a wild dog into a gorge to where six packs waited, their own infighting put aside awhile, and—you watched—at the cost of dog after dog after torn-apart dog, they bit the rampaging babirusa apart.

You were there again when it awoke from its second egg.

The third time a great bird of a kind gone now from the world hauled it skyward and dropped it. The fourth time the grandpiglets and great-grandpiglets of its aunts placed poisoned plants within its food. Thereafter, when it rose again—to find you—it lived alone. The fifth time a forest fire took it.

—You were hurting her when you came, you told it, the second time it rose, and the third. —Perhaps her belly wasn't made for lightning. You were tearing her open. She couldn't have lived. I helped her.

You remember the hot warm weight in your hand when you eased it out.

—That's the only time I interfered, you said to it, when it came back.
—That first time.

You had put the piglet down. Retreated into the river and watched the bleating newborn thing with rills of lightning playing upon it while it called, and you'd seen the pig tribe come to the water's edge, to claim it.

Those first few lives, how could you not follow? Read your lightning brother like the symbols of the mystics of the valley, straining to glean insights? And if, in its resolutely ordinary rummaging, its scratching of its back against bark, the days of remorseless unremarkable pigness, it was resistant to such parsing, surely you needed to read harder. And in those other moments, when energies built up in it and its bristles went stiff as its tusks and the blue arcs overtook its eyes and it rampaged until trees were down and rocks were smashed and animals were dead and it wheezed and snorted and came back, if then it was opaque in the flat dreadfulness of its violence, what could you learn from that about yourself?

You left it for centuries. Spent them alone or with tribes or in cities, killing ruling loving hiding standing still.

At last you could not disavow that curiosity, the care, and you crossed oceans, tracked stories of hooves and murder amid impossible storms. At last you descended a found ladder of roots to a humid gulley and there for the first time in many lifetimes the deer-pig was before you.

You smiled and raised your hand. It regarded you and for the first time it did so with something like hatred.

When it walked away, for all the years of searching it had taken you to find it, you did not follow.

Seventeen years later you found it again and it growled and you left again.

Three years after that you found its egg fresh and freshly opened and it still dripping in the wet mess of its resurrection, and weak with returned life as it was it squealed to see you and flailed its head to try to gore you.

—She would have died anyway, you said.

You came back to it after two more civilizations rose and fell and this time when you entered those old lands you knew, you could not say how, you were certain that the pig, in whatever of its lives this was, knew you were coming. In the smoldering ruins of a village, this time—people had come by then back to that continent—you found the deer-pig or the deer-pig found you and it stared at you from atop a stinking pile of human dead, and it screamed. It hurled itself down the slope of corpses.

It fought you hard, screaming the whole time, and no matter what you said in what tone of voice it would not calm.

You killed it. You buried its remains deep. You left that land. You took a longboat with far-traveling people to the cold north. You built a legacy as a hunter of bears and monsters. You let the nomads tell stories that claimed you were a dragon. You killed a woman who called herself empress of the trolls. You killed her great-grandson who came to avenge her. And a part of you, you would come to know, a part of you was always waiting. Because one night late when the moon turned the snow of your estate to silver, you saw a shaking at the stockade, and you stood in the doorway of your hearth and hall, and when you saw the babirusa step forward, all the way across the globe from where it had been born, in cold that would have killed its siblings, when you saw it ignore the shouts and spears of your guards, and when you saw its rage and caught its black and desolate eyes across the night land, you were not surprised.

How does it find you?

Whenever you kill it you disperse its body as dust, or weigh it down with iron and sink it in the sea, or take it to the deepest cave you can and shake down the mountain upon it, or throw it into lava. And as well as however long it might take the gusting ash to reaggregate, the world is big, and a pig has to walk a vast distance to hunt you down. There are only so many ways a pig can cross seas. It takes it a long time.

Perhaps it might come to know that you saved its mother from pain, and be grateful. Perhaps it knows, and seeks you, and to end you, for other reasons, every time it wakes. It has seen you so many times.

You have killed it quickly when you could. Slowly when you had to. You have killed it on every continent.

It has killed you too, three times. The first time, in a market in the Fertile Crescent, while the shoppers wailed it stamped you down and rended your belly with its teeth. Perhaps, you thought in those hazy bloody moments, this is the time. But when you woke from your egg, nothing was different. This death, at this animal's doing, brought you no nearer to anything.

All there is left to you now is to hope for many years between each time of finding.

It was a century and a half since last you disposed of the deer-pig's body. You threw each handful high, and watched the motion, a thin line of dirt coming apart in the wind, like the pillar holding up a temple whose time has come. Until it is born again, this pig can fly.

This time you have the tattooed strip of its belly skin.

One hundred and sixty-seven years pass.

You approach a city of arched kiln-shaped buildings. You raise your hands as you come and throw your spear and your shield down. Arrows fly past you from the guard towers by the gate but these are warning shots and as loud as you can you shout: I am here without weapons, I need the help of the shamans.

You wave a little leather scrap.

—I come with the sign of the god, you call. —I am the ink bearer.

The sun slips behind a peak, and now that it's not so silhouetted, you can see the town more clearly. You can make out the sign over the gate, painted in blood. A circle. Two stylized curling lines to either side, jutting, protruding.

Two of the five shamans want to kill you. So far you have spoken to them in the trade creole of the pass, not their own language, in which they cast their votes. So they are startled when now you say in their tongue, That would be a mistake. I would come back. And all I want is to ask about your god.

You hold up the tattooed flesh again, with the town sign upon it. They look at it so reverentially.

—Teach me, you say. —Tell me about this.

The chief shaman takes you to the longhouse.

—What are you? she says. —How do you know of us?

—I'm a knowledge seeker. I spoke to the Church of the Teeth and they told me where to find you.

She spits.

—Heretics and traitors.

—They say that of you. I don't care who is right. You share a god. I know it. Teach me everything about it.

—When it visited, we marked it in thanks, she says.

—I know, you say. —I am amazed it let you. I took your sign from its body.

She stares at you.

—You're the god-pig's brother, she says at last. —One of the children of the lightning.

When you can speak again, very slowly you say, —One of?

She is saying—what is she saying? You can make out what she's saying, can't you? You will concentrate again, very soon, you'll strain to make sense of what she tells you, that's why you've fought lions to come here, because since you killed it in that rocky land you've heard stories of giants, heroes, devils. Children of the lightning, the gods. And you don't know, do you? You don't know what the lightning wants, or how alone you truly are. And you must know.

—Ever since the spirit of the first quiet was interrupted by life, spirits enter flesh when they need do business here. They ride flesh.

The puns works in many languages. She mimes opening a door and thrusts her arms like a cock. She bucks her hips first as if mounted then in an exaggeration of coitus.

—Their children, the children of the lightning, are moths, the woman says. —Butterflies, she says. The children of the lightning sleep in their pupal sacs.

You feel as if you are dreaming. As if you've eaten an herb to make yourself fly.

I remember everything, you say to her. I'm older than my pig brother and I remember everything, you say, so he must too.

No you don't, you don't say it, you mean to but you don't speak, you only think the words.

I was in a chrysalis before he was, you try to say.

There are how many children of the lightning? you want to ask.

But she cares only about the pig.

I was in a chrysalis before him, and as you strain to say that, it comes to you that though you do not remember the times within your egg, you know that it is a lonely place. And you are shocked and stop up your mouth with your hands because that revelation might make you weep.

I am a lightning child, you do not say, like the pig, and we are tools, and only broken tools know they are tools.

A HIDDEN GOD

DIANA KNEW OF B'S CAPACITY FOR A TERRIFYING ATTENTION, and of what his body could do, the vast deviation of its limits from those of humans—or other humans, as she might put it to herself, depending on her feelings about him on any particular day. Extrapolating and considering Babe, she expected it to maintain something of its focus, the rigor of its rage, to be less distractible than others of (what appeared to be) its kind. So, after her first sight of it, Diana waited some hours before returning. Until, unable to resist the urgency of her fervor to learn, she made her way back to the viewing room before she was fully awake. B was still there, still looking through the glass at the deer-pig within. The animal was still rearing and jumping and hammering at the glass to get at him, had not slowed, seemed as full of energy as ever.

"When will it stop?" she said. "Will it stop?"

"It will," B said. "Eventually. It'll crash and fall asleep. If I'm still here when it wakes, it'll start up again."

"How long since it saw you?"

"About 250 years. I'd have to do some counting to be exact."

"It's like this every time?" she said.

"Not always," he said. "But for most of the last seventy-eight thousand years, yes."

"Why?"

"Revenge for something. Hunger for something. I don't know."

"You must have some ideas."

"Some."

"What's your best bet?"

"That every time it wakes," he said quietly, "it can tell I'm there. And I'm the only other thing that hasn't changed. So it thinks I have something to do with what's happening to it. It blames me for itself."

They watched the animal stamp and circle, swinging its head, denting a steel locker.

"Most tranks won't work on it but I'm sure you'll find something to do the trick," B said. "Your bosses must be keen for you to get to work."

She looked at him.

You know what works, don't you? she did not say. And you won't tell us. "You feel sorry for it" was what she did say.

"Is that your big insight?" B said.

Stamp stamp stamp scream scream bite gouge kick. From his pocket B took out a scrap, held it toward her.

"Be gentle," he said. "It's seventy-five thousand years old." He laid it flat upon her palm. A dark soft patch of leather.

"Jesus," she said. "This should be dust."

B shrugged. "There are things you can do to keep things fresh."

"This . . . this is from it." She gestured at the window, at the howling pig. "This used to be its skin. In another life."

"Can you make out what's on it?" he said.

She moved into better light. The leather was a gray so dark it was nearly black. She squinted and made out an infinitesimal distinction in pigment or the subtlest of ridges in the skin itself. A circle. Four marks.

"Someone tattooed it?" she said.

"It was one of the cults that worshipped it," he said. "For a while there were nearly as many cults of it as there were of me. In fact during the worst of the ice age, it had more. Their numbers dropped off since Charlemagne."

"What did they believe?" she said.

"The usual mix. That it was an angel or a devil. Sent by death or the void. Or God. Or something. They didn't agree among themselves. That's not my point. My point is that so far as I knew, this . . ." He pointed at the leather. "Was the last time he let anyone get near, except to kill them."

"So?"

"So whoever did that had some kind of special relationship with it, at least for a moment. Remember the tunnel? Thakka? The deer-pig didn't come in through the warehouse where we did. It came from the other end." He squeezed his eyes shut as if against migraine.

She said, "Are you OK?"

"I'm feeling like there's something just out of reach," he said. "I guess kind of like I'm trying to remember."

"This is where I remind you of your perfect memory," she said.

"Yeah," he said. "I know. And it's you who keeps telling me that memory's not as simple as it seems. You're not the first person who's told me that, to be fair, but you're maybe only the second who's really changed my mind about stuff like that. All the work we did on remembering my mother, there's something I never told you," he said. "I don't know that I ever told myself, but I think I knew it even if I never said it to myself. Is that knowing? Come to think of it, is that remembering?"

Diana waited.

"I saw her once, arguing with my father. My human father. They were trying to keep quiet. I couldn't hear but I could see them. She had something in her hand. I've never put this in words before. It was—" His eyes did not open, but his hands sketched out a shape. "A diadem. Bright. Feathered. A little bird crown."

After a time Diana said, "Did you put it on?"

"It looked like nothing anyone in our band could have made," he said. "And the way my father was staring at it . . . I'd just been with him, clearing out some neighboring tribes. So no one would attack us." He inclined his head in gracious skepticism. "We'd been on the hills, and we heard a crashing in the sky, and saw lightning, over our village. Not like that that birthed me. Red this time. Something new. We rushed back. No," he said, "I didn't put it on. I've had eight hundred centuries to think about it and I think my mother meant it for me. I think it was a gift. I think it was to . . . well, to fix me. I never put the crown on because my father took it from her and threw it into the pit."

He shook his head and opened his eyes and looked at her.

"Why didn't you get it?" Diana said. "You could have."

"She wanted to save me from what I am," he said. "He wanted me to surrender to it. That crown was a gift to her, and from her to me, from the red lightning. It frightened him. Maybe I didn't fetch it out of the ground because I agreed with him. How would you save me from myself? Maybe that's not a gift you want. Maybe I didn't want rescuing. Maybe I didn't want to disappoint him."

"Maybe that's a distinction without a difference," Diana said.

"In the tunnel," B said at last. "Where the pig came. There was a ladder at the end. An entrance I didn't even know was there till later."

"What?" Diana said. She started to speak, stopped, started again. "Why are you showing me this?" She pointed at the pig leather.

"Maybe the tattoo was the same kind of thing as the headpiece. A protection. A gift. I'm showing you this," he said, "to tell you there've always been people out there who want to walk in the babirusa's footsteps. There was a ladder in the tunnel beyond Thakka. And at the top of that was a trapdoor. That's how I got out. It had been closed. I found the hoof tracks down there with Thakka, but that can't have been all. No matter how smart or strong or special that pig is, it didn't get down there without opposable thumbs. So it wasn't there alone. It's not just the pig that has something to do with whatever happened to Thakka. Someone let it in and came down with it. When whatever happened to Thakka happened."

                                                                    . . .

IT WAS A PRETTY SMALL HALL AT THE BACK OF THE BUILDING. IF YOU DIDN'T want to come through the front, through what had once been a showroom for washing machines and was now a large and sprawling thrift shop, there was the rear entrance. That was how Stonier entered.

"Hey."

He stood on the threshold. A smiling woman about his age approached him. She had her hand out from halfway across the room. Behind her the whitewashed room was clean. There were eight others there, looking around and smiling at him briefly before continuing to top up a vat of coffee, sift through papers, pin notices on a corkboard, scroll through documents on laptops. In the center of the chamber, an elderly woman was arranging cheap orange chairs in circles.

"Ideally," the approaching woman said, seeing him watch the setup procedure, "we just want the room to be just one circle, but we're getting too many to fit, now." She shrugged. "A nice problem to have, I guess. I'm Marlene."

"Jeff." He shook her hand.

The other parishioners approached. Their smiles made Stonier close his eyes for a moment in dismay. They were so very friendly.

"Hi there, I'm Edgar." A hand. A big guy with very wide eyes. Stonier shook.

"Sam." A nerdy young person with severe bangs.

"Tree." "Mike." "Sean." Tall friendly white woman, quiet dark-eyed man, older man with an Irish accent.

"Welcome." "Welcome." "Welcome." Shake shake shake.

You fucking sad-sack weak pricks.

For fuck's sake, go easy, killer. Was that Stonier's own voice in his head or Thakka's? Yes.

"You here for a meeting?" Marlene said. "That's great. You're a little early, but if you give us a few minutes . . ."

"I don't know," he said. "I didn't know about the meeting. Maybe I'll come back another time . . ."

"Jeff," she said. Smiled at him and it could have been teasing but no it was not. For an instant rage came up in him, but it subsided, so fast, so soothed by her voice that he shocked himself.

"... I guess I wanted to ask some questions," he said.

This was the third time he had traveled to the hall. The first time he had entered.

"Sure," Marlene said. "Of course. I'll be happy to tell you anything I can."

"I just ..." Stonier said. And then had nothing more.

Marlene stood looking at him, quite still, quite silent. He could say nothing. She took his arm and gently pulled him to one side.

"Let me guess," she said quietly. She looked him up and down. "You feel dumb being here. This isn't the kind of thing you'd ever consider. You hate all that self-help crap. Right?"

"Nah," he said, "that's not fair ..." But he let her continue.

"Someone recommended this to you. Right? Friend, therapist? Your ex? Your mother?" She narrowed her eyes. "And you're at the point when you feel like you need to try anything because you don't trust yourself to go on but this all sounds culty and stupid and you hate that 'feel your feelings' stuff and anyway all you want is just to take a breath ... How am I doing?"

He shrugged at last.

"OK," he said. "Look. I don't even know what this is. I don't know what you do. Someone told me Dr. Alam's name, is all."

"What do we do?" she said. "I mean, we don't do anything, exactly. It's not like we're a religion. And we're not an MLM. We're not going to ask you for more money to get you to OT 2. In fact we won't ask you for any money at all, although, sure, if you're in a position to donate, it all helps keep us in coffee. What we are is a group of people who know ... who have come to learn how important it is to make life mean life. And no, we're hardly the first to do that. And no, it's not as simple as trying to Ack Sent You Ate the Positive, which is no bad thing to do, exactly, but even if you do that absolutely it does not mean pretending you're not in pain. We all are. The idea that you have to choose between the two is the problem. You have to be able to inhabit both. And what we think . . . what I think, I should say—I don't want to talk like we all have a group mind." She smiled and hesitated. "My point is, I think you're here because you're an addict, Jeff."

She held up her hands.

"I'm not attacking you," she said, as if he had remonstrated. "I'm an addict too. We all are. Everyone in this room. And plenty more outside."

"You know that it's bigger than that." It was a tall thin man who spoke now.

Stonier had not noticed him entering the room from the depths of the building. He was middle-aged and blond, in chinos and a loose blue shirt, and he too held his hand out, and he smiled, and Stonier had been ready for just such an entrance, and had, he understood as the man spoke, been hair-trigger primed for a shit-eating grin or the unctuousness of a time-share vendor or the neon-white tooth glow of some Tony Robbins-wannabe. But this was, fuck it, a lovely smile.

"Charles Alam," the man said. Stonier shook his hand.

"You said you've read the literature," Alam said. He did a comedy wince. "I'm sorry, I know some of it is a bit . . . It's 'cringe,' isn't it? Isn't that what young people say? I never know how my tone's going to come across until after."

"Yeah, I read a bit," Stonier said. "About your history and such. It was you and your partner who founded this. But you're new to Tacoma."

"Newish," Alam said. "Yes, we got our start back East, a long time ago. After a few years she went on her way, but I knew there was more we could do. Hence, here we are."

"Here you are."

"And here you are, Jeff. Anyway, you know what we're saying," Alam said. "It's our society that's addicted. To negativity, I don't mean this in a power-of-positive-thinking way, not that I have any problem with thinking positively. But that's become kind of meaningless, these days. If you really start to think about what it is to think positively, it's a lot more effort, and a lot less cozy, than that cliché makes it sound. It's tough. And that's right, it should be. Because we have to break an addiction. Our culture is addicted to negativity, and that means being addicted to death. It's a death culture. That's what we have to break."

"That's a big ask," Stonier said. He laughed. "I mean, death happens, doesn't it. It's not like you can avoid it."

Alam narrowed his eyes.

"I can see it's touched you. I'm sorry for that. The same's true for all of us."

"So I'm addicted to death?" Stonier said.

"Not just you. Our whole society."

"What does that mean? And how am I supposed to break it?"

Alam shrugged.

"You're here, aren't you? That's the first step. Stick around and find out. The meeting'll start soon." He looked at Stonier, then, almost teasing. "Maybe you even feel a bit better already."

Stonier set his face. Because ridiculous as it was, disloyal as it felt, he did.

ON AL MOATAZ STREET, UNUTE LEANED AGAINST A PALIMPSEST OF OVER-
laid and ripped-up posters. He wore a baseball cap and a gray thobe and few people glanced at him in the ferocious brightness. But the woman who emerged at last from the beauty parlor opposite, her hair fixed and newly unmoving, made up, splendidly sullen, looked across the traffic straight at him. She stared at him for a long time, her mouth falling open. She shook her head.

She mouthed Arabic words he could read on her lips.

Come to tell me where I have to go?

He crossed without looking to either side, leaving a wake of blaring horns and braking.

"No," he said.

"I told you," she said, switching to the English he used. "You remember what I told you?"

"You were only eight," he said.

"I was six, and fuck you 'only.' I meant what I said and I say it again." She stuck out her chin at him. If she was afraid it did not show. "I'm not my great-great-grandfather—you can't order me around."

"Great-great-grandfather," B said, "and I didn't order him. I made a suggestion and he followed it. Pretty eagerly."

"I don't care," she said. She walked away from him. He followed and said nothing while she lit a cigarette and pushed through the crowds. "You never made me an offer. And if you did I'd tell you to go fuck yourself."

"Fadila," he said. "I'm not arguing with you. Your decisions are yours. I told you that when you were a kid and you put your hands on your hips, exactly like you did a minute ago, by the way, and told me I couldn't tell you what to do. What did I say then?"

She stopped walking.

"You said you agreed."

"I told you the same thing in every letter I sent, and on every call to your parents. I paid for you to get out when the war started, and I told you the same then."

She turned to him.

"And I paid to get back in." She jabbed her finger at him. "In more than just money, believe me. You got me and Mum out. Thanks. Have I ever asked you for anything since? You know what this life did to her . . ."

"I never asked her to do it. You're not angry with me: you're angry with her. And with her father. And his father. And his."

"Yeah, and who got him started on all this?" she said. "So now what's happened? Another elsewhere, and you're here to tell me to relocate? Where to this time? What shithole at the end of the world are you directing me to?"

"No. There hasn't been another elsewhere. And, Fadila." Unute shook his head. He even smiled. "You're right. You're the one who crept into Raqqa when Daesh took it over. No one asked you to do that."

"I knew they'd fall," she muttered at last.

"And you were right, but don't tell me those were easy years. So this whole 'I'll go where I want to go' thing is tendentious. I know why you came back."

"Why are you here?" she said. She moved and a spear of sunlight pierced her hair and she looked powerful.

"I know why you came here," he said again. "Your mother had to leave the book behind and after she died you found out it had been taken to the museum. You came back for it."

"I came back for her."

"Do you have it?"

"I wanted it for her," she said, "not for you. Why are you even asking me? If there's been no elsewhere? What do you want it for? You never even needed it in the first place!"

"No," he said after a pause. "But I wanted it. Ritual matters. Especially to me. And I'm here because I want you to be ready."

"So you are here giving orders . . . "

"I needed to know you have it. I told you, there's been no elsewhere. But . . . other things are happening. And one way or the other, the past's back. I mean, not that it ever goes away . . . "

"You're telling me that?"

"I feel like things are heading to some kind of conclusion. And you know I never kept the book just for the hell of it. It's always been to solve a puzzle. So I need to know where it is, in case I get more puzzle pieces. I need to know you have it. That's all I'm here to ask. I knew you came back for it. I never knew if you'd been successful."

They stared at each other for a while. She moved and her sunlight corona went out.

"I was," she said. "Successful. I have it."

He breathed out.

"Good," he said. "Keep hold of it. I think before long I'm going to get more data. So don't do it for me, do it for your mom, but keep hold of it. In case I need it."

"If you do," she said, "will you take it this time? Like you were sup-posed to? I thought that was the whole ritual. Will you take it to where you die?"

He did not answer. He did not wait for her expression to change. He turned and walked into the crowd and the wider streets toward the Euphrates. He crossed back, all the way to that small country wherein was Thakka's tunnel tomb.

CALDWELL TURNED HIS BACK ON THE WINDOW, ON THE DEER THAT HAD returned, to look again at Dr. Shur.

"So he bought it?" he said. The deer ran away, unheeded.

Shur folded her arms.

"It isn't a question of buying something," she said.

"Please," he said. "Don't be coy. You tell yourself whatever you need to to get up in the morning. I'm just concerned that you and I understand each other."

"OK," Keever said. "Now, look . . ."

"Keever," Shur said. "Help me out. You have your soldiers' interests at heart. I'm sorry if you think I'm being a bit precious but I consider it important to be exact about what we're doing, and respectful of each other's expertise."

"Sure, Doc," he said. "I think what Caldwell is saying . . ."

Caldwell drew breath. "My apologies," he said. "I understand that I can be abrasive. It's not intentional."

"I was recruited, Dr. Caldwell," Shur said. "I didn't ask to come here. Your people asked me."

"And they were right to," Keever said. "We're all after the same thing here. Stonier's a good man. We all want him to be OK."

"And not to do anything stupid," Caldwell said.

"That too," Keever said.

"All right," Shur said. She sat and clasped her hands. "You understand my job? I've worked in the services my whole professional life. The last nine in SpecOps. And what that means is, as well as dealing with psychological responses to extreme situations, alongside individual patients, I also have a responsibility for the mental health of, if you like, the collective. The Unit. I've spent a long time proving that there's no contradiction between those two. My job's to ensure that our soldiers can hold themselves together as people, members of the Unit, and that the Unit's taking care of them for their sake and for its."

"What brought you here, Doctor," Caldwell said, "with all respect for your expertise, and in the spirit of a frank assessment of where we are, was the attempt on Unute's life by the now late specialist Jon Ulafson. We can all agree that Ulafson was crazy"—Shur tutted and shook her head—"to think he could hurt Unute, or even cause him anything but mild inconvenience, no matter what hoodoo he wrapped his bomb in. But the point is that he tried, costing us three soldiers and $4.7 million worth of damage. And severely hurting morale. None of us can pretend it's been the same since Ulafson. Including, I think we all know, with Unute himself. Which is why it's important that you can be an outlet, Dr. Shur, that the men and women of this unit feel secure that they can tell you anything in absolute confidence."

Caldwell paused and inclined his head.

"And which is also," he said, "why part of your job is to report back every one of those confidences to us. So can we please get on with that?"

"Your sense of the . . . uniqueness of your work is clearly important to you, Dr. Caldwell," Shur said at last. "I hope it doesn't puncture that too much if I tell you that the unusualness of this unit isn't so much because we're dealing with phenomena most people would consider impossible. I'm sorry to break it to you—and I wouldn't if I weren't one hundred percent certain you don't already both know—that the army also has a cryptozoology unit and a khesheph unit, the marines have an effective pataphysics unit, that the air force ATF, Anomalies Task

Force, is second to none. And so on. That's been my career path. It's not the parascience that makes us stand out here. What it is, firstly, is that we work alongside the object of these researches. Secondly, that it appears to be human." She set her lips. "And thirdly, that it regularly kills us. Even if it generally apologizes afterward. That"—she narrowed her eyes—"unique relationship of comradeship and fear in which your people hold Unute creates a very particular mental strain. Combine that with the pressure on social bonds when—inevitably—he causes pain, injury, and/or death to his own comrades, and leaves those still alive with a weight of guilt and resentment, all of which are countervailed by a duty to put up with this, and you have a hothouse.

"I'm not surprised at Ulafson," Shur said. "I'm only surprised that he was the first, and so far the only one, to attempt to, as he appears to have thought it, free the world of the scourge of Unute. That's why I'm here."

Ulafson's brief letter had arrived the day after his death.

I've seen too many good people die. You don't need me to recite their names. How much longer do we stand by telling ourselves we're using a weapon while all the while it's being used against us?

"Perhaps he did," she said.

"His dumb trinkets," Keever said. "He should've known that wouldn't work."

"This is why I've been worried about Stonier," Keever said.

"Sensibly enough," she said.

"I too am eager to know what Stonier's been disclosing," Caldwell said.

"This is exactly why we discourage romance on the job," Keever muttered.

"But the heart, notoriously, wants what it wants," Shur said. "I understand this is the first time you've had the loss of one half of a couple. To be clear, it's a very long way from saying that Stonier loved

Thakka to saying that he's now a danger to his comrades, let alone to Unute."

"He is one hundred percent definitely not a danger to Unute," Caldwell said.

"Point taken," Shur said to Caldwell. "It's a long way to saying that he might attempt to be a danger to Unute, with the damage and disruption that might follow. But that obviously doesn't mean he's not depressed, or grieving, or full of resentment and confusion. If we were dealing with a civilian, I'd keep him under observation. As it is, I've prescribed him some meds, and I'm pushing him to find creative outlets for his energy. Of misery. Release trauma from the fascia, be in the body. And to find group counseling in the city, distinct from me. Obviously, it's only with me that he can be really honest, but I think—and I've told him this—that acting as if his grief is more quotidian than it is is going to be the best way, the only way, for him to become part of a wider community. A community of the bereaved. Which I think is what he needs."

"That," Caldwell said, "is exactly the sort of thing I was getting at. If you don't want me to say he 'bought' that suggestion, what verb do you prefer?"

"What kind of kooks have you sent him to?" Keever said.

"Really, Keever?" she said. "'Kooks'? I wouldn't waste his time or yours. Your people ask me to ensure that none of your soldiers become a danger to themselves or others, and that's what I'm doing. Keep an open mind." He was not sneering: his face was calm. And Shur was staring not at him but at Caldwell. "Have you seen the stats about the mental-health benefits of, say, having a dog? Or a hobby? Or standing among trees?"

"Forest bathing," Caldwell said.

"I don't like that term either," she said, "but the results speak for themselves."

"I like trees fine, Doc," Keever said. "So you told Stonier to go stand in trees?"

"No. There's no one-size-fits-all. Stonier's grieving, and he's in danger of getting stuck in it, not going through it."

"Melancholia, not mourning," Caldwell said. Shur glanced at him, her surprise evident.

"Often I'd say what's important is to come to terms with the reality of death. But no two cases are the same. This is a man who deals almost exclusively with death. He deals it out, witnesses it, faces it, and now it's taken the man he loved. It was very early days, but I think he was making progress. He was moving. It was a purer sadness I was beginning to see. Which is good. And then . . . there's this equipment failure and it turns out Thakka wasn't dead." Caldwell said. Shur did not look at each other. "And it's as if he dies all over again. And Stonier's pushed right back to the beginning, only worse than ever. As if Thakka died all over again. In his case, I think he needs to be allowed to, one, take moments where he's doing something else, not to forget but to let his body move, to let it keep going, and at the same time, two, to do the opposite, to really go in on it, let himself focus on what a scandal death is. To inhabit the grief. I want to tell him not to accept death but to focus on life. And that will make him sad, and even angry, because Thakka doesn't have life anymore, but sadness and anger are OK. What's more dangerous is getting stuck."

"As if he died all over again," Caldwell said. Keever gave him a warning look. "So where did you make Stonier go?"

"I can't make him go anywhere," Shur said. "I gave him options. Both for type one and type two. Put it aside and go in on it. Whatever it takes. Try anything and everything. As much as he can."

"So what did you recommend, then?" Caldwell said. "In the second category?"

"Anything and everything."

"You heard her," Keever said. "I know a bit about some of these places myself."

Shur pursed her lips.

"Let me tell you something," she said. "There was some research. Someone was going to prove once and for all whether Freud was right, or Adler, or Lacan, or Klein, or psychodynamic therapy, or object-oriented therapy, or whatever. So they tracked a bunch of patients over their treatment, in all these various paradigms, took stock at the start, and then at the end of the process. Care to take a guess? Who was most improved? Which paradigm came out on top?"

"Go on," Keever said.

Shur smiled.

"There was no difference," she said. "Not significantly. They're all as good as each other. And as bad. But. They all did considerably better than the control group, which had no therapy at all."

"Which means?" Keever said.

"Which means talking is better than not talking. And it almost doesn't matter who you talk to. Or how they talk back. I wouldn't go quite that far, but what it does mean is that for a long time now I've been making lists of groups that practice, you name it, meditation, discussions, twelve steps, therapeutic interventions, rebirth, group hugs, whatever. I've vetted them all—they're harmless. Nothing that's actively toxic. Which is, yes, a judgment call, and that's my job. So I can pull out the names of those that score high on whatever axis I think my patient needs. Now, Stonier, in shock like he is, what he needs is something I'd call positive-slash-life-affirming. So I've recommended a bunch of nice little groups in Tacoma. Whatever was top of the pile." She dared disapproval.

"And he agreed to go?" Keever said.

"It wasn't easy for him. But any of them'll be good for him. If there's any danger—which there is—that he'd get angry with you, or Unute, or the Unit, or the government, these should help minimize it. And in any case, the pills I prescribed have a few other active ingredients beyond the SSRIs. To help make him amenable to suggestions." The men considered this. Shur looked at Keever. "Speaking of the aftermaths of grief, how was Joanie Miller? You went to see her."

He hesitated. "Struggling," he said. "But, then, I'm getting the sense you knew that. And your point is taken."

"I'd heard she wasn't doing well. That's the kind of bereavement that can go bad. That's what we're all keen to avoid. Hence my approach with Stonier. Ulafson was before my time, but if we'd had some of these structures in place then, who knows?"

"Well," Caldwell said at last. "Good work, I suppose. I bet you'd love to talk to Unute himself. Now, there would be a subject!"

"No I wouldn't," Shur said, a cold calm about her. "I'm interested in how humans think."

Caldwell smiled at that.

"Sometimes things go our way," he said. "This makes me come across all Dickensian. It makes me just want to say, 'Bless us.'"

"Is that *A Christmas Carol?*" she said. "It's hardly the season."

Caldwell laughed. Another disappointment. It had been how long a time since he had spoken that code and heard it spoken back, seen the cool stare of gnosis and shared purpose?

Still, no, he did not at all think he was alone in the Unit, in having another, hidden loyalty.

Secrets beget and attract secrets. Walk these corridors and nod at your coworkers in passing and among those soldiers of this particular deniable conspiracy you must, surely, greet a mole from some militant offshoot of the Templars, and/or a prophet of a Kabbalistic sect, and/or an assassin sacred to some other occult purpose than raison d'état and My Country Right or Wrong, snuck into the official operation to pursue their own duties and the rites of their church and the desiderata of their other hidden superiors.

Nor did Caldwell believe this was much of a scandal nor any great insight. Just as in a mid-sized office, a certain level of stationery theft should be considered inevitable, so the commanders of the Unute Unit

FOR AN INSTANT, PERHAPS, SHUR LOOKED AT HIM WITH STILLNESS THAT went beyond surprise or incomprehension, but just as abruptly that impression was gone. And Caldwell was sitting in her office, regarding a thoughtful woman in middle age looking at him with nothing but polite curiosity.

must expect that a non-trivial number of their staff would cleave to various hidden agendas. Much like the canny activist in a leftist cell who knows that police agents work alongside her, and has to get about the insurrectionary business, for all she knows they are her enemy and working for their own ends and against her, keeping her eyes open and deploying this enemy's necessary kayfabe against them, the trick, surely, was to pursue the objectives anyway. If it was the FBI who was paying for your revolutionary leaflet, well, at least you got a leaflet out of it. So, surely, must be the mindset of Caldwell's official, or officially unofficial, superiors: in such a way, however dug through by moles the Unit might be, never minimizing diligence or declining to lay mole traps, at least the Unit got committed agents, scholars, killers.

So it was, he suspected, that those unseen eminences in drab corridors who controlled the Unit must consider that as long as the research was being done and missions carried out, there was little point in getting preemptively pissy about infiltrators, whatever their intentions or worship on the sly. The bosses would be ready, though, for when such agendas ceased to move in phase with theirs.

Which did not mean, of course, that he would advertise his true allegiances. He, Caldwell, mole, had to dig tunnels for the Unit to use, however much his burrowing aims were distinct. He kept his codephrase fishing rare, careful, disavowable. Not least because, if all proceeded as he thought it might, it would not be very long before, precisely, his true aims and activities, and those of this government, did in fact deviate.

A succession of dead faces passed through Caldwell's head. Josh Barrientes. Weatherly Knighton. Jon Peters. The last shock and surprise of archaeologists and priests, sellers of maps, of gimcracks, of information, as he had closed his hands upon their throats or slid a slim blade up beneath their ribs, their eyes dimming with disappointment, their fingers fumbling as he took from them what it was they had wanted to withhold. Carved figures of Unute older than the oldest figures on a cave wall. Scrolls of poems in forgotten script telling the adventures of the child of death, the avatar of ancient stillness. A slow amassing of information, to be shared with and withheld from the Unit in careful titration and camouflage.

Bless us: bless us: bless us. The slogan of his nameless cabal, seekers of power. Whisper it to those who might help, inducted into the mysteries of the immortal. Whisper it back to those who spoke it. Such a stupid pair of words, such a risk of inadvertent false fellowship, but it never seemed to happen. By a configuration of context and person and tone of voice, those to whom it was spoken in its secret meaning were like those to whom a cop shouts, "Hey, you!", always recognizing, whether they knew it or not, that they were its object, and giving up an answer that defined them correctly, by choice if insiders, as if by choice if not. Bless us: that was what divided goats from other goats. Segmented off those who had striven for years, alongside Caldwell, some worshipping Unute, if that was the verb, some more instrumental in their attitude, some considering him a demon to control, but all yearning, striving, to tap his powers. And not for any of their countries—what an odd choice for fidelity, those fleeting and contingent polities—but for their own devices. Call them demiurges if you like, if they succeeded, secondary miracles, full of energies derived from a higher power.

So? Where is that power? It doesn't care: once, twice, in a moment's amusement or pique, it spat Unute—and the pig—into the world, then settled back into indifference so great as to be indistinguishable from nonexistence. Leaving those who siphon from the batteries that charge Unute—or those who command that which so siphons—to rule. Whatever Unute might have to say about that.

"Dr. Shur," Caldwell heard Keever say, "I'm going to require you to digitally record your sessions with Stonier and upload them to a secure folder. I'll send you a link. Those of us in this room will have access. For due diligence. We can't have another Ulafson."

Shur's mouth twisted, but she nodded.

"On that topic," she said. "I have a request. As you say, we can't have another Ulafson. I want to request that ex-members of the Unit, and perhaps even bereaved relatives of those soldiers who died in the line of Unute duty, and I mean specifically at his hand, are offered sessions with me."

"Doctor," Keever said. "You know that's not my decision."

"I know, but if you're in favor, it'll sway the brass," she said. "I think this could be important. For healing. And, you know what, if you like, also for intel too. If any of them take me up on it, I'll do it here, in my office. The recording equipment will be set up, so it'll all be available for you to check over."

Keever considered her proposal.

"It was you who told me that our duty to them and their families doesn't stop at death," Shur said.

Keever went still at that. "I'll see what I can do," he said.

A knock sounded at the door. Shur called, "Come in."

Diana entered. "You missed the meeting," Shur said. "We're almost done."

"We've been discussing Stonier," Caldwell said.

"I'm sorry I'm late," Diana said. "I got waylaid. That's what I need to talk to you about. Stonier. Well, not him exactly, but . . . We need to talk about Thakka and everything."

"Calm down," Caldwell said. "Research is ongoing, as well you know. In fact, Diana, I meant to tell you I've had a rethink about one of our leads—"

"That's not what I'm talking about," Diana said. "I mean what this whole thing is doing to B. He's gone again. He's gone hunting."

NIGHT IN A COLD AND GLINTING CITY. THE FINANCIAL DISTRICT. BELOW: A sea of neon and headlights prowling like the bioglow of benthic beasts. Rising like black smokers, the vertical landscape, tower after tower.

Ingress from a roof. There are a score of ways to do it, even without air support. Even alone. Hundreds of ways if you are strong enough to hold your weight the full height of a skyscraper while you scale a corner, to punch holes through reinforced glass.

Unute crept through the stairwell. He did not pause at the

entrance to the topmost story, empty but for piles of cardboard boxes filled with styrofoam. A baffler against listening drones.

Weapons ready. Pistol in his hand. He breathed in deeply, to calm that voracious oddity within him, eager to take his body over.

The floor below. Storage for doomsday intervention: sarin, knock-off Kool-Aid, explosives. He hesitated at the reinforced door, took in the light around its edges. But he would not be able to disable these things without alerting his unwitting hosts to his presence, and he had questions. He would seek answers before he dealt with what of this he could.

He slipped the lock.

He descended again. Quietly through the third door down. Unguarded at this level, because who expected ingress so high, above so much security? Beyond the door, an LED-lit vestibule, offices, a door marked with the name of the biotech company housed therein: Mochyn Industries. Its logo a circle bisected by an equal sign.

He slipped the lock.

The offices were open-plan and half-lit with the swirl of screen savers. He'd known the cleaners would be at work, which was why he put away his gun and let a dustcloth dangle from his hands, why he wore dark overalls, walked with the slump of someone working late, past tired figures carrying buckets and mops. Corridors toward the executive offices. Where he knew the board was meeting.

A labyrinthine route, longer than seemed possible through interiors of intricate design. This is how to hide a stronghold in plain sight.

Dark-paneled double doors without windows. He sent them flying open onto the guardians of the sanctum. People in dark gray, jumping up as he entered, bringing their weapons to bear and starting up with the usual shouting, and Unute, out of some momentary pity, another wince at the inevitability of murder at his hand, actually saying something along the lines of "Stand down and I won't kill you," pointless as he knew it to be, watching them not listen, as he'd known they would not, so bringing his pistol up, ducking sideways pulling the trigger sending a bullet straight down the muzzle of the rifle of one man and another into another's face and a third into a woman's neck.

Unute heard an animal scream.

From cages sprung open in corners of the room, two dark shapes hurled toward him.

Dogs. Dogs?

Huge things with outlines like distorted German shepherds, dark-furred and slavering, but not since dire wolf days had he seen canines of such size and speed. Amid their bared and glistening fangs were larger teeth. These dogs were tusked. Ivory stilettos protruding from the lower jaw, two more curling through the skin of their snouts.

They leaped. The first hit him and bit down hard on his left arm and Unute shouted in pain that shocked him. He brought his right fist onto its head. He stared because it yowled but did not unclench its jaws and Unute knew the blow would have decapitated a bull.

That ecstasy came up in him. It had been a while.

But he needed to be clear, he had questions to ask, and hurt as it did, and strain as he must, and unnatural as it felt, he emitted a clotted trace of a scream of effort and squeezed his muscles and pushed the trance back down.

Two swift hammerblows struck his left side and bullets tore through his ribs and meat and he staggered to stay upright but he would ignore all that because the first dog was still on him which shouldn't be possible and it was still conscious, and it was snarling through clamped tusks and a froth of spit and Unute's blood, and now the second dog had reached him too.

"THERE," CALDWELL SAID. THE ORDERLIES PUSHED THE LOLLING BODY OF the babirusa on the steel gurney. He pointed them through a maze of machinery in another, deeper, lower lab, past rows of flasks and flesh-filled jars. The crew steered their cargo into a niche behind the computers and the generator that Caldwell had had put in place, alongside the chamber of bubbling dark liquid, an unclear shape within.

Even without Unute's help, the techs had cobbled together a combination of radioactive particles, ketamine, and an aura-dampening cage that, after a few distressing failed attempts and a titration of elements, knocked the babirusa out. The flesh mound twitched and drooled, its legs drumming in its drugged sleep. It strained against its bonds—shackles derived from Unute-containment work.

Alone, Caldwell pulled up a map of the world. The edges of its coastlines flickered as he scrolled through history, outlines changing with the eons, ice ages, geologic shifts. Across that, a fountaining spread of red threads, a repeated animated cycle, guesstimates of millennia of the deer-pig's routes.

Caldwell tap-tapped again. Overlaid on the pig's journeys, now, appeared the reconstructed routes of Unute's voyages, and of the spread of technology.

I've been working for so long, Caldwell thought. Old texts, heretical hymns, trails of tachyon distress, oddities and anomalies. I won't pretend it hasn't taken effort to put this together. And if that's so to trace you, Unute, how much more so for a pig?

He followed tangled routes.

Where have you been, pig? What have you been doing? How do you know how to find him? And what is this? He touched a place that seemed to be one where the pig had settled, still, for a long time. And this, and this, and this? Places and times when the pig had walked for lifetimes to move far away from Unute.

Does he know? he wondered. He told us you hunt him every time you come back. Does he know there are eras when you go out of your way to go out of his way? What do you look for then? When you avoid him?

He put his hand on the quivering pig hide.

Of what do you dream?

Caldwell closed his eyes. He listened, as hard as he could, as if the creature's guts would whisper to him, as if its bones would tell him secrets.

He whirled around and stared into the cold glare of the room, into all the corners, where walls met scrubbed floor, at the thresholds. He was alone. He stood very still and for a moment he held his breath and strained to hear a scuff, an infinitesimal tap.

Caldwell shook his head at last and breathed out.

I'm tired. I'm running on fumes. I'm excited.

Sorry, Diana, he thought. I know you're extraordinarily eager to get to work on this, too, to find a new route to the blue, to where the lightning comes from. I call shotgun. Caldwell stood by the curved glass of the great tube, there in the deepest part of the base. He put his face up against it. Looked through the fog and fade of his own breaths into the heart of the dark preserving liquid, that darker dark. He stared through the glass as if it were he who was a specimen.

He looked back at the pig. Like Unute, he thought, this has plenty of life. Plenty of life for a vector of death. Too much life. It won't die: like him, it has life to spare.

Caldwell lifted a cable from the gurney and slotted it into an inlet in the base of the tank.

Cut you, do you not bleed, pig? he thought.

He turned on a gauge that glowed green with measurements of current, of quantum packets, of ill-understood energies.

And then, Caldwell thought, if I cut you, doesn't your bleeding stop? Do you not come back?

He flicked the dark gray zip tie on the hooves.

Shouldn't be necessary while you're out, he thought. But just in case. Our Fenrir's bonds, Diana tells me Unute said. Should work on a pig as well as on a wolf. Which is to say, not perfectly, yet, but not badly at all.

From a rack of equipment he unclipped a rotary saw.

I can be precise, he thought. I can take you to the edge of—let's call it death, even though we both know that's not accurate. I can take you to that point and keep a log of exactly how much pressure I've used, how much blood you've lost, how much current I've applied, how deep I've cut, the neutron foam and waveform agitations. I don't need to wake you: I don't see why pain should be part of whatever engine all this is. Of which you're a cog. I hope for your sake that doesn't change. I can keep tabs on how fast your heart beats, your temperature, your respiration, your beta, theta, gamma, and lambda waves. What happens at the rim of that abyss into nihil, and the instant that I push you over, if I decide to do so. What energies are released. Particles several times smaller and more boisterous than the smallest dancers they've noticed at CERN, all the way up through this . . . He tapped the creature's damp mouth. Up through this emergent totality, this body, and beyond. Our feed from NASA will alert me of sunspot activity, flares, shuddering in the Van Allen belt.

And then I'll keep tabs on you while you sleep your pupal sleep and the slop of you reconfigures in the caul and I'll track what happens at the instant when you push through the membrane and come back. The casual way you and Unute turn entropy on its head is inspiring but maddening, too. You make it seem so simple. Would that that were so.

Caldwell put his ear to the dark glass.

Because all the while you and Unute just keep on living, your neighbor here stubbornly refuses not to be unalive. I know that's an ugly formulation but no language I speak evolved to deal with the paradoxes of your kind or its. So you'll have to forgive me.

Swish, swish. Liquid whispering beyond the glass.

Some of us have deeper aspirations than merely to build immortal warriors, Caldwell thought. Some of us—Bless us!—have more interesting aims, want the real secrets, the true powers, to tap the purest energies, such as those in Unute. In you?

He put on a clear visor. He turned back to the wheezing babirusa. He checked the connections of the cables, and the saw.

Caldwell thought, You have life to spare, and that life is never more metastatic than when you get close to death. I'm in the business of tapping. He opened one-way gates from the babirusa to the power that charged the liquid pillar.

He turned on the saw and lowered the whirring blade to the deerpig's throat. When it touched the skin, even in the deeps of its haze, the animal kicked, shifted, twitched, whined.

· · ·

KILOMETERS BEYOND THE CITY OF SKYSCRAPERS. NOT IN FOREST BUT A
rocky zone. Half-sunken into the cliff, overlooking a gulch, a house of
great cost and beauty, mahogany, pewter-colored steel, glass that
darkened at the late-day glare.

No roads ran here. On the helipad in the basin where the building
emerged from stone sat an AgustaWestland 109, its rotors bowed and
motionless. From windows glowed the sepia of household lamps.
Staff passed in front of them.

In the control center, a man in his early middle years, muscular
and tall and shaven-headed, listened to his security chief. When the
briefing was done, he nodded and thanked him and left the room and
took the wide corridor up curved staircases. He passed three maids
and they nodded their heads and he responded in kind.

His bedroom was a disk-shaped chamber on the highest floor, its
roof level with the plateau. It jutted from the slope, held up by but-
tresses in the rise, glass-floored in the bay of its window, so the man
could stand there and look out and down into the sky. When he opened
the door, he felt cold air, and the lights did not come on. He knew instantly that something was wrong. But before he could close the door
again and press a panic button, a voice came from the darkness.

"No," it said.

The man stood still.

"Come in," the voice said. "Don't make a sound."

A darker silhouette against the lesser dark.

The man hesitated for one second, then went in.

"Good. Now close the door."

He did. He stared into the shade and it seemed to him that he saw
two flashes of cold blue.

"That was sensible," the voice said. "I think we both know your
chances of being alive in four minutes are low, but they're not zero.
And even if you don't make it, the manner of your leaving is up for
debate."

In the shifting dimness the man saw a hole punched through the glass of the floor.

"Do you know who I am?" the intruder said.

The man struggled to speak. "You're the enemy," he said. "You're the devil." He was shaking, but he stuck his chin up, and if you had seen him, you'd have known he was trying to be brave.

"No," Unute said. "See, that is the garbled result of a long, long time of handing down half-truths. Like that game Telephone. Like your corporate logo. Cute, by the way. How long's it been the same as your holy sign? And how long do you think that sign has looked like that? A few hundred years? A couple of thousand? That sigil's the result of laziness. Do you know that?" Unute made two quick sweeps with his index fingers. "It's quicker to do straight lines, so that's what they turned into. It should be curls. That's what it used to be, coming off the circle."

"I know," the man said. "Tusks."

"As to me being evil . . . It's your so-called god that took a disliking to me. I never had any problem with it. I wanted to help it. You know the sad thing about all this? I never had any beef with your predecessors. They were fine to me. I learned a lot from them, right back to when they marked its skin. Your people were the last people it let get close. I'd have been quite happy leaving you guys to your rituals and rites. You worship whatever you want. Worship a mochyn, a pig. Yes, I speak Welsh. I speak everything. And you know what? I'd be glad for you guys to keep doing your research, too. After all these years of you going high-tech. Could be useful."

Unute hurled a big shape out of the darkness. It arced up and tumbled and landed with a heavy dull thud and rolled, coming to a stop on its tusks, its big eyes staring, tongue lolling all the way to the ragged fringe of its own neck. The owner of Mochyn Industries stared at the head of a pig-dog.

"Gods and monsters," Unute said. "Aliens and avatars. Entropy versus change. Death versus Life. Ideals, ideas, and dumb luck. We've all got ideas about what I am. What kind of avatar. I know where you guys stand. Sometimes that was the least bad option, as far as I was concerned, to be the devil. These days I'm kind of over it. I like to think maybe some kind of 'a machine planted by curious intelligences vast, cool, and unsympathetic.' That's Wells. But I'll give you guys this: your 'god,' at least, made sense. You could see it, and it did stuff nothing should be able to do. And there've been worse gods than boars. All gods are disappointments, but if you're going to be disappointed, and you are, being disappointed by a pig isn't the worst thing. Imagine being disappointed by Goodness. Or Truth. Or Light. Or Life! Back in the day some people who hated me said I was death, and that the god of life was on their side, and wanted to kill me. I always wanted to say, Why the fuck would you think life would give a fuck about you?

"Those things were strong," Unute said. Still shadowed and hallowed in the cold. "Your dogs. I got past them to your board. Obviously. They gave you up. Obviously. But your dogs hurt me more than they should have, and they took more than they should have from me. Do you know how hard your predecessors tried to train boars to do the guardwork? But pigs aren't nearly so pliant. Still, you people made a pretty good fist of your compromise. What do you call them? Tuskdogs or something?"

"Babirusas," the man said at last.

"Of course. Why let the fact that they're more dog than pig get in the way of that homage?"

Unute stepped forward, into the lesser darkness of the room, and the man saw pools of shadows for his features.

"I never thought I was the only one to have a little remnant from the old god. That tattoo your founders gave it. You guys have been busy with whatever you had. Cloning, splicing. Building your warriors. Maybe it's not just dogs, eh? Some of your priests and paladins got big teeth, too? Got strong stomachs? You people." He shook his head. "It's always about immortal warriors. Admittedly, you've gotten further than most others. And you know what? I don't even care. You haven't been standing in my way. I'm not here to tell you to start doing something or to stop doing anything you want.

"I'm here for one reason only. I want you to tell me who came for it. Who was with it."

"That's not one reason," the man said into the darkness. His voice quavered but not too badly. Defiance was always admirable. "That just begs the question, What's your reason for that reason, devil? Why do you want to know? What are you looking for?"

Yes, defiance was always admirable so Unute admired him for the moment he deserved, and he let that admiration batten down his startlement at being interrupted.

"That's *raising* the question," Unute said. "Not begging it. Every-one gets that wrong. When I visited your colleagues, I'd come to think that maybe you actually had a connection with it. You could still get close to your god, that it let you, the way you did that once. But your colleagues told me no. That it hasn't let you people fraternize with it since the tattoo. I gave them every opportunity to revise that infor-mation," he said, and through the man's mind went the images of the bodies in the boardroom. "And they didn't. And I'm pretty good at telling when people are lying to me. And I think they were telling the truth. So it's not you who's been keeping it company.

"But I also know that you people still know that pig and everything about it better than anyone else in the world. Maybe it's better for you this way. Nothing more thrilling than a god that keeps its dis-tance, right? A hidden god. So faith can become a wager. But for folks like you it may be hidden but it's not that hidden. You've kept a closer eye on it than anyone. And a closer eye on everyone keeping a close eye on it than anyone. And this is what's going to decide whether you stick around and keep breathing. And if you don't, how it is that you check out. So consider your answer to me very carefully."

Unute took another step, and now the man moved back from the dead dog's head, at the exhausted anger in Unute's scarred and heal-ing face.

"I'll ask you again," Unute said. "For the last time. Who's been walk-ing with your god?"

The Wife's Story

MY FATHER WAS A SHEPHERD. MY MOTHER WAS A SHEPHERD AND then a shepherd's wife. My brothers, in order of their births, were a shepherd, a shepherd, a brigand, born dead, and a fool. My sisters were two weavers and dead and a novice, and I, the youngest, was to be a shepherd.

I was seventeen years old and not yet married when the soldiers came to our village. They killed my father and mother and two of my sisters. Before they dispatched her they ravaged my mother, and they did the same to my father, though when I told that part of my story in the later years an abbess told me not to say so. The soldiers dressed in the priest's robes (they had killed the priest) and they laughed at him and bade those of the village who were neither fled nor dead to laugh at him too because of his babblings. He smiled at them no matter the sobbing of our neighbors because our older brother was one of those soldiers, had gone months ago and had now come back and was singing to him the songs of our childhood. I had already seen my soldier brother lead his comrades to our parents' fields and seen him watch while they killed them so I was not surprised that he stood by as those of his new company strung the poor simpleton to the tree by his neck and heaved the rope to raise him and, shouting and sporting that they were witness to a miracle of flight as he kicked, said he danced and cut capers too and sang to accompany him.

I lay in the ditch and shed my own tears without a sound.

That night the stars were hidden. What awoke me was a hand upon my lips.

It was a man. I struggled but he held me. I saw his face in the glow from the soldiers' fires. The man whispered that he would let me speak to tell him what had happened here. I breathed slower and he took his hand away.

When I was done with the telling he nodded and placed his finger to his own lips and stood in the field and walked toward the fire. I heard a soldier shout, Who's this? It was my brother's voice.

My other brother, the dead and dangling one, faced the fire as if he, too, watched the approach.

The man whom I would marry met my treacherous brother at the edge of the field. My brother raised his musket. The man put up his hands. I heard the shot and I saw blood from the man's palm as the ball passed through it.

So slowed, he caught it in his other hand and put it in his pocket.

He made a rising sound like a storm and took my brother's gun away and threw it, and the other soldiers fired upon them both and their balls made my brother dance as ugly a jig as had our poor natural upon his last ascent and the man who had awakened me pulled my soldier brother's arm from his shoulder and swung it in a gouting arc hard enough to knock the fratricide's head from his shoulders into the forest beyond.

The other soldiers stared and went still. Began to wail. Light sparked from the newcomer's eyes and hands. I witnessed the visitation of his might.

Young as I was I had seen terrible things. But I had not known that the human body could be took apart in such ways as my husband-to-be took apart those soldiers.

When he was done, when I could summon motion in my limbs, I stood. I did not tell him then—I never told him—that he had killed one of my brothers in vengeance for another.

He beckoned. We left that place.

I do not know the year we married in Brno but that it was after the first and before the second battle of Breitenfeld. By then we had traveled years and long shared a bed. I had no shame for this sin, because I did not doubt he loved me, from the fervor of his declarations and the passion of our couplings, and because in our wanderings across Europe's ruins I had seen such depths of degradation that I had come to damn the God that allowed them, to consider his edicts the rantings of a madman. This had made my bedmate smile.

Thus I was astonished when he said, Marry me, and in a church, he said, For whatever the priest who so joins us believes, if the God to whom we consecrate our love yet exists and is capricious as you say, then let us challenge him with the insincerity of our declaration of fidelity to him, which he will know even as the minister does not.

I do not like to consider the ceremony. Neither he nor I flinched nor laughed at the mention of death parting us.

What name should I take, said I, and he told me that as he had no family name I should choose my own. That is why I have since then been, to myself at least, called Immerfrau, the wife of always, because I had seen enough—him pulling pikes from his innards, digging bullets from his neck—to know that my husband would never die.

Every morning I woke he whispered that I had given his days their purpose, that he now knew that I was what he needed.

While the world swooned in agonies of war we found gladness in each other. We helped some people and ignored others and took what we needed on our way and my husband inflicted on the perpetrators of some violence torments of his own. He gave me to understand the signs that would come when the spirit of the maelstrom overtook him, when I must leave him be, remove myself from his company, until the bloodlust left him, and he breathed deep and stared amid the slicks of what he had done. Then would I emerge and lead him by the hand and clean him.

How came you to be? I asked him.

I was sung into the world, said he.

How live you still? said I.

Death will not take its own, said he. It has ever watched me. Betimes, said he at last, in the morning of my life I saw it watch me from the darkness in the stares of beasts and folk, behind the windows of their eyes.

What are you?

I am a tool, said he. I am the ending.

Perhaps you bring it but you are not death, nor its herald, I said to him, whatever you may say and whatever you have been told or you believe. I have seen death and all it is is ceaseless quiet. You, my love, are all motion and noise, even when you say nothing.

That made him thoughtful.

In the ruins of a town in Silesia I told him that all I lacked to make my life complete was a child. I said that once and only once, for though I'd long known that he was fear itself to others, that was one of only three times I was afraid of him myself. He did not put his hands upon me but told me in a dread voice that he would not subject himself nor me to the issuance of the dead. Thenceforth when it was my fertile times he would exit my body and spend upon me.

For all that lack, for all the apocalypse of the war, and knowing that it may make me sound a monster, I was happy then. And he told me he was happy too.

In Antwerp we learned of the Peace of Münster. I was glad for the masses of Europe but I could see my husband was overcome by sudden sadness.

It is the clearest single moment in my long life. I saw everything change for him, and in him, in the space of one breath.

He did not glory in tragedy so I knew the war's end was not what troubled him. I begged him to tell me what it was.

I must go, he said to me. Our time has ended.

I could scarce believe what I heard. Of course I was now in middle years, while time itself remained afraid to attend to him, but still each morning I had woken to his stares and if he lied when he told me of his delight then he lied every morning for decades and never once did I know it.

He said, I must go.

I reasoned. I teased. I raged. I played the seductress. I pleaded.

He said, I must go.

He said, You will not see me again.

He went.

Three years I grieved.

For eleven years I worked as a baker, grew hardened to the fact that I started each day without his eyes upon me. I strove not to think of him.

When I had been resident in the south of Madrid for eight years, word reached me of certain dissenters.

My agon against God was less by now, not from reconciliation with any force so wicked as to allow such suffering but from growing indifference. Not being immortal, I kept my counsel on such matters, and attended Mass as was appropriate. I have no great interest either in the tenets of the church nor of those who set themselves against Rome. From my wandering years, however, I retained fascination with warcraft and the shifting allegiances of factions, and to make sense of such turbulence I knew enough of Jansenists and Ranters and the like. A person like myself, who had willy-nilly found themself concerned with—and of possible interest to, too, had ever been my fear—enthusiasts and the fervidly devoted, heretical and canon both, could not but come to know the signs and jargons of such currents. Having myself in my role as consort of death been the subject of fancies and fallacies and exaggerations, from the spinning of which yarn busybodies cannot refrain, and having marveled in the much more grandiose tapestries of falsehoods pertaining to my erstwhile companion himself, doubt is my nature. But even I could not restrain a certain grue and foreboding to hear tell of the new gnostics. Secret adorers of the bastard children of pagan powers, of those in endless occulted war, devoted on the one side to such a principle as Order, on the other, to Alteration. Or, too, to more sinister aspects. To Flux itself, at any cost and all. Even, contrariwise, to an utter and virtueless inertness, a cold quiet underlying the noise and motion of the world. This was the year of Venner's Rebellion against England's restored king, and thus it was that I knew of the Fifth Monarchists. Now I heard talk of such schisms in the Antinomians of that current, a diaspora of heretics among heretics searching throughout the continent. There were those among them, some said, who worked against the Crown, others to whom the Palace gave their orders.

To the blasphemous tenet that the Saved, being Saved, were not bound by the Ten Commandments, those known as Unutarians added the doctrine that a new Christ walked among us. That he above all was exempt from the strictures that governed lesser men. That he might thus commit bestial acts in the service of his Godly mission, which was, by the deployment of death—by mechanisms occluded by a cloud of unknowing—to put death itself to flight, that all might live forever, someday, as did he. They would follow him, they said, and fight for him, and against his foes, not sparing those with whom they had of late broken bread. For others, erstwhile of their larger company, declared for opposing Brummagem-ware messiahs, entreated fidelity to archons of eternal life itself, the declared enemies, said they, of the Unutarians and the lightning son. And thus and so.

Of course these beliefs garnered my attention. Such lost souls were not the first of whom I had heard who, to some partial knowledge or hint of my husband's existence, had added favored verses, proverbs, aspirations, and called the resulting gallimaufry a faith. They were, though, the first to connect me to their dreamed-of savior or Beast.

The first time I opened my door to a young man who entreated me to tell him what I knew of the comings and goings of the immortal, that his own master, the child of life, might destroy him, he did so in English, which I did not then speak. It was only his use of my husband's name, and those rumors I had heard, that gave me to understand the nature of his intervention.

I do not know how he found me. Aghast, I pretended not to make out even what little sense I did, and I closed the door on him.

His erstwhile comrade in faith, now zealous opponent, who visited me the next month, was a stocky wild-eyed Dutchman, not so easily dissuaded. He pushed past me into my kitchen. With no little anger he told me in broken Spanish that my duty was to the coming Kingdom of God on Earth, that I must tell him the location of the chosen one, that he might go to him, pledge fealty, warn him that his adversaries approached.

I forbore informing him that I had heard nothing from my husband for more than ten years, since that day when the love was gone from his eyes. Instead I told him to quit my house and not return. I grabbed up a boning knife and held it to him. He took his leave but he said to me, I will return, you must help us. We need him.

Thus it was that when I was woken by a knocking, two days thereafter, I was not surprised. I descended and threw it open, ready to tell him once again to leave me be, but it was not he who faced me in the moonlit street.

Three men were at my door. In the middle, gripping those to

either side, unchanged since the day he had walked away, was my husband.

The sight of him had me staggering and gasping his name. His companions fell forward into my house. I saw that they had not been standing, but had been supported in his grip. I saw that they were my previous visitors. I saw that they were dead.

My husband closed the door and locked it. He crouched and turned over the bodies of those he had killed—with, it looked to me, remarkable gentleness for him. I, able at last to speak, told him he was not welcome. I kept my voice cold and my face too and I am proud of that. He paid me no mind.

I asked him what he meant by killing such poor deluded creatures.

He said to me—these were his first words that evening, and he did not look at me when he spoke them—that he was done indulging or protecting unwanted pilgrims of or against him. That it was such as these, those paladins who styled themselves deathkillers and were committed to his destruction, and, no less, his own aspirant worshippers, who threatened the equanimity of his endless years. He might once have let the two of them take care of each other, but no more. They were tribulation, he said, more than the hog and its church—by which he meant I know not what.

Should they come to me seeking their god, he said, in me or in the enemy they imagine for me, I will grant them their wish. Though not as they expect.

I've never seen you so cruel, I said to him. It was a lie but I continued. But for your final cruelty to me.

He looked at me then.

This is not pleasing to think upon.

I told my husband that he must go, never to return, as he had said he would. I told him to take this evidence of his crimes and, had he any decency or soul, to grant me now the solitude he had bequeathed me.

When he spoke, his voice was quite changed, had a brittleness and cold to it like that of a swordsblade in a frozen lake. He called me ugly, and old, told me I was a liar who was alone because none but him would ever have had me.

These are not days or nights I choose to recall. I could recite everything he said to me in these months of our second life together, the middle panel of the triptych of our marriage. I will not do so. They filled me with shame then, and do so now.

He did not raise his hand against me. He did not follow me from room to room. Stronger than the fear that he spoke the truth about me, far greater even than the shame that what he said provoked, is the shame that I did not remove myself. It is true that that little house was all I had, but I had had nothing before, and have had it since, and I do not fear that. Not only did I not take myself therefrom but nor did I from the bed, which he now claimed. Nor did I await his renewed touch with dread, but craved it, reached out for it, asking him if he did not still love me, if he would not treat me as once he had. And touch me he did. But even as he did, he told me all the same things he said during the days, and whispered to me that none but he would deign to do as he was doing.

He did not trap me in the house when, each day, he left with the rising sun. He would only mutter one of his new cruelties, would quit me, leaving me uncertain as to why I did not go. When he returned, oftentimes bearing the body of another of his unwanted worshippers or their enemies, to dispose of in my ovens, he complained of their stupidity and cursed first them, then me.

I do not choose to know exactly how many months it was that I lived thus. I know that I was complicit in a good deal of murder. That he did not soften in his invective toward me, of whom he had once spoken tenderly. And I know, though I could wish it otherwise, that what kept me there was not some glamour but a part of me that wished for such degradation, that thirsted for what it knew was poison.

He brought back bodies less and less often. One by one, the cells of believers in the town met what they sought, their Immanuel or Adversary. Until, having cleared out the scourge of those with hope in him and those with hope that he could be ended, he was done.

This time, when he left, he left without a word.

I went to England.

What I told myself, and it was true, was that I was no longer safe in Spain, that I needed a sea between me and the site of my husband's crimes. I have come to believe that I also chose to journey to where the greater part of those who had tracked him had set out from. To an island where some knew more about him even than I.

I did not ever seek them. In that at least I can take pride.

In England I found a source of greater shame still, which honesty demands I tell. That is that good man whom I met, and who, I know not why, loved me.

I let him marry me as if I were not married. I was bitter to him. I told him he was of no worth, repeated words that had been said to me, that were it not for my pity none would take him. I saw the pain such words induced and tangled therewith; I saw, too, love, as if a cat played with two balls of twine at once. I wish I had not sought to hurt him as I did, and that he had not forbore, as he did, as had I, with he whom had hurt and left me.

It was death which released my lesser husband, after twenty years of suffering me, and I am glad he is free of me, or the me I was.

Three years have passed since, three years when I have been wife, bigamist, and widow. No matter how age bowed me, I never believed I was done with the first of my husbands, or those who sought him.

A year ago word came to me of two travelers to my village. Rumors reach the ears of even such as I, who lives beyond the boundary and whose accent is strange, whose neighbors relish shunning her, call her witch, which is a lie, and wicked, which I cannot deny.

Through the whispers of the children who come as close as they dare and do not know I listen, through the blurted words of those who seek the poultices only I know how to make, I learned that one of the two was tall and wore a cowl and a mask and covered himself with robes and walked stiffly and would or could not speak. The other was a rough-haired man who spoke like one from afar, they said. When he learned that the villagers believed that it was plague that had disfigured his companion under his coverings and left him mute, he stood in the center of the village on the last day of their visit and embraced the other through the robes, that all might see, to prove that no miasma surrounded him.

He spoke of healing, said one farmer's wife to me, as if I would answer her, or speak a word. He said that he and the covered one traveled the world seeking to heal, to spread God's love, to bring life, to banish death and the devil. I have heard a hundred men and women say as much, but she repeated these familiar promises as if they were of immeasurable price.

Two seasons after that, on an autumn morning, I came down to put water on the fire and my husband was sat by the hearth awaiting me, staring at the embers.

I did not start. I did not drop the water. I put the pail down and sat beside him in what had been my other husband's chair.

My first husband had not changed, of course, since Madrid, but that his face was sadder. My heart beat steadily after one moment's surge. I knew then that I had awaited him for more than twenty years.

I have heard, he said to me. Someone came. A masked man. One who walks with him. They seek me and do not wish me well I think. Nor you perhaps, as my once consort. You should, when they return, stay away from them.

An hour went by, and neither he nor I said a thing.

At last he said: I have said goodbye to so many people. I think I'm done with pain and then it comes back to me and then I think I'm done with it again and then it returns. I think I'm done caring that I kill and then I care greatly. Sometimes I say I can't love and have never loved and sometimes I say that I love easily, all the time, and sometimes I believe that I am saying the same thing in two ways. Would it not be loving, he said, to protect your lover from the pain of your own pain?

And how might you do that? I said to him.

Perhaps, he said, by making them dislove you. By being dislovable.

Am I, I said at very last, to be grateful to you, then?

It was a while before he spoke again, his voice without emotion. Cold not like winter but the steadiness of a long autumn.

He said, I regret your pain.

I damned him to hell and cursed him as a coward.

When I was done, he said to me, What did they want? The masked man and his companion? Did you speak to them?

I wished him boils and sores and a dried-up prick.

When I was done he said, Of what did they speak?

I told him I did not know, that none in the village would speak with me because of the aura about me, which he had left upon me like the stink of night soil.

You are right, he said, I am a venom, and I regret your pain. Keep your distance from the travelers.

My husband rose to go and I cursed him for a cur and in the deepest part of my heart I felt sorrow for him. In the deepest part of my heart I wanted him not to go. I shouted at him to go. I let him go.

It is the end of the year, now.

Yesterday, a knock sounded upon my door as the sun descended.

The part of me I wish I could exorcize hoped it was my husband again. But it was neither him nor was it a man with rough hair and a silent strange companion in a shroud, as I had supposed it would be. Perhaps hoped for that, for all, or because of all, their intentions. It was a small figure with gray hair, and a face it is hard now to recall.

They looked me straight on. You were married once, said they. I do not speak of he who died, he to whom your neighbors say you were unkind.

I told them I knew whereof they spoke. I said I would speak to them for the sake of my latter husband, the dead one, who had deserved better.

Where are your friends? I asked them. The masked man and the other?

I am not their friend, they said. Not yet. I follow them. The better to seek your first husband, as do they. We share a mission, though they know it not. To find the source of sorrow.

There was a great calm about this visitor. Listening to them made my heart slow.

That man who came looking is a child, they said, though he but vaguely knows it. He puts his faith in his companion to find who must be found and do what must be done to him. To it. Which will not be efficacious. When that companion is gone, and not before, I shall come to him, and tell him that what power he has is his own, not that of the baubles of his overflow. And you: I am here to talk to you of healing, they said. About the end of pain.

I wanted to be cruel to them, as I knew so well that I could be. But I could not.

Tell me of your pain, they said, and it made me catch my breath, raising in me a kind of hope in hope's end.

I stood there, on my step, speaking to that stranger. They made it easy to speak to them.

Know you, said they, where walks a boar after he with whom once you walked?

He spoke of it once, said I at last. That is all.

What then will you tell me of your husband? they said. Your first husband?

What do you wish to know? I asked. And why?

They said, Because we all seek him, because we would see sorrow end.

And I said I would tell them everything.

There burrows a maggot in my heart that loves my immortal husband and always will. But looking into that visitor's face I felt a calm, and something changed. As I spoke my inmost pain, I felt a freedom from the shame and regret that had curdled me.

He is death, they said to me.

I knew the truth of that. And if a piece of me still loves him, it is death and hate that it loves, and I can hate such love in me, and wish for freedom from it, and so it is that I said all, will do all to aid those who would end its reign.

UNITS OF HATE

SHUR SAT WITH HER HANDS ON HER LAP. SHE WATCHED Stonier, sitting across from her.

"So," Shur said. She smiled a little. "You seem better."

"Yeah," Stonier said.

His look was of great uncertainty. The look of a man shy of his own gladness. He folded his arms, biceps bunching under his shirt.

"It's going OK," he said. "I tried out some of what you said. I went to a bunch of places. I thought it was fucking stupid, to be real with you."

"I know," she said. "That's OK. I'm grateful to you for trying it even though it felt stupid. That's more admirable than if you hadn't felt that way."

"Yeah, I went to a bunch of the places, and I ended up . . ." It was his turn to smile. He shook his head. "It's so dumb."

"Let's be dumb together," she said.

"It's clappy-therapy-churchy-group-huggy nonsense, just like I thought it would be." He rolled his eyes. "It's stupid. Even while I'm there it feels stupid to me. 'Now I want you to turn to the person next to you and tell them that they are alive.'" He made a vomiting noise.

"You are, though," she said. "Alive."

"Yeah, I am." A shade came back across his expression. "He's not."

"No."

"And I'm as sad about that as ever. But I guess if I'm going to be real with you, I do feel more . . . energized. More galvanized. Even though it still fucking sucks that he's not alive, and even though I full never thought I would."

"Tell me about a session," Shur said. "What do they do? What happens?"

He was silent awhile.

"I been thinking," he said. "About other people in the same situation as me. Who lost people. Who lost people to him, I mean." He jerked his head. "What they would think of this." He looked confused, as if he was trying to remember something.

"Tell me about the sessions," Shur said.

"It's hard to say," he said.

"Hard to explain, you mean?"

"No, I mean I've only just started and there are other things later, they said, but you know, we go in, we talk, like a group session, then the main guy, Alam, talks, we listen . . . I don't really remember more details."

She frowned. "You don't . . . ?" she said, then stopped. Tried again. "Perhaps it's not about the details," she said carefully.

"Yeah, maybe. Yeah, that's what I've been thinking. It's the company, maybe. I do talk a lot about him, I know that. When it's my turn. That much I remember. And about being alive."

Shur put her hands together and considered this.

"It seems like you've found a milieu in which you're not being asked to get over anything," she said. "Or be less devastated, or miss him less. But through that sadness maybe you can reach another state."

"It's not happiness," he said. "But it is alive. I feel alive. I didn't realize that I didn't, for a while. Feel alive. Life is a lot. It's everything."

"You said."

"Even things that would have . . ." Stonier shook his head. "That would have sent me spiraling not long ago. It's a bit different."

"Can you give me an example?"

"The token."

"His token?" It took her a moment. "Of you, the one you took when you found him the second time? What about it?"

"I . . ." He held up his hands. "I lost it."

"Oh, Jeff. I'm so sorry. What happened?"

"I don't know. When I thought he was dead, the first time, I knew he had it in his pocket, and that hurt, but it was good, kind of, to know it was there. That he had a piece of me with him. Then when I found out he'd been . . . that he wasn't dead . . ." He kept his face controlled. "I came, and I could see, straightaway, that he couldn't last. He was holding it." He blinked. "I held his hand. Since then, you know, I always have it . . . had it . . . in my pocket. And then, a couple of days ago, I was rooting around, and . . ." Very slowly, he shrugged. "It's just gone." He swallowed. "What I want to think is that someone stole it," he said. "You know? When you can't find something in your house and you feel stupid so you start telling yourself you've been burgled and the burglar just took that one exact thing because there's no way you'd be so dumb as to lose it."

"I know that feeling."

"Right. But I have to take responsibility. I don't know how or why but I fucking dropped it. And I know what you're thinking, Doc."

"What am I thinking?"

"You're thinking, 'Oh, he unconsciously threw it away. He has all kinds of resentment or he's self-sabotaging or whatever.'"

"Is that what I'm thinking?"

"Yeah. Time was, I'd have told you to shove that up your ass. Now . . . I don't know." He shook his head. "And listen, I'm not glad I lost it. I'm fucking crushed. I miss it. And I feel so fucking stupid. But here's the thing. I know I loved him. I know I miss him. And maybe . . . Hell, I don't know how I lost it, and maybe, who knows, maybe you're right, maybe I did unconsciously get rid of it."

"To be clear," Shur said, "I haven't said any such thing."

"Yeah but just listen, Doc. This is my point. My point is that I lost it, and . . . I'm OK. I am, really." He sounded astonished. "I'm OK. Maybe I did get rid of it behind my own back, or maybe my pocket just had a hole in it. Maybe I'll find it. But even if not . . . My point is, I'm OK. I wish I hadn't lost it. But I'm OK and I'm alive. Something's working. I don't want to keep it to myself.

"I keep thinking about Ulafson," he said. Shur's eyes widened. "I know he was before your time, but you know what happened. I still have some numbers. Some family of people from the Unit. Who didn't make it. Whatever's working for me . . . I think there are some of them it might help, too."

SWEEPING IN LOW AS IF PUSHED BY THE ROLLING CLOUD, AS IF CHASED BY

thunder, an unmarked black chopper. The storm was loud enough to catch up and muffle its staccato exhalation. Even allowing for that, to those within, the noise wavered in and out of amplitude in stochastic stop-starts unrelated to the whirling of the rotors, less like turning down a volume dial than a repeated glitch in the nature of sound waves themselves. They had been briefed about the effect. This was from the experimental dampener on the shaft. A spin-off technology derived from Unute research. A something something of the something field: Keever had not paid much attention. An early-days prototype of cloak technology, was about what he'd gotten. Give it more tweaks, and in a few years they might release it to those "secret" wings of DARPA considerably less secret than the Unit, from where its existence would then be leaked to the ever-reliable assets at *The New York Times*, psyops to cow the enemies of the nation and to prime future grunts.

Among his other work, Keever had always known he was on a product-testing team.

He watched the ground shift underneath, darker black against the black.

"We don't normally pay too much attention to these kinds of group-lets," the briefing officer from Africom had said. "They're mostly just students with too much time on their hands. But these guys have been making a few links we don't like. And with the money they're getting from some enemy governments, it's going to be easier for us—for you—to cut the head off the snake now. Intel has it they've been making overtures to some jihadi groups in the gulf, and that we will not stand."

Hence, Keever thought, preemptive retaliation.

Unute stood at the roaring door of the aircraft, leaning into the throat of the night. In he'd come, to the Unit base, after more days out of any contact—another hunting trip, he'd vaguely said. Here he was, back again.

Ranged around him, strapped in position, Delgado, Tranh, Stonier, Beech, others, briefed, ready to go. The pre-drop rituals Keever recognized. Tranh folding wads of gum into his mouth—"I don't want to die with bad breath," he'd once said. Beech kissing the St. Christopher at her neck, Delgado mouthing the words to some heavy metal song. Stonier, standing still, quite calm. Quite calm.

Keep watching, Keever told himself. Are you going to pop, Stonier?

"You OK, son?" Keever had said quietly at the briefing's end, standing just so in the middle of the room, taking his time with his bergen, so the next thing you knew it was just the two of them there. "You good to go?" Staring right into his eyes.

"I'm good, sir."

"There's no dishonor in taking some time, you know."

"I know, sir."

Keever was used to quietly cursing the resistance of his soldiers to admitting their own troubles. He had been ready to order Stonier to stand down. But he knew how to look past bluster, and it had surprised him to see in Stonier's eyes something approaching calm.

"Sir," Stonier had said, quietly. "I promise. I'm good."

Well alrighty then.

As they were walking to the chopper, B had leaned back and whispered to Keever, "How's Joanie Miller? You still seeing her?"

Keever had widened his eyes in a moment's surprise. "She's not answering my calls anymore," he said.

"I thought it was she who called you."

"At first. Now she won't pick up."

"Maybe that's a good thing," B had said at last. "Maybe she's moving on."

"I guess maybe."

"What were you saying to him just now?" B had said. "To Stonier?"

Well shit. Keever hadn't even known they were being watched.

"Just what you'd imagine," he'd said.

"I listened to one of his sessions, you know. With Shur."

Keever had said nothing. Had just kept walking, as if he had known that Unute had known of the recordings.

"He was in a bad way," B had said.

Keever was not used to seeing even so fleeting an expression of sorrow cross B's face.

I'm glad you came, he had thought. Wasn't sure you'd join us. Thought you might be off hunting, still, so you didn't have to sit with yourself. Maybe this'll do as well for now.

And now here they were. Coming in so close to the top of a compound wall that they could almost have reached down and touched it as they hammered above it, toward the hidden HQ of the Thomas Sankara Front.

"Ready?" Keever shouted into B's ear.

"Why do you think they bother lying?" B said. "You're not a fool, Jim. You know the Sankarites and Lumumbites don't work with the Salafis. The brass knows that you know that. And they know you'd obey orders without them conjuring up some bogeyman Islamo-socialism. And they know I'll help them if they help me. So why? It's like they think they're supposed to lie, that that's less undignified than just telling you to kill some reds because they say so." He shook his head. "It makes no sense."

"My country right or . . ." Keever began. But B stepped out of the helicopter before he could finish, and Keever swore and followed him down on the end of his line, down into a courtyard already filling with screams and cordite and the first glints of cold cobalt glow.

Keever stayed low, shooting in controlled bursts, sending enemies slamming red and spattered against concrete walls and shooting dogs in the face, always keeping close enough but not too close to B, who was, yes, in that state now.

Blue-white crackling ecstasy. A rushing plowing drive through his enemies, through anything nearby. His grunts more like the shifting of the earth than spit in a throat. His punches just kept going through the bodies in their path and he drew his fists back at last in rainbows of blood and lightning, to the appalled stares of those whose last sight it was.

Keever saw Delgado and Beech and Halberstam doing their work, this was a good one, this was tight, no casualties so far, maintain the momentum, and he saw Austen and Bullmer and Stonier in the same professional states, and looked up again at B, don't ever let yourself lose track of what the asset's doing, but this one taking moments to follow what was going on behind Unute. Keever watched Stonier swing his weapon up, securing rooms in the aftermath of Unute's rampage, and the look on Stonier's face was almost beatific.

They moved toward the central chamber, wherein according to intel was the head of the cell, ready for termination, along, yes, sure, now that you mention it, with the artifact they were also tasked to grab, seeing as they were there, the box, don't open it, a rust- and age-stopped box, its lock mechanism millennia older than any such should be, in charge of which should be Unute and only Unute himself, that he had been ordered, requested if you prefer, to bring back.

DIANA SOUGHT B, AND FOUND HIM IN THE VIEWING CHAMBER, LATE. HE smelled of fire and blood and his clothes were ripped and filthy and his skin smoldered. He watched the corpulently muscular body expanding and contracting with heavy breaths and drool spread upon the steel of the table while the investigation team gently sliced its tough skin and took slow-motion high-def macro footage of the fibers reknitting. Measured the waveform of the EKG. Tapped those splendid tusks and bored into them, removed thin sections of their cores.

"Welcome back," Diana said.

"What did you do to it?" B said. He gestured at the pig. The marks upon its skin, near its neck, still-diminishing keloid traces of what had been much longer, deeper slices.

"Not me," she said. "I don't even know who's worked on it last. Everyone wants a piece of Babe. Good of it to heal, between sessions, so we can all take a turn."

"Nothing has ever hated me like that pig," B said to her.

"Sure? Not even the boss of Mochyn Industries?" She saw his admiration when he looked at her. "The late boss, I should say? Their share price is tanking. If his death wasn't enough, those files you leaked have done them in. They probably won't be around for more than another couple of weeks. I hope you got what you wanted out of it."

"Not as much as I might have hoped," he said. "I thought that they'd persuaded it to let them worship, again. That they'd been walking with the babirusa. They denied it. He admitted they'd heard that someone had been, but he didn't know who. I believed him. How did you know?"

"It wasn't hard to work out that was you. And, really, you're always reminding me how long your life has been. Can you really say that in eight hundred centuries you've never pissed off anyone or anything as much as you did that thing?"

"Oh sure I have," he said. "But take that Mochyn guy: how long had he had to hate me? Thirty-five years? Forty-five? Whereas that animal has had almost as long to hate me as I have to be hated."

"OK, I get it," she said. "Let's figure it out then. What's the unit of hate?"

"Hm?"

"What's the most universally hated thing in the world?" she said.

She was always pleased when something she said provoked interest in him. "Child molesters?" she said. "Hitler?"

"Not Hitler, unfortunately." They were both silent awhile. "Mosquitoes," he said.

"OK," she said. "That's good: they're small, so they're good for units. So, let's say the hate aimed at one member of the Culicidae family measures one, I don't know, culicid. A cull! Which means," she said, "that if you hate something as much as you hate ten mosquitoes, your hate is ten culls. A decacull. That's, say, dog shit on my shoe. Now, the Westboro Baptist Church, say, I probably hate ..." She shrugged. "A good seven or eight kiloculls."

"You enjoying yourself?" B said.

"I am. Let's say you piss someone off enough that they hate you as much as I hate the Westboro crew, and you're in their life for ten years. And they think of you every single day. That's ... more than twenty-nine megaculls."

B folded his arms.

"So Babe, there," she said. "Let's say it hates you that much. Eight kiloculls a day. But it's hated you almost its whole life. Call that ... what? Call it seventy-five thousand years?"

"A bit more but go on."

Diana took out her phone and pulled up the calculator.

"So that's ..." She counted zeros and frowned. "I'm getting lost in Greek prefixes," she said. "I think that's more than two hundred and eighteen gigaculls." She gave a slow whistle.

He looked at the unconscious babirusa again. He was not smiling anymore.

"And I don't hate it at all," he said.

"Did you have any luck?" she said. "Getting any useful information from the Babe-cult people? The ones who worship it? We're not so dumb as to stand in your way," she said, "but we do our best to keep track of what you're doing."

"Like you say," he replied after a minute, "the pig's been around a long time. Those cults may be the only ones who think it's actually a deity, and even if they have to worship it from afar they keep good track of who else is interested in it, and sometimes even have a few ideas why. So yeah, the pope, as it were, gave me a list of leads, people who they heard might've been asking around about it. Too many leads, really. It's hard to chase them all down."

"Have you looped in Caldwell and Keever? We could help you."

"Maybe I will," he said after a moment. "When I've done some legwork. We need to figure out a bit more about who might have been with it. In the tunnel, with Thakka."

What are you keeping from us? she thought. And why?

"Anyway, I hear the mission went well," she said.

He shrugged.

"I brought back what Caldwell wanted. They had it in a safe, he was right."

"I heard," she said. "Well done." She held out her hand. "I'm here to bring it to him."

From his inner pocket B took pitted metal about the size and shape of a cigarette case, clotted with age and oxidization.

"It's no skin off my nose," he said.

She started at that. He kept his face inscrutable.

"Somewhere in your office," he said, "I'm pretty sure you have printouts." He put his head to one side. "Ranking theories about me. Or what's behind me. What caused me. We may not have been working together that long, but I know how smart you are. You wouldn't conflate hunches with analysis. I know you don't believe it, but I'm betting 'god(s)' is still on the sheet, with a question mark. Fucking gods." He shook his head. "I've met so many people who called themselves gods. Most of them were so full of shit you could see it behind their eyes."

"Most?"

"Well, a few of them believed it."

"Did you ever believe it?"

He looked at her.

"Once," he said. He glanced at her and hesitated. "Maybe once and a half." He looked down at his own hands. "Anyway, what's after 'god(s)'? 'Alien intelligences,' question mark? 'Time travel slash parallel dimensions,' question mark. Does it say 'Purpose,' question mark? 'Tool slash weapon slash message slash warning,' question mark exclamation mark?"

"You're wrong." Diana waited a beat. "I combine question marks and exclamations into interrobangs. They're more efficient."

"Someone left a message for me once," he said. "Written in my own blood. That was the only ink they had around. I always thought it was important, but I couldn't read it. Someone else had smudged it out. I don't mean to give you shit," he said. "You're good at what you do. You've helped me. More than anyone has for a long time. I just want you to understand that there's nothing, not a theory you can come up with about this"—he tapped his chest—"that I haven't asked myself."

Diana frowned. "What about your berserks?" she said. "I wanted to ask you, have you seen the lingchi photos in Georges Bataille's essay? About the 'ecstasy of pain'? It always reminds me of your descriptions of what happens to you." He frowned. "You talk about your immortality a lot more than you talk about your rages, do you know that? Your 'riastrids.' I take it you took that word from the *Táin Bó Cúailnge?*"

"I knew Cú Chulainn," B said. "He was an asshole."

"Thomas Kinsella translated riastrid as 'warp spasm,'" Diana said. "What is it that's warping? Maybe it's more than just you. What if the reason you get even stronger, what if what pushes you into that state is that you're a conducting rod, and you're not just changing yourself, you're changing the world around you? What if space and time are different when you berserk, B? What if you're a key? To a door?"

B looked at Diana silently for a while. She held her breath.

To a vast space beyond. She held her breath.

B looked at Diana silently for a while. He dropped the flat metal box into her hand and walked away.

She exhaled slowly, and descended.

. . .

HERE, IN THE WINDOWLESS PARTS OF THE UNIT'S COMPLEX, CORRIDORS

had been designed by architects of peerless vision to always imply that this was the wrong way. Even Diana, familiar with the route and with the business that was conducted there, had to overcome a sense of allergy as she proceeded. Doors marked with DO NOT PASS and, under them, in a much smaller font, OOBU. Down steel stairs into tunnels, a sunken zone of subtly dimmer fluorescent lights.

Diana found Caldwell.

"I saw from the logs," Diana said. "You've been working on Babe. Alone. What's that about?"

"An idea," he said. "I wanted to try something."

She said, "The marks aren't fully gone yet: you've been treating it hard. What have you been—"

"Experiments," he said. "It's government property. I'm a government employee. I've no less right to it than you."

They walked.

"I was thinking about what you said to me," she began. "And I've been paying attention, and you are right. Every time he mentions gods, his disgust is palpable."

Caldwell raised his eyebrows. "Go on," he said.

"The way he keeps negating that idea—that might be evidence that, whether he knows it or not, that's exactly what he does think he is. And his distaste also feels to me like disappointment. Maybe gods disappoint him by not existing."

"Or maybe by existing," Caldwell said. "Do you ever wonder if he knows what's down here, Diana? His pass reads ACCESS ALL AREAS."

OOBU: out of bounds [for] Unute. A tighter loop of corridor that would (attempt to) deny his AAA ranking. Past rooms beyond handspan-thick windows wherein technicians worked. Ranks of servers and monitors, clear cylinders of preservatives and wrongly shaped flesh blossoms.

"I don't think he's interested," Caldwell said. "Had he been, he would have gone looking, would have found this, and simply have entered."

"Come on," Diana said, "those doors have been built to withstand a nuclear blast at one hundred meters, and they've been made with those experimental materials…" Caldwell glanced sideways at her and said nothing and she sighed and nodded. "Yeah," she said. "He would have. Eventually."

They walked past shining cylinders. On a trip to London, Diana had taken a tour of the Grant Museum of Zoology. It had struck her then as, from a certain perspective, too good to be true, for all that it was real. That it was a film set, a bit too on the nose, all spindly skeletons and fusty taxidermy against a perfect backdrop of dark wood paneling, the rows and rows of old jars with conclaves of preserved moles and tightly wound eels and misbegotten, unborn sports pressed up against the glass with the unique pathos of the pickled. Here, it was of those jars that she was put in mind, at the sight of these greater containers, for all these were of a uniform size, and modern design, and crystalline and reinforced and with colorless liquids within, rather than the piss yellow of old preservative, and even though not all the specimens herein were quite dead. Not in the same way as were those antique animal corpses rebuking rot in London.

There was no mistaking the tight somersault curves of fetal animals in some of what they passed.

"Which isn't to say he has no idea," Caldwell said.

She turned her attention from the striae of embryos.

"You think he does know and just doesn't bother coming down?" she said.

"I don't think that," Caldwell said. "I simply don't know that he doesn't. He's always been unmoved by the specifics of our research. As if he doesn't care."

"More than once, he's said to me, 'Build your supersoldiers if you can.'" She shrugged. "He asked me if I thought we were the first to try that. He was mocking me."

Caldwell pursed his lips.

"I wonder," he said at last. "If any of the earlier attempts were successful."

They walked on.

"Well," he said. "We know he knows something."

"We don't," Diana said. "But we should err on the side of assuming he does. He's just always seemed indifferent."

As if he knows what he knows, Diana thought. As if he knows what he wants. You'd have to be a child to believe that about yourself: what is growing up but realizing that you don't understand yourself? And he was never a kid, not really. How can you be a child if you're standing within days, fighting in weeks, killing in months? How can you be a kid if you can't forget anything? B talks a good game, and maybe he even believes that he knows himself, she thought, but I've got enough faith in his humanity to think that's a crock of shit. That's what makes me like him and that's what makes him dangerous. That and, you know, the rest of it. And I do like him and I'll do what I can for him but not at any cost, and not—I'm sorry, B—not at the cost of this, this knowledge.

She held her breath again.

Of the source, she thought. It's a part of you that's standing in the way, B. I'll still keep at it, of course I will, but it's your subconscious or your unconscious or your shadow or call it what you want but it's you in the way of getting there, and we'll keep on, I'll give you the pills, I'll ask you the questions, and on we'll prod toward what made you, you have to be a conduit, you tap it every time you glow, whenever you kill, but unlike you, B, I don't have thousands of years, unlike you, time, for me, is kind of of the essence and we need to get moving because I want to know, I want to see, I want to understand. And take hold.

Breathe out again: her exhalation accompanied her footsteps, in time to her speeding heart.

And I'm sorry, B, but you're no fool, and you're no more an altruist than I am, we're both in this for what we want, you've said so yourself, and if it's easier to use the other B, Babe, as a way in, because pigs don't have a subconscious (do they?) and they don't stand in their own way, and there's something to be said for simplicity, and if I can get the right operations, press the right buttons so to speak, get my hands on its mind and heart and soul and get through, to where the lightning is, not a god then if you don't like that, but with what it can do whatever you call it we both know the stakes, the source of everything, of your power, of you, if I can push through whatever meat pathway there is, touch that place myself, let it touch me, back through—

Caldwell was staring at her, she realized, with narrowed eyes. Diana unclenched her hand and met his stare.

"If you, we, get him what he wants, that mortality he thinks he craves, then why would he care, I suppose?" Caldwell said. "I'm certain he has some idea of the sort of thing we're doing with his samples. I can't imagine it would shock him. You said it yourself."

"He must know we have offcuts," she said.

"He does," Caldwell said. "I showed him a hand, once."

"You what?"

"Don't look at me like that. You're no more a stickler for process than I am. After the business in the museum, that extraction a while ago, I showed him the hand we got. Nor do I imagine it's the first time he's seen his old parts."

Yes, B had told Diana, in fact, that there had been times when he had lost bits of himself. That he had, perhaps, on occasion, entered one of those periods of brief cessation that she sometimes called "little deaths," that he had pupated, had emerged from the rind of his old matter, newly perfect, in the slop of revivifying albumen, to kick aside remnants of his own carcass left behind.

Even so. How strange to hold your right hand in your right hand.

"He said something about it . . . he made a joke . . . when he gave me this," she said.

She handed Caldwell the metal box. He stared at it hard.

"Did he say anything about this one being different?" he said.

"From any he'd gotten before?"

"No."

"Good."

"This was the so-called wart, yes?" she said. "The one you changed your mind about and decided you did want after all? Care to explain yourself?"

"I will," he said. A complex look went across his face. "When I'm sure. We've all gotten our hopes up too many times."

"Caldwell," Diana said. "Whatever you have on your mind, it's your job to share it with me."

"Oh really?" he said. He spoke mildly. "Sanctimony doesn't suit you. You bide your time, I'll bide mine."

He began to move the stiffened oxidized dial on the box back and forth, grinding its hidden gears, ruthless despite its age, as he came to a stop before a last glass window. In the lab beyond, attended by more specialists, a final cylinder. Eight feet tall, full of churning liquid, this time a dark brown like strong tea. It was hard to make out anything within.

"If it's true he suspects what we're doing," Diana said at last, "he's doing us a favor by staying out. It would feel impolite of him to look at this."

Deep at the center of the roiling liquid was a darker shape still. She muttered. Caldwell looked up.

"What's that?" he said.

"'Life is everything,'" she repeated.

"I wish you'd tell that to our friend in there," he said. "What do you mean by it?"

"I don't mean anything. It's something Stonier said to Shur. And that's exactly what I was thinking, about the contents of that tube. Life is everything. In various ways, we're all after the same thing. Even Unute. If you think there's no life without death, or at least its possibility. And it comes from somewhere, Caldwell, death, and life, too." And whether through him or not, she thought, that's the trail I will follow.

Caldwell looked at her curiously, still working his hands. Studied her hunger.

"Where the lightning lives," he said. He hissed abruptly in triumph as the box lid twisted. He put his hand on it, as if keeping it closed, and waited.

"What is it?" Diana said. "If it's not a wart. More for the collection?"

Caldwell said, "Every time we get wind of one of these things, you know how it is. Whoever owns it is all 'It's the most important artifact in the history of the planet', they're all 'The heart and soul of the world', et cetera et cetera. I'm as inured as anyone to hyperbolic claims."

"Still," Diana said. "You're hesitating."

He nodded.

"I am. There's something about the way people whispered about this one . . . There was once a cave, is how the story goes. Where a long war was fought. Full to the brim of blood and flesh. A thousand rotting Unute heads, ten thousand fingers and toes, a lake of his giblets, acres of skin."

"Jesus," Diana said. "I've heard this."

"And all of that was shed to find this one piece. That's how the story goes."

He took long tweezers from his pocket, opened and reached into the container. Brought out a pale flake.

A sliver, no bigger than a fingernail. A sharp nub of dry white flesh.

BUFFALO, NEW YORK. A DOORBELL SOUNDED.

"Jesus! All right, all right already, Jesus Christ!"

A woman opened the door. She was tired, white, with drawn eyes, a scar at the corner of one. She smelled of smoke and coffee. Her hair was tied up tight.

"Christ almighty," she said. "What do you want?" She shielded her eyes from the morning light to peer at the figure on her porch.

"I'm sorry to bother you, ma'am. And I'm sorry if this is difficult but I wanted to talk to you about Daniel."

The woman stayed still.

"You're Mrs. Clemens," the man said. "I'm here to talk about your husband."

"There's nothing I can tell you." Sally Clemens set her mouth. "He's dead. Which I guess you know."

"It's more what I can tell you."

"What? Are you from the army?"

"For what it's worth, ma'am, I truly know how you feel. Can I come in?"

DIANA WAS FAMILIAR WITH ALL THE INTRICATE AND COMPLEX RULES RE-garding what she could and couldn't take out of the office and work with at home. For the most part she even obeyed them, though there was always leeway—a certain degree of transgression was expected, she and Caldwell had agreed. That was part of the understanding. The faceless powers above her and her colleagues would err on the side of paranoia, and she would gently tweak them back toward a sensible compromise, without straying too far. Certainly she took security seriously: not out of respect for the idiotic default Top Secret-ism of the military, so keen to slap warnings on the most banal memo, in constant wolf-crying, but for the sake of her own research and her own safety. If a burglar tried their luck at her downtown duplex, they would find no compromising paperwork, and any attempt to access her computer without the passcode would destroy it and its contents.

It was surely that professional caution, she had thought for weeks, that lay behind her constant sense that she was being watched. That, she reassured herself, was reasonable, given that she might have been.

How, then, to distinguish degrees of such a feeling? What was she to do when, after coming home late that night and throwing her keys onto the table, she stopped pouring a glass of Sancerre and went suddenly very still. Felt abruptly more regarded than ever.

She remained frozen. She waited, but the feeling did not pass. The creak and play of the wood of the stairs, the minute motions of the house in the wind, sounded to her more and more like the breath of a watcher striving to be quiet.

Diana raised her head. She looked around the room, its dark and muted paintings, the stained wood and old film posters.

She would not pooh-pooh notions such as instinct or hunches. She worked, did she not, on arcane fields and on engines to measure and to adjust them. Would it be stranger than Fleming's mold juice killing bacteria, than observation nudging particles this way or that, to learn that such tinkering at the femtoscopic level of reality might have led to leakage in the structures of her own synapses? Might not her intuition, now, be offering real glimpses of unknowns?

The feeling neither waned nor waxed. Another jagged change, and she was certain she had just seen motion.

Diana went to her laptop and opened it, logged in to the cameras and e-ears that kept watch over and listened to her house. None had registered unsanctioned ingress.

She went silently to her bedroom. From her wardrobe, she took the "broom," a bug wand for close-up double-check scanning. Room by room, Diana swept painstakingly along every surface. Nothing registered.

And then she froze again, at the tiniest sound.

She crept into the hallway, reached for her handbag hanging among the coats, weighed down by the tiny pistol within the lining.

Motion again, at the edge of the room. Low, by the floor. Fast and skittering. Her heart sounded hard within her. Could this be a mouse? Had she indeed been altered into some new version of a human, the edges of her reality bending and hazing into a more slippery relationship to multiversal potentiality because of her physics-altering experiments . . . and thus been granted the insight that she was being watched by a mouse?

She heard an edge of panic in her own laugh.

There, once more! A rush like a windblown leaf, like a bug, something continuing now along the length of her hallway, no, not animal not even insect motion but a puppety jerking rush along the dark carpet, too fast for her to catch sight of it, she could only register its aftermath, and she pushed a chair aside and at its clatter and the crash she ran and stumbled and reached for it and with a spurt of acceleration whatever the malevolently scuttling little presence was it went faster, the pile of the carpet rustling and a line scored through it and now that pile was bending back toward her as the unseen thing changed direction and flitted like a sliver in a storm right up toward Diana so she stopped and staggered and fell toward the kitchen putting her left hand out to catch herself and her right hand up in defense and something whispered through the air and she let out a gasp and touched motion hard and fast and she closed her eyes and felt a scoring scratch along her face.

She rolled and pushed herself upright in a jujitsu guard. Let her eyes cross the lamplit room.

Nothing moved now.

Diana stayed still for a very long time, as she had been trained to. She straightened and took her phone from her bag.

"B?" she said. "I know it's not usual for me to call you, and I'm sorry. I wouldn't if it wasn't important. Something's happened, and I don't know what it is, and I don't know what it's got to do with everything else that's going on, but I think you should come over. I'm going to report it, too, but…But I want to talk to you about it first."

She felt motion on her face. Put her left hand quickly up and touched moisture and looked and there was blood on her fingers. A long scratch, beginning to sting, to drip.

Diana said, "I've had a visitor."

brother

IF YOU COUNTED BACKWARD THROUGH EVERY STEP OF YOUR RELENT-less life in a number trance, you could tally all the frozen mountains on which you've walked.

The first time is easy to recall. You, still a child though with the body of a man, before your first death, with your weapons held high. This, Father? you had said. These people are a long way from our valley—how can they threaten us?

They aren't close, no, he had said, but they know of us and they want what we have. We won't be safe until—

So you'd gone in and brought the walls of that frozen palace down, and that's the point when your memory smooths over, because that was when the spasm, the berserk, had come upon you for a while. When the textures came back, there you were atop another mountain on that mountaintop, this smaller peak all corpses, red and boned and sliding, and nothing breathed anymore in the hidden city but you and your companions. Looking at you in that way they had had.

Now you wrap your furs about yourself in very other icy heights. You are not indifferent to cold. Even your fingers can grow sluggish, your teeth rattle like a snake's tail. Of course it will not kill you, of course your dying skin will be renewed by waves of blood, but why suffer chilblains if you don't need to? And there may be travelers, even this high, and you'd as soon avoid the suspicions of witchery and the drawn swords that a man unclothed in frost might provoke.

Look. Are those lights ahead?

Your horse is dead a ways back. Speed up, one foot in front of the other between walls of sheer flint.

I can see you, you shout. I can see your torches. Friend or foe? I'm here to find the child of gods.

The wind swallows your voice. The guttering gets closer. Friend or foe? you shout. I'm in no mood to fight.

No one answers.

The gorge grows wider, and a vortex of snow limns you, and the moon watches, gibbous and hazed behind the snow but bright enough to sketch out this bowl of black stone. A warmer light from torches. Six men, three with hatchets, three with arrows nocked at bows and aimed at you. Shrouded in fur above the curls and filigrees of armor.

You raise your hands.

I'm not looking for trouble, you shout over the blizzard. I'm looking for the godkin.

No one lowers their weapon.

Is this how you welcome strangers? you shout. In the cities of the plains they told me that the mountain people are honorable and cordial and hospitable. Were they wrong?

We're not local, the lead man says. We're here for you. We know who you are.

You sigh. You tilt your head, and, yes, you can hear footsteps behind you, closing the ambush.

Let me pass, you say. You sound as tired as you are. Just let me pass. We've hunted you a long time, the man says.

He gives an order in a language from a long way away, and the bowmen pull back their strings.

I was there when your church was born, you tell them. The saddest part of this, you say, is that you don't even know what it is you're about to die for. I know; you think you're here to honor your god Dukkra, which has charged you to seek and destroy the Shaitan of the seven islands: me.

It's too dark to see their eyes or faces but their stillness is uneasy.

You say, You don't know where the seven islands are, or why I'm their devil. And you don't know that Dukkra isn't a celestial judge with an elephant mount, as you think.

One man fires. His arrow goes into your thigh. You wait. No one else moves. You take another step, in new pain.

Your priests added that rider, you shout, more than seven hundred years and six major religious schisms ago. Before that, Dukkra was the elephant.

Another arrow. It misses, skitters against the rock.

Dukkra was an elephant for a thousand years, you say. Initially a mammoth. In your earliest icons, you tell them, that mammoth has a notably small trunk. The reason being that it wasn't originally a mammoth.

An arrow from behind, this time, passing right through the side of your neck. You hiss.

Before that, it was a pig, you say.

You are close to the waiting group now, and those with hatchets heft them, but they don't look ready to fight.

It was a pig, you say, and what you fools don't know is that your holy order is a split from a split from a hundred splits from the original group, who were just watchers, of a pig. Nervous swineherds. And your epochs-long war, and that of the others in the same genealogy, against the Devil Who Walks the Earth, me, is the garbled results of some of those swineherds' observations. Namely that the pig on which they kept an eye does not like me very much. That's it. Your struggle against the end of the world means absolutely nothing at all.

They know they're going to die, but—give them credit for bravery—they creep closer.

I am tired, you tell them, this time in a language long dead, of being your designated apocalypse.

And you hear the gasp of another arrow and you move faster than any woman or man can move and the arrow breaks on rock and your blade is up in the belly of the leader of these soldiers, and before his shock registers, while it's still just a glimmer in the corners of his eyes, that almost comical Wait a moment you've seen many thousands of times, you pull the blade up and through and out and end him in a cataract of blood, and you sidestep an ax and bring up your free hand with fingers stiff and crush the throat of its wielder so down he goes and begins the pointless business of failing to breathe and you turn to some poor young lad who is spilling his arrows all over the place whispering prayers to the elephant rider of whose existence you've just disabused him, sorry young man, you think, would that it could be otherwise—

But you do not kill him. For once it is not you.

As you step forward you hear the hiss of more arrow shafts from behind you and the boy is riddled with them, staring as he staggers in his final stickleback form. And as you take a step his comrades all sway too, suddenly like nail fetishes, stuck all over. And they go down.

Shapes rise from the rocks. Archers' silhouettes. Bows not aimed at you but ready.

I'm here, you call to them at last, looking for the godkin.

Yes, a man's voice answers. We heard you say so to the brigands.

They weren't brigands, you say. They were holy knights. But they were wrong.

Whoever they were, the man says, they had no business here. Nor do you, but the way you moved against them . . . you've proved yourself worthy of an audience.

He descends, comes close enough that you can make out the professional fascination on his grizzled face.

Not many are worthy, he says. But you . . . Come with us.

When you don't die, you become a taxonomizer. By the fourth or fifth century of your life, every event that occurs in your vicinity reminds you of another, then another and another. By now, all people you meet remind you of someone, all food brings to mind another meal or many, all stories you ever hear are variations of others. You organize them in your mind, moving through the world placing like with like, accumulating experiences in distinct sets, comparing the sizes of the piles. Things may occur that are uncommon, but nothing is ever new.

It's never been rare to hear stories of demigods. There've been places, and there have been days, when every person who felled a tree more quickly than was the village norm was declared such. Few of these tales have warranted investigation.

But there is the pig.

Even separated from it by countless miles and centuries at a time, there has now for a long time been the deer-pig. Of which you saw the moment of conception, the blinding orgasm of the sky. Your porcine half brother's agon against you is a source of grief. But brothers fight, don't they? Estranged you may be, but that's the way of families. This beast must be of your blood. The son of the storm, the answer to pig lament and prayers. The child and the gift, as your mother said to you of you, of a god.

So there are such children. Your certainty that you were alone has been disproved.

Which is why you've gone back into your memory, to look again at all those stories you once heard. Given the pig. Those very few that remain worthy of curiosity. If it is the fact, as it is, that centuries of pursuing this story of this warrior son of this god, and that hymn of that immortal monarch who is the daughter of that supreme being, and so on, turns up nothing but the quotidian propagandas of cultures in which some command the many, there are also—yes—a handful of attestations not so simple to dismiss. Rocks broken and marked by the signs of knuckles. A lord and his so-called son and his so-called grandson who shared a name and a face so closely that their oldest parishioner confessed to you she never believed them different people but one who would not die. Signs and portents.

And if you have been disappointed hundreds of times, you stick to your decision that the next few millennia are for investigations. You couldn't say if that is grit or hope or what.

You have not, for a long time, followed so rich and tenacious an oeuvre of poems as those of this God-Son Lord of these mountains. And walking now with these silent warriors, repeating to yourself all the warnings not to get your hopes up, to keep your heart from breaking, you cannot stop that remorseless heart beating faster than it has for years, at the thought of family.

On a cloudless morning, between three peaks, you look up at a stone castle cut into the flint. You take a narrow ridge with your escort. You wait with them while arbalesters reposition on the battlements at your approach and soldiers shout a sequence of passwords and the great door opens.

A courtyard wherein grow trees with no business thriving at this altitude, through air much warmer than blows outside. The people here crowd to watch you, in bright colors. They stand with shoulders back in proud curiosity.

A passage into the mountain's interior. The soldiers let you take the lead. A hallway lit not by torches but glowing unflickering light out of hollows in stone. A door of foreign wood, carved with a thousand hymns. You read the pictures: God-Son crossing the water; God-Son subduing the mountain monsters; God-Son building his throne; God-Son feeding the maidens; God-Son taming the moon.

Wait, shouts someone behind you, but you push open the door and stride into a bright-lit chamber sheathed in tapestries of gold and blue and red and guards in shining armor range with quick expertise into a phalanx between you and a raised throne, and advance on you with the points of their spears ready for your throat,

while you stare into the eyes of the man in the chair. Tall and tough. Wearing an intricate headdress. Blue eyes, eyes as blue as yours.

Stand down! he shouts in a mountain language. The guards slowly lower their weapons.

The man rises. You see how he stands, how powerful he is, how perfect are the lines of his face, how bright those eyes against the dark kohl around them. He steps down from the dais.

You see a glint, a flash, a lightning spark from his blue eyes, and for the first time in centuries you gasp.

He smiles. He holds out his hands.

I heard you were coming, he says. I saw that you were coming in the flights of the birds. But I didn't believe it. I've been disappointed before. So I kept my counsel and sent my best officers to seek word and watch the path and I prayed to my father for guidance and patience and to understand his plan, and I discerned in his silence an excitement I hadn't felt for a very long time.

He walks toward you, past his guards. You know that they hate you in that moment for disrupting their lives, for instilling in their lord this eagerness. You raise your arms palms out, to show them the innocence of your intent, but he, their king, throws his own arms wide, shouting at you, Wanderer! You came, the birds flew true.

The man grabs you and pulls you in while his soldiers stare. He grips tight to the bright thread of his robes your sodden filthy furs and frozen dirty skin. He shouts, very loud, Brother!

For hours you just hold each other, weeping and howling, first you then he then you then he, and he shouts Brother! again.

I never thought, you say.

It's been so long, he says.

When the God-Son tells his bodyguard to leave the two of you alone they hesitate. He has to order them a second time. Alone with you, he says, Tell me your life.

I was born in a valley to my mother and the lightning, you say. He nods. That was the start, you say. I learned to kill, you say. I learned the dance of murder when my eyes go bright and I must break apart that which is whole, you say, and his smile has recognition and sadness in it.

People bring you food and drink. You tell the God-Son of the civilizations you have seen. It sounds like nothing, all those years. The telling does not take so long.

I've been looking for you, you say.

So too with me, the God-Son says. I've been waiting for a brother for a long time. I was born to my mother and the lightning in a plain a long way away. I learned to kill. I learned the walking sleep of violence, too. You have no home? he says.

Everywhere is my home. You stay in one place? you say.

For many years, I sailed to the green country, I went to where the volcanoes are. I came here. There are people in the valley below. They know I will protect them if they need it. They bring tribute. You can cease your wandering, brother. If you want to.

I want to, you say, and saying it you know it is true.

Mountain God-Son says, Let's rule together.

Your room is full of pillows. A window looks onto a gentler slope of the acclivity. The warmth of the castle courtyard rises from great vertical tunnels bored down to chambers below where slaves tend fires of rubbish and wood and coal.

Caravans of travelers from the valley tribes bring grain and vegetables and salted meat and beer. The sons and daughters of the noble families in this skyhouse take turns to lie with you.

You swap stories with the God-Son.

Did you ever spend time with the wetland people beyond the hills to the north? you say. The ones who made figures out of the crocodile hides?

No, he says.

You tell him that you lived among the slope-browed people until the last of them died during the ice.

I spent centuries with the eagle people, he says. Do you know them?

No, you say.

They have feathers for hair, he says. And when the moon is full they can fly.

You do not reply to that.

Have you found any others? you ask him at last.

He looks at you for a very long time. Only you, he says.

And you didn't find me, you say. I found you.

He inclines his head. Someone had to stay still, he says. He looks splendid in the headdress he never removes, with its horns and bones and teeth. What I've been doing is collating, he says. I have collected stories of gods and powers.

I have hundreds, too, you say. You were the best of them. Saying that, you smile.

And you were the best of those that I heard, he says.

What was the second best? you say. After me?

He thinks for a long time.

Vayn, he says. The Church of Vayn.

And now you start, because that is a name unknown to you, and you thought you knew the name of every god humans have created.

What's that?

I don't know, he says. I couldn't find out much. Very far from here. I sent messengers and spies. It's a secret. That's why I was interested. Because most of the stories are of people who proclaim themselves, but this one seemed to reach me by accident. Glowing eyes. The child of Life itself. And when I sent people to track it, the channels didn't open up, they closed down. As if they realized word had leaked and were being careful.

You say nothing.

But you were the best. By a long way. When I read the old poems.

How your flesh heals. The trance. The spit and glow of blue from your eyes. I knew then how I must look to those who saw me.

In the fourth week, he says to you, Some of the river people are late with their tribute. They sent a climber last night who asked for another month. I must go and punish them.

Is it worth punishing them? you say. If they only need more time?

We have spies, brother, he says. They're lying. Their silos are close to full. They're trying to sell it, then hide the coin and claim a blight.

You say, Oh.

You arrive at dusk at the head of three hundred men.

The headwoman says, Mountain God-Son, you honor us. Then your brother turns at some sound you do not hear and stares into an upper window of an overlooking building and out of it an arrow flies and he leans to one side out of its path and it lands in the chest of one of the men with you who stares at it with the stupidity of the dying and tips slowly sideways and now more arrows come and more of your men fall so here you go again, so yes up comes your weapon and you look around a little weary for a target.

To see the God-Son of the mountain, your half brother. Hands clasping his own face.

He runs, then, lowering his hands and bringing up his scramasax and slashing down shattering the woman's ribs, and he snarls and growls with an abstraction coming over him, and you see the blue fizz and froth and glow of his eyes.

And you do not enter that fugue yourself. You only fight and block and punch and kick and kill to keep yourself out of the fray. You follow the God-Son on his howling way, and you watch him.

Until many villagers lie steaming dead and the rest run, screaming that they will bring all the food, begging for mercy, and the mountain fighters gaze at their glowing-eyed leader in awe, and your mountain brother breathes more slowly, the light dimming from beneath his brows.

His eyes come to rest on yours and he smiles. On his right forearm, one long slice from a flint knife adds his blood to the blood of those he has killed. He is otherwise untouched. You raid the silos and go home.

You catch yourself looking at his forearm cut the next morning, during your shared breakfast. The flesh on either side of the cut is red and puffed and it seeps.

He sees you looking. He does not lower his arm out of sight, as you expect him to. He does not cover his arm with his hand or with the cloth of the table. He looks himself, raises the forearm.

Yes, he says. It's taking its time.

Thus he buys hours of you not telling yourself what you already know.

That evening when you come to him to drink wine, your heart sinks to see a bandage over the cut, dark with healing herbs and mud. You know that you have been hoping that you are wrong, and that those hopes are dashed.

Again he sees you look. Again you wait for alarm in his eyes, for challenge. Again there is nothing. He only smiles and says to you, I've had my doctors attend to this, thus to enable the divine healing.

You lie unsleeping all night, staring up into the darkness.

When you meet at sunup his arm is still swollen and he winces when you touch it.

You say, You always wear that headdress. May I see it?

He looks about to ensure that you are not observed. He says, My father gave me this and I do not like mortals to see me without it. But he lifts it off his head and offers it, and you take it, and turn it over, and feel the weight of it. And you find the little pouches in its sides, over where his ears would be, the existence of which you have surmised. You pull at the opening thereto and he nods at you, encouraging you to seek the secret, and you sniff at the dust within, the astringent smell of it.

What is it? you say.

Saltpeter, he says, from the shit of bats. A little charcoal from pinecones. A tiny part of brimstone. Crushed-up dried berries of a particular fruit, he says, for the blue. That gives the color.

When he presses them, curving-teeth channels release the powder near the corners of his eyes. Those channels' tips are flint, and double as spark stones.

I make the blue glare and sputter and glow of the death trance come from my eyes, he says. To honor my father.

He smiles.

And you smile back at him. There is no defensiveness to him, no appeal to complicity, no intimation of revelation. It is a look unguarded, ingenuous, trusting, glad, fraternal.

This is what he thinks it is to be the child of a god. Mummery and tricks. Mimicking the stories he has heard, the stories of you.

You can't even hate him. You can't even hate him for lying to you, because he did not lie, poor warrior, poor foolish champion mistaking story for life.

So you don't punish him. You wait until his back is turned. When you kill him you do it quickly, so he never knows.

His face, when you turn his struck-off head in your hands, still smiles.

You pass the night with the headless body and bodiless head of he who is not your half brother. You pass the head from hand to hand and tell it you are sorry that this is how it has turned out. When the sun rises over the mountain your cheeks are wet and the edges of everything are sharp like knives and you remember that's how tears make light work.

Out into the corridor. Past the guards, moving so fast that they do not even follow you, the look in their eyes saying, of the gory remnant you hold, I must not be seeing what I see, I must be wrong, I have not understood, this is a mistake. You ascend the dais in the throne room to a rising chorus of alarm and shouts at last of To arms! and Guards, what has he done? When you face the crowd of suppliants the soldiers have their spears up and all courtiers and viziers and officers have ghastly expressions, and you hold up the head and raise your voice.

Mountain people. Your king wasn't Heaven-seed.

You hurl the head into a wall, where it leaves a smear and a spatter of blood and rebounds spinning over the crowd to come rolling in its irregular investigation into the center of the room to lie eyes up and open and mouth still with the remnants of the smile now crooked from your rough treatment.

The bravest guard steps forward. Hefts his spear. You bare your chest and gesture for him to throw.

His aim is good and his arm is strong and you have to take a step back as the spear slams into you below the breastplate, goes deep enough and slips to the side of your spine. You stand tall and take in the room, the shaft bobbing as you turn.

He was a great warrior, you say, and gesture again at the head. He was a fair ruler. He was not a bad man. We'll honor him because he was not a liar. I believe he believed his story. He was wrong, is all, and that's not a sin.

Bring to me the four finest craftspeople in the valley. Have them build his statue, to stand in the center of the courtyard. It will stand when this keep falls. It'll stand when the mountain lowers, and when the children of your children's children's children to the twentieth degree dig in what will be a valley, they will uncover it and say, This must have been the king of this place, he must have been a great king, perhaps he was the child of a god. He can be remembered as what he thought he was. That'll be our gift to him.

I need no statues, you say.

You leap. You jump straight up, from the lip of the dais. Spread your arms and legs wide belly-down like the gliding squirrels of the far-off forests, the shaft of the spear inside you angled straight down, and you fall hard so the floor drives it right up with your weight all the way through your body, so when you land in a low alert crouch on the tips of your toes and the tips of your fingers, the spear points at the ceiling.

And everyone in that room is still and staring and afraid when you stand. You walk to the man who threw the spear. His bravery pleases you: he does not run.

You reach behind yourself and pull the spear all the way through. You offer it to him.

Take it, you say. Use it against the enemies of this castle. Serve me. You gave yourself to a holy child. I am he.

The man takes his wet weapon. He kneels. Everyone in the room kneels.

No, you say.

Most leave, cursing the skies. Some argue, plead, demand. Them you kill.

You will rest, is what you tell yourself. You eat as much as you can. Your shape does not change. You drink the strongest liquor, for days at a time, and grow drunk, but never as drunk as you wish. You dance until everyone with whom you dance has fallen over in exhaustion, pleading. Sometimes you give them the mercy of sleep. Sometimes you drag them up and keep dancing with them until they die in your grasp.

Generations pass. You await holy warriors who will attempt to exorcize you from the mountain but none come. Once the people of the castle rise up against you. These are the children and grandchildren of those who were there when you arrived, and perhaps they believe that their elders' stories about you are myths. You kill the ringleaders in various ways.

The commander of these insurgents is a young cook. You have her brought to you for your judgment. You stare at her and try to work out to which of her family you did what, to parse the nature of her desire for vengeance. But you've never seen her before and her ancestry is nothing.

Why? you say.

Because fuck all gods, she says. She meets your eye.

You tell your court you'll burn her alive at the base of the mountain.

Every month the local people ascend. Every few months your officers descend to lay down manners. Some weeks you receive visitors who have followed the stories, who have striven to find you, to petition you to heal their sick or bless them with luck or wealth or to fight their wars.

You descend with her and cut her bonds and tell her she can go. She stares at you and will not let you see her relief and you like her even more.

Be afraid, she says, and walks toward the river.

Fifty-three years pass. You wait for her return that whole time but she never comes back.

The darkest night for decades. You hear buzzards. You lie in your bedroom, amid sprawled and snoring bodies and wineskins and the smears of food. You alone are awake.

You hear the slow sound of steps. For a moment you think this is a courtesan wearing wooden-soled shoes, but the pattern is wrong.

The door swings slowly ajar. You stare at a dark and heavy shape beyond.

It steps forward, noses the door open the rest of the way, walks slowly in to stand at the threshold, staring at you as you stare back.

You breathe out a welcome. The pig has found you for the first time in centuries.

There you lie, crusted with come and slip and liquor and sugar and salt. You peer across the half-dark at its tiny black and glinting eyes. It stands like a household spirit, like something seeking to understand, like a memory.

Hello, pig, you whisper.

You found me, pig.

It's been a long time.

There are many guards. There are miles and miles of freezing mountain path. In your mind you see the babirusa's passage. Waking from its egg, on some foreign shore, in years long gone. Its trotting hunt, through cities, learning skills of stealth and patience quite alien to its form, smuggling itself onto ships, swimming, walking through forests, breaking apart the predators that came for it. The loneliness of that pig could make you weep. If not that endless mission, that search for the other immortal, what would it do? Ascending the slate of the path, tap tap, hoof echoes in the cut, determined as no animal should be or have to be, quieting its own snorts, plunging into rivers to minimize its gamy smell, making itself invisible through sheer brazenness, perfecting a proud non-skulking pigness that leaves trained experts thinking, I am seeing things, I am hallucinating a pig in pigless halls, crossing the world to be here. To stare at you.

How many pig-lives ago since you saw it like this? Quiet, not snarling, not scraping the ground, not spreading its jaws so its slaver stretches and snaps in its eternal campaign of violence against you? Just watching.

Come then.

You raise your head. Your own motion surprises you. But there you are with it, here it is, and this is what you are doing.

Present your throat to the pig that hates you with the hatred of a faith.

Tear it out, you whisper.

You've come so far, you whisper, you've worked so hard, I'm tired. I'll rest awhile. Send me to my egg. Shall we go together?

The pig looks at you for a long time.

It turns its head and you, your throat still up-thrust and needy, watch the deer-pig stare into every part of the room, at everything and every-one within it, that slow gaze returning at last to you.

And what you see in the pig's eyes you have never seen there before.

Disdain.

It turns and walks away.

Pig, you say. Hey pig.

The pig trots quietly down the corridor and out of the castle.

Hey, you shout. The bodies around you move sluggishly as you raise your voice. Pig, you shout. Tear it out.

It does not turn.

Hey, you shout. What happens now? What happens if you don't do it? You can't ignore me!

But the pig is gone.

He could not read, your predecessor, but he understood the importance of writing, and in a high wing is a library, and therein a chest full of scrolls that he had his scholars recite. You read fables and dreams and invocations, riddles about the deities and their families.

Not all are about you.

The people of the castle will not enter, not when you have warned them against it with your expression, but they clamor at the entrance as you unroll the documents and pore through these dead and living languages.

King! they shout. Why are you forsaking us? they shout.

You say nothing. You unfold a list of supposed gods and powers beyond gods and demigods and demons. The fury of the quiet abyss when the world arrived, flitting from body to body in its fight. The archons of endings and beginnings, of death and life. You find your name written among the latter. A scroll pleads with its reader to find pity for you, the dry-loined lonely sad-eyed son of the void. A scroll tells you that Vayn the daughter of Life opens the ears of the dead and fills their lungs again, and awakens the cold clay, and the unmoving matter of the world, so that it may dance and smell out her enemies. An ancient parchment scripture sings of her adversary, the oldest thing there's ever been, stillness itself, which death can only mimic.

Outside the room guards tear off their armor and cut their chests to prove their loyalty. No, one vizier shouts. You will fight me before you abandon us. Kill me, but don't discard us.

You unfold maps of hidden churches.

This is your child, someone shouts, and you look up and out the window at that, and someone else calls, And this, and held high above the crowd you see two babies, three, fitful in their swaddling. Very likely you and their mothers have fucked. But as if you don't know by now, as if you haven't had it proved in a succession of sad still cold little bodies, there is to your essence something inimical to any womb. You turn back to the tracts.

At the bottom of the box, a fragment of parchment. Hold it up to the light.

Such antique pictograms. You remember this script, it came and went quickly. Cavorting stick figures, intricate minatory sigils, a sibilant language of a people who spoke in whispers.

The Hymn of Vayn, you read. The songs of the immortal child of life lightning.

This is all I'll take, you say to the civilization you're abandoning. The castle, the food, the fealty, the weapons—everything else is yours.

Let us worship you! someone shouts.

Your god still watches you, you say. His statue is in the courtyard. Would you be so ungrateful as not to give thanks for his care?

When you walk out of the keep, setting out for the first time in a long time, and for the last time, down the steep and rocky path, only children watch you go. The rest of the people of the mountain are holding hands and circling around the weathered stone figure with its stern face. They are burning meat to the statue of the first God-Son, throwing flowers into the bonfire, and the man who threatened to fight you, knowing you would kill him if he did, is leading the chants and laments already taking on the rhythms of ritual. The people sing to he whom you killed before they were born, begging for protection.

KEPT IN HONEY

KEEVER WOKE TO THE RATTLE OF HIS PHONE AGAINST HIS nightstand. He sat up. Still dark. He blinked. Blocked number. He put it to his ear.

"Keever."

"Yeah." A cautious female voice. "Who am I talking to?"

"Who am I talking to?"

"OK, yeah. This is Lieutenant Carstairs from the San Antonio Police. Sir, do you know a Joanie Miller?"

"What's happened?" He was on his feet.

"I'm calling you," the voice said, "because you're the last message on her phone. From a few days ago."

"Where is she?"

"I'm sorry, sir. There was an accident. She went off the road on Fall Edge Road north of the state park."

"Is she OK?" Of course not.

"No, I'm afraid she's not."

"She's dead," he said.

A moment.

"I'm sorry, sir, yes she is. Serious injury to her head and neck. No one else was on the road and her car rolled right out of sight, it was a couple of days till anyone . . . I'm very sorry. What was the nature of your relationship?"

"We were friends. I worked with her husband."

"That would be Kaz Miller?"

"Yes. He served under me."

That did the trick. The woman spoke more respectfully. "I see, sir. This would be Kaz Miller who recently . . ."

"Yes."

"And . . . sir, if you don't mind me asking . . . how was Mrs. Miller . . . ?" He waited out the silence for a while. "Not doing great," he said. "As you can imagine. Why?"

"It's just that she had a lot of alcohol in her system. I'm really sorry to have to tell you this."

Hey, you're just doing your job.

Keever realized he was not speaking aloud. He heard the woman say more but not what she said. As she spoke into his ear he parted the slats of his blinds and looked into the sky. Hey, he said, not aloud, he realized again. You never know what someone's going to do, how they're going to react. Grief makes us all crazy, doesn't it? Crazy.

I WAS SO EXCITED, CALDWELL THOUGHT, WHEN WE FOUND AN EYE. WHEN I started all we had was a leg and a half. A few bits of viscera, like jerky. A handful of bone shards.

Once more he positioned the subdued pig beside the cylinder. Once more he attached the sluices and the cables.

Gather a few ugly relics no more magnificent than anything the Vatican could muster, and then an eye? Of course it looked like a raisin when we found it but I knew. Get it right, it'll swell back up. And here we are. Now with our new piece.

This whole line of research had come from the most unlikely source. Caldwell had been watching a movie.

It was soon after he had joined the Unit. He had returned home one night, exhausted, and turned on the television: back then he still might occasionally watch or read something completely unrelated to his work. The paradox, he supposed, was that he wouldn't waste his focus like that now, but it was doing so that had given him this fecund area of research.

He had come in a little way into a movie starring, and presumably directed by, Polanski, of all people. He'd been mildly surprised that they were showing it.

Caldwell had been eating, half-watching at most, until that one scene. Polanski's character lying on the bed, drunk, talking to Isabelle Adjani.

"Cut off my arm," he said. "I say, 'Me and my arm.' Take out my stomach, my kidneys: I say, 'Me and my intestines.'" Caldwell remembered how Polanski had gone on: "Cut off my head. Would I say 'Me and my head' or 'Me and my body'? What right has my head to call itself me?"

Caldwell had sat up very straight at that moment. Thinking of that leg and a half. Unute's scraps, which he had inherited. What right did this or that bit have to call itself him? What of Unute was ontologically Unute?

And might thus, appropriately prodded and awakened, undie?

That approach had quickly become a priority. To chase down every story of every scrap of every bit of Unute that had been pickled, dropped, buried, venerated.

You'll never be finished, he thought of and at the shape within the cylinder. We could always paste more pieces into a better approximation of the shape of which you're discards. But you're more complete—completed—than plenty of true-born humans, or than I ever thought you would be. What will it take? What must I do to say hello? What kind of current or energy or field or vibrations do I need to pour through you to wake you up?

I could hardly expect Unute to look kindly on you, he thought to the figure in the glass. But.

Each relic they'd found since that revelation had come to him with hush and ceremony. Gloves on, with all due reverence, lifting whatever organic scrap it was from its housing. Reading any documents, details of its emanations and provenance.

In the Year of Our Lord 1372 Simón de León of Seville was given the task of protecting this, the littlest finger struck off of he who is called the Hidden Saint by the Brothers of this Order.

I Fatima Al-Khouri swear that I am the bearer of the lobe of the ear of the nameless soldier who protected the Prophet Muhammad Peace Be Upon Him and whom Allah blessed or cursed with eternal life—the jurists do not agree on this matter.

Sixty winters gone. Stranger came, fought a bear. Penis torn off. The man's. This is it (another grew where it had been). I have kept it in honey.

Some of us, bless us, want the powers of the energies of Unute. And Unute himself is not a reliable source of access to himself. But, as if generously, he does leave trails of his own discarded self. Which is an opportunity.

I didn't need that, he thought. I don't need that much.

Eighty thousand years. There must be enough Unute biltong and slivers to build a whole towerman in dried-up flesh. That thought, as it always did, put into Caldwell's mind an image of a clumsy ragged giant stamping through the ruins of the world.

Now the image that came to him was a memory of the real results of his searches. A man-sized mound of pieces and parings, clutched and sunken, added to the Unit's collected gobs of innards, bones older than the oldest art in the deepest cavern, fixed together, slowly stitched, sutured, heat-sealed, organic-epoxied into the roughest approximation of their erstwhile configuration.

There was only so much that even the most bleeding-edge—ho ho—biotech could do to rewind the aging of such tissue. But there was brain matter within the brainpan: the crusted remnants of thought. An adequate homunculus.

If only, Caldwell had thought, we didn't have three spare hands, all left. If only we had an eye for each hole, rather than four ears. But it had been time to try.

Channeling current through that cool hypercharged elixir. Sluicing into meticulously reconstituted veins harvested blood. Pushing the whole into a quantum-catalytic state by the cajoling of incompossible wave-particle interactions, according to the arcana of Unutology.

And absolutely nothing had happened.

The liquid had churned, the lights moving within it like the spirits of fish, eddying in complex vortexes, just Brownian motion and fluid dynamics. Nothing more. Not that time, nor any time since.

Death doesn't want Unute, Caldwell thought. But no matter what we've done, life doesn't seem to want his remains, either. Surely the pig might have some extra to share, it seemed like a reasonable bet, but not so far. Do you, Babe? If I try again? Prod you? All the way back to the edge? Maybe shove you over, this time? Get your life rushing back so I can siphon a little off into our project?

What do you say? One more try? And then, Plan B?

"DIANA?" B CALLED SOFTLY FROM THE ENTRANCE TO HER HOUSE. HE WAS backlit by the glaring white of the streetlamps. He read NO JUNK MAIL PLEASE, near the mail slot. Looked down at the mat to wipe his shoes: WELCOME! thereon, and a picture of a puppy wagging its tail. A little nail protruded from the wood by the door, where once perhaps had hung a mezuzah or a dream catcher.

"Diana?"

"It's open," she said from within. He pushed the door gently. "Come through."

She was sitting on the floor in the living room. She had her laptop open on the low coffee table, was staring into its cold light. To one side of it was a mug of coffee; to the other, a small pistol.

"Diana," he said.

"I'm OK," she said. She patted the air as if to reassure him, as if he were agitated. "I'm OK."

"What happened?"

She gestured for him to sit on the sofa, so he could see the screen over her shoulder. But first he leaned down and reached out and took gentle hold of her face. She let him, half-closed her eyes. He looked deep into them, took in her features. She could feel his slow breath upon her and her own breath caught.

"It didn't hurt you?" he said. "Whatever it was?"

"No."

He frowned and rubbed his thumb along the mark on her face.

"What's this?"

"It didn't hurt me, but it . . . well, it touched me. It scratched me. Gave me a scare."

"Tell me."

"Sit," she said. "Look. Maybe you can tell me."

He sat. She gestured at her laptop screen.

"Have you ever seen a ghost?" she said.

"It was a ghost that attacked you?"

"I didn't say that," she said. "I don't know. Have you? Seen a ghost?"

"Not counting when I look in the mirror?" When she frowned he said, "A ghost is something that doesn't stay away after it's died." He cocked his head.

"OK," Diana said. "So you're a demigod, an alien weapon, a genetic sport, a force of silence, a chaos, and now you're a ghost. Anything else? One of these days you're going to have to make a decision."

"No I'm not. I have no problem living with contradictions."

"Have you?" she said. "Seen one?"

"Don't you think that would have come up by now?" he said. "You said it yourself, B—a lot of things have happened to you. And remembering isn't the same as it occurring to you. You don't always know what's worth mentioning. You told me that."

"Fair," he said. "OK. So, have I ever seen the spirit of someone who died? In eighty thousand years I've never seen that, any more than I've seen a plesiosaur in Loch Ness or Okanagan Lake. But if you mean have I ever seen anything that I couldn't explain? Many times."

"Something uncanny," she said. She nodded at the screen. On it he saw a green-gray image of the inside of her house, through a camera's low-light-enhanced vision. She pressed a button and tides of pixelation passed over it, shadows as she fast-forwarded, the infinitesimal shifting of a corridor. She let it return to regular speed and a second thereafter the eidolon of herself passed through the hallway.

"Wait," she said.

They watched.

A skitter. The tiniest disturbance of the carpet. A shadow in the shadows of the wall.

"There," she said. She paused the screen and brought up still images. All of that corridor, all in that slice of time. Enlargements of the patch of darkness. Formlessness. "I've gone through it a ton of times," she said. She gestured at a swirl of black. "I can't get anything. Whatever it was was too quick."

He was up, then, and in the hallway. Crouched down below the prints and the childhood photographs, crawling below a sculpture from Benin, his face right by the floor, fingertips feeling like antennae. He sniffed. He shook his head.

"What did it feel like when it touched you?" He returned. "And how do you know it's gone?"

"I don't know, but I … " She frowned. "I just don't think it's in here anymore. It felt like the air went empty. And what it felt like … " She gestured at her face. "It felt like a nail," she said. "A fingernail. And it has to be connected to what's going on."

B looked up at the ceiling.

"Pattern recognition," he said. "You owe pretty much everything to it."

"You?" she said. "You mean me or humans in general? Second person—you're discounting yourself?"

"Sure," he said. "You know that. What I'm saying is pattern recognition is what got monkeys signifying. And it's also what gives you paranoia and psychosis."

"And?"

"And I understand. The babirusa comes back for me. And whoever was walking with it is still out there. And there's Ulafson. And Thakka . . . and now this invisible infiltrator. It seems like it's all got to be part of the same moment."

"Also you," she said. "There's you to take into consideration. At the best of times, that's a curveball, but recently? With how you've been? Something's on your mind, B. Preying on you."

After a moment, he said, "OK. Add that. I get that it feels connected, but that kind of certainty isn't your friend, Diana. We have to be dispassionate. Something came in here. Touched you. During a cluster of mysteries, yeah. But if we decide in advance that everything's linked, we're not going to be investigating, we're going to be telling ourselves a story."

"You're saying you think this is coincidence," she said. "That these are all unrelated."

"No. I'm saying we shouldn't 'think' we know what this is, and still less that it's necessarily all connected. Look for patterns and you will find them."

"Mm-hm," Diana said. She took a sip of her coffee. "I understand," she said.

They stared into the dark corners of the room.

At last she said, "You don't believe any of that, do you?"

"Not for a second," he said.

"You're as certain as me that these things are all part of something bigger, aren't you?" she said.

B said, "One hundred percent."

"COME IN, COME IN, COME IN."

The door at the back of the hallway let in a wedge of sunlight. A cluster of figures stood, backlit and hesitant.

"Come on in! I'm Marlene. I'm sure happy to see you." She hurried over and threw the door fully open; three men and a woman waited within, hunched into their warm clothes.

"You-all get on in here," Marlene said.

She grabbed a muscular man with short-cropped dark hair, whose eyes widened in surprise when she hugged him. "You must be Himchan," she said. She bundled him in. She took hold of the tough-looking white woman with a scar by her left eye. "Sally, right?" Marlene hugged her too. "And you're Jonny." A tall man older than his two companions, with gray in his black hair. He hugged her back.

"Pleased to meet you," he muttered.

"You too, dear, you too. Jeff's told me about you."

Stepping in behind the newcomers, Jeff Stonier embraced Marlene. He pulled the door closed and gestured his companions to chairs in a circle, by a vat of coffee and a plate of cookies. When he sat, his companions did the same.

"Well," Marlene said. "Here we are. I am so glad to meet you. Let's get started. I'm sure grateful to you for coming. I know some of you have traveled a long way to get here, and I know Jeff's told you a little, but I'm sure you must be wondering what the heck it is we can do for you."

Stonier nodded gently at the newcomers.

"Sally," Marlene said. The tough-faced woman met her eyes. "If it's OK, I'll start with you. Ladies first. Jeff told you he'd let us know a little bit about you." Sally nodded. "And I want to thank you for trusting us enough to come here. So. Your husband, Don, worked with, with . . . Jeff's husband, right? In contracting?" Sally nodded. "I know you lost him too. Also to an accident."

"Sure," Sally said. "An accident."

"Sal," Himchan said quietly. He didn't look up but he reached out and took her hand.

"Himchan," Marlene said. She turned to him. "You used to work with them both, right?"

"I didn't see the accidents," he said. "I wasn't on duty either day."

"No," Marlene said. "But you were close to Don. And that's why you stopped working there. After what happened. Too many memories."

He paused. "Kind of," he said. "It's a dangerous business, and it wasn't just Don and Kaz that got me sick of it. It was . . ." He nodded at Stonier. "It was Arman too, and it was Ulafson, and . . ."

"I get it," Marlene said.

"I doubt that," Himchan said.

"And it was Bree, too, wasn't it, Himchan?" the last man said. Everyone turned to him.

"Yes," Marlene said gently. "Your Bree. It's a terrible thing to lose a child, Jonny. I know what I'm talking about, Jonny, I do." Jonny met her eyes. "I'm sorry you lost her, Jonny, I am.

"Now, Jeff's been coming here for a few weeks," Marlene said. "He told us he was going to get in touch with you. He told me he understands what you guys have been going through, and he thought you could get something out of this, just like he did. And the way I'm thinking, if you're here, he must have said enough to get you interested.

"So." She clasped her hands. "You've all lost people. The details aren't my business, of course." She made a locking-key motion at her lips. She leaned forward. "I know you're angry with death. And you know what? Me too. And I'm willing to bet that part of the reason you're here is because of what Jeff told you, right, that you're not wrong to be. That life is everything, right? No one here's going to tell you to learn acceptance. Or look for closure. No one here's going to tell you that you need to move on. We're here to tell you that you're right. Death sucks!"

She smiled sadly and sat back.

"I'm not here to talk about circles of life and yin and yang and that kind of thing. Death is the worst thing in the world. It's the worst thing in the universe. Wouldn't it be better if we could just end it? We want our people back! Right? Right! And if we can't have that . . ." She hesitated for a long moment. "If we can't have that, then the least we can do is fight death. And then . . . what if we could do both?" Jonny, Sally, and Himchan glanced at each other.

"I know you want to know what we do here," Marlene said.

She stood and went to an internal door and opened it onto a dark cupboard. She entered and the three newcomers furrowed their brows at her wheezing and huffing, the clatter of matter. At last she reappeared, dragging something behind her.

"Here we go," she gasped.

A large wooden base on tiny wheels. Atop it wobbled a tall, vaguely human-shaped outline, a dense foam figure on a sprung base. She pulled it into the center of the room and clicked up the wheels so it braked and was abruptly still. The armless, legless black torso swayed back and forth with a juddering noise.

"Death sure is my enemy," Marlene said. "I'll bet it's yours too."

The foam curved at the top, a rough head. A striking target for boxing and kickboxing. Where the face should be, a skull was painted on the dark rubber, something between a Posada etching and a malevolent cartoon rictus.

Marlene went back into the cupboard and came back out with four aluminum baseball bats. She held them up.

"Come on, you-all," she said. "Let's show death what we think of it."

The newcomers looked at the bats, and at the punching stand. One by one they turned their gaze to Stonier. Jonny rose slowly.

"You are fucking shitting me," he said to Stonier. "You bring me here for this? Fuck you."

"Wait, wait," Stonier said. He stood with his hands up. "Marlene, they can skip these stages. They're ready, they're ready!"

She hesitated, her smile frozen.

"Would you get Alam, please?" Stonier said to her. She nodded uneasily and headed for the door. "Tell him I want my friends to go straight to the final phase," he called. "They're ready. I promise." She nodded and did not look back.

"Jonny, listen," Stonier said. "Sally. All of you. Please. Just give me ten minutes. You have to meet Alam. There's more. There's more."

·   ·   ·

CALDWELL LET THE BRIGHTNESS OF THE LATE SUN WASH OVER HIM.

He finished drinking his coffee and sat before his laptop. He played the silent video of his recent unpleasant task. He pressed buttons to slow down and speed up the explosions of blood and the swirl of the dark liquid in the tank. The last shaking motions of the pig. Eventually, the first fitful motion of its staticked flesh and blood crawling back.

More nothing, more motionlessness from the innards of the tank.

Flesh Caldwell watched the little Caldwell on the screen check the laboratory readouts of the wired-up pig corpse and the tank and the tubes connecting the two. No reverse vortex of energy registered, no wind-back of entropy, no spurt of life ex nihilo.

"Fuck," Caldwell muttered. "Damn. I really hoped."

Wherever was the life it needed, Caldwell thought, he had not found it even in the full transgression of death that killing the pig had wrought. He could siphon no power into that patchwork thing, even as it came back from the void.

OK, he thought. Plan B it is.

He took out the metal box, and opened it. He looked in at the tiny nub of hard, pointed flesh within.

"So just what do I do with you?" he whispered. "Where do you go?"

Caldwell pulled up the image files of the microscopy of that remnant.

"How do you help me? What do you do? What are you?"

Dermatology was hardly his field, but years of scouring through offcut data had given him an acquaintance with cell structures of most regions of the epidermis, even those ruined by time. He knew what keratin looked like. He recognized densely matted hair. This nub partook of all such, but was simultaneously too abstract and too vague for him to recognize. And it was, yet, unnervingly distinct in its hardness and triangularity.

Does it matter? he thought. If I just stick you on anywhere? Are all the stories I get snatches of nonsense? Were you ever even part of him?

I will make you his third eye. Right in the middle of the forehead. Like the little girl's curl. Are you good or horrid? Time to find out.

What are the stakes if I get it wrong?

What if I've been thinking about this wrong? he wondered. Maybe it's not about the amount of life: maybe it's about how you get out of death. How you push through, out of not-life. Maybe we just need the right equipment.

DIANA PUT HER PHONE ON B'S TABLE.

"Do you feel unsafe?" he had said. "In your house?"

"No," she had said, but had hesitated. "Unsafe" was not the right word, but she had realized then that she did still feel something. Surveilled. For all that the two of them had gone through her house again, through every room, and found no trace of whatever it was that had been within.

They had driven to his.

It was not the first time she had been there. The sumptuous furniture and dark shades of the art—original paintings, posters like her own of classic movies and of albums—reminded her of his preference for a certain office chair. Why would his house not be just exactly so? Why would it be a shell, a modern cave? Why would it not be lovely?

B stood by the stereo, pulling album after album from its sleeve and considering them.

"If you don't mind," Diana said, "I'm going to record this." She indicated her phone.

"Go ahead," he said.

"I know from experience not to leave anything to memory," she said. "Not a problem you face."

"No," he said. "But on the other hand, you know that remembering everything isn't what it's cracked up to be."

He blew all around the grooves of what he had chosen and placed it down, and she could not help but smile at the inimitable thunk and crackle when he placed the needle.

"Never had you down as a hipster," she said. "Vinyl's just a warmer sound, you know?"

He was silent through the solo piano of "Splanky." When the other instruments came sliding in he looked at her and, affecting the same earnestness, said, "With Basie, it's all about the notes he doesn't play."

Diana laughed. "For a lugubrious immortal," she said, "you're a funny guy."

"I mean, it is true," he said. "About vinyl. But for me the appeal's less sound quality, real as it is, and more slowness. Ritual. The use of hands. I'm not hating on tech. If I had as little time as you do I'd be all about workflow and convenience too. But the point of convenience is to eradicate the journey to the telos. In my shoes, what's the point of that? You want to rack up as many teloi as you can—"

"You're describing jazz albums as teloi?" she said.

"I guess. And good meals, and nice shoes, and books. Anything. You have only so many years to get them under your belt. But when I get to the end of any of them, all there is to do is reach for another. Might as well linger en route. If I were recording you, I might fuss around with tape ends."

"You're saying you've got an old reel-to-reel somewhere?" she said.

"Sure." He jerked his head toward the attic. "Always enjoyed playing with the spools." He gave a sad smile. "Spoooooool." Are you a Beckett fan? He liked the way I said that word. Put it in a play."

"Are you telling me he wrote *Krapp's Last Tape* because of you?"

"No, just that line. He liked how I performed it though."

"You acted?" Diana said. "For Beckett?"

"Sure," he said. "There were only twenty people in the audience—it was the back room of a pub in County Clare. This was 1975—he was exactly the same age as Krapp. He told me he'd been suspicious of someone as quote young as me playing the role, even with the makeup, but he thought I'd done an even better job than Magee. He said, 'No more laboring the angst. I believed you didn't care at all about being old. And that was perfect.'"

He shrugged.

"Sometimes," Diana said, "especially recently, despite what you've told me, I feel like you are ready to die."

"No," he said, taking his time in turn. "I don't think so. I don't think I think so. But I do feel . . . bad."

"Bad?"

"About Thakka." He looked fascinated by his own words. "And Ulafson. All of them. You'd think that if you've been responsible for as many deaths as I have, it would be impossible to feel bad about any one of them. But you never know. You never know which ones will get you, or why." He sat across from her. "So," he said. "Let's talk about whatever was in your house."

After a moment, Diana said, "You know what it was, don't you?"

"No," he said. "But I am reminded of things I've seen before. I'm thinking about times I've encountered certain things. Infiltrators. Spies. Moving too fast, or wrong, like you've described. Like on the video. Too fast for animals, and different, anyway."

"Microdrones?" she said.

"Long before drones. And quicker than any drone."

"So tell me," she said at last.

"I've said, you guys need to get out of the mindset of thinking that technology began in 1950." His eyes refocused on a middle distance of memory. "A lot of years before the last ice age. I was attacked by a flock of stones. They were being directed by flint wranglers." He held up a hand. "Don't ask, it was a long time ago, and everything about the Duchy of Bosheen is dust now. And there was a time, sixteen, seventeen thousand years later . . ." He pursed his lips. "In what's now southern Macedonia. A woman warned me that I was being chased by what she called wolves. But when they came, they were made of dead wood and metal. They were quick. I destroyed them. Threw them into the sea. And there are other times I could tell you about."

"Do!" she said.

"I'm just saying," he said, "there've been times—presences—that remind me of whatever this is."

Don't rush him. There's no urgency to get to the telos, Diana. Let him take the journey. But after two, three minutes of only Basie and his orchestra, she could not restrain herself.

"So what are you thinking?" she whispered.

"I don't know why," he said. "Because there was a lot about it that was different from this, from whatever that was." He gestured at her screen. "But something happened to me that I can't stop thinking about now. A lot more recent than these others. Only a couple hundred years ago. For whatever reason, the footage of what was in your house reminds me."

"Of what?" Diana said.

"It was on a ship," he said. "It was at sea."

CALDWELL STALKED FROM ROOM TO ROOM OF HIS APARTMENT. HE MOVED his long lean body with agitation, excitement so great it almost looked like pain. Twice he lay down, once on his bed, once on his sofa, and closed his eyes. You have to sleep, he scolded himself, and he lay with the hard light of the streetlamps across his chest. You're no good to yourself if you're exhausted. He breathed deep, impatient with his own tiredness and with his inability to sleep. He rose, went into the kitchen, turned on the small lamp at his table, took out his notebook, put it away again, shook his head and rubbed his eyes.

I have to get back, he thought. Then: You're not thinking clearly. Focus.

Caldwell opened his notebook again, and sat staring at a blank page. He brought his pen down and wrote the date and one word in capitals across the top of the page.

SUCCESS.

His pen hovered above the paper.

Too early to be sure, he wrote at last. Caruncle changed energy flows. Subject still dormant but readings consistent with change in (hypothesis) brane polarities (?)—possible chiral anomaly/quint ramp-up. Tiny / discernible shift in mass?! Energies! New state??? ≠ previous ≠ unlife

Caldwell froze. And put his hands slowly down upon the table. Blinked and turned his head.

He tried to bring back to his mind the sense that had just passed through him. The sense that something had scuttled through the room. He frowned. Reached out very slowly, turned off the lamp.

I'm no field operative, he thought. But I can move.

He went low, quietly, toward the stairs. Froze again.

A dark-clad figure stood in his doorway.

Caldwell kept his face still. His heart did not accelerate. He put his right hand in his pocket and moved forward, and the figure backed away and Caldwell sped up and stood and brought his switchblade out and brought it forward and up but before it touched anything air whistled and something hit him very hard on his chest.

Oh.

He was lying on his back.

Oh, he'd flown backward, and was lying there. All the air was out of him. He struggled to breathe. Whipped his blade back and forth in front of him and kicked himself away and pressed his back against the wall and tried to rise.

Another rush of air, a sting like a hornet. Caldwell's right arm went numb. He dropped the knife. Another impact, this time great pain, a rip of shirt then flesh on his left arm and he cried out and shouted some furious word, incomprehensible even to him, flailing his bleeding left arm as if flies were upon him, and whatever tiny cutting thing it was that hit him hit him again and again. Went deep. Hit and cut and dug through and Caldwell felt wetness spread across his clothes, across his skin. He slid down with his back against the wall, his legs out. They trembled.

Again, again, switch switch, two more spinning slashes, against his face, up one cheek down the other.

Silence then, but for the faint sound of his own bloodiness and dripping.

Blackness crawled in from the edges of Caldwell's sight, darkening the dark of his house.

"Hello, Caldwell." It was a man's voice.

The air before Caldwell vibrated, whispering distortions crossed his vision. He strained to speak.

"What is that?" he gasped. His voice was faint. "What hit me? Who the fuck are you?" What is it you cut me with? Or: What are you doing? or Who are you? again, and a gout of blood emerged and he felt it slide out of his mouth and down his chin and he closed his mouth.

Someone walked toward him. It was hard to make out. Caldwell felt cold. Someone was kneeling slowly next to him and looking closely into his eyes, without pity. Was that disgust in those eyes?

"Do you know why I'm here?" the voice said.

Caldwell looked inward now, inside himself, toward where a last dream was starting.

"That poor animal," the man said. "I'll admit I'm surprised I care, but it grew on me. I wasn't with it long, but I walked with it. Well, just behind it. That was how it preferred it. So it didn't have to look, could just feel my vibes. It led me where I needed to go so I could find out what I needed to know. I thought that was the end of the relationship, and I guess it was. What a way to go. Even temporarily. You're not a nice man, Caldwell.

"This is what happens to you when you choose this way," the man said. Caldwell could not make out the details of his face. Of anything. Heard the voice through a roaring in his ears. "You chose to give your life to this organization, and you know what it is? It's a force for death. The death of everything. For the purest, coldest end, for entropy. There's nothing grand about your mission, you know, whatever you told yourself. You're just a functionary in the bureaucracy of death."

Caldwell thought, You have no idea, and tried to say it, and could not. Oh, so close! he thought, sadly. All those years, climbing the ranks of the Unit and the other ranks, too, the steps toward illumination, initiating the layers of the mystery cult, so close, so close. Oh.

"Why would I waste my time with you?" the figure said. "You're nothing. Do you know that, Caldwell? You're a tiny, petty little agent of death and the negative. I want to be productive. I want to aim at the big death and the big death only. For the sake of life. The sole reason I'm talking to you is the energies coming out of your lab. The accidental progress you've made. What you've found. I've seen it all. With my other eyes. The fact that you're going to help me with that. Focus me. Help me channel. I know you have the relic. And the mission is the only thing worth doing. The only thing in the world."

You have no idea, Caldwell thought again, hazily, and clenched the muscles of his stomach, tensed the muscles of his neck to turn his gaze at the eyes that looked down on him.

"One problem," Caldwell managed, at last, to whisper, through bubbles of spit and blood. "For you . . . you won't . . . get a chance . . . to use me . . ."

Give this fucker a long look, Caldwell, he thought as the darkness came in. Make yourself laugh at him. Make that your last thing.

The Stowaway's Story

I HEARD HUGH CURRIE TELLING JOHN BROND THAT HE WAS GOING to hide himself away aboard the *Oban* and I asked him to take me with him.

"Hush, Peter," said he to me. "You're too wee."

I said, "I'll sneak aboard whether you help me or no so you may as well."

John and Hugh I knew from the docks, where we would ask the sailors for pennies. I'd come to Greenock with my ma and pa near two years before but my mother left on the third night there and consumption took my father and since then the old woman who ran the boardinghouse let me sleep in the kitchen because the minister had told her it was her Christian duty and every week when he visited I heard him say, "How fares the boy?" to which she'd say, "Tolerably well," though how would she know? She never gave me food nor any but the coldest attention.

We were stood outside the baker when Hugh told John of his plan and I knew straightaway it was what I wanted too. In truth all that the world would have needed to move me to action was the possibility of a life elsewhere where more food might be available for my howling stomach. Hugh at twelve was three years older than I, and he liked to mock me as a bairn, but when I told him I too would stow away my fervor was such that John said, "Me and all!" and though Hugh did not like it John was the best of us so Hugh had little choice but to pretend it was a grand plan.

Now, boys—and for all I know girls too—announce scores of plans every day and most such castles remain in the air. But Hugh's mother was not kind to him and John spoke often with a great look of wonder in his eyes of the animals and wilderness of Canada and as we pledged ourselves to the endeavor I believed we all meant it. I was surprised when, two nights hence, amid the creaking ropes and doleful chain sounds of the harbor, it was only me and Hugh who met in the shadow of the iron-hulled three-master. We waited but it was not long before Hugh whispered, "We'd best try another night, John's no' here."

But I said to him, "I'll not wait."

Perhaps Hugh heard that as challenge. When I stole on board hand over hand on the ropes, my bag heavy with stolen victuals and beer bottles full of water, Hugh climbed behind me, astonishment upon his face.

We descended through intricate wooden byways where I saw hatches and spools of rope and nooks behind stairways and barrels and the between decks and ribs of the ship. A thousand hiding places. Why, this would be the easiest thing! Down we went, on every ladder we found.

Amid the cargo, at the heart of a maze of crates, in the smell of coke in the cramped and creaking darkness of the hold, Hugh and I ensconced ourselves beneath a stiff tarpaulin. We listened to the noises of the ship and ate the first of our paltry rations.

"We've to wait until the ship's at sea," he whispered, "then emerge and throw ourselves on the mercy of the captain. We'll be put to work and fed and made sailors."

Neither of us slept. We held our tongues, our eyes big in the darkness, a tattoo of footsteps around us, the rough voices of men calling instructions. We prepared for motion. But what came to our ears first was the scrape of nearby chests, men coming closer, hefting and hauling things aside, shouting to each other.

"Fuck all!"

"Nothing!"

"Hee-haw. Nothing."

I could make out Hugh's eyes. He mouthed at me, They're looking for stowaways.

I had not known that they would do so so soon. Many years later, I wondered if Hugh had. If he had wished to be found.

We backed farther into the wedge between the casks, and I heard a man's voice shout, "Whist now, come here," and an abrupt shoving of sacks and bits of wood and a glare of illumination as someone yanked the tarpaulin away.

The man stared down. He swore. He was looking, I saw, at Hugh. I was still half-covered and in shadow. I realized he could not see me. He grabbed Hugh by the top of his ear and hauled him up, bellowing, "Cost us time and money and provisions, will you, lad?"

Hugh howled that he was sorry. The man cuffed him across his face and blood spurted from his nose.

"I'll thrash you before you go home," the man roared, and he pulled Hugh away, and Hugh's eyes went wildly from him to me, but he said nothing. He spoke no words as the man pulled him out of sight and I heard the dreadful punishment he gave poor Hugh, who wailed with every strike.

I thought that Hugh would call my name and the brutish man would return and give me the same treatment, and that I too would be yanked abovedeck and returned, tender all over with new bruises, to the shore.

But no one came.

I cannot know whether Hugh's silence as to the fact of me was born of fear or loyalty, or whether he so resented my part in placing him into this situation that he held his tongue knowing that what punishment I might receive on discovery would only increase the longer it was delayed. I have never known whether to pity, thank, or curse my erstwhile friend.

A long time thereafter, I felt the ship move and sway.

I heard water to all sides, but my terror of discovery was greater than that provoked by the knowledge that I was deeper than the waves. I screwed up my courage and crawled farther into the darkness, by broken wood and iron bars, links of chain, boxes and their lids, nuggets of coal, sacks, oilcloths, splinters, and rags. I almost cried out when I thought I felt a monster's fur but these sticky fibers were oakum. I tugged it and hauled it aside and made another little hollow deep in that lowest hold.

And there I stayed.

The *Oban*'s voyage took it up into climes the cold of which I felt keenly, wrapping myself as best I could. Even so deep a little illumination reached, faint enough to be more a dream of light than light. Once, I do not know how many hours into the voyage, a hatch above was thrown open and I could have died of fright. But all that entered was more of that gray light and the sounds of men, who closed it again, and left me to myself.

I gnawed at my bread and sipped at the water. I found a sack and felt coal within it. I found a rag and answered nature's call then covered what I left with the coal.

Certainly I was afraid of the darkness. Assuredly I populated it with devils and the most malicious of maritime spirits. Yes, every rumble of the ship became the growl of a leviathan. It was not courage that kept me still, nor, much later, had me creep out at last, after many hours, in the darker dark, to learn the limits of my new universe. For courage I had none. I was simply more afraid of capture by the mortals above than of unearthly bugbears.

In my tar-smelling nest, I slipped eventually into a numb stupor.

I made out the edges of boxes, gradations in the shadows. All I could do was wait.

I think I must have remained such, all but motionless, for a day and a half at least, before a new sound shocked me back into fear. A long, slow scraping.

I clamped my hands over my mouth.

This sound did not float down as had the clatter of the opening hatch or the calls of sailors. It was close and it grew closer.

It slowed down, paused. It started again.

I held my breath. Tried to believe that what I heard was a rope swinging slowly against a box as the ship pitched, but the rhythm was not that of the wind or waves or chance. It had intent behind it. A rat then? But it was not furtive, was too deliberate, not abrupt enough to be even so noisome a fellow stowaway. And still it grew closer, and I felt as if my heart would burst me.

When it stopped again I took hold of the tarpaulin over me and pulled it and raised my head just a little. I stared into the pitch-smelling pitch, and at the gray edges of lashed boxes and sacks and walkways amid the shade. The scraping sound returned.

I saw something. Something like a collection of sticks and bits, and then it became, and seemed then always to have been, a tall and shrouded figure, and it was moving.

It stalked between boxes, slow, quiet, reaching out.

I was quite still. I did not breathe. It threw up two thin and irregular robed arms, with a strange, silent, flailing movement. It lowered one hand and touched its surroundings with the gentleness of a nurse. I heard a sound as at a nail on wood.

And the thing turned its obscure head and looked in my direction. I screamed without a sound. I held myself curled up as tight as I could. I heard the thing approach, the tip-tapping, that curious touch. It came toward me, braced itself against the motions of the ship, clopping with a sound like wood on wood to my hiding place. My eyes were closed. I wept with fear. I prayed as well as I knew how.

And nothing happened. The noise ceased.

You can be sure it was a long time before I moved again.

I looked at last. Beheld nothing. I stood and stepped out into the walkway. Nothing moved.

Had I been grown perhaps I would have asked myself whether I had slept and dreamed. As a child I knew I had not. But no matter how deep dread is it cannot last forever.

So, later, I moved and ate and drank again. I relieved myself again. I heard footsteps above. I piled up coal to throw, to defend myself against I knew not what.

Twice more, I froze, thinking I heard that scrape again, farther away, distant enough that I was not sure either time.

It cannot have been so many days before I had only one bottle of water left, and only half a loaf of bread, and that so stale it was like chewing dust.

My horror of the dark shape I had seen notwithstanding, my fear of the crew and their rope ends and masculine fury was barely less present in my soul. Otherwise, I would have hammered at the hatch and begged to be released. It was not fear of my unseen companion but hunger and thirst that sent me tiptoeing to the ladder.

I planned to wait until nighttime to creep about and find the galley. But as I looped my arm around a rung, full of rising dread, a sailor by chance stepped upon the board above my head and roared something to a nearby unseen comrade and I dropped in shock and I saw again in my memory the beating Hugh had received, and my tears began. I shuffled by fingertip back to my little space, dragged the oilcloth over me, and sobbed my hungry self to sleep.

However. When I awoke, many hours later, it was to the smell of food.

My eyes widened. I folded back a flap of the tarpaulin. There on the creaking floor of the walkway between boxes of cargo was an earthenware jug of water and a plate of boiled meat, bread, potatoes.

Nothing could have been more ambrosial.

But who had done this thing? I thought of the jam and ends of cheese by which you trap mice. I waited. I strained my eyes with searching. When, after long seconds, I made nothing out, I reached for the plate, licking my lips.

I heard that tap-tap again, and froze.

Perhaps my father had come down from Heaven to look after me because I'd been a good boy, I thought, but I was a stowaway, so I knew I was a bad boy.

I saw movement. What had seemed the very lines of the hold itself now came toward me. That dim and angular figure. An arm descending. Reaching.

I understood at last that the motion was not one of predation but of encouragement. Of invitation. It gestured at the plate.

I need not tell you of my shock. I began to eat. The thing nodded.

After the meat I ate the bread. After the bread I ate the potatoes. The watcher watched. I divided my attention between it and my plate. When I was done, my observer nodded once more. It raised its arms and tilted its head to one side and slid stiff and awkward this way and that way, jiggling its midriff. I gawped in alarm. It looked like nothing so much as one of the puppets I had seen performing on the commons, and it came to me that it was doing a little jig. To amuse me it did not, but I felt a kindness in the gesture and I made myself smile.

The thing placed its hands by one side of what passed for its head, like a pillow. It was telling me to rest.

I returned to my cave. I let the curtain fall again and hunkered into the prickly oakum, rolling myself in it for warmth, warmer by far now with food inside me. The last thing I heard before sleep took me was the gentle brittleness of that hard thing ascending the ladder.

When I awoke, the plate and jug were gone, and I was alone.

That was how it went for days. Never did I reach any pangs of near starvation again before sustenance appeared before me. Not every time that my secret sharer thus aided me did I see it. Sometimes for all my peering I made out no movement in the darkness and the angles of the ship did not transform into its blocky shape. Even so, I would smile my thanks in every direction at the start and end of my meal. Other times I saw the waved greeting of that draped figure watching me from the dark. I would wave back and whisper my gratitude. Once I found a rough blanket alongside the plate and jug. The hold, indeed, was growing ever more cold. Thereafter came thick socks, much too big. A man's shirt.

I grew accustomed to the faint sounds of the other hold dweller. I no longer started if I heard its strange perambulations.

As I ate a tough ship's biscuit one day, in the dregs of light filtering from above, I made out the scarecrow outlines of my benefactor. So I spoke.

"Whit are you?"

The figure seemed to tilt its head to one side.

"You're no' a devil, are you?" I said. "You'd no' help me if you were. Are you an angel then?"

Even in its snapping jerks and tugs, more like a tree in wind than the gestures of any person or beast, I discerned, or told myself I did, curiosity. Consideration.

I knew it would not speak. I was not expecting it to move closer with that ungainly grace. The thing that watched over me reached out with something draped by cloth and moved it across a box beside me and I heard a faint grinding. A scoring noise. On it went a long while. When it was finally done it lowered its limb and I saw it had with some sharp and hidden finger scratched jagged letters upon the wood.

It waited. So I squinted at the words.

"Oh," I said. "I see. Thank you for helping me. Why are you here?"

It reached again. It scratched again, for a longer time, adding more to its missive. It stepped back. I leaned in again.

"Oh," I said. "What will you do now?"

It scrawled once more and I looked at what it wrote.

"Why do you help me?"

It wrote. I made as if to read.

I did not want to disappoint it nor to discourage it from discourse. So I nodded at the sigils that made no sense to me, and I told it thank you, and it seemed satisfied.

Sometimes when it came back thereafter, with the food it brought to keep me alive, it might take a moment to scrape more words into the wood. Whenever it did so, I made great show of examining them, and acknowledging them with nods and mimed consideration.

Once I was particularly lonely.

Into the darkness I whispered, "Will you tell me a story?"

And there the jerky thing was. That lumpy outline under its old sheet reached out, still concealed within its drapery, and wrote awhile again, and I fell asleep to the sound of its scratching.

Thus we continued for many meals. I might lie there, hearing the faint clamping of my companion on the ladder, on its way up, and wordlessly I would wish it success on whatever were its secret missions above. One of them, I knew, being to find provisions for me. I heard it rise, and heard it descend again.

Until I did not hear the latter. Until one day or night neither the sounds nor those provisions were there anymore. And my hunger began once more to grow.

I grew weak. I grew thirsty. My throat grew dry and strained. I whispered. My pleas went out into the cobwebs. At last I rose with the end of my strength. I wandered the sunken walkways, listening to the footsteps above, craning my neck, straining my eyes.

"Are you there?" I whispered.

"Where are you?" I said.

"I'm hungry, will you no' help me?"

"Where are you?"

"Please help me."

I still recall that as I wandered, begging for my supper, famished and fearful, I felt, too, concern for the presence that had saved me.

"Where are you?" I whispered as loud as I could in the swaying hold, to the unlit candles and the odds and ends.

I lay down again and my hunger grew and the cold grew and I did not know where we were in the oceans of the world. Whatever spirit or ghost or frightful hobgoblin it was that had come to look after me was banished, it seemed. I would die if I did not rouse myself according to my original plan and find food. And now to my fear of the crew was added sorrow for my lost savior.

When I was very weak I learned that a death from thirst would not be restful. So I raised my head, and I heard myself crying, and my head spun about, and after a time I heard a hatch, and I blinked to clear my eyes and saw a figure approach, and my eyes hurt as it glowed, and I called out in joy, but the noise died in my throat, for there was light pouring down from the between decks, and it was not the swaying benefactor that came toward me but a man carrying a lantern. A bearded man. The sailor who had caught and punished Hugh.

"There you are," he bellowed. Speech so loud was strange to me.

He grabbed me by the arm and shook me and I lolled and flopped like a figure made of rags. My placidity enraged him. He hit me and my ears rang.

"Every bloody night!" he shouted. "Food and drink!" He hit me again. "What else have you stole, you little bastard? You're a sneaky one, I'll give you that. You'll get what's coming for you."

Another blow. The man loomed over me. I closed my eyes.

I heard a fast faint galloping. The man dropped me. There came a rush, a sharp exhalation. A wail, the crash of boxes.

I looked again. The man crawled amid splintered and spilled wood and coal. That dark and shrouded figure loomed above him. Draped beneath a sheet, a filthy ghost.

It raised its arms and brought them down upon my attacker's back, smacking him down again, and he screamed. It hauled him up and the sailor gasped for breath and the figure clutched his throat with draped digits.

Everything went still. The shaded figure tap-tap-tapped upon the floor with its leg.

I heard my own voice.

"There you are!" is what I said.

My friend tapped again, drew the man's attention, and mine, pointed to one of the boxes. We both looked, and it leaned in and I heard that scratching upon the wood. It wrote with its digit poking through the cloth on the wood of the box's side. The sailor read. He looked up with terror. The figure in the shroud stepped closer to him and pointed at its words, and the man cringed and threw up his hands and called, "I shall, I shall, I beg ye, I shall!"

He stumbled to his feet, put his hands to his bleeding face, staggered to the ladder, and climbed. I heard the banging of the hatch, and my savior and I were alone again within the hold.

Quickly, on an unmarked part of the wood, it scrawled more lines. I leaned and looked at them. I nodded. It did not move. As always when it was motionless, had I not known otherwise, I would have thought it the innards of the room.

"Thank you," I whispered.

I don't know how long it was after that that I heard the hatch open again. This time, though, the descending steps were slow and deliberate. Whoever had come down walked between the irregular outlines of the cargo.

Through a slit in my oilcloth, I saw a figure appear. A tall broad dark-clad man with a well-trimmed beard. He stared into all the shadows. Two, three more steps and he would see me. I held my breath. I strained to hear the skittering of my feeder, but all I heard was that newcomer, and fear gripped me again. Because he was coming closer.

But as he passed what looked like bits and debris, that concatenation of stuff moved. It was my companion. For all the blankness of the coverings upon its face, in that looby motion I believe I saw in it shock, fear, resolve. It raised whatever served it as a hand and grasped him. It squeezed.

The man hissed and what gripped him took tighter hold and seemed to grip him steady and stare at him. And I would swear that it seemed to hesitate then. Not to be afeared, but uncertain. And the man snarled, truly, like a beast, and made claws of his hands, and seemed about to rake them across what held him, when my companion resolved whatever were its doubts and gripped him harder and the hold was abruptly filled with a cold blue light that seemed to outline my sticklike friend, and out of the man's open mouth came a dreadful sound, and a rush as if of wind lifted him from his feet and there he hung in the air, his body crumpling as if he was squeezed, and there came out of his lips a blinding burst of that same light, as if a moon rose within him.

My eyes stung. I blinked to clear them. He twisted in the air, the thing's limbs upon him but not seeming to support him. Still the glow came out of him, from his ears and eyes and nostrils, too, now, seeming to pour from his attacker into him. His skin rippled like the sea.

The man curled and coiled and his face went through agonies, and his body now seemed to inflate, as if he would burst, and he turned in the air. The figure that held him turned what passed for its head to me. In, I believe, triumph.

And as it did so, the man's eyes opened, his mouth closed, he clenched his jaw and his hands and his body and he dropped to the deck. Stood tall. He shucked his arms so fast he broke my savior's grip. His own left hand whipped up and grabbed the figure's throat in turn.

"I don't know what you are," the man whispered. "I don't know what that was that you just did. Or how you did it. It's been a long time since anything's felt like that."

He slammed his right hand into the shrouded chest and sent the thing flying back with a tremendous noise, to collapse to the floor.

The man said, "It didn't work, though, did it?" He stepped closer. "I will tell you something else." He pulled up his quarry. It moved weakly. It looked now like rubbish wrapped in cloth. It flailed. He shook it. "Something like you," the man said. "Something so strange as you. There's a story to you, I'll be bound." He grasped it. "I don't care. There are always stories."

The man ripped the cloth away.

For what I saw in the gloom, for the first time, clearly, I have no words. It was nothing but mess. Its head, a half-sphere of wood conjoined to bundled sticks. A broken end of ladder where its chest might be. Broom handle one arm, tight-wound rope and sack the other, digits of screws and twigs and spikes. A morass of man-shaped trash, shaking in the grip of what it had tried and failed to fell.

"Look at you," the man said. Calm as ever. "Yes, there'll be a story of you."

Without features as it was, I cannot say why I am convinced of it, but convinced I am that the thing was staring helplessly at me, pleading.

The man punched its faceless face. The man wrenched off a flailing arm. My composite friend staggered.

"I wonder whose story it is," the man said. He tore matter from it and threw it. The thing spasmed. Piece by piece he scattered it. "But I don't wonder very hard."

The last of rubbish-thing tried weakly to crawl away. The man straddled it, rained down blows into its tangle, brought his hands apart in plumes of ruin.

"I could tell something had happened to Maxwell down here," he said. "I can imagine the sort of thing you did to convince him to stay away. He tried to keep it from me. But he's more afraid of me than he is of you." He kept tearing. "I don't know where you come from, or what business you think I am of yours, what wrong I did you or your mistress or master, if they exist, or when I did it, or what you wish. Nor what it was your strange touch did to me, just now. It's new to feel like that, it's true, so full of life it hurt. But I no longer care to hear all the stories there are."

He brought its own parts down in a makeshift mace, and the wood that was its head flew from it and arced into the darkness of the hold.

After the clank and clatter of its unseen landing came silence.

"Perhaps you know what that was," the man said to me at last.

He flung away the last of what had saved me. He turned and walked straight to where I hid and flung off the sheet and looked down at me.

"Perhaps you know its story," he said.

"I dinnae ken anything," I managed to say.

"This kind of thing, a thing like this that shouldn't walk," he said. "A construct like this? I've not seen one such for a long time. I've not seen them often and not for a long time but I've seen them. Why do you cry, boy?"

"You'll do awa' wi' me," I choked out. "And you killed my friend."

After the longest silence yet, he walked away, back toward the ladder.

"Come" is what he said, without looking back. "Bring some of your friend if you wish, to remember it."

I wiped my nose upon my sleeve and stood.

He was patient. He must have spent minutes listening to me scrabbling in the dim, gathering debris, whispering a pledge not to forget. Perhaps he had to exercise self-control not to laugh at the sight of me when I came, stinking tearstained thing shuffling into view in my ragged clothes, clutching a bundle of splintered slats of wood as if it were a babe. He turned and climbed into the light, not bothering to watch me, trusting that I was following him, as I was.

This is not the place to tell of the days that followed. Of my ensconcement in the secret adjunct to the captain's cabin wherein the man passed the journey, ignored with a resentful fear by the captain himself, fed by the no-longer-fearsome Maxwell, now entrusted to bring plates of food for me (he would not meet my eyes) and to cut down patched-up men's clothes to fit my slight frame. The long, cold days and hours of silence in the tiny cell, me on tiptoe staring out the porthole at the gull-flecked sky and the chewing jaws of the sea. There are no tales, in truth. Though we were together therein, not before nor ever since that time have I spent so long without speaking or being spoken to. Sometimes—this was as much attention as he ever paid me—the man watched when I ran my fingers over my relics of my lost benefactor.

Yes, on certain days, according to obscure exigencies, he might lean out of our disguised panel door and mutter to the captain or to Maxwell, but I never knew what business he discussed with them. He did not correct nor touch nor mind nor entertain nor seem very much to notice me.

When we arrived across the world, he led me down the gangplank in a cold that made me shake even through my jury-rigged warm clothes. I rolled, unsteady, on the stone beyond the jetty, watched without curiosity by the stevedores.

"Here," the man said. He gave me an envelope. "Don't open it now," he said. "I wish you luck. I am sorry about your friend."

He turned his back to me and walked away, and there I was, a new and terrified Canadian. Who said, aloud, watching the words coil as smoke into the foreign air, "I will never cross the water again."

The envelope contained money enough to keep me a month or two. The years that followed were their own stories. The first cold months. The fear, the apprenticeships, the fights and loves, the travels, the sins of which I will never speak, the rising through the various concerns and fallings, and risings again, the marriage and subsequent abandonment, by and of whom it depends which version of the, yes, tale you hear. None of this is what I am here to tell.

Here I am, a cobbler in a mid-sized city. Few cobblers know better than I do how miserable is life without shoes. Here I am, a man with one story to tell, telling it, for the first time. And the custodian of another story, a secret story, that I do not know.

It was more than two dozen years after my arrival in this sprawling country that I had the security to turn my attention to my letters. And in truth, I think I had held back as long as I could, fearful of what would be vouchsafed to me when writing gave up its secrets.

When at last the kind teacher assured me she had done all she could for me, I could delay no longer. So it was that when she left my humble shack, I drew a deep and shaking breath and brought out all that wood I had carried with me since my return to land. That I have still. The slats I took with me from the hold of that ship. I had cradled them when I took them out, tended them gently, let the man who took me see. I had hoped then and I hope now that he thought them my friend's strange remnants, the ruins of its body, not, as they were, those of the crate on which my friend had scored its messages to me.

My fingers trembled as I unwrapped them, for the first time in more than twenty years.

I spread them out. I fit them together, as best I could, edge to corresponding edge, reconstructing the wooden face of the old box. Much was missing. I had not found every word. But I was able to lay out on my tabletop partial answers to my questions and my plea, and a warning, though not for me, for Maxwell. For the first time, I ran my fingers along the discolored grooves, jumping the splintered gaps, breathing through those spaces, sounding out and speaking the messages' remains.

i am no devil i am   of the world   life and alive
to save   the world   hunt for Death to end it
not know always been certain   I will feel the presence of the
enemy, the end of energy is dread miasma to my new
soul   my makers and we followed trails but i feel nothing
upon this ship so we were lied to perhaps   i will search
again.

boy it hurts me to see you weep
Once upon a time the children of the daughter of Life went hunting.
With them came quiet stuff she woke and they woke from the endless
rest into this ceaseless clamor

thought and purpose and a mission to be as
bloodhound, to sniff out Death

This last was on another segment, in larger letters:

go and never come back here say nothing leave the
boy alone disobey and i will end you and consign you to the
flames

Poor devil. It told me it was not a devil, and I believe it. But it threatened Maxwell with death and the flames and Auld Nick is known to be a liar, so I do not know. Perhaps it only implied that it was of diablerie to protect me.

It told me a story.

It sought death, it knew that it would smell it, in that ship, that it would feel it, and it did not, and it thought its journey was for naught, and then it found me and a new purpose, and it went hunting for its quarry, to be quite sure, in every cranny, while I wept, and it found it not and delivered me, and then death came for it and even all its life could not defeat it.

None of this is what I am here to tell. I am not here to tell you of my growing sadness, in later years, which came to me with a wondering whether staying hidden until I wept, I'm sure I wept, I remember weeping, meant I was bait, a last snare, to be sprung but not by the target for whom the poacher had hoped. He had come later. If my hunger and fear might have been a payable price for a greater mission.

In any case, I am the maker and keeper of a promise, and he to whom the promise was kept.

Poor thing, in any case, whatever it was, to face that quiet man.

THROUGH THE GLASS

"**K**EEVER," DIANA SAID INTO HER PHONE. "I JUST GOT A MES-sage." She was still blinking, only just awake, eyeing the text she had received from the blocked Unit number: RSVP via scrambler urgent. "What's going on?"

"Ma'am, I'm not your goddamn liaison—"

"Keever, please!"

She heard his hiss.

"Caldwell's missing."

"What? What do you mean . . . ?"

"Ma'am, listen. He's not responding on any channels. We've checked up, and he came in last night, we've got him swiping in late," Keever said. "Leaves again half an hour later. But he never got home."

"I don't understand."

"Me neither, ma'am. I have to go. Get in here, they want a full roll call."

"But Keever, none of this makes any sense, what do you . . . ?"

"Ma'am, I've told B, I'll tell you: get here. I have work to do."

He hung up.

Do you know about what's been going on with me, Jim? she

thought. She stared at her phone. Looked about her house again, guardedly. Do you know about my invisible spy? If everything's connected, what's that to do with this that's going on now, with Caldwell? Should I tell you what happened to me? If I don't, what damage am I doing? If I do, what secrets and protocols am I breaching?

She called Unute but he did not answer.

I knew it was a Faustian bargain, this job, she thought. I'd pay whatever I had to for this access to the foundation, to what made Unute. But I do hate the game-playing. Who knows what about whom and why? I can't keep track. And I wish I had the option of not caring what's going on right now.

But how could she. Not, right now, that she could do anything about Caldwell, or any of it.

Diana froze.

Or can I? she thought.

"TALK TO ME." B WALKED THE CORRIDORS. THE WOMEN AND MEN OF THE

Unit around him did not run, but they walked quickly in all directions. B's fists were clenched.

"We don't know much." Keever's face was grim. "It could easily have not come to light at all. Here's what we do know. No one can get hold of him. The kids on duty let Caldwell in," Keever said. "They say he seemed 'urgent.' A little zoned out, one of them said. 'Talking too loud. Seemed a bit confused.' Does that sound like him to you?"

"It does not. So what?"

"So nothing," Keever said. "Except these guards have worked with him for months, and it didn't take too much for them to admit they hadn't actually bothered with protocol. Didn't do a full trunk check or inside or mirror check of the car."

"When was the last time anyone checked yours?" B said. "Or the last time anyone did an iris scan, come to that? When did you last fill out a daily sitrep?"

"Long time ago," Keever said, "I hear you. I know and you know that it's not fair but I know and you know how it goes: we all cut corners, and nobody cares until something goes wrong. And then even if it's got nothing to do with any of the corners you cut, if you're the last corner cutter, you're fucked."

"How fucked are they?"

"They're pretty fucked."

"How come you asked them how he was?" B said.

"We asked them when we couldn't find Caldwell or get him on his phone. Like I say, you double-check when something goes wrong. Here's the sequence. He gets here late last night, zero three forty-seven. We've got his Lincoln leaving twenty-seven minutes later. But what we don't have is him in the feed from outside the front of his home. And we can't find the vehicle. No one knows where it is. We sent a team to his apartment."

"And?"

"And he's not there. But take a look at what was."

He held up a sheaf of garish photographs.

B stared. "Whose blood is that?" he said.

"His," Keever said.

"That's a lot."

"Yeah," Keever said.

"So," B said. "He leaves here, dumps his car somewhere, walks home, sneaks in, somehow? To where . . ." B gestured at the images. "There's a welcoming committee?"

"Maybe. We've got no sign of anyone else getting in before him, or getting out again."

"I've been kind of busy," B said. "What's he been working on?"

"Judging from his digital footprint," Keever says, "mostly the usual. Except, in the last few days, he'd had the pig . . ." He paused. "It wasn't recorded properly, didn't make much sense at first. But he did work on the pig."

B turned. "What's he been doing to it?"

"I don't really know," Keever said. "Uh . . . took me the help of a techie but it looks like, killing it."

"What?"

"Yeah. At least once."

B took the paper and read. "So he's doing this to it, then he just disappears . . ." He went silent.

"What?" Keever said.

But B was moving now, fast. Keever swore and went after him.

B raced past startled guards and turned at corridor crossroads, ignoring the elevators to slam his ID at doors to the stairwell and leap down the half flights, pulling farther and farther ahead of Keever with the slam of his descending boots.

"Fuck's sake, B," Keever called, and followed to the lower floors, losing him halfway there. Soldiers half-raised their weapons in alarm. "Goddamnit, don't you point that thing at me," he shouted. "Follow me." He gestured to them.

They found B staring at the main lab window. Keever came closer.

"Hey B," he said. "I'm an old man. You got to give me a head start next time, son. What's got you worried?"

"Look," B said.

Keever stared into the laboratory. Strapped on the steel was the scabbed ichor of the babirusa's regenerative egg.

"I'm surprised," B said quietly. "And I'm always surprised when I'm surprised."

"What? You weren't expecting to see the cocoon? I told you Caldwell killed it."

B said, "I wasn't expecting it to be here at all."

"Huh?"

"I thought that must be what this was about. He does something to the pig, and someone does something to him. I thought if he was gone, the pig would be too. Stolen."

"Why? For what?"

"Research," B said. "Everything's connected, Keever. The pig is the new thing here. The variable. It's got to be what this is about."

"We'd have known if the pig was gone, B," Keever said. "They've got more tags and tracers on it than on nukes."

"Yeah," B said. "And tech like that never goes wrong, right? And no one ever figures out a way to fool it."

"Fair point," Keever said. "But look. There it is. Right there. Asleep."

"It's not asleep," B said quietly. He watched the faint throbbing of the membrane. "Whatever goes on in there, whatever that pig is doing, whatever I've done all those times, it's not sleeping."

He entered. Through the glass, Keever and his escort watched him walk counterclockwise around the pig egg, his left hand upon it, feeling the shuddering reconfiguration deep within. By that ritual, B, Unute, let himself slip into a minor trance, quite different from that which accompanied his greatest violence.

Unute left. One of the guards began to follow him, and Keever gestured for her to stay back.

"Give him space, soldier," he said quietly. "He'll call us if he needs us."

Methodically, Unute began to sweep the buildings.

He entered restricted zones and moved without politeness or hesitation between other teams on their investigations. He did not doubt their expertise, how they tracked Caldwell's digital and physical trails. Out of doggedness or boredom or meta-curiosity or sheer perversity, B had sometimes, over the centuries, pursued research into subjects that did not naturally light a spark in him—among his seventeen PhDs were those in accountancy, land economy, and food science—but there were other skills at which he had only ever acquired adequate expertise. Computers represented one, even though he never disputed their usefulness. On that he was happy to let the Unit's internal detectives take point.

"Come on, brother pig," he whispered.

He went into every place he had ever seen Caldwell. He scanned walls, edges, darknesses, inside each drawer and cupboard in each office. Opened the man's locker. Sat in the chair Caldwell preferred in the canteen. Watched while techs shone black lights into gravel on the basement level of the garage where Caldwell's car had been.

A hazmat-suited woman said to him, "We've found a few blond hairs and jeans fibers. No DNA match yet. Any luck?"

"No," B said. "The trick is to distinguish true intuition from the false. I'm getting pretty frustrated."

"Because you're not getting any, uh, hits on your intuition, sir?" she said.

"The opposite. Because it's ringing like a bell, everywhere. I'm getting it everywhere I go."

"Maybe," she said, "if you're getting it everywhere, it doesn't matter where you go."

He considered this. "Let me try something," he said. "Bear with me."

He sank slowly, hands to the ground, as if he were about to spring.

"I've been thinking I keep finding things out," he said. "And finding them. But maybe you're right. Maybe something's been finding me. Maybe I'm being followed."

Very suddenly he placed his head down sideways, his right eye by the ground. Swiftly he moved his head. Seconds passed.

"Boss?" one of the techs whispered to the woman. "What do we . . . ?"

The woman clicked her fingers twice and put her finger to her lips. Unute shot his arm out and scored his finger through the gravel, rummaged in among the little stones. When he drew his hand back, he held something between his index and middle fingers.

"What are you?" he said to it. He sat up and looked at what he'd found, and all the soldiers and investigators and technicians squinted and leaned down and peered, too, to see.

A tiny blanked and tabbed piece of thin wood or cardboard. A jigsaw piece.

"Tell Keever," B said, to no one in particular, to all of them. "And Diana."

. . .

THE YOUNG SOLDIERS OUTSIDE CALDWELL'S OFFICE SALUTED AS DIANA AP-
proached.

"Ma'am," one said. He raised a hand. "I'm sorry, ma'am, but there's an investigation. Keever said . . ."

Diana raised her badge, with its ostentatious green triple A across it.

"I know what Keever said," she said. "I know there's an investigation. Why do you think I'm here? You're aware that Dr. Caldwell is my closest colleague? I know what he's working on better than anyone. So stand aside."

The man hesitated. When he complied, Diana considered that she was not, strictly, lying. She was one of Caldwell's closest colleagues. No need for this soldier to know that she had no idea what Caldwell had been doing recently, where he was, or any idea about how to find out.

She took in his crowded office, the books in battered leather bindings, the big wooden globe, the tchotchkes of antiquity that seemed designed at least as much to declare the character of their owner as to be functional. We all put on a show, she thought. She examined the stapler, lamp, calculator, pen, the papers on Caldwell's desk. She opened his laptop, and frowned at the password prompt.

Let me guess, she thought. Some showboating joke in cuneiform. A pun that works in seven languages, five of them dead.

Diana hesitated, considering the protocols that would destroy her own hard drive after a few too many attempts at ingress.

She typed 1234567. Password. Password123.

Nothing. Worth a try, she thought, and closed the lid. She picked up two shreds of paper from the bin. She squinted at the scrawls. *inner room?* she read. *Life?*

Why, she thought, is everyone talking about life?

Her phone buzzed. She read the message. Her eyes widened. She swept out of the room and walked quickly back through the hallways toward the front of the Unit's complex, turned in to the lighter corridors. She knocked at last on Shur's doorway, opened the door and walked in without waiting for an answer.

"The fuck?" someone said. A young woman in fatigues was lying on the couch, staring at her.

Shur stood. "Do you mind?" she shouted at Diana.

Diana did not look at her, but at her patient.

"Get out," she said. "That's an order."

The woman set her face and glanced uncertainly at Shur. When Shur did not speak, only stared at Diana, the woman stood and left and closed the door behind herself.

"How dare you?" Shur said.

"Save it," Diana said. She held up her phone, so that Shur could read the message. Shur's eyes widened.

"I don't understand," Shur said.

"A jigsaw piece," Diana said. "B—Unute—found a jigsaw piece."

"What are you talking about? Who knows how much garbage there is in the parking lot. And what's this got to do with me?"

"In fact there's barely any. Garbage. They sweep it—in both senses—every couple of days. And I've worked with Caldwell for a fair while, and I may not know everything about him, but I promise you that jigsaws are not among his vices. But I heard the tapes—I know Stonier told you he lost a token. You can stare at me all you want but you know we had access."

"So?"

"He said it was something he used to finish one of Thakka's games, remember? He's a videogamer. But Thakka did puzzles. Thakka took the last piece of the first puzzle that Stonier finished with him. As a memento."

Again Shur's eyes widened.

"This has to be Thakka's," Diana said. "And then Stonier's."

"What are you saying? That Stonier was in Caldwell's car? And dropped it?"

"Maybe."

"But he told me he lost it a while ago. And if they rake the garage as often as you say . . ."

Diana frowned.

"I don't know. Stonier has no official reason to be dealing directly with Caldwell," she said. "Let alone to be in his car. Or under it. In fact you know he was avoiding him. And I'm sure you've heard, whether you're on the official coms chain or not, that Caldwell's missing." She did not wait for Shur to reply. "Whatever holes there are in the story, this is a lead. So maybe we need to find out everything we can about Stonier, and fast."

"What do you want to know? You've heard the recordings. There's not much to say . . ."

"I found some notes in Caldwell's office," Diana said. "How did you direct Stonier to the Life Project?"

"This again? I told you, I directed him at everything."

"But why that one?"

Shur shrugged. "It was on the list provided to me by the Unit when I got here. I had admin get me a list of all relevant organizations in the city."

"You didn't vet it?"

Shur set her lips. "Of course I did. It's a self-help group, like a thousand others."

Diana held out her hand. "Give me anything you have on it."

Shur nodded. "I'll email it."

"I don't think," Diana said, "that that would be a good idea. Let's keep it hard-copy." Shur's eyes widened. "Would you please write it out? Let's just say I work better on paper."

IN HER STUDY SHE TRACED CONNECTIONS, UNPICKING GENEALOGIES FROM Shur's data, poring over the gloss on the LP's website, the brief histories she found of the self-help splits that had led to the Life Project's birth and development. Reviews and write-ups.

Among the countless positives, a few one-star reviews.

I thought I had found what I was looking for but well let me tell you settle down and let's get into it.

Wow. Just Wow.

Those voluble dissidents slammed the organization they had left, though not because of human sacrifice, of dread sciences or philosophies of terror, but because the convener in their branch had ignored their request to stock a different brand of coffee or to reschedule a meeting. She read two-star references to what one woman called "icky glassy-eyed kumbaya-ism." But mostly, even those who mocked themselves for it stressed the comfort they found in the rah-rah repudiation of death.

Diana logged in to the Unit search engine, which, as well as the usual internet shallows, trawled a growing proportion of the Deep Web, a colossal archive of deleted pages, rolled straight through most password protections and cross-referred with results from various secure, plausibly denied government agencies.

Life Project, she typed. History. Ideas. Criticism. Alam. Stonier.

She made notes by hand, her scrawls covering sheet after sheet. She took screenshots of relevant searches while the light beyond the windows waxed, waned slowly, then fast. She turned on the lamp on her desk and circled certain words in certain documents in red.

The Life Project had been born of the Glad Project, which was a development of the You're OK! Project, which was begotten of a merger of refugees from Keep Light and the Yes Group. Eight years ago, the Life Project had passed into the leadership of Alam and someone called S. Plomer, about whom there were vanishingly few available details. Diana ran searches on that unfamiliar name. The two had been veterans of many organizations, passing through them together at every step on a long pilgrimage. But a year after their joint ascension, all references to Plomer disappeared from the LP's literature. And indeed—even more remarkable—from the internet at all.

After that, the Life Project, now under Alam's leadership, had bounced around the United States. "Opening branches," as it described the process, without disclosing that with each new opening came a closing of the previous. Alam and his cohort—minus S. Plomer, wherever they were—traveled every few years or even months from place to place, holding their workshops, then moving on. To settle in Tacoma, in fact, scant weeks ago. Between Unute's discovery of Thakka's brief afterlife, it turned out, and his return from his own resulting disappearance.

Diana sat back and looked into the dark. Her eyes narrowed.

What have you been chasing, Caldwell? she thought. Were you looking for Plomer? Is that the life you were looking for? What did you find? How did you hide it? What am I missing?

She wiped her search history. As if that would do much against anyone prepared to hunt, with the right help. Especially here, with the powerful central mainframes and servers. The thought of such ferreting, her curious imagined colleague watchers within these walls, whatever their aims and agendas, stopped her moving, and provoked her into consideration.

I've got to get ahead of this, she thought. She locked her office behind her. I have to find out what you knew, Caldwell, about all this, and anything. And I'm sure not going to be able to break into your records.

The soldiers in the AI department stood and saluted her.

"Ma'am?" one woman said.

Diana smiled as if flustered. She did a bad salute back. Yes, the Klutzy Civilian thing provoked the scorn of some on the base, but you could make it likable too. Deploy it to give off Look After Me vibes.

"I'd be grateful for some help," she said.

"What do you need, ma'am?"

"So, I've been collaborating with Dr. Caldwell. I know you've heard that Caldwell is . . . that we can't find him."

"Ma'am."

"Obviously we all hope he'll be back soon, but I have to keep on with this project, it's very urgent, and he's not around to tell me what he got up to. If I give you the keywords, I'll be grateful for whatever they flag up in his recent searches." Diana was careful to place her ACCESS ALL AREAS badge on the desk.

"Ma'am," the soldier said, after only a second's hesitation.

Diana slid across the paper on which she'd written "Alam," "Plomer," "the Life Project."

The soldier worked quickly at a terminal. Her machine chugged for a while and spat out papers, which she handed over. Diana skimmed, saw nothing at a glance that she had not already found. It looked as if Caldwell had, if anything, looked less deeply in this direction than had she. Certainly on the Unit network.

"Do you want Sergeant Keever's searches on those topics too, ma'am?" the woman said.

Diana froze. Just for a moment. Continued shuffling the papers.

"Jim?" she said. "Caldwell had him working on this too?"

"His name was the only other one that came up when I ran those terms. I took the liberty." The woman slid over a single paper. "This is his log."

Diana checked the header. Keever had researched this topic weeks ago.

"THERE YOU ARE," KEEVER APPROACHED B OUTSIDE THE BABIRUSA LAB again. "Came all the way back. Should have known. You OK?"

B shrugged. "I don't mind not understanding things, Jim. I've never minded that. But I don't like not understanding plans that include me, let alone that I think have me as a target."

"Come on. What can they do to you?"

"It's the principle."

"This guy here helping you?" Keever said. He gestured at the pig egg through the window. "Won't be long now, will it?" B shook his head. "They're not getting any matches on the hair they found."

"Are you OK?" B said. "You look worried."

"Of course I am."

"OK, or worried?" B said.

"Both."

B nodded. "What do you make of this?" he said. He held up the jigsaw piece.

Keever looked at it. "I have no idea," he said, and shrugged. It was less than an inch on each side. Its back was dark cardboard, hard and sheened. On the other side, the line of a tree. A clutch of leaves ending at the edges of the cut, the blank. Brown—a branch.

"I think that's the edge of an apple," B said.

Keever nodded. He tapped it with his nail. "It's coated with something." He took it.

"I don't know," B said. "Clear nail varnish? Acrylic? To protect it? Make it harder."

"Should I understand what I'm looking at?" Keever said. He turned it over several times, and handed it back.

"How does it . . . make you feel?" B said.

"Huh?" Keever saw the hesitation on B's face. Looked down at the thing again. "I don't know what you mean," he said.

"I don't really either," B said. "It feels weird to me. But not bad. Which, I don't know, surprises me. I don't know what I mean either." He took it back, set his lips, and put it in his pocket. Kept his hand therein, gripping it, turning the little piece over and over with his fingers. "I wish I could know what this pig has seen and done," he said. "Who it's spent time with."

That was the moment the sirens started.

Throughout the corridors of the center, klaxons wailed. Lights flashed red in on-off time to the blasts. From everywhere came the sound of running feet, the slamming of doors, the percussion of magazines clicking home into rifle housings.

Keever had his radio to his ear and a sidearm in his hand. An armed squad came running.

"LOCKDOWN," a voice announced throughout the halls. "CODE NINER. LOCKDOWN."

"Jim?" B said.

"Say again?" Keever was shouting. "A what? Soldier, say again . . ."

There came the sound of smashing. Another, close now, only two, three turns away, and here came more soldiers in Kevlar running, and B joined them, with Keever on his heel, shouting, "Wait . . .," another vain pursuit, already, and here now were reinforced doors to another wing, and behind them, beyond the glass, a stretch of empty corridor and far off near its end and beyond all the sounds and lights of alarms, the glare and jackhammer slam of bullets. A man's body flew out of a side hall in the distance to land with impact he could not have survived. Two more soldiers came into view, retreating carefully, laying down fire.

One was grabbed abruptly by something too quick for even B to make out, hurled into the other to tumble in an ugly heap. Around the corner into that inner sanctum beyond the glass a new shape came.

A naked man. A naked manlike something. A naked something. Something naked.

What stamped toward them had the outline of a human with skin of mishmashed hues, greens, grays like ash, the darkness of death and frostbite, white like fish flesh in formaldehyde, all crisscrossed by wire. Its arms clotted and lumpy as if with lymph as well as strength, skin rags hanging from bones and boxy rigid muscles. It dripped as it approached. It raised its arms, and both its left hand and its right hand were left hands. It walked fast, swaying, uncertain, furious. It turned its head and stared through the triple windows with a coldly burning blue that B knew.

This thing that began to run toward him, roaring like a bull in pain, was stitched, ruined, burnt, frozen, tanned like hide and rotting like fungus, but B could make out the underlying features on its face, and they were his own.

And he was not surprised.

life

WHEN YOU DON'T DIE, YOU CAN CHOOSE CONSTANCY OR CA-
price. It will make all the difference in the immediate term, and
almost none in the long.

On your way, stay vigilant for cold stillness before, behind everything.
Setting out from the mountain, you search for this Vayn. Another lightning's child! The hymns say Vayn makes dolls and the dead move.

You pass through pretty blue flowers and a hawk's music and think,
I'll be a horse thief, I'll be a doctor, I'll mine tin, I'll bake bread, I'll fuck,
I'll be notorious. I'll evade the enemy and find Vayn, child of lightning
and Life.

You stand on a crag.

I'll do whatever I want. That dangerous thought again, bringing in its
wake, as it always does, Which is what?

On your way you talk to those you've killed, in your head, and to
those who have killed you, that vastly smaller number. You tell them
what you've seen on your travels.

Walking through empty lands, sometimes you roar to accompany
yourself. You dream of your mother. She puts her hand in the center of
your chest and says, Son, why are you screaming?

· · ·

A buzzard is hunched by the fire. You look deep into its eyes but see the glint of avian consciousness, no portal into emptiness that, for reasons occult to you, you dread to see. So you bid it good morning. You'd be welcome to share my breakfast, you tell it, but I have none.

When I was young, you tell it, before I died for the first time, my mother asked my father, my sky father, for a gift to help me. When I came into the village I saw that she was holding something like you. A bird. Not a bird really, a little crown made of feathers. She was worried about what my manfather had me do, and I think that feather helmet was to let me rest. I don't know how. She and my manfather fought. If I'd worn what she held I'd have looked like a peacock god. Maybe found relief. Been able to die.

You stop. This is the first time that occurs to you, as a potential liberation.

They didn't see me see them, my parents. My father hit her hand and the gift went down the pit. I don't know why I pretended I had not seen. Why I did not climb down. Or jump down and break my legs on the bottom and wait until they fixed again and climb back up with the feathers in my teeth.

The buzzard stretches its neck.

I've never gone back there, to dig through thousands of years of accreted earth to see if I can find it. I don't know for sure what she considered rest, my mother. Now I want to find Vayn. Another like me. I think that's what I want.

I've seen a sphinx. I've seen stone that walks. I've seen the pillars of Iram. But I've never seen a person who knows what they want.

The buzzard snaps its beak in clack-clack language.

I have nothing, you say. You turn your pack inside out and upside down and the buzzard watches the dust fall out, and cocks its head.

You're a demanding guest, you say, but you smile.

Take your knife from its sheath. Pull up your skirt. Put the blade to the top of your thigh. The buzzard waits. Draw the metal sideways and red blood comes quickly out of you. It is not that you don't feel pain, it isn't that you don't mind pain, it is that you are very very used to being hurt. You set your teeth and press deeper, pulling the blade through skin fat muscle, blood pouring now. You slice off a piece of flesh several inches long, half a palm wide. You peel it off, hold it up dripping and the buzzard makes a sound. Cut off a tiny end of it, then throw the dripping rest to the bird.

It catches it in its beak and swallows it down.

You're welcome, you say. You hold up the nub you've kept. Roll it up. The flayed part of your leg throbs. You put the flesh into your mouth and chew and swallow. That taste again. You've eaten of yourself before.

It does nothing.

The buzzard flies away.

Before you begin your quest for Vayn the daughter of the other force, that which brings plants out of mud, you detour to a port town famous for its spires and bridges and machines and spindly ships brought from Kumari Kandam by merchant-priests before that continent disappeared, and you set up a soothsaying business in the Foreign Quarter from where you gull the credulous and build up substantial savings and one day a sub-vizier comes to ask you when their brother will die and they are very beautiful and you tell them that you have been living a lie and have no mantic skill and they say they'll ask you a riddle to decide whether or not to hand you to the guard and you know the answer to the riddle, it is An egg, and they reward you by spending the night with you and you spend ten years together and you show them you are immortal by pushing a stiletto through your eye and out of the back of your skull and they run shouting they never want to see you again and four days later they come back and have you tell them the story of your life and you tell them bits of it and they say they still love you and you stay together five more years and they tell you only one thing is missing and though you know it can't end well you surprise yourself with hankering too and the two of you hire a wombwife and your lover is to lie with her but on the night you lie with her too while your lover strokes you both and the wombwife grows big and you hope against hope but when the baby is born it is dead and the color of ash and the wombwife too sickens and dies too and you and your lover lament for the prescribed time and you live together in your seaside tower until your lover is very old and they tell you you have been the best thing in their life and you say the same which is not true though you are fond of them and you say you will never forget them which is true and then they die and then you bury them and then you give away all your possessions and then brick by brick you pull down the minaret you built together while the townsfolk say yours was the love that will never die and then you walk away with the rubble behind you and then you decide that that is enough procrastinating, and you pull out the scroll with the hymn upon it, about Vayn, and you allow that it really is time to get started.

You are killed four times following Vayn's trail. Each time, as the teeth close about your throat or the ax pushes under your ribs or the fires take you, you steel yourself and tell yourself to keep paying attention all the while. But when you wake, into the blood-warm mulch and light through the egg case, splitting it and falling out like a mucal gout to gasp breath into new lungs, you can't be sure whether the dim sounds, the sensa-tions, the tides of affect that still buffet you are memories of what reached you from outside in your reknitting cocoon, are the dreams of an immortal between bodies, or are imagined retrospections born when you opened these new eyes.

Anyway, on you go. Another few hundred years.

You neither declare your intent nor hide it. You know how fast word travels. You are never shocked to arrive at some crystal-flecked nunnery or louche bazaar or whatever to have a local wise woman or town crier or infomancer whisper to you, You are looking for the Church of Vayn.

What follows is roughly twelve false trails to every one that helps.

With enough time, and the expertise and tenacity time bequeaths, almost anything is possible. On an isolated island, at the end of a trail of stories, you track down the descendant of the cook who threatened you in the mountain. Your great-great-however-many-times-it-was-great-grandmother was a brave woman, you tell her.

I know, she says. I've heard the stories. I know what you are.

Well help me find out more, you say. Come work with me. She said, Fuck all gods. Shall we honor her together?

You teach the woman to read and share everything you have. You part for months and come together again, again and again, and she tells you what she's found and you tell her what you have and together you go on.

I have a lead, she says. She takes you through wet forest. I followed word of a pig, she says, and that makes you stop, but she's going on. It found its way here, she says, is what they say.

You keep the spike of jealousy that passes through you to yourself and you and the woman fight a tribe of simians that talk like people. She limps on past their dead, beckons. Points.

A great crater, a steep declivity that grows drier and more barren within, at the dead center of which is a hole in the ground.

This is Obukula, she says. This is the way into the hollow earth. This is where the child of Life, of the lightning lives.

She crawls down the scree with you.

It's dangerous, you say. This isn't your quest.

Didn't we find the Living Ax together? She sings a fight song. Didn't we eat the berries of the damned?

All right, you say. Come.

You lower yourself to the stone lip, squeeze into the darkness. You strike fire and light a torch.

This is what the sot in the inn described to me, she whispers. I think I can remember where to go. From her pack she takes a spool of twine. Ties one end to a stalagmite. She unrolls it as she goes.

In the torchlight with shadows scudding the hugeness of these hidden chambers makes even you gasp. In corners are designs that do not seem like the random artistry of time.

The woman pauses, closes her eyes, and you know she is revisiting the rooms of her memory palace, rediscovering all the information she has heard. You go on. For a long time.

Until she crawls through a hole in the stone and you squeeze after her and her torch goes out and you haul yourself up in absolute darkness and hear from the reverberations that this is a vaulting space. In its deepest reaches, you glimpse figures. Human, and other.

You hear a whispered commotion.

Unute, your companion says, don't be afraid.

Arms grab at you.

You pivot on your hips and lunge but whoever had taken hold of you is gone. You stumble.

Stop, the woman who led you is saying, Unute stop don't be afraid. My great-great-grandmother was wrong, I want to help you—

You stand, and feel something strain, and understand that what you'd felt a moment ago was a slipping of chains about your arms and waist.

Unute they're afraid of you, she calls. They insisted. It's just to reassure them. I promised you I'd get you to Vayn and I have. This is it! This is for you. Be still, they just need to know you're no threat. You should be together! Two children of two gods. Balance—

There's motion all around you and you strain against the metal and from around the enormous chamber fire comes up and you see your companion mouthing her pleas and reassurances and all around her a congregation in dark robes and featureless clay masks and swaying beyond them in the rim of darkness are trembling constructs moving like nothing should.

Unliving life, edging like nervous animals. Figures in wood, in stone, in bronze, in lines of all such. Bones and slate and glass. They writhe and they totter.

You strain and turn, and see that your chains extend back yards across the uneven stone to a dais by a deeper doorway. There is not a crowd restraining you. Only one figure holding the metal, bracing against you. Stare at her a moment. Her expressionless mask.

You prepare to bunch your body, to break the links. Light arcs through them. A jolt of energy sears into you. Makes you buck. Makes you scream.

Stop! the woman who came with you shouts. What are you doing? He's come looking for you, let him speak!

But you lose her words against the racking pain of that current. You fall and jerk and dance and drum your heels upon the floor.

Stop! you dimly hear her call.

Then all there is space for is your pain.

Who knows how long until you come to? You have no memory of the hours when you were unconscious, any more than you do when you berserk, any more than of the times when you are, temporarily, dead.

You can see faint spectral silver edges when you come back. Look up. Make out a hole in the rock roof way overhead, for moonlight.

You have been dragged to a new chamber, smaller, but large enough. Your chains have been layered and layered and folded in towering piles on every limb, hammered into the stone wall. Into a network of metal rods and thinner chains and wires, which spread out, connected like a spiderweb, across the walls, enclosing the whole chamber. Beyond the pillar of lunar light a spindly figure watches. It is another wire framework, a tangle of bits in the roughest armed legged headed shape.

We've been getting ready for you, you hear someone say. For a long time.

Out of your reach, clay-masked members of the church watch. Some are scribes, with rolls and styli.

One comes to stand directly before you. You feel energy come from them.

You strain against the chains.

After all this time, your interlocutor says, you want to get away again? You've found what you've been looking for. You've found us just like the boar.

It is a woman's voice.

It tasted me, poor thing, what a shock. Followed the trail, when it came in I could see that it thought it would find you. Imagine its pleasure and surprise. It doesn't hate me. It rested awhile, then set out. Did you meet it again since then? You wouldn't know, of course. You don't know how long I've waited.

You go still.

At last you say, You are Vayn?

You want to not be alone, she says. You want there to be another, or others.

After all this time you think you're the first other person who claims to be the lightning's child? you say.

No. But I'm the first you believe.

You can't even tell if you hear her in your ears. You can't tell what that voice is like.

But the real question, she says, is why? What is it you think that company will give you?

You say nothing. To that you have no answer.

You're ashamed, she says. You think it sounds foolish, don't you? It does. You want family. Two questions, Unute. Why do you want that? And why would you think I, the lightning child born of Life, would want to be your family?

You, she whispers, making your bones vibrate, are . . . my . . . enemy.

Wait! You hear the voice of she who led you, from beneath one of the masks. You promised . . . What about the woken stuff? They didn't sense him, he's not poison to them nor they to him, and you said he would be—

Be quiet, Vayn says. We're all still learning.

She reaches up as she says this, and her hands touch the wall, and you realize what she will do as her fingertips reach a seam of the metal, and you open your mouth to shout as she sends forth from somewhere within another burst of energy, that, yes, lightnings out of her, through the metal and into you, and you arch your back so fast and hard you feel and hear it break, and you hear the cheer that ugly crack raises among those there, and then you're out again.

And back. Straight into another burst, and out again

. . .

blast you

again, and back and again

Again, crawling, for the energy to return and quickly

back. And silence. The room is empty now but for you. You wheeze, and breathe, and lick the sweat and blood from your upper lip, and wait. They are somewhere, sleeping.

Whatever is in these bonds you cannot break them, you cannot. And it comes to you that you will rise again as many times as they choose, collapsing, hatching, collapsing, hatching, falling to rise to fall to rise to fall. And if the life of their leader is endless as is yours, and why would it not be, and if she has fidelity to this mission, which why would she not, she will kill you, you will die in pain, over and over, for the rest of eternity.

And at that even you make a miserable little sound of fear.

Later you hear the noise of an approach. You raise your head.

A robe-clad masked figure stands alone with you, at the only entrance to this chamber. You pull at the metal again.

It won't work, she says.

It is your erstwhile companion.

She navigates the uneven surface of the cave, pulling herself around jags. She does not take off the mask.

I know, she says. You feel weak. It's those bonds. It's the lightning.

That's its paradox, life that weakens.

Her voice is full of sadness.

I'm sorry, she says. They've shown me things. They've told me the truth. They don't know I'm here now. They told me not to come here. They said whether you know or not what you are, you are what you are, and it's a tragedy either way, and talking to you can't help.

What are they doing to me? you say.

They're filling you with life. To end you, in the end. You can't be allowed to be.

To end me? How? How do you kill with life?

She says nothing.

How can that be? you say. What have they told you?

When she does not answer that, you say, What am I then? Your voice appalls you. What am I?

She whispers, You are Death. And it's time your reign ends.

At last you say, I told you that when I met you.

Yes, she says. But I didn't know it was true.

I told you it was true, you say.

You did, she says.

And what do your new comrades want from me? you say. What do they want with death?

She won't come closer to you. She won't take off her mask.

They want to know everything, she says. Everything about you. And how to snuff you out. I came here to tell you, she whispers, in case you don't know that you're evil. In case you are as you always seemed to me.

So that you can end it, now.

What?

End yourself. It will be better.

Have you not heard anything I've told you . . . ? you say.

I know what you told me, she says, low and urgent. But now's the time to let your powers go. Now's the time, for the sake of the world, to die. To die quickly and quietly. For your sake and the sake of the world. Because . . .

But she can't say what it is she dreads.

All you can do is laugh. She whispers desperately at you to be quiet. I can't turn it off! you shout. Even if I wanted to! Which I do. I told you. You did, she sobs. But I didn't know it was true.

When you can stop your pained laughter, you say, Well. It is. True.

Then I'm sorry, she manages to say. I hope for your sake you are death. That you are evil. Because then at least there'd be a point, there'd be justice, to this finally. And even if you are, truly, I'm truly sorry.

She turns. You can hear her crying. She walks away. You will not call after her.

And hours later the church returns, a score or more of people in their robes. They are not accompanied now by any swaying statues.

You will not say anything while one of them, that leader with the body language that, yes, you remember, Vayn, whom you recognize now, steps again to the wall and you breathe deep and bite down, and the scribes get ready to take notes again, to perform their work of observation, and Vayn says, Are you ready?

The scribes nod. Their leader touches the metal again and makes your heart stop and makes you die.

And back you come into your mind, waking into consciousness, mid-thought, that thought being Again, as out you come, however long it is later, slipping, slopping out of your sac like a young dogfish from its purse, before a gathering of those robed bastards, onto a bed of metal prepared for you, at the touch of which you hear your own shout of despair and into and through which metal comes an instant burst of energy, and you awake again naked and crusted with the dried slime of your rebirth, chained again, in this place of torment. Watched over.

More spurts and sprays of power through constraints, and in the agonized seconds before they jolt you into darkness, you feel distinctions in their nature, some energy stronger, some sharper, some more diffuse, hurting or stunning or devastating you or even once or twice filling you with instants of new strength, sudden and unexpected, as they experiment with energies, followed fast with blasts that simply debilitate.

No one feeds you. Hunger won't kill you.

The scribes record the bolts and your responses when the lightning flows. You spit and curse.

Torturers are lower than slavers, you shout. Lower than maggots.

You think this is a pleasure? someone calls. It's her. Not everyone's as base as you, Death. Sometimes the only way to learn is through pain. Would that it were other. Even for you.

She calls an order. Five worshippers step forward. One holds an iron hook, another a trident. Two hold knives, one a hammer. You growl and shake in your bonds. As weighed down as you are, as locked into place, as exhausted from all their ministrations, you cannot fend them off as in they come in a choreographed attack, and use their weapons, this time, weak as you are, to take you apart.

The last thing you hear, this time, is the leader shouting to the scribes, Note whence the blood flows, note how the scabbing begins—and then you're gone.

                          to fall out of the egg onto the metal again, to howl to be subdued again, to wake again, to face the church again, armed now with their new tools, scissoring blades, a file, pincers, boiling pitch, always that burning blue, so you scream with miserable laughter and demand they bring it to you, which they do, and as a heavy sword comes down through your trachea you hear

                          nothing and a short time's timeless

mercy

and Hello again, the channeler says.

A pit of venomous snakes. Garrote. Fire. The lightning keeps you alive and weak or agitated or sluggish or strong or foolish or kills you. As does a rock to the skull. Cave bear. Flail. Lightning. Drowning. You pray to your mother. You bite out your tongue. Return from the egg. Molten metal. Yes you're used to pain but so much so fast so repeatedly so often so overwhelming is harder and harder and harder to bear, current keeps you around, ends you, back you come, arrows and the lightning, the scribes taking notes and the channeler, Vayn, the child of the lightning itself telling them that they must be growing close.

It's taking longer, you hear through blood, it's taking longer for him to return, each time, we're learning, keep going, hatchet ants boiling water, dead and alive again, and you plan and plan and plan, over the years, the years of this, noting the configuration of the room ten thousand times. Once when you awake half out of your egg you manage to hurl yourself through and down to land with your neck right upon a spike hard enough to rip your own head off and go back to the calm memorylessness untime between egg-births

to hatch again, the leader saying to you, Very clever, but what did that gain you? You helped us.

You see that the spike that you used last time has been flattened.

Now we know that isn't the last of it, either, Vayn says. Suicide. It's all research. It's all research for us.

choking pulled apart stabbed crushed current water fire, the world will end the sun will grow fat and red and slow and waterfirestabstoneclogearthyears and years and every second that you are alive you scream in your mind to your mother and both of your fathers and any of the dead to end this, to take you from the moment, and moment, and moment of your death, to let you truly die, Let them kill Death, you think, you ache, willing the egg not to return, it not to grow here in the mulch of your pain

and

you

wake again,

and push out of your egg

and you

are

alone.

On your hands and knees you wheeze, cough out the last gluey liquid from your lungs. You stretch your fingers against—sand.

You look up.

Into a cloudless sky wherein a white sun pours forth heat and light, and you shut your eyes against the agony that follows light after lifetimes of darkness, but there is none because these are not the eyes acclimatized to that gloom, but new ones.

The slip dries on your skin.

You stand amid dunes. You are out of the cave. No one is hurting you.

Your scream is very long and loud, and it is of joy.

You run for a long time out of the delight of being unchained. You relish the new thirst of desert desiccation, so different from that of jailers' withholding. There are ways to find water in such places, and when you are ready you drink.

At last, in a hollow, in the gentle dark of night, you consider. You aren't minded to count the times you've come back, but there

were very many. The sac out of which you've emerged has always constituted itself out of the matter of your remains. You do not understand,
and have never before experienced, this new energy, which your very
anguish must have wrought on that process, spurting your selfness, out
of that place of your long torment and repeated murder, to take seed
and grow somewhere quite new.

How far from that of your last dying? How long thereafter?

How did you do this?

Can you do it again?

How do you do this again? How do you do something again when
you do not know what it was you did?

Vayn has wanted you to die and you have not died. But something
has happened. These are the questions you must address. What is it that
has happened?

And Vayn, it comes to you, and Vayn's people, have lifetimes of research that might help answer that.

You must find something to kill, that you may skin it, that you may
have its skin, and you must have a fire to burn a stick to tip it with char,
that you may write down what matters about this moment. In an ancient
script of which you are the last scribe, you will make the marks for Torment, for Antique Land. For the Month of the Moths, diacritics to indicate the start thereof. For Newly to a Desert.

But you remember everything, remember? Don't you? You have said
so for many millennia. So why must you write this down? But write it
you must.

You find an oasis. You grow stronger. You set out. After weeks of trudg-
ing, your skin blistering and healing in endless cycles, you reach a town
and learn that you are an ocean and half a continent from the hole of
the hidden church. Of Vayn.

Who, it occurs to you, has seen you die and not return. Who likely
believes their experiment over. Successful.

Who will not expect your return.

You steal a fortune. You buy a ship. You commission a crew. You sail. You land. You fight. You continue through unforgiving places. You fight again and escape and buy a horse and ride it and exchange it for another and ride on. You kill many people and animals and are nearly killed once.

Very many years after you cross the ocean, you stand again at the rim of the crater.

You wait awhile. For the part of you within to declare, as you know it will, that you have no need to do this, no need to see what if anything is left of this cult below, that if there is another godkin there, under the ground, they hate you, and you do not need to know it. When that part of you has had its say, you tell it that they have studied you and that you have questions. Questions about what you are. And how you died. And were elsewhere. And you would know their thoughts on that. And that in any case, if the truth is to be told, you have sought for too long to know whether you are the only one of your kind, and you will not resile from that knowledge now.

And, yes, you allow, with a certain brutal humor, a certain anticipation, that while many have hurt you, none have hurt you so utterly, so terribly, for so terribly long. None have made you scream. And if you owe Vayn and their followers a debt, because in their very cruelty and the relentless tenacity of it they have taught you something new about yourself, they have broken you from the constraints of your own dead locale, the nature of your self, your body, it was knowledge very bitterly come by. And if you owe them this insight, that does not mean you don't wish to repay them in their own coin.

You imagine again their voices when the gobs they left of you, years ago, did not crawl like slugs and snails back into that columnar pupa, did not spit fibers and interconnect and ready themselves to receive you again.

Look!

It's done!

Look we have ended the cycle!

Look we have done it!

Look we have killed death!

It comes to you that you, too, had thought you might be made mortal by all that death, by the piling up of your bodies. When you had dreamed of the end of that pain, it had always been to end altogether. Never what occurred, never that elsewhereing, this travel by death.

What did they think, thereafter, when death continued, in the world? What did they think they had done? Have you been concerned, you think as if shouting to those imagined celebrators, have you been troubled by all the death that has occurred since you believe you witnessed mine? You killed death, didn't you? So what's that about? Have you not heard the fables? Do you not know the moral? Do you not know that no one who attempts to kill death does well out of it?

You rise in the moonlight and stalk toward the hole.

FIRST SILENCE

THE HOUSE WAS BEHIND BUSHES, SET BACK FROM THE STREET.

Diana ascended the wooden stairs. Cat flap. Battered chair on the porch. She rang the bell and heard it echo within.

After a minute, a woman opened the door and smiled up with tremulous and polite uncertainty. She was in her mid-sixties, plump and white and shiny-skinned. Over her blouse she wore a schmutzy white apron with four words printed on it: MY KITCHEN MY RULES!

"Hello?" she said. She wiped flour from her hands onto the cloth.

"I'm sorry to bother you, ma'am," Diana said. "I'm looking for a Mrs. Bennett."

"I'm Aggy Bennett. Can I help you?"

"Mrs. Bennett, my name is Diana Smith. I need to speak to you about something urgent."

"OK," the woman said. "That sounds serious." Her eyes flickered nervously.

Diana took a deep breath.

"Does 'the Life Project' mean anything to you, Mrs. Bennett?"

She watched her closely, saw nothing.

"No. What is that?"

"It's an organization up in Tacoma," Diana said.

"Oh Lord, I haven't been to Tacoma for years. And I'm not interested in buying anything, so, thank you…" Smiling uneasily, the woman began to close the door.

"Wait," Diana said.

"Thank you, but I'm not interested."

Diana said, "Is Plomer interested?"

The door stayed open that last inch. Diana was still.

It opened again. The woman put her hands on her hips. She looked up with a face quite changed. No aggression or hostility, but a new suspicion, implacable and unafraid. She folded her arms. When she spoke again, her voice was cool.

"Who are you?" she said. "How did you find me?"

"This is … well, a matter of life and death," Diana said. "I have to ask you some questions."

The woman stepped back, pulled the door open, and inclined her head. Diana stepped inside, onto thick carpet. The hallway was in pink-tinted beige, pastel paintings and prints on the wall. The door closed behind her.

"Let me tell you what this is about…" Diana said, and something slammed violently into her from behind, shoving her face-first into the wall. She lost her breath at an expert kidney blow. She knocked two picture frames as she went down, and glass cracked. On her knees, Diana stared at them as she heaved for breath. A photograph of a river. A watercolor of a deer looking at a sunset.

The woman spun her around and held her by the lapels and hauled her up too easily, pushed her heavily against the wall again and put her right forearm across Diana's neck and put her weight on it.

Diana tried to speak. With her free hand, the woman went through her pockets. Drew out Diana's ID and her Glock, threw the pistol to the far end of the corridor.

Beneath her fear, Diana was aware of awe, that the hand that held her was too strong. That the physics of the room were disobedient.

"I'm not shocked you're here," the woman said. "I've been waiting for years. But what I can't work out is why someone would come to my door rather than just try to kill me. So you have one chance to tell me who you are and what this is and if I don't like it, you're not going to be telling anyone anything again.

"Did Alam send you?" the woman said. She kept her right hand on Diana's coat, drew back her left in a quick motion, with the fingers metal-stiff, a wedge to crush a throat.

Diana flailed. "What?" she wheezed. "No no no. I'm not from the LP, I want to know about them . . ."

"How did you find me?"

"Look at the ID," Diana gasped. "It's government. I work for a . . . secret department . . ."

"How did you find me? Last chance."

"Reviews!" Diana said.

The woman did not move.

"You left a review . . ." Diana swallowed. "I know Plomer and Alam ran together for years, and they took over the LP together." She held up her hands. "A few months after that, Plomer disappears and that's the last of her. Then two weeks after she leaves, a comment appears on Google's reviews page for the Life Project. This one's different from the others." The woman's grip on her was softening very slightly. Diana took a breath. "For one thing it's one of the few criticisms that gets taken down, a few days later."

"So how did you see it?" the woman said.

Diana gestured. "Archives. There are ways if you've got the re-sources. This message . . . all it says is 'You are being lied to. All of you. Made—'"

"Made into monsters,'" Yes. How did you find me?"

"The comment was anonymous but I got the IP. Yes, I know it was years ago and it went through Tor, but, resources, again. I told you. I'm a G-man!" She did not like how breathless that sounded. "This is gov-ernment stuff. So I did a trawl on Tor searches originally from that same IP. Lots of stuff on pagan cults and archons and antique civilizations, Mesopotamia, Sumeria, and alchemy and embodiment, avatars of gods."

She waited but the woman still held her tight.

"Is that so weird?" the woman said. "You could get that kind of mixture on a D&D forum."

"You're right," Diana said. "Turns out that there are a fair number of people who are interested in that sort of thing. But there's not so many who are interested in ancient magic and who are also investigating the biology of echidnas and platypuses, and who are big fans of Solange Knowles and Millie Jackson, and who speak German and Polish and Farsi and who are very keen on baking. Plomer is one."

The woman relaxed her grip.

"Still," the woman said. "No one's unique, no matter how much we'd like to think so."

"No," Diana said, rubbing her neck. "Even that still left a few. But here's the thing: I could trace the searches of the others back for years. There was only one person interested in all that who seemed to suddenly get interested in it just after Plomer left the LP. And not because she had a sudden series of epiphanies. Because she didn't exist before then. Sure, she's got records, but I know retconning when I see it. Plomer disappears, and twelve days later Mrs. Agatha Bennett—and her past—appears and starts looking the same stuff up online that Plomer had. And I'm here because some of what she's been looking up is stuff I urgently need to know about. Right now."

At last the woman said, "You better come in." She stood aside. "Kitchen's that way."

Diana brushed herself off.

"So that's real?" she said, gesturing. "I thought maybe you had a pre-floured apron by the door, for disguise."

"You've seen my search history. Baking's how I relax. Lucky for you."

BEYOND THE REINFORCED WINDOW CAME RUNNING THE CRACKLING, STAR-ing, grimacing, hunched and stamping thing. It stared with a single eye. It came with a motion at once awesome and pitiable, faster than the full-bore sprint of any human, a rolling gait of vitality, agony, energy and injury, loping leaping stumbling running falling knuckle-galloping and crawling beyond any parsing. But

no more time to consider because it had arrived at the glass.

B met his own eye. He was gazer and engazed. Dorian Gray and his portrait. Strange meeting. With this chimera of infinite scraps. Oh B, he thought.

You, he thought as it drew back its right left fist, its agglomerated fistmass, on a farrago of an arm, on a stitchwork welter of a shoulder.

B, Unute, watched this other him blossom with the slurry that approximated blood from a pattering of shots, making that multitudinous body a garden of black and dripping flowers. An errant bullet hit the window and made spiderweb threads. What separated Keever and B from the inner section of the Unit's complex where the thing stamped was a layered composite of glass, acrylic, and polycarbonate, security level way beyond IQ, able to withstand direct mortar fire.

The thing leaned back, braced its neck, slammed its head forward. Unute could see glinting in the center of its forehead a tiny speck of hard white flesh.

It butted the window with a sound like rockfall. The glass went white at that impact point.

More bullets hit the creature from behind as it fumbled at that spot. Reared back and brought its head down again. A crack appeared. It hammered with its skull and the lines began to spread.

The composite Unute worked at the window, staring at its unitary self.

DIANA SAID, "WILL YOU HELP ME?"

The woman turned off the oven and hung the apron on a side door. She sat at the table and gestured for Diana to sit opposite. Diana smelled cinnamon and spices.

"That depends," the woman said. "On a lot of things."

Diana sat. "What do I call you?" she said. "Plomer?"

The woman shrugged. "Stick with Bennett," she said. "Or better yet, don't call me anything. Say what you have to say, listen to what I have to say, and then we can be done."

Diana clasped her hands.

"I have a colleague," she said at last. "He's gone missing. He's disappeared and we're trying to find him. And I think it has something to do with the Life Project. What can you tell me about them? Why did you leave?"

"Let's turn it around," the woman said. "What do you know about it?"

"Self-help group. Positivity. Living your best life . . ."

"What do you know about its real agenda?"

Diana hesitated.

"I think they have a . . . a hatred for death," she said. "I think they have something to do with my colleague disappearing. I think their leaders might have some kind of techniques to, I don't know, hypnotize, or something, some of the people they work with." She frowned. "I think they get people to do things they wouldn't otherwise do." She hesitated once more. "I think you know a lot more about this than I do."

"The LP," the woman said, "is supposed to be about real life. Some of us, at the top, have—had—techniques that could maybe have been used to change the whole relationship we have to living. To make it as long and fruitful and creative and exciting as possible. And what that means—I don't mean it's all it means, but it's part of it, it's one part of a program to maximize life—is opposition to death." She folded her arms. "We were never stupid; humans have to die." She did not look sure of this. "But even if so, that doesn't mean we should be in a hurry on our way, does it? And however long it takes, and however we do cross that last bridge, there's death and there's death. Right? Death is a horizon, yes, but the nature of the journey to it and over into it depends on a lot of things, no?"

"I mean . . . sure," Diana said after a moment. She frowned.

"I can see you thinking, 'What is this bullshit?'"

"No, I just don't understand. If this is how you feel, why leave? I mean, this is their line too, isn't it?"

"Because of Alam," the woman said. She closed her eyes for a moment. Opened them again and looked carefully at Diana. "Oh, Alam. The work . . . There's no more honorable work. I still know that's the truth. But the question is, How do you go about it? If part of the job is opposition to death, what does that mean in the day-to-day? What do you do to 'oppose death'?

"You might say," she continued, "that you should live as rich a life as you can, for as long as you can. That might be one way of fighting death, right? I mean, we're all going to fail in the end, supposedly, but what's wrong with failing better? But what if what you decide is that you have to literally go to war against death? What would that mean? What techniques might you use? And what's more important is this: if you decide that that fight is so important, then does that mean everything else is secondary? That you'll lie, cheat, control—and, yes, kill—if that's what you have to do?"

She shook her head.

"Alam's his only name. He's gone through first names like you might go through socks. Can you imagine what it's like," she said, slowly now, "to realize, after years of working with someone who you truly believed was a good person . . . who you still *know* is a good person, with noble aims, which is what makes the whole thing so much worse . . . Can you imagine what it's like to realize that they're so committed to their version of the project that you thought you shared with them, that they'll do anything? That they'll do wrong? Things they know are wicked? That they are your enemy?"

"The ends," Diana said, "never justify the means."

"Oh, baloney," the woman said. "Sure they do. If I knew, if I was absolutely sure, that his methods would work, then I'd never have left. But they won't. I don't believe they can. And it's one thing to be the necessary evil. But if it's not necessary, or even if it is necessary but it's not also sufficient, then it's just evil. And that I won't do. Not even for this."

They sat without speaking.

"What kind of relationship to death is that? What is it Alam's doing?" Diana said at last.

"What do you know," the woman said, her voice calm and flat, "about Unute?"

WITH THE EAGERNESS OF A DRUNK THE CREATURE SHOVED ITS FINGERS INTO the hole it had battered in the glass and began to pull, and the window came away, not breaking but unpeeling with loud reports and a heavy flapping like that of a drying pelt as the resin sealant curved, parting like curtains, like sagging flesh lips or a sea, coming down in slabs and bangs. And here came the escaped scrapbook of memories of B, through the portal.

A chorus of noise, the shouts of orders to and from the officers behind B now as well as behind that which he faced. Voices calling his name.

Do you mean me? he thought. There are two of me now.

The alarm was still screaming. Amid the cacophony and blaring glare of the fluorescent lights, and amid agents and soldiers running to their places, it was as if B were in the silent dark alone. Staring into unstill water. Into broken obsidian.

A horizontal rain of steel slammed through their flesh.

They were alone, B and counter-B, the one and multiple.

Am I your horizon? B thought. Are you mine?

Which walked forward first? B or the collage of B-ness? He came for it and/or it for him in an elegant and thuggish pas de deux, and they punched and their knuckles met, a fistkiss hard enough to crack sound.

B moved fast and though its parts seemed barely contained by keloid seams and scarecrow stitchings so did his fractured other, a fight of two armies with the same face.

Some of the soldiers dropped to their knees and you could not gainsay their bravery, they contained their terror and laid down fire and the dragontongues licked the child and other child of the lightning and hurt them. B saw the patchwork man reach for those battalions and he grabbed for it and shouted at the operatives to get back. His counterpart shouted too, its voice was full of earth and gravel, and it spoke a mash of slangs dead before the continents changed, and what it said was "Here I am again."

"Son!" B heard.

Hello, Keever.

But the other him moved too fast, and B knew the push that rose within him now, that uncoilingness, filling his sight with blue, his ears with static, prickling his hairs up and out and filling all his muscles with lightning and his mind and soul with a prophet's fervor.

"Get back," he cried out in the last moment that he could. "Get away from me, give me space." Because here it came, the riastrid, the warp spasm, the blood dwarn, his thoughts receded, and fight joy rose in him—

"UNUTE?" DIANA SAID.

"OK," the woman said. "I can see you know the name."

Diana exhaled. "Honestly, I thought perhaps that the LP people . . . you . . . knew something about that."

"Him."

". . . Him."

"What he is," the woman said, "is the child of death, which is the stillness under it all. He's the first and onlyborn of the Enemy." Diana could hear the capital. "Nihil Messiah. Entropy's Child. The name of what birthed him is the Thowless."

Diana held her breath.

"And then," the woman said, "there are those of us who are to the life what he is to death."

You could see her pride.

"Do you know your Bible?" she said. "Ecclesiastes 8:8. 'No man has power over the wind, or over the day of death. And weapons are no use in that war.' Something like that. It's not true. There is someone with power over death. And they have weapons, too.

"There was a time when *fundamental forces* walked. Call them what you like, just don't waste my time pretending not to know what I'm talking about. You came here, remember? They walked among us. The child of lightning was in the world, and so much life poured out of her, so much of her parent's energy that it made the inert dance."

"The child of lightning?" Diana said. "Life?"

"Vayn."

The way the faithful could make a name resonate! The word raised prickles on Diana's skin.

"The first daughter," the woman said. "She knew her enemy: Death and Nothing, the blankness she'd escaped by opening her eyes. She walked alone for a long time. The story is that when life started on Earth it's because she stirred a rock pool with her fingertip." Bennett/Plomer shrugged, but that due diligence didn't dampen the ardor in her eyes. "I don't know how literal that's meant to be, but she kicked out life like a furnace does sparks. Like Unute kicks out death. And not just us and the rest of the rock-pool slime: touch the unliving the right way, she could wake them too. And not just for the hell of it. This was always a war, from the moment she breathed. A thing like that, the idea was that unlike us who were alive in our *form*, at least for a moment they'd stay so close to the lifelessness they'd been freed from that they could still smell life in them they were toxic to it. So they'd know when the enemy was coming, and be weapons against it. That was the plan. A long time ago."

· · ·

AND B WAKES TURNING, SEEING AGAIN, STANDING AGAIN IN THE CORRIDOR, dripping with blood and the darker ichor of the other him. Staccato images rush through him and he does not know if it was he who tore his own face or if it was the other or if that makes a difference.

The sirens hurt his ears.

Why was everyone so still? Who was it who shouted, "Easy, easy!"?

And why at him?

Where was his enemy?

He saw a slime trail on the floor, smelled the chemical stink, old blood extended from this wet place, and wherever it veered from the straightest line a soldier lay dead or screaming and broken, and on went the spoor again.

"It's out!" someone shouted.

And B learned then that there were in him urges stronger than curiosity, that intimate allergic tenderness he had felt at staring into his own miserable eyes. Because Keever lay on his back with his hands fluttering, while medics tended to the hole within his body where fingers had gone right in. He stared right at B and mouthed his name.

"Jim. What did it do?"

B knelt and put his hand on Keever's shoulder.

After a moment, B nodded.

"OK," he said. "OK. I'm really sorry, Jim."

"These painkillers are the shit." Keever smacked his lips and swallowed. "Listen to me. I'm sorry about this," Keever whispered. "Never wanted you to find out about this thing. Sure not like this."

"Jim, it's OK," B said after a moment. "I told Diana and Caldwell they could do what they want. I know Caldwell's been collecting

"Shut up," Keever whispered. "I know what's what."

"Son . . ."

"Stay quiet," B said. He looked at the gouting hole. "Let these guys—"

offcuts, and it wouldn't have been hard to guess what for if I wanted to. I thought he couldn't wake it up. Guess they solved that problem—"

"No," Keever whispered. B put his ear to Keever's mouth. "No they didn't. That's just it. Whatever woke it up, it wasn't us. And that's not all."

"Jim, let it go, it's OK—"

"Goddamnit will you listen?" Keever coughed and blood hit B's ear.

"The . . . Franken-B, that's the brass," Keever said. "Caldwell's idea. Not the LP. That was . . . me. The stories . . . It was me who suggested it to Shur, son." B looked at him, half-closed his eyes. "Before Stonier, before what happened to Thakka, even. I heard stories. Alam . . . I heard he can do things. Bring people back. I never really believed it but I thought if there was any truth, at all, we could use it . . . You kill a lot of people, son." He smiled sadly. "I know you don't always mean to and I never blamed you . . . but if we could bring the right ones back . . . "

"Jim, what are you saying?"

"What they say," Keever whispered. "That Alam can do . . . And now this . . . It's all fitting together . . . But why would he want . . . ?"

B pushed his ear close. Keever's lips did not move.

And B sat up and spat some curse and looked at Jim Keever's body in that unique motionlessness of death. The furnace of his heart going out. The eyes looking as intently at nothing as they ever had at anything in life.

"Fuck," B said.

All gazes were upon him. Every soldier, every tech, every medic, every scientist and orderly in the site of contestation watched him with terrible wonder.

"Close his eyes," he said.

The young medic stroked Keever's face gently and his gaze was gone.

"What now?" she said.

"I go punish what did this," B said. "That's what. I find that thing."

"What did this?" she said.

He turned to her and she said nothing more. He saw her face settle through fear into careful stillness. He looked back down at Keever, who had been so close to him. Right by his side when the lightning came. He looked up again. Saw Keever's people looking at him, their expressions of resentful wonder. Angry sorrow.

"Jim?" B whispered. "Jim."

He held his hand before the hole in Keever's chest. It fit.

"Which of me?" he said to the medic at last. "Which of me was it?" She did not speak. Oh Jim, he thought.

B felt a strain within him. But this one was not where his heart was. It was lower. It was in his pocket. He put his hand inside it. His fingers closed around the jigsaw piece.

"HOW DO YOU KNOW ALL THIS?" DIANA HEARD HERSELF SAY.

"Alam . . . came to." The woman inclined her head. "Remembered himself. Or enough of himself to get started."

"What? Out of nowhere?"

"Out of nowhere. Years ago. Told me the stories, what he remembered." She shrugged. "Then it was years of research. Vayn had to go in the end. Looong time ago. But when she did, she left her children behind, her blood children and the woken, her other children, to keep the faith and finish the mission. Win the war." That last she almost whispered. "To bring the kingdom. Unute's the son of the first silence, and what he spreads is the kingdom of the dead, which is everything she stood against. And what Alam and I stand against, too."

"How did he remember?"

"I don't know. I never knew." A shade passed across her face.

"So, like I said . . ." Diana asked after a moment, "why did you leave the LP?"

"Told you. It's not me who changed my mind or forgot what mattered. Or lost my loyalty. I was his . . ." She hesitated. "He didn't always know the truth."

"I could work out when Agatha Bennett got invented," Diana said. "But she's only existed since you split, the name stolen from a kid born about when you were, who died young. But Alam? He's really been around the whole of his life. I saw his birth certificate."

"I'm sure you have," the woman said. "And if you'd seen photos of his father or his grandfather, you'd have seen more than a family resemblance." The woman regarded Diana without expression.

"My God," Diana whispered. "How old is he? Another immortal."

"No," the woman said. "No. Whatever he might wish, he's not immortal. He's lived a long time, yes. But he just kept mooching along. You might think if you just kept on living after everyone around you dies you'd know something's up, right?" She shook her head. "Not necessarily. Not everyone. Not if you're walking in a kind of fog, for I don't know how many years. He didn't know how many, either. Just changing his name when he had to. From one Alam to another. I'd been with him a few years, and it was OK. All I knew was that he was kind of a vague guy. Deep down he must've been waiting for me to grow old, and die, and to move on again." She closed her eyes. "But something woke him up."

Say nothing, Diana told herself. Say nothing into this silence. This woman wants to speak.

"There used to be a few of them," the woman said. "A church of Vayn, disciples, and a bunch of Vayn's flesh-and-blood children. But one by one—after long times, for some of them—they died. Some because of Unute. They'd been hunting together with Vayn's other kids, the stones and such, but whatever it was their mom had hoped they could do, the woken couldn't do it. Couldn't finish it. So they died too, some when they met him. Vayn's kids had kids, only some of whom knew about their grandma or the mission, and those kids had kids, and generations go, and they may have a touch of Vayn and live way too long but it's getting weaker, and even if a few of the kids can wake the unwakeable too, it's not easy and they're not so strong, and even if they know the job they fail too, and they get weaker and weaker, and eventually the last of Vayn's line forgets who he is, and just keeps wandering. Changing his name every lifetime. Until he marries someone who loves baking and Millie Jackson, and they have a nice quiet life, though she wishes he could have a little more oomph, sometimes, maybe.

"And then he remembers that he's on a mission. That that's what he's for."

This time her silence stretched out.

"What did you say when he told you this?" Diana said.

"I said, Bullshit!" the woman shouted. "I thought he was losing his mind. I told him he was crazy when I could feel it. Literally feel it inside me, when it poured into me. When he learned what to do, when he touched me, in a certain way . . ." She smiled. "I kicked your ass like a twenty-year-old, no?

"'I have to forget the woken,' he told me, 'that's what they've said.' 'Who?' I said. 'What have you been reading?' 'The people who know about this,' he said. She frowned again. "'It never worked,' he said, 'it was a dead end, a parlor trick.' Instead he wanted to push life right out where he needed it to go, not into the world's junk. Like I say, all this changed him. I don't just mean what he could do, I mean his mind. I sure got that oomph I'd been missing." She smiled. "I never regretted that. This isn't 'Be careful what you wish for.' You come face-to-face with something like this, you feel the life he learned to emanate, it changes you, too. As it should. It was good. It still is. It was beautiful. Watching him come into what he was supposed to be. Watching him grow in confidence."

A look of delight abruptly crossed her face.

"If I had any doubt left," she said, "he got rid of that the first time he woke a woken."

Don't say anything, Diana thought.

The woman shook her head. "Even though he'd said he wasn't going to." She smiled proudly. "It wasn't even deliberate. Just spilled out, a little life into stuff with no business being alive. He made a pen spin."

His servants are objects? Diana did not say.

"Could only ever do one tiny little one," the woman said, "but while it was there he could see through it, see what it saw." She smiled again, into nothingness. "A pen, spinning . . . and he didn't *control* it, he asked it what to do!" She shook her head and her happiness ebbed quickly away. "It only lasted a minute but the next day he threw that pen away. He was really agitated, said he couldn't go down that route again, that it was a mistake, he mustn't be tempted. I think maybe it was . . ." She shook her head again. "Kind of addictive? And a dead end, he said. But just to see he could do it in the first place! To know he was a soldier. And I was too.

"And I'm still loyal, like I say." Her eyes snapped back into focus on Diana's. "To the cause. But he'll just keep trying, and he'll keep slipping further into the pit, with whoever joins him. Doing everything he does because he 'has' to." She clawed the air to show quotes. "He believes it, Alam. He's just wrong. Death is evil and I'm not saying we should accommodate ourselves to it, I'm saying . . ." She was quiet for a long time. "You know that saying, 'The best revenge is a good life'? We should be building communities that are committed to that, that's how we win. Not a war. Don't pick fights you can't win."

"Why are you hiding?" Diana said. "Why not have this out in public? Or at least among the faithful?"

"Because Alam is a saint. Get on your knees and pray that you never, ever have to deal with saints. Because they are lunatics. When he realized I wasn't going to join his crusade, that I had my own ideas, I could see him decide that I had to go."

She closed her eyes and swallowed.

"He'd be sad about it," she said, her voice steady, "like he is about any death, but it had to be, for the greater good, for the cause. And no one in the group even knew what he had in mind. They're lost souls, most of them. They don't know much of this. I thought about trying to split the group—that's when I put that first post up—but I had no one with me. Alam's always been more persuasive than me. And way more powerful. Blood.

"So I had to get out and keep my head down. Live as best I can. Alone. And take precautions. But if you've found me, then Alam can too . . ."

She bit her lip.

"What am I going to do?" she said. "What are we going to do? Does he know you're on to him? How many of you are there? What are you, some kind of cult task force? It's going to get ugly if he pushes this. Alam's not Vayn's direct child, he's a descendant. That's why he can't face Unute down. He's not his equal, he's just one of the children of the children of the lightning's daughter. That's why he's been looking for something to boost him, to boost that power."

"What?" Diana said. "You said the woken don't—"

"Not the woken. I don't know exactly. He wouldn't tell me. That's when we started . . . That's when I realized we didn't see things the same. He started talking about it one day. Maybe one of his disciples told him, I don't know, they sure as shit were talking more together by then than he was to me. He said we need something to strengthen life. A protuberance into another place. He called it a name in an old language, said that meant the usherer-into-life."

Wait, Diana thought. The children of the lightning's daughter?

"This doesn't make sense," Diana said. "The children of lightning's children are all born dead, I thought . . ."

The woman stared at her. "What are you talking about?" she said.

"Unute can't father children . . ."

"Unute? Unute's father is Death! Of course he can't have children, he is the child of unlife! If Death's enemy, if Life has a child, why the fuck would that kid not be able to create more life? That's what it would be for. Alam's lineage is Life."

Her face almost glowed. Then fell, far and hard.

"Which is why it's so sad," she said, "that he's lost it."

And then, as Diana shifted in her chair, the woman looked at her. Something went over her face.

"How do you know that about Unute?" she said.

Diana stared at her hard. "I've been working on this project a very long time," she said. "I've, uh, read all—"

The woman put her hand to her mouth. "You're . . . Oh dear God," she said. "Jesus Christ."

"Now, hold on," Diana said.

"You're not here to find out how to fight him," the woman said. "Oh dear sweet God, you're working with him. You're not his enemy, you're mine!"

"Listen to me," Diana said. "Just listen."

"You're on the side of Death!"

With a single smooth movement, the woman bent and reached below the table to just where Diana had inferred she had a pistol hidden in a strap, pointed directly at the seat to which she had carefully directed her guest.

Which was why Diana was ready. Holding her own handbag, ready and aimed on her lap, with its disguised tiny pistol in its inner pocket. Did not even have to waste time raising it to fire. Pulled the trigger, three four five times.

The woman went spinning in a nasty pirouette, her arms up, clawing at the walls, stumbling into the side door, taking accidental hold of the apron, falling, adding blood to the stains of flour.

The Orphan's Story

I SAW THE ZEPPELIN THAT KILLED MY FAMILY, AND I THOUGHT IT beautiful, like a whale, and what with war being so quick and loud and rattling there was something wonderful about its implacable slowness, how it did not scurry over the city but made its way sedately through the uplights. I was on the bridge when booms blossomed below that airship, as it delivered what it had come to deliver. The blasts did not increase its urgency. It pivoted at its own pace and set off north.

Later the rabbi told me the name of the ship—I will not repeat it. He told me it had come from another bombing raid on the Skierniewice engine yard and had for good measure made its way northeast to release what it had left on the sidings of the city. The rabbi told me I was a man now, that I must be brave, honor the family name, and he intoned the hope that the memories of the dead would be a blessing. I nodded and thanked him and did not say aloud, Fuck you, rabbi, fuck your blessings, and fuck God.

My father was a rolling-stock man with a high braying laugh and whenever you told him that it made him sound like a donkey he laughed that donkey laugh more. My mother was short and sharp and did most of her talking with her eyes and was more eloquent with them than most are with their mouths. Awiszal was two years younger than me but much cleverer. Dajcha was seven and would boss me around like a teacher with her hands on her hips. The house came down on them all. It may be the bomb was meant for the yard over the way or maybe some aerial spite overcame the dirigible's captain, and he knew the nature of the buildings over which he passed.

My mother's sister took me in. After a while her husband wanted to reprimand me—I could hear them argue—about my nighttime visits to the rubble but she said, Let him be, you brute, and he grumbled and did not speak to me about it, or anything.

From afar explosions look soft. Like cloth. I could not let that lie stand. I wandered the piled-up ruin where I had been born (they put up fences to keep us out but I was not the only person who crept over to explore, though I was the oldest and the only one whose home this had been). I sat on the chunks of brick and slate and would not allow myself to pretend that the detonations had been as they had appeared, like curtains or mist or silk or expanding dough, but made myself dwell upon them as they were, a million sharp edges and rocks, and consider that my family had not been enveloped in a kindly final bosom but stoned to death as if in punishment for parlaying with the dead.

The city promised to clear the remains of the house but the authorities were stretched and we all knew the trash was not going anywhere soon, and I was glad. It was my stone garden, my hill of memories. I visited at night to sit with the absence of my sister and my sister and my father and my mother, and to talk wordlessly to them.

After weeks had passed I tried to bring Agata Faber there for a nighttime visit. She had been with Julian Biterman and Aleksander Melamed and she had already let me put my fingers inside her that very night but when she saw where I was leading her she pulled away.

"Are you crazy?" she said. "What is this?"

She would not let me explain. I could not have explained, even to myself.

Now I think I sought a ritual of my own. I do not know why I thought that fucking with Agata, my pants down around my ankles, her skirt about her midriff, the two of us scraped by the mortar of my past, might have been such a thing, but I am grateful to her that she did not let me try. Instead I went alone and climbed to the top of the pile and looked up at my erstwhile neighbors' houses from angles impossible before. I rummaged amid the stones.

I found a book.

When my house collapsed it left uncovered the walls of those to either side, raw parts of them hidden, until then, for decades. You could see scraps of wallpaper, the ghost shapes of staircases and cubbies. I made out, protruding from a chink, stubs of pages between boards. I reached for them. I could not reconstruct whether this had been a secret compartment, once, or the underside of floorboards, or what. I drew out a small thin notebook, wrapped in leather, very filthy and battered and untouched for a long time.

It did not have so many pages and no more than half were filled in. For the first few double spreads, the entries were pasted carefully with adhesive flat upon the paper. The first several of these looked like antique parchment of great age, marks upon it faintly visible only in certain light, impossible for me to decode. A few sheets in, more recognizable entries began, on the paper itself, each in a different faded ink. I tilted for the glow from a streetlamp. They were in languages I did not know.

It did not take me long to recognize the language of those most recent as French. With my wages from the clerk's office, I bought a small French-Polish dictionary. With its help and that of the larger volumes in the library and of my coworker Tomasz, whose grandmother was from Lorraine, it was not so hard to decode what was written.

The first entry of which I could make sense: *Drowned, Seine, 1 February 1737. To Benin.* Others:

Fire (painful), Istanbul. 14 March 1753. To Providence.

Fall, Reykjavik. 14 July 1763. To Dhaka.

Pig, Carpathians, 1 January 1801. To Mosi-oa-Tunya.

The most recent entry read: *Shot (secret police). Warsaw. 25 February 1861. To London.*

Before it, a century of violence with a global reach. A hanging in Lichtenstein. Crocodile frenzy in the Gold Coast. An earthquake in a place called Wairarapa. One violence, one place, one date per line. Then a gap, then the next. I will not list them all.

The penmanship was not the same. In the first entry it was more curvaceous than in the last. But it was close enough that I thought it all written by the same person.

So. Why did whoever hid this notebook, let us say, I asked myself, make entries and carefully pretend they dated back from nearly two hundred years ago, and very much further, all the way through to fifty years ago?

Below that question there was a rebuking answer. I knew it was there though I did not entertain it. It never left.

There it remained, for years, and there it was, jumping to the fore, long after the war, in 1927, when I heard a knocking at my door, very late, and opened it in my robe on to a tall man, a dark man, with dark clothes and sad dark eyes, when he said to me, "You have my book."

And I was not surprised.

We stood together in the low glow beneath a streetlamp opposite the site of the house where I had been a child and wherein my mother and my father and Dajcha and Awiszal were crushed. A new house rose there now. I thought it ugly. A light shone in the uppermost window and I imagined a scholar at work, an old woman at table, a couple wishing to see each other as they shared their bodies.

"How long have you watched me?" I said.

"Your family died in 1914, yes?" the man said. "I came back to the city two years ago. It was in your neighbors' room that I left the book, but when I got back in there, no sign. I didn't think it had come down in the blast, and there was no record of any fire. It took a bit of hunting. But you haven't gone far."

It had taken us twenty minutes, no more, to walk here from my new house.

"And what if it had gone?" I said. "Been burnt or shredded?"

He shrugged.

"Then I'd be without it. Perhaps I'd start again. It'll certainly go at some point. I'm surprised it's lasted as long as it has. Pleased, I allow."

He turned to me and held out his hand.

"How do you know I brought it with us?" I said. "How did you know I have it?"

He put his hand back down and looked at the replacement house.

"Everything is a wager," he said. "You collect data and you make your wager. I'm wrong, sometimes, but not very often, by now. To watch you, as I've watched you the last year, is to learn about you. To make a wager about the sort of man you are, and the sort of boy you would once have been. What you would have done, and how you would have done it, in the face of tragedy."

"Tragedy?" I said. "Is that what it is that happened to my family?"

He shrugged, not without kindness.

"Sometimes," he said gently, "I wish I could avoid becoming a metaphor." He did not use metafora when he said this, but przenośnia, and I was surprised. "But it's in the nature of life."

I did not reply.

"At times it feels insulting," he said. "As if it only matters what we are insofar as we mean other things. That condition afflicts us all, but I think I'm even more of a metaphor than most. There's nothing I can do about that. Nothing any of us can. And perhaps that's all right. Perhaps it isn't a bad thing."

He said, "Death . . ." He paused and thought. "Death is a journey. I have even less interest in similes than I do in metaphors. Death is not *like* a journey, it *is* a journey. We all know that."

I took the book out of my pocket. I held it up. I do not have any doubt that he could have taken it from me but he did not. He watched and waited for me to hand it over.

"What is it that's recorded here?" I said.

"I think you know," he said. I looked at him and knew him to be much older than my country.

"How can I know?" I said.

"I think you know more than you believe you have the right to," he said. "Death is a journey," he said, and sighed. "But what if it ends up right back here?"

I listened, sisterless.

"What I have found," he said, "is that most journeys take you back to where you left from. But not all. A very long time ago I learned that at the end of some journeys, you start again somewhere new. They don't happen very often. Such journeys as those. So when they do, it's worth taking note." He gestured at the book. "In any case recalling has never been a difficulty. But there are ways of seeing. See too many and it's overwhelming. If you're looking for patterns, there is a line between too little information and too much. So this is data."

"And this," I said, holding it up, "is enough? The perfect amount of information?"

"No," he said. "Not nearly enough. It might be enough in a long time. And when I write in it, as when anyone writes in any book, what I record is accompanied by the infinite ghosts of that which is not recorded."

"The ghosts of everything," I said.

"Yes. And the task for the recorder, for the clerk is to discern those ghosts, those might-have-beens that matter most, from those that matter least. Take this book," he said. "I hope it might help me. That

I might learn why I open my eyes sometimes to different skies from those under which I closed them. And you'll find . . ." He looked to the sky now, and chose his words. "Consider some of the ghosts unpresent within this book, unrecorded because unoccurred. Impact by a meteor, say. The result of transgression against King Shaka. Assault by that which moves that should not ever move, table-tapping of the most boisterous kind, I mean. There's no record of any such in here. But that doesn't make them equal in their absence. I never entered Shaka's wives' isigodlo nor did I spit nor sneeze in his presence and he never had anyone raise a hand against me. There are by contrast secret ways to know where spacefaring rocks will land, and I have learned such secrets and I have chosen to stand to meet them. I woke in Kaali after one such challenge. But that is just it: it was in Kaali that I was ended, and in Kaali that I opened my eyes. The ghost of the third instance is the most important here. For a while I thought some dancing oddity would earn its entry here, because they've certainly sought me, and sought to close my eyes. But they've never done the necessary work. It's been some years, it was on a ship at sea, that I ended the last such chase. I will never know if I would have been right, had that meeting gone another way, and if so, why. That, you see, is a pertinent ghost. Meaningful. This is a book to solve a mystery, and while the first two might-have-beens are merely not here, that last absence is very present in its pages."

I could tell he was not Polish but he spoke without an accent and I understood every word he said except for that foreign one, isigodlo. The true sense of what he said in that gentle sorrowful lulling voice was quite beyond me. And yet, for all that I understood nothing, as if I listened to an exquisite piece of music, I felt communicated with. I experienced no frustration.

"How does it work?" I said. "That book."

"We all make rituals of our lives, and for them." I looked up sharply at that. He continued: "I could keep the book in one place, yes. But what if there is something in the thereness of the destination that matters? Or is that too easy? Surely the causally important place must be that of the setting out. So. This started with the first journey that took me somewhere else. I made my way back whence I had left. But mindfully this time, as decision. I made an entry, stored it where I started from. Went about life and time. The next time it happened, I journeyed back to where I'd stashed it. Recorded the information of the next journey. Took it with me back to the starting place of the last journey, there to secrete it again. And so on."

"So you last . . . began a journey worthy of the name from War-saw?" I said.

"On the anniversary of the Battle of Olszynka Grochowska," he said.

"So the fact that you are here now . . ." I said. "You have something to add. That's how it works?" I held out the book. "You're here to take it, add an entry, take it to a new place, your most recent place of departure?"

He took it. Opened it, drew out a pen. He wrote, waved the book in the air for the ink to dry, and handed it back to me.

I read: *Dragged behind car, Damascus, 3 September 1880. To Bagamoyo.*

"So," I said. Very quietly. "Now this goes to Damascus. That's right?"

He nodded.

We stood together.

"The sound of it," I said. "I think Awiszal would have heard it. The ship. She goes to the window and pulls aside the curtain. That's how I see it. My mother tells her not to, to behave herself, help with the dishes, but Awiszal is twisting her face up, looking into the sky—"

"It won't help," he said. He did not raise his voice but the inter-ruption almost made me stagger. "No story you can tell, I won't say you won't be able to get something from. But alongside that, how-ever compelling, whatever the story, will always be the facts."

"Those," I said, "I can never touch."

"No. But nor will you be able to stop yourself from reaching for them. I'm sorry."

"I miss their voices," I said.

"Yes," he said. "Death is quiet. It is the first quiet, and it will be the last."

"Do you think so?" I said. "The first quiet is older than death, surely." He stared at me, at that, and blinked. "And for all I would give everything I will ever own to hear them in the world again," I said, "I do hear their voices within me."

"If that's a comfort to you," he said, "take it."

"It's no comfort," I said. "It's merely one of the facts. I don't find death to be very quiet, in truth."

He looked at me again. I felt respected. As if I had surprised him. He held my gaze. Something came across his expression. Something like curiosity. I did not nod but I was ready when he spoke again.

"In Damascus," he said. "There is a small park. At the corner of Sharia Al Jalaa and Aziz Al Seoud." He looked not at me but at it, in his mind, there in Warsaw. "Repeat that to me."

"Sharia Al Jalaa," I said, "and Aziz Al Seoud."

"You seem to me," he said, "to be a man who wants a journey that leads somewhere other than to where it began. I suppose there's no reason it has to be me who brings the book back to the last departure point."

"I don't understand."

"Certainly you do," he said. "I don't know why, but I'm going to make another wager. Come back to this spot tomorrow, two days, three days, and see what happens. If I'm wrong, and my journey starts here, as most do, there will be a scene, or strong signs of the authorities doing what they can to hide one. I'll be with you, then, in a few days, to take back my book. But if I'm right, if this wager succeeds, there'll be nothing here to see. Then you should go to Damascus. In one year's time, at this exact time by the local clock, be at that park. You remember the location? Be there. And bring the book. Because if I'm successful in my wager about you, and I can't be sure I will but I'm sure, I'll have another entry for it."

He smiled at me. He drew a pistol from the inside of his jacket.

"No," I said.

"Death is a journey," he said.

He put the barrel of the revolver into his mouth and pointed up.

I tried to speak again. He fired.

My ears rang and dogs barked and I saw the flash light up his cheeks from the inside and flare them out as if he were a trumpet player and with wet smacks what had been within his head hit the wall behind us.

I heard my own screaming.

He stared at me. He adjusted the gun in his mouth, pointing in a slightly new direction. He fired again. And again, and again.

I backed away, watching him stagger as he poured bullets into his own head and I could hear more and more shouts and screaming from nearby, and he kept firing, and I began to run, and he slumped against the wall, and he withdrew the pistol from his blood-pouring mouth, and opened the chamber, reached into his pocket, his fingers shaking, drew out bullets and reloaded and snapped the chamber shut and put the barrel back into his mouth and began to fire again, gesturing with his free hand for me to go.

I ran.

And I came back two days later and the cobbles were stained with blood, and that was all.

I came back a day after that, and the blood was gone.

I waited another week, and another week, and two more, and no one has come to claim the notebook.

And my wife has told me I have gone mad, and that she will not come with me to Damascus.

EYE AND EYELESSNESS

DIANA STOOD OVER THE BODY, HER BREATH RUSHING, HER heartbeat fast and ragged. She kept her weapon up. Even with the little suppressor the shot had been as loud and ugly as a window breaking. She waited. A dog barked somewhere, but cheerfully enough. Blood pooled on the kitchen floor. The dead woman stared at the underside of a cabinet. Diana heard no cars approach, no oaths or shouts of concern.

She put her bag back on her shoulder, its new hole smoking. Her hands trembled. She'd never been good at this aspect of the work. She knelt and ran her hands quickly through the woman's pockets. Found nothing. She stood, took out her phone. Dialed B's main number.

It did not go to voicemail or ring, only sounded a hollow echo, of course, as usual. She disconnected. Diana stepped over the body, toward the door, and stopped.

She pulled out her phone again and considered her options. She dialed again and it connected on the second ring.

"Unite Cleaning."

"My name's Daisy," Diana said carefully, "and I have a spillage."

"What spilled?"

She glanced at the body.

"Red wine," she said.

"Where?"

She gave the address.

"What service do you require?"

"Full," she said. Exhaled shakily. "Deep scrub."

"Keys?"

"Standard," she said. "No alarms."

"Hazards?"

"Unknown."

"Fifty minutes."

The connection broke.

I'm not the one who changed my mind, I know the truth, Bennett/Plomer, had said, or something like that. I'm loyal.

Diana looked up the stairs. She thought of Keever and Caldwell. Both had searched around the LP.

I'm not brave, Diana thought. I'm a scientist, not an operator or a detective. I don't know what Keever and Caldwell were looking for. I need to get out of here.

She looked down at the dead woman.

It's true, what you said, about how you moved. No amount of CrossFit could do that.

She dialed Keever.

"Keever," she said when it connected. "It's Diana." She heard a commotion in the background. "Jim, I've known you for a while now, and I need to ask you something. I found out that you—"

"Diana!" Above noises of shouting and running, it was not Keever's voice, but B's.

"B? Thank God! I need to talk to you. You need to be careful. Is Keever there? He—"

"Shut up," she heard. "Keever's dead."

She gasped and her mouth worked.

"What happened?"

"One of your science projects got loose."

"What?" she whispered.

"Your patchwork puppet in the cellar woke up."

Her eyes widened and her left hand fluttered in front of her mouth.

"B, listen," she said. "It was never my project, I just—"

"I don't care," he shouted. "I don't care who stitched it together or that you wanted a more pliable me, but I do care that it . . ." It was rare to hear him hesitate. "It killed . . ."

"B," she managed to say. "It wasn't asleep, B, it was never alive. It can't have woken up. Caldwell could never fix that . . ."

There is someone with power over death, she heard in her head, in Plomer's voice, and her own voice ebbed.

"Tell that to the soldiers it's just ended," B said. "Tell that to Jim." The connection ended.

"WHERE DID IT GO?" B SAID. HE PUT KEEVER'S PHONE GENTLY BACK IN THE man's pocket.

The young soldier to whom B had directed his question stared at him with that awe B recognized.

"You were . . . you were fighting it, sir, you hit it, and it hit you, and it kept trying to get past you, and then it moved just too fast and—"

"Not trying to kill me? Trying to get past me?"

The man looked confused.

"That's what it looked like," he said.

Orderlies covered Keever's body with a sheet and wheeled him away.

B turned at the sound of firing from a few corridors away. The crumps of grenades.

"It didn't get out?" B said. "It's still here?"

He ran. Through these least secret of the secret hallways, past noticeboards with information about movie nights, pickup basketball, book groups. Through security doors and up, through the big cafeteria bright with daylight pouring in through high-up windows, below which Formica tables and chairs lay scattered and hunkered soldiers called and bled and the air smelled of shot.

"Where did it go?" he shouted.

He followed old blood and groaning soldiers through stairwells. He ran through the blare of information issuing from speakers, insistent screams, he overtook armed figures. Followed spoor. A random route, that of a panicked or desolate consciousness appalled at itself. These were admin blocks, now, meeting rooms, offices. The fleeing himself-thing had left the labs and the arsenals of the wetwork warriors behind.

B was alone for long corridors at a time.

In one of these upper hallways, three men were gathered around an injured comrade writhing on the ground, while a woman guarded them, a handgun in both hands, braced back hard against the wall near a junction. All five were in civilian clothes, but the woman covered them with expertise, and Unute saw pistols held as well in two of the men's hands.

"Thank God!" one man gasped at the sight of him.

The woman frantically made *Hold on* motions at him, then jerked her thumb to indicate *Around this corner*. From beyond it he saw the dappled light that came through trees, through an unseen window.

"Sir!" one of the men whispered. He was a tough young man with blood across his gray suit. "We thought it was you, at first. Then we . . . we saw . . . What is that thing?"

"How long?" Unute said.

"You . . . It came through about three, four minutes ago. Took a swing at Daniel." The man winced to look at his wounded fellow. "Simone got a few shots off but it just ignored them. Kept going past us, round that way."

He looked behind Unute, who glanced back to see a growing wetwork squad approaching, their rifles up and ready, their visors down. Unute put his hand behind him, palm out. The approaching squad froze.

"And?" he said.

"And it's still there," the woman said, looking past the corner. "I heard it stop. I can . . ." She swallowed. "I can see it. It's just . . . standing there."

Unute pointed at the woman and gestured for her too to stay back. He reached out and she gave him her pistol. He turned the corner.

At the end of the hallway that window onto vivid green. Between him and the gleam, close to the last flight of stairs up, stood that conglomerate mockery. Its back was to him, the staples, scars, and sutures straining on its slick skin. It swayed. Entranced, it seemed, by the light.

"What did you do?" B said quietly.

He raised the pistol to point it at the base of the scrapwork neck. He walked forward. His boots echoed through the hall. He fired.

The shot resounded, and the thing jerked, and swayed, and dark slime dripped from the bullet hole, but it did not fall.

"What did you do?" B said. Somewhere, what he felt was disappointment. Hurt.

It would have been good to be wrong about Caldwell. And about Diana.

"What do I call you?" he said to the thing's back. "Medley? Me? Unute 2? Franken-B, like Keever? I know, Frankenstein was the scientist not the monster, blah blah I've always been both. Which means you have too, right? How come you're here? What was it got you up?"

He put his hand on the thing's shoulder and turned it to face him. What B saw in the shattered reflection was bewilderment.

"You don't know, do you?" he said.

To which it swayed, was all. Swayed again, and something was missing in it.

And that look in its single eye saw not him but some emptiness, something nihil, the relief of ending.

He felt the shoulder he held slip, the arm fall away. He heard the sodden percussion of meat on the floor. The eye looked through him to an ending. And as he watched, the face, the chest, the other arm and the belly and the penis and hips and legs began to slide, coming apart along the seams and transforming in instants with the elegance of liquid from a crude sculpture of himself into a sliding cascade of black and red and the white of old bone and the slurry of antique organs, and in that moment as he stared at the last of its face, as its forehead dissolved, and both eye and eyelessness were gone, Unute saw that the nub that had broken the window was gone from its forehead.

"YOU DON'T UNDERSTAND," DIANA SAID. "I NEED TO GET IN. I NEED TO SEE Unute."

"Ma'am, I understand just fine," said the soldier at the passageway from the initial to the inner complex. She was tall and stood impassively blocking Diana's way. Plastic barriers had been erected across the walkway, and more soldiers stood by them at several points, having similar arguments with other non-military staff—including those, like Diana, of the highest rank.

"No one's answering my calls," Diana said.

"Lockdown, ma'am. All unauthorized signals are out." The whole base could be made a dampener, if necessary.

"Are you calling my phone calls unauthorized?" Diana said. The soldier shrugged.

"Soldier . . ." So close to her own office, Diana was growing agitated again. She could feel adrenaline swilling inside her. "Soldier," she said, "I take no pleasure in using this line for the first time in my life, but do you know who I am?"

"Yes ma'am. I do."

"So stand aside."

"Maybe I wasn't clear." Now it was the soldier's voice growing tight. "I know who you are, ma'am, I know you're Access-All. And I know what my orders are. Code Tau lockdown supersedes all other codes, and absent a direct in-person order from my direct OC, all other protocols remain suspended. I don't know much about what's going on, ma'am, because it's a lockdown, but what I do know is that some people, including, it sounds like, some friends of mine, are dead. So until I get a direct order to the contrary, ma'am, I'm going to do my job. Which means not letting anyone in. No disrespect, ma'am, but that includes you."

Diana turned, her lips trembling.

"Are you OK?" Diana said.

"Dr. Shur!" Diana said.

Shur came to her, her face creased with concern. "Do you have any idea what's going on?" Shur said.

Diana flapped her hand at the soldier.

"This person . . ." she said. Shur led her away, and Diana let her.

"I know," Shur said. Out of earshot of the guards, her voice grew more urgent. "It's been like this for hours," she said. "They're only letting uniforms through. I don't know what it's about."

"But I think I do," Diana said.

"Whatever's going on, you're not going to be any help to anyone if you're having a panic attack, Dr. Ahuja—"

"For Christ's sake I am not having—"

"Please don't look at me like that. You're not far off. This is literally my job. Come to my office. One advantage of being a support worker with basic clearance: my room's not in any trouble zones."

Diana let her lead again.

In the consulting room, Shur gestured for Diana to sit and brought her water from the cooler. Shur sat, too, not behind her desk but at a chair close to Diana's. She waited while Diana drank and took deep breaths. "OK," Shur said. "Tell me what's going on."

"I mean, isn't it obvious?" Diana said, and gestured back the way they had come. "There's a crisis and I need to get in—"

Shur narrowed her eyes. "There's something else, too," she said.

Diana took another long sip.

"You're good," she said after a while. "I killed someone today."

Shur nodded slowly.

"I thought perhaps that might be it," she said. "Your first time?"

"In this field?" Diana shook her head. A brief image of a collapsing would-be assassin went through her mind, her first time, a cleaner headshot, a more clear-cut business. "But only my second. I didn't like it then and I don't like it now."

"I'd be worried if you did," Shur said. "OK. Let's take a moment. We'll find out what's going on soon."

"I've already found out more than I want to know," Diana said.

"And I need to tell B what I know." She hesitated, then said, "Keever's dead."

Shur nodded.

"I know," she said. "Word gets out. He was a good man." More silence. "Listen, if you want to talk about it, whatever it is that's happening, what you've found out, it won't go any further. This is what I do."

"Yeah?" Diana said. "Like Stonier's sessions don't go any further?"

"Come on, that's different," Shur said.

"How come?"

"You're more senior."

Despite herself, Diana smiled.

"I'm asking because . . . Keever had been talking to me, you know," Shur said. "About Stonier." She hesitated at the sight of Diana's expression. "I thought that's what you were getting at, about finding things out."

"I knew he was looking into things, I didn't know he talked to you," Diana said. "What did he want to talk about?"

"Stonier and the Life Project," Shur said.

Silence again.

"What do you think's been going on?" Diana said. She let Shur struggle to find an answer. "I've never known exactly what you know about Unute but you've got to have the basics. What do you think is going on with him?"

"I don't know," Shur said. "I try not to wonder too much. I stick to my own work. I don't know anything about him or how he thinks."

"Isn't it your job to read people?"

"People," Shur said. "Exactly."

Diana appraised her. "You probably realized a long time ago that it's my job to figure out what he is," Diana said. "Sometimes he likes to . . . I think of it as him teasing me. He tells me he is a god after all and I tell him no he's not." For a while she'd wondered what the source of her pain was in those exchanges. Now, it came to her that it was hard to see him, to see anyone, strive to be beyond caring, and to care so much. As when someone asks for help by saying, You cannot help me.

"I go around a whole gamut of theories. A mutation. An alien. A tool. A weapon. An agent of change. At least I'm not talking about a god."

"But?" Shur said quietly.

"But. But I met someone today who definitely believed we are talking about a god. And she gave a pretty good argument."

"What was it?" Shur said. "A good argument that this is about gods?"

Diana looked up at her. "Gods'?"

"Isn't that what you said?" Shur said.

"What I said," Diana said, "was 'a god.' Why would you think she was talking about gods plural?"

Shur's face stayed still. "I guess . . ." she said at last, and then she sighed.

and she was in front of Diana, then, her forefinger to Diana's lips, and at the touch of her, Diana's limbs went stiff and cold. Shur's whisper went deep into Diana's ears.

"Whoever heard," Shur said, "of there being only one god?"

ACCORDING TO MOTION-REC SOFTWARE, THE PHONEMES THE FRANKEN-B had been shaping with its lips as it rose through the compound might have been the word "Why?" in a tumbling torrent of languages. All as silent as were B's own words now.

It feels like we should have learned something from each other, B said without sound. I told someone once that you can't choose not to be a metaphor. And here I am, staring at a me, made of eighty millennia of discards. That's got to be a freighted scene, right? And for the life of me—heh—I have no idea what it means. What you and I mean.

So how can that be a metaphor?

Even as he thought that, he knew he was wrong. Just because he did not know what it meant, just because it was contradictory, opaque, did not mean metaphor failed. Such moments might be its vindication.

He turned and looked expectantly at the operator of the workstation behind him.

"I'm running over the data from when it was in its tank," she said. "We still can't get anything on how . . . on why it . . ." He saw her glance in the direction of the cylinder in which the thing's collapsed remains were again stagnating. "The last person to do any work on it was Caldwell." She squinted. "A few times. But nothing happened. Then, the last time he came in, energy was flowing in. Through some kind of focus. I've never seen readings like this before." She shook her head. "I don't know what he did."

"A focus," Unute said.

He left. He wandered.

Oh look he found his way to the regeneration pod of the babirusa. He entered, put his hand on the egg, and felt the movement within. He went out, and on again, past crews who nodded at or saluted him or turned away in nervousness. He did not consider where he was going.

B took staircases up. He sought solitude. Walked for a long time within the more secluded and locked-down sections of the complex.

He proceeded at very last along a deserted topmost story, where he had not been for some while.

Why am I here? he asked himself.

A window at the hall's end overlooked the forest. He was in roughly the same section wherein his mimic had fallen apart, a few corridors over, and down.

Oh, right, he answered himself.

He slowed a little, only thoughtful, not hesitant. Up through more locked-down hallways.

I guess it would be nice to understand, he thought. Maybe if you understand something you can stop it. He looked at his own hands. You don't always get to become what you want to be. And sometimes you start off as something you'd rather not be. Maybe you can never understand that . . . but maybe you can. And maybe that helps. Maybe that might change things.

He made his way at last to the room from which, he understood now, someone would have come running to intercept the composite him where it had stopped on its way up, called somehow in this direction, from the laboratory. There to reach out, take something from its forehead, steal back to this chamber for which Unute was heading now, with its roof space overhead, its cameraless approach, its triple security, a room no one would dare come to without authorization. Which he reached and entered now, as dusk approached.

His office.

It was empty. He did not sit at the desk but took the lamp and slid into the darkness in the corner of the room, and waited, and waited, wondering lightly what it was he was thinking.

There he stayed for a long time, imagining the blaring sounds without, the screams of "Where'd he go?"

What he found himself considering was a revelation offered to him in blood, and obscured so he could not receive it, millennia ago.

He faced his own desk. He stood with his back against the door. Unute waited a long time.

WAS IT MIDNIGHT WHEN B HEARD A NEW SOUND ABOVE HIM?

He stayed silent. He watched the panel slide away, fingers emerging from the revealed darkness. Saw arms brace. Saw them tense, and haul, and the body of a man swing down into the unlit room and tumble in without sound.

A silhouette rose and moved toward the desk.

The man did not move when B turned on the light and pointed it at him. He only blinked and put his hand in front of his eyes.

B said, "Hello, Caldwell."

B ACK DOWN INTO DARK.

What is this feeling that rises within you?

The world is infinitely older than are you, and you are sure creation is infinitely older than the world. Your own life is only a fingernail less minute than are the spans others are allowed. Every feeling you have ever felt is a wrestling with its obverse, an entangled war. This, now, as you walk through the rock tunnels you last trod many years and a body ago, is relief, eagerness, anguish, and lament.

You stop at junctions you remember. You can hear only dripping.

New life has made this tellurian kingdom its own. Mottled glowing fungus on the stone. Perhaps you brought their spores in on your breath on your first ingress: perhaps after all the barren years, all the cold gray ragdoll-dangling babies, this is the only life you will ever usher in, your only child the luminous energies of rot.

All these halls are empty. Not even ghosts for you to visit. Lift your torch, let oily shadows explore. You were unconscious when you were dragged from here to the torture chamber, the execution chamber. So you take each dark tunnel one by one. Walk slowly; nothing will come past you. Take as long as you like, for this investigation. This revenge.

So, you are not above revenge. Very well.

These are channels. For days, you press on. Track your way.

You hear nothing that whole time. But when finally you push through black slits narrow enough to make this an inverse birth into a pillar of moonlight you have seen before, moonlight that descends from a split above to glint on metal veined in the walls around you, as you crawl upon an oxidizing pile of ancient chains, you are in a morass of sticklike desiccated bones, a mulch of your own remains, overlaid scores of long-rotted bodies. And it is no surprise to you that you are not alone, not even counting your dead selves.

A woman sits upon a throne of those cold and ruined chains.

She does not move as you stumble to your feet. Her gown was white once, is streaked and filthy now with lifetimes' muck. She holds something you cannot make out. Only when she tosses it to the stone and it cracks wetly can you make out that it was half a clay mask.

This woman has dark hair and eyes as sad as others have told you yours are.

"Hello again," she says. "Brother." Her voice is quiet. "I knew we hadn't killed you. You took longer than I thought you would. Listen."

She stands. Her eyes widen, then, because you do not say a word, and only swing your arms and leap straight as a spear at her. She moves as fast as you but your fists hit her chest like a battering ram against a city wall and hurl her into jagged rock and she twists as she impacts the stone and takes the blow and pushes off again into the dim with inhuman grace, new dirt upon her shroud.

You brace for her counterattack. She does not move.

Careful now. You feint, duck left slide right and lunge but she side-steps and you go past her.

She stands still.

So you attack again and she says nothing and you come close to connecting but she is never there when your knuckles go by and you bite down hard enough to hurt your teeth and it has been a long time since you have felt a rising tide of actual anger and what it brings yes, here is that glow, the blue glow, the trance light, and your self withdraws within you, at last, receding behind eyes like windows, and you hear the roar of your own ecstasy and your own voice spitting out, This is my berserk, and You'll die now.

Wake up, Berserker.

You stand to the wheeze of your own bloody breath, amid the piles of body parts.

It's a daylight shaft that comes down through the hole above now. There is the woman. She stands with her palms flat against the wall. She does not look afraid.

"You're quite the dancer," you say as your energy returns.

She says, "I won't fight you."

"That's up to you," you say. "But I'll fight you."

Try again. Punch hard enough to sink a ship. She is gone when the fist connects and your hand splinters with the flint.

"Was it years?" you call. "Or centuries? That you tortured me?"

You dance amid your mummies and smears. She's always an inch beyond you.

"And you've never tortured anyone?" she calls back. "I'd have done it differently if I could. But please, listen to me."

"What are you?" you shout.

andbut

to ask that, to see her face at the question, a readiness, an eagerness, her mouth begin to open, to answer you, is to know, though not why, that you do not want to hear it

so

and so

here it comes, your phase again, you go quickly into your fugue before she speaks, her face falling to see you succumb, and there's a new sense to the sensation, a new frustration, because it has not been sated, her blood is still in her, and you're howling because all you've done is break yourself and rocks and that won't still the hunger of your thanatic trance

oh in and of hellven joygany miserecstasy

pullpushgougebite

be fought and fight

time rushes it must be the last days and

you make yourself yourself

see your clawed hand rip at not hers but your own face and time is perfectly still forever and ever and ever and ever and this happens this occurs to sluice through you in release your violent investigations against these features like your own, your self,

you

blink and feel your breath slow

have let you go," she is saying as you emerge

She is untouched.

The noise you make is strangulation, grief, hunger still unabated.

"What fucking are you?" you shout again. As if you would hear her response.

"I'm trying to say," she says. As if she's begging. "I would have let you go. As soon as I understood. I should have known when the guards, when the constructs didn't react. As soon as I knew I'd been lied to. It was never your pain I wanted, I just sought to end you, and that without hate. We were both lied to."

"All I wanted was to find you!" you shout. "I've been so lonely."

That surprises you.

"Me too," she says. "Please listen." Immediately you run at her but she will not stop speaking. "When you died and didn't hatch we thought we'd done what we came here to do, found just the right modulation of the energies, or achieved enough years of violence against your body. But I felt nothing inside, and I realized you'd woken somewhere else. That's when I began to understand I'd been lied to, but at first I got the lie wrong. Before I knew that, I'd sent I don't know how many children, breathing and not, into the world telling them to keep trying. But no matter my guilt about anything I can't even end myself. So listen—"

She opens her mouth to tell you the truth she wants to tell you and alarm fills you again, and for the third time in an hour? a day? a week? eighty years? your thought submerges in the roaring tide of fight blood, and your sight fades out

and this time when you wake you're on your knees. Sapped, dribbling from mouth and nose. And your erstwhile captor is on her knees too, by choice.

"Please," she says. "I have that in me, too," she says. "That energy'll drive you mad if you let it. I've had longer to work on it. But you have to try to control it, now."

"The pig," you say at last. "Like me. It found you."

"Many times," she says. "It's more like me, too, than I'd once thought. I always knew I was the nemesis of entropy, and is it so foolish to think that's death?" She stands. You grip stone. "I knew you'd come back," she says. "I set out to learn the real truth in time, so I could be here for you, waiting, because you deserve—"

You swing your hand and wrench rock up out of the earth too fast for her to dodge this time and her blood explodes from her. She turns her half-face to you and hisses.

"Are you mad?" she bubbles. "Listen to me—"

Quickly! quickly! bring it back!

It's back, thank gods!, the riastrid blue, the force that pushes the flower to grow, the seas to roam, that pushes you to kill and kill, it is unweakened, oh that relief, it is drowning her out, and you're wailing like the wolves that fear you, telling her in your wordless way that you'll not let her go unpunished and that whatever she is you'll end her and whatever she has to say you will not listen.

She's screaming too.

"Stop it!" you faintly hear. "You're doing this to yourself! Don't you want to . . .?"

And a part of you would say yes, sit and hear her, but you came here for the violence that flows, so let that take over, stop up your ears.

". . . lied to!" she's screaming, ". . . you and I . . ." but you're less and less there to parse any such information, ". . . was told to . . ." and you don't care what she was told, by whom

"Stay!" she shouts. "Don't be a coward! Don't fugue—"

and this time

as you stare into the chamber

from behind that blue light of your eyes

the last thing you make out

as you surrender to berserker trance

is such light glimmering in hers, too.

to wake yet again
but with a new feeling.

A feeling of you. Look down, you think you'll see the sodden slip of bloodslime and the flawlessness of a new body, an egg. That she, Vayn, has killed you in that last fight, and another cycle started. That you are elsewhere.

But you still wear your stinking clothes. But your body is still marked with the little accumulated scars and abrasions that, according to whatever rules there are, will not be healed this time around. You have not little-died.

For the first time, you look across the floor at the atomies and remains. The chamber is dense with the remnants of sagging sacs that once held you, a nidus of empty eggs, from which you turn your face, the number of which you will not count.

You have not been reborn, so how then can you feel as you do? Strong? Very alive, so renewed, so vim-full, so vigorous? Where is she? Is there one more relic here than egg?

Vayn is nowhere. You are alone.

Quickly. You sink to your knees below the hole. You crawl in a spiraling circle, running your hands over the ground and through all your remains, feeling for evidence that she was here, that anyone but a thousand yous were here before. There's blood on your palms, though they are not cut.

Your memory is without flaw. But though you don't forget, you must wonder what happens when your mind goes too far to make memories at all, and if some of those you do have are of things that did not happen.

Was Vayn here? Don't look back now. Were there bodies?

Above the crawlway through which you entered you see a streak of your blood.

You stare at it, you are familiar with the sprays of wounds and this has no business being where or the shape it is. You make out strokes, where fingers have smeared it on the wall.

Letters.

We are, it says, visible to those who know how blood dries, in a hand you don't know, in an ancient alphabet. What follows that, the object of that verb, though, is too thick, too clotted, too dripped, too smeared, too obscured and effaced to make out.

You cannot know what Vayn's message was. Is it just this? That you are, that she is? Or did she write an answer to a question, something she intended you to know, that she was shouting as the tide of fightness overcame you? She wrote it in the only ink she had. And then, and you cannot know why, she must have smeared out what she had written.

Punished you with ignorance. And then she left. Left you. And left you alone.

And you get out. And you seek her, a bit. It feels like a duty. At which—the knowledge is there and you'll neither deny nor dwell upon it—you don't wish to succeed.

So you look for Vayn for centuries but she has gone, and you can breathe out. After several lives of searching you stop. And after more lifetimes you stop searching, too, for her children, you'll let them come to you if come they will, and you stop your hunt, as well, for any other children of your own lightning father, as you do for those of her father or mother or motherfather, who hated yours, it seems, or for those of any gods at all, because you grow to be sure that you are the only one, and anyway you don't care, or care to know, and underneath it all is always the vorago, watching, claiming you, underneath it all is the silence of ash.

AN INSECT CRAWLED

CALDWELL MADE AN UGLY MOTION. IN THE FAINT LIGHT FROM outside and below, his face was very drawn. He spasmed.

"Hello, Caldwell," B said again.

Caldwell's lips worked, faster and faster, as if what B saw was the recitation of some long soliloquy.

"Hello, Unute," Caldwell said at last. His voice emerged from the unceasing twitches of his mouth.

"What are you looking for, Caldwell? You're confused, aren't you?"

"Unute," Caldwell said. "Unute." His lips kept moving.

"It never made much sense," Unute said. "You get in, in kind of a state according to the guards, do whatever it was you did to wake up your patchwork doll, then—*someone leaves*, but there's no sign of you anywhere." He shrugged. "So obviously it wasn't you who got out. I think there are things here you still had to look for, maybe. I think we both know you're under orders. Not many people could have broken back in from outside with the base under lockdown, but if you were already here? Someone else drove out—someone who came in in your trunk? So you just had to get back to a secure room inside, where no one would bother. And you knew just the room."

"Well well." Caldwell said. His jaw worked and he took a deep breath. "I admit not see you this a matter chance or made a sense of has would grateful help I don't I'm thinking clearly as I to think maybe I and came back and frightening to can help think you can stand against time is now help afraid."

Caldwell's eyelids were blurring open and shut, as fast as were his lips. He seemed to be listening for instructions.

"You don't know what you want anymore, do you?" Unute said. "Or what it is that you're being asked to want. Instructed."

"Confused," Caldwell said.

"Sure," Unute said. "I'm not going to call anyone. Because the thing is, I'm tired of this. And I don't know what's going to happen now, so it's just you and me. I want you to take me to whatever's telling you what to do."

"Confusing," Caldwell said, "to die."

"Yes it is," Unute said. "Even more confusing to come back, right?"

He reached but Caldwell moved faster, shoving Unute open-handed with a strength far greater than he should have and sending Unute flying across the room to the floor.

"Well damn," Unute said when he could. "You've come back different."

He rose, shoved Caldwell back. Impossibly quick, Caldwell braced, stopped himself from falling.

"Where's your controller?" Unute said. He put his hands up in a wrestling pose. "Did they come in with you? Hiding in the back? You think because you came back once you can keep on doing it? Do you want to risk that?"

But he gasped, because Caldwell stepped forward and smacked him in the chin and got back out of his range again.

"Tell me," Unute said. "Or I'll take you apart like you took apart your doll."

Caldwell blinked.

"Yeah," Unute said. "All that effort to wake it up, and then the moment you did, you get told to send it back to sleep. Permanently, this time. That must have stung." He took a step forward. "It sucked, right? You didn't want to do that. You took away what woke it up. After I fetched it for you. Where did you put it?"

Caldwell straightened up. His face went slack. He opened his mouth. Stuck his tongue out, pointed it right at Unute. At the very tip, a sliver of hard white flesh, slick with his spit.

"There you go," Unute said. "There it is.

"There's the egg tooth."

HE REACHED.

As his thumb and forefinger touched Caldwell's tongue, Unute heard a scuttling and a crash behind him, an impact, but before he could turn Caldwell brought his teeth together into the meat of Unute's hand.

Unute hissed with surprise and yanked but the bite held. Unute saw his blood on Caldwell's mouth. He swung with his left hand to break that jaw, but Caldwell caught the punch and twisted, and a gust of something passed through the room and Unute lost himself for a moment, came back to hear Caldwell make a sound, could have been "Now!"

Someone came from behind and slipped a noose around Unute's wrists, together as they were up in front of Caldwell's face, and yanked hard with a ratchet sound, Caldwell stepped back and here was another such at Unute's ankles, drawing them together. He fell to his knees, and looked up.

Black uniforms, balaclavas up, ranged around him, Unit soldiers. Unute strained.

The thick cordlike ties around his arms and legs creaked. He tugged at them and they seemed to tighten and tremble as the space in their vicinity shimmered with their unorthodox planar properties. He heard himself growl, bunched his muscles.

"You've improved these," he said at last, and let his arms slump. The ceiling hatch through which these others had followed Caldwell dangled open. The man who had slipped the Fenrir's bonds around his wrists stood over him, pulled the covering from his face, and stared into Unute's eyes.

"Stonier," Unute said.

Four figures moved, weapons leveled at him. Unute felt his breath change, the rhythm of rising riastrid.

This, this sense, the proximity of the fight, sent him spinning back to a cave, and of all the thousands of times he had lost himself to this frenzy why was it that time, that moment that came to him?, and oh, yes, it was, he knew, a proximity of opposites, because that was when he had striven to tip himself into it, to slip out of time, just as fiercely as he struggled to control himself now, to remain here. He clenched his teeth hard enough that a molar split, pinning himself into consciousness.

"I'll make you a deal," he managed to gasp as his muscles twitched. Everyone was still. "You think I won't get out of these?" he said. "You know I will. Shoot me and you'll only piss me off. Even if you get really, really lucky and put me down you'll just delay me for a while, is all. And I'll come back for you. Caldwell. Who brought you back? I want to make them a deal."

No one spoke.

"What's your endgame?" Unute said. "Whoever you are, I know you came here to finish me off, forever, which is . . ." He shook his head. "But you should hear me out. Whatever special plan you think you have to kill me, you want to know what I have to offer. And look." He sat up. He brought his knees quietly up and showed them his wrists. "I'm not resisting. I'm sitting quietly. Quiet as the grave. You stop listening, I start fighting. Even trussed up, that won't be fun for you. So there's an easy way or a hard way for you to try out your plan. Who was it brought you back, Caldwell? I want to talk to them."

A man stepped forward. He let the rifle hang by its strap over his shoulder. He lifted his mask. He was older, with a kind, lined face, and gusting blond hair. He met Unute's eyes.

"My name's Alam."

"Yeah," Unute said. "I met your mother."

"OR," HE SAID, "MAYBE YOUR GRANDMOTHER, OR YOUR GREAT-GRAND-mother, or your great-great. I don't know. Do you know?"

Alam did not move.

"How much of all this do you know, Caldwell?" Unute said. "Can you even understand me? Can he?" he asked Alam.

"You're death," Alam whispered. He did not sound energized with hate. He sounded almost as if he were dreaming. "It's been so long," he said. "You're the enemy, and we're here to end you."

"Your whatever-mother was on a mission to kill me too," Unute said to him. "I get that a lot. She hurt me badly for a long time. And then . . . Then she stopped. Maybe she decided there was nothing she could do to me. In the end, she just gave up and left. And now you . . . Her kid or grandkid or whatever is back on the mission."

Alam said, "I didn't know. For lifetimes. Not until a few years ago. Someone unlocked me. Before that? You might find it hard to believe how strong denial is. I'm part of Life's lineage. I just kept on living, changing IDs when I had to, and I just didn't think about it. I didn't need to. My wife would have noticed, if things hadn't changed. My last wife, my best wife. She was with me when I was told about my bloodline. Why I'm here. It made sense. Of my life, and hers."

"The last time I saw the pig," Unute said, "before this time, I mean, I thought maybe we'd turned a corner. I thought it might have reached a new peace. How did you find it, Alam?"

"A lot of effort. I've been following it."

"To find me," Unute said. "Did you do something to it to make it want to find me again? Or was it tracking me anyway?" He sounded plaintive to himself. He looked into Stonier's eyes as he spoke to Alam. "That's how you found Thakka," he said.

"Was it deliberate, Alam?" he said. "Or are you a little out of control, sometimes? It was a mistake, wasn't it. You didn't mean to bring Thakka back to life—life just kind of spills out of you sometimes like death spills out of me, right? But no reason not to use it. You got Thakka to tell you . . . where we are. So you come to Tacoma. Then what? You couldn't keep Thakka alive?" He looked at Caldwell. "It looks like you've gotten better since then."

"I've had help. I've had a focus."

"Of course," Unute said. "Yes. Well I hope so for Caldwell's sake." He looked at the consternation on Caldwell's face. "Is his body still hurt? How long does it take to fix? It's got to be hard, your first time. Thakka was your first time, making it happen, wasn't it, Alam?"

"First time with flesh."

"No wonder he was so confused. First him. Then we found so much of your blood, Caldwell: no one said it but you had to be dead. And here you are. And that patchwork thing waking up. Life where it shouldn't be? This has been bringing to mind stuff I haven't thought of for centuries. I'd call them mysteries but are they still mysteries if I didn't care what the secrets were? I was never in the decoding business. Things like that have started to matter a little more since Ulaf-son. I figured that whatever had poured life into Thakka had done it into your funhouse-mirror me, too, but then I saw it up close. Thakka was because of Alam following the pig to find me. And I know you were trying to use the pig's energy to bring your puppet to life, Caldwell, but you couldn't have woken that thing like that. That was never alive in the first place. Just the residue of deaths. That needed that last scrap you found, Caldwell. That you had me bring you." Unute extended his right forefinger. "Here's its equivalent on this body," he said. "It doesn't normally come off, I guess, just kind of ebbs back into the body. This is the caruncle I must have used to rip myself out, last time."

He tapped it, tough fingertip against his thumb.

"This," he said, "is what's left of my last egg tooth. What you had me find for you was its like, an old one. One of the rarities that came off. I think I know from which lode, too. That's what you pushed into that slurry that you managed to convince was me, Caldwell. That's what woke it. With some help from your new friends."

The egg tooth. Life-giving jag. The hard spur—true tooth, keratin, nail, matted skin—with which a baby bird, a baby frog, a snake, a spider, a monotreme breaks the container, its tool to emerge into new life. To be absorbed back into the body. Or to fall from it. Residue. A rejectamentum of the hatching.

"A babirusa doesn't need one," B said. "Not with those tusks. But soft little me, it turns out, could do with the help." He sighed. "You came down from my office and took it from the quiltwork's forehead. And took that life away." Like Rabbi Loew rubbing at EMET on the golem's forehead, leaving only MET. From Truth to Dead. "Why do you want it, Alam? You found out Caldwell had it, sent him to get it from his experiment. Help you control yourself? Focus? It was you who brimmed into it, wasn't it, newly primed? It was you who sent Caldwell to get it, right?"

"It'll help me channel," Alam said. "It isn't easy, you know. I had to know it worked. He'd already deployed it. And then when I came to see?" He raised his eyebrows. "I'm still learning." He clenched his fist and glimmers of light seemed to pass over his skin and he made a rueful expression. "With the tooth having started the work, when I got close my bloodline woke the thing right up."

Think of what such a tooth does! Splitting the skin of the cocoon, that liminal place, to push out of unlife into life again. How could it be a surprise that it would shove you or the broken echo of you that last little way into these lands of breath?

"Caldwell, you'd done a good job making me skeptical of gods," Unute said. "I'd been coming toward your way of thinking, I'm a tool, blah blah. Deployed by something that wants things to keep moving. To alter things.

"But this changes things, doesn't it? Looks like we were both suckers. It's one thing that there are people out there who think I'm the god of death and hate me—that's old news. But then it turns out that they're pledged to another god, that that god is your father's enemy, that the child of that god, or that child's child, is here, and they have powers, after all the millennia you wasted looking for any such thing . . . You have no idea," Unute whispered, trembling with an emotion he could not name, "what it is to find that out. To hear that they actually can bring life."

He held his breath until it came out smooth again.

"So," he said. "Let's say that I am, in fact, born of Death. Death's enemy is Life. And Life also has a child. Vayn. And she could have children. Of course. She's life, I'm . . . not. I don't know how you do what you do, Alam. What energies you tap. You can bring people back to life. Maybe you *can* kill death. And the truth is, I am tired, I am truly tired of people dying." He surprised himself with that, and with the relief of saying it. How good to be surprised. "I know why you're here," he said to Stonier. "You're right to be angry. I'm sorry."

Unute looked at each of the soldiers, slowly.

"I don't know who you all are but I'm sorry," he said. "Whoever it was I took from you. I know you've been hurt by death. By me." He gathered himself. "What happened to the bereaved who didn't accept your invitation, Stonier? Ask him," he said to the others. "Ask him what he would have done if you'd said no. Ask him where Joanie Miller is." By the time the last word was out of him, he was past anger again. He watched the soldiers look one to the other. They did not lower their weapons. "Maybe you expect me to fight you," he said at last. "I would, too. But I'm very tired." He sighed.

"So, I'm going to offer you a deal, Alam," he said. "I don't think you can kill me. But I know you'll take your shot, whatever it is. And here's my promise: I'll lie there like a lamb. I won't fight. I'll let you do exactly what you want."

Unute did not say, I do not think you can kill me but what if you can? What if you can bring silence? No more of all this death. My own or others. And then there's this: even if you can't end me outright, what if you can bring life deserving the name? Can you end immortality?

"To get me to cooperate," he said, "all you have to do is kill death one more time. In one more person."

THEY BROUGHT A GURNEY. THEY PUT HIM IN A BODY BAG, THE BONDS STILL

securing him. Zipped it all the way up but for a slit for his eyes. Hidden, he strained his arms. He felt the complex structures of the shackles strain, strain hard, alter uneasily, hold.

The faces of his companions were hidden, but Unute could see the glances passing between them as he lay on the stretcher.

"This wasn't the plan, was it?" he said. They avoided his gaze, all but one tall man who would not look away. "This wasn't how it was going to go down." They were looking to Alam.

"If you move," Alam said, "in the bag . . ."

"Then you'll do what?" Unute said.

Alam turned from Unute to face Caldwell, who met his stare with an intense stare of his own, his body trying out a hundred tiny motions, as if controlled by something quite unused to such a machine. Alam held his hand up and out.

After a moment, Caldwell slowly extended his tongue again. Alam reached out and plucked the skin fleck from its tip. Closed his fist on it and turned back to Unute.

"If you move," Alam said to him, "I won't do what you ask."

"If I wanted to raise an alarm by now, don't you think I would have?" Unute said. "Isn't it me telling you where to go? Where you won't be disturbed? So you can do this?"

Alam tilted his head. "Why?" he said quietly.

Wouldn't it be a trip if it's you who gets me what I've been after all this time? And Unute actually gasped, then, as Alam pulled the zipper up around him, because just as if he'd spoken those words aloud, Alam nodded, slowly, and narrowed his eyes, and something came across his face that looked to Unute like pity.

As she lay still, he heard a whisper, right up close, by his ear, through the bag. A new voice.

"Her name was Bree. I'm her father and I want to hurt you very fucking much. So please move."

Motion. Long corridors. The hiss of elevator doors. More hallways. Footsteps approaching. No change in the rhythm of the wheels beneath him. Stonier's voice: "Jacobs, Denton," answering grunts, receding steps as they pushed on.

Was this what it was like when his body reknit? In this enclosure? In this enclosure?

Another elevator ride. The gurney slowed.

"Delivery," he heard Stonier say. "And we're here to relieve you."

"We can't—" a woman replied.

"We have orders," said another. "There's been a lockdown—"

"Why do you think a combat unit's here?" Stonier said. "You're in danger. Get to your assembly point and wait for instructions."

When their footsteps were gone, he heard Stonier say, "I'll go kill the feed."

Sounds of another door, a hiss, cold, the percussions of steel.

A very long time of nothing at all. Could he play, Unute wondered, like this, at being conscious in his egg, as he never was? In his enclosed darkness, on his way between, a moment's intense claustrophilia, that cosseting otherwise denied him.

The bag opened.

Unute sat up and shook himself free of the cocoon. Looked into the glaring lights and reflections of the morgue.

His abductors—if that was the word, given his voluntary presence— were stationed ready around the room. One of them pulled a balaclava off Caldwell's staring face.

The tall man, the one who had whispered to Unute, tapped buttons, and the wall of windows that granted a view onto the corridor polarized, became mirrors from without.

Alam ran his fingers along the handles to the refrigerator drawers.

"You be careful," Unute said.

Alam brought his hand to a stop on the one marked KEEVER, J.

"Careful," Unute said. Alam pulled it open. Drew back the sheet covering what lay within. Looked down on Keever's gray face.

Alam met the dead man's gaze, then Unute's, with a quizzical look.

"You owe him," Unute said. "He told me. It was him who checked you out, recommended you to Shur. He'd heard the rumors of what you could do. I think he hoped, even though he didn't believe." He should have believed but not hoped.

"Is that what you think?" Alam said. "That he found us? It isn't that hard, you know," he said, "to put ideas in people's heads. And make them think they've thought of them."

Unute's eyes narrowed, but he turned then at the opening door, at Stonier's voice.

"Feed's dealt with," Stonier said. "But there's a complication."

Behind him was Dr. Shur. Unute felt a tug, a shift about him at the sight of her. Shur looked at him with vast hatred. She pushed a wheelchair. On it, breathing, bloody, her eyes moving wildly, her breath sputtering past a gag, was Diana.

"GET HER OUT OF HERE," UNUTE SAID. HE BROADENED HIS CHEST AND FELT the bonds tight about his wrists. "She has nothing to do with this."

"When I got out of the signal-dampening zone I had a message," Stonier said to Alam. "I've filled Shur in."

Diana hummed, frantically.

Shur gestured at Diana. "She knows something," she said.

"Why didn't you just take care of her?" Alam said.

"Because we need to know who she's told what," Shur said.

"Let her go," Unute said. "Or I'm no longer quiet."

After a silence, Shur took a pistol from her pocket and placed the barrel against Diana's temple. Diana chewed on the cloth in her mouth.

"Now look," Shur said. "The deal's back on."

"You think you can threaten me with someone's death?" Unute said. He felt as if an insect crawled through his clothes. "If you don't kill her she'll be dead in a moment, anyway. Sixty years at the most. Do you have any notion how short a time that is? You think it would make any difference to me? And you said yourself, you need to know what she knows and who she's told."

"I'd like to, yes," Shur said. "But if we have to prioritize matters . . ."

A look of excitement so lubricious it shocked him went across her face. "Because I can't believe how close we are to the end of it. To the death of death. So I'd like to question her, yes, but if it gets tricky?" She shrugged. "And to your first point." She would not look at him. He could see her hate was too intense. "I don't know what pangs of conscience have gotten you to this point," she said. She gestured at his bonds. "This deal . . . Nothing's more important than this, so do what you've promised, and think about this—we don't need to kill her afterward. I think you know we'd rather not if we don't have to. And let me add." Now she managed to look at him. "If you make me shoot her, it's you who'll have killed her."

Unute felt another tug as if from within him, a spasm. He saw something in Shur far from Alam's stern purpose.

"I don't care what you do with that guy," Shur said, gesturing at the refrigerator drawers, "so long as we fulfill the mission."

"You promise me," Unute said to Alam, "that you'll keep her alive."

They were all motionless in the silver of that chamber, in its chill, its reflections of blades and bulbs. Underneath the sounds of metal, Unute heard cloth as Diana shook her head. He heard her struggle to speak. Alam gave what might have been a nod.

"Now do what you promised," Unute said after a moment. He gestured with his restrained arms. "Kill his death. Then you can try what you want."

Alam stared into the cold drawer.

"You're not without honor, Death," Alam said at last. "There was no one to explain why I kept not dying. I just kept on until Shur found me, told me who I am."

He unclenched his hand. Kept his thumb and forefinger together, as if he positioned a tack between them. Held his hand, with the gripped speck, above Keever's motionless face.

"I'm the end of death," he said.

He brought the egg tooth down on Keever's cold forehead. Touched Keever's face with his other hand. Whispered, "Live."

From every corner came sound like faint bells. The flasks and beakers and tiny blades, the retorts and stands trembled, a dance of objects. Unute half-closed his eyes against a light, coming up, light in that too-light room, a glowing growing where Alam's hand touched Keever's face. A crackling blue-white shine.

The fluorescent lights went off, came on again.

And light rushing through, taking Unute back to those arcs along the metal in walls beneath the earth, and the current poured out of Vayn's however-many-times child and into Jim Keever's body, and that body snapped and jerked, danced like the metal of the room, drummed its heels, noise rising out of him, and as the lightning went in, the sound changed from the lifeless gasp of escaping gas to the cry of a man, and

Keever sat up.

Somewhere, B heard Diana's straining breath, her spit and hack. Keever stared. Little arcs of blue light spasmed along his limbs. He opened his mouth wide at the sight of Unute. He let out a gasp.

"OK," Unute said. "You really can do it. Wow. Hello, Jim."

Keever stumbled from the drawer, staggered, naked, shivering, his expression between vision and pain. He spoke in a rattling voice like chains on concrete.

"Hey happened to?" he said. "Where've I feel like all the in, and come out do hurt alive. Can that be know died, I are you did you help? Unute. Thank you son."

Unute strained again. The quantum-fritzed latticework did not break. It felt so strange to be so held.

"Happened?" Keever said. Stonier took hold of him gently, led him to a corner of the room.

"OK?" Alam said.

B breathed out.

"OK. Keep him alive."

Alam came forward. "Let's see how honorable you are," he said. He did not look afraid.

And Unute found something in submission.

I'M READY, HE THOUGHT. LET IT HAPPEN. HOW LONG HAS IT BEEN? LET IT BE

now. He heard Diana scream into her bonds.

Now faced with it, with whatever this was, there came up in him uncertainty such as he had not felt in millennia, and he did not know, he could not tell if it was, it could not be, no, he could not be afraid, could he?

His hands hurt. His ankles hurt.

This is what you want, a part of him said to another part. They can't but what if they can? And another part said, He brings life not death, how could he end death, you're death? And then came calm sadness back again.

"What do you think you can do?" he whispered to Alam. "You can't bring death to me." Across the room, he saw Caldwell look at him with new attention, mouth his name.

"What I'm going to give you," Alam whispered back, "is life."

Oh, there it was. Belief, in Unute, again. Hope. If he's Vayn's chosen one, if he can bring life, my endlessness is ended. Because whatever it is (I am), endless life is not life. I am not alive, so what will life do to me?

And he shook the shackles again, and this time he knew that he was not trying to fight or struggle but to stretch his arms and chest forward, to lean into whatever this was.

Alam said, "I'm going to give you so much fucking life."

He brought his hands down. Unute felt a hard edge like that of a nail between his eyes. A rising sluice of something beneath. Alam put his other hand on Unute's chest. Light surged.

. . .

BLUE-WHITE OUT OF ALAM, INTO UNUTE. HE SNAPPED INTO RIGIDITY LIKE

stone. Nerves and muscles, marrow, and for the first time since that subterranean house of pain, another's light overtook his sight, and he could not breathe and was full, full, fuller of life. He was bloating with it, expanding, as if he grew heavier and lighter at once, as if he would explode.

Beyond the bright glow Caldwell mouthed his name again. Keever gazed. Diana shook. Shur's smile was of triumph.

Unute felt something tug at him, again, more powerful now in all this new life, pulling hard, stronger than emotion.

He shook, his body effervesced, felt himself suspended in the air bent backward as if held in strong arms, felt the boundary between himself and the universe begin to breach, and he started to fight because he could tell that this very life would be the end of him. That he was overflowing, his edges quantum spume like foam on waves, like the shrill call of stars behind matter, not dying, never dying, but too small to contain all this life, his remorselessly reknitting flesh fighting and overwhelmed by the scattering of his self, not death but life so utter it diffused him throughout the everything, sprawled him so wide lost, everywhere and nowhere, that this was how he would disappear, his edges blurred, his I stretching so omnipresent, so thin, it would be with immortality more ego-eradicating than any mortal death, and maybe that was as it should be, he thought, in another great wave of surrender.

More caustic life went through him, and strengthened him too strong, drew him up and dangled him and his arms and legs flew apart and the world winced at that ontological crack of his shackles and life went into whatever it was that moved again, that moved against his skin, in his pocket?

What?

It was not some inner tug made haptic.

Boisterous with the spillover of his new overwhelming energy, reviving what had been all but spent, tugging out of him as he might from an egg. The jigsaw piece. It tore through the cloth of his clothes, into the air, spinning, before his eyes.

Everyone in the room stared at the hovering thing.

"What did you do?"

Blearily, through the terrible pain of life, Unute recognized Shur's voice. He turned his eyes; she was looking not at him but at Alam.

"I told you never to make one!" she screamed. "I said I'd go if you ever, ever did!" Something too deep and resonant in her voice and a look of rage and revulsion in her eyes.

"I didn't even mean to," Alam shouted. "He brought it in and left it on his chair and when I picked it up I just brimmed into it and when it moved I could feel it, sometimes I could see through it, as if it had eyes! How could I not? Why shouldn't I? Aren't I life? You were never supposed to see it, but I was using it! To find what we were looking for, though!" He was pleading. "For the mission you gave me!"

"You fool!" Shur shouted.

"But it was all used up!" Alam said. "It was gone!"

The thing was full again now, of new ruach, spirit-breath, the over-spill from Unute, realive, reawakened, stinking of love and hate. And how was it that Unute could feel those emotions, essence and mis-sion, pouring out of it, subliming off it with its own surplus quiddity, the energies of revivification?

How could he feel this was a little echo of something he'd once dismantled in the bowels of a ship, that it was born an avatar of life itself to be allergen to its own opposite. So how did it not burn him now? And why had its looming ancestor, brought to being by Vayn's bloodline precisely to hunt him with the energies of her lightning, not felt him enter that ship's hold? How had he surprised it? Was he not its purpose, was he not death, her obverse? How then did its energies not negate him? Yes, that wood-limbed thing had weakened him when he fought it, with its own too-much-life, a preview of this at-tempt, but he had overcome it. And now, why was Unute not the ob-ject of the blistering focus of this its tiny accidental descendant, this mooncalf feral love token? And where, against what, if not him, was its hate directed?

andbut

Unute heard Diana spitting her gag free, shouting, "It's a lie she's lying to both of you!

The Thowless isn't death! It's stillness!

shouting, "Alam's not your opposite, Unute, his lightning's blue, too!"

THROUGH MAELSTROMING VISION, UNUTE SAW THE LITTLE TABBED PIECE

twist, spitting lightning as well, lightning as full of agon, seeking out the opposite of energy, to negate its essence, and he saw Stonier stare at it in shock and recognition as the thing spun like an ill-shaped wheel, straight for Shur.

Who as it came stared at Alam with shock and the fury of betrayal and

grabbed a bone saw with a speed beyond Unute's own, brought it down upon the trinket, to split it into two with a deathlike clapping sound.

Stonier cried out.

"They were never venomous to me," Unute whispered. He hung still, racked by the pain of toomuchlife.

Where did Vayn go? "Where did Vayn go?" he gasped.

Alam looked at him. And, louder, Unute said again, "Where did Vayn go?

"Stonier," he shouted. "Shur killed your token because it knows she's not of Alam's party. The made-alive don't hate death, what they hate is *entropy*, Alam, Vayn had me, clearer than you do now, and when I came back, she wouldn't hurt me anymore. She tried to tell me something. But it was me, I . . ." Unute winced and made a sweeping motion, as if wiping lipstick from a mirror, paint from a wall. "She'd been lied to. Alam, you've been lied to."

Someone was shouting, saying it was too late to change his mind now. Unute kept on, louder than what was tearing his body apart.

"At first Vayn thought she was life and I was death. It was a lie! Alam, I'm not death and you're not life. *Our lightning is the same.*"

He turned about himself.

"My fathermother and your grandmotherfather were never enemies," he said. "Vayn and I weren't enemies. You and I aren't enemies."

and all that toxic new bloating life roared out of him and he fell and smacked against the gurney and to the floor and lay amid the wet of sweat and fizzing blood, and his skin crackled, trying to regrow, with the sweet relief of not so much life within him.

He stood. Scanned the room, tremulous as a baby. To see Stonier staring, and Diana bleary-eyed and Caldwell blinking and mouthing words and Keever with the stunned expression of a newborn, and Shur, in her fury, and Alam.

Alam shook his head. "No."

"You know it's true," Unute said. "Your lightning. Vayn's in the cave was blue, too. It was never red, it was never some 'gift' to fix me, whatever that was. Vayn told me she'd been lied to, and then she disappeared."

"If she realized, why didn't she tell you the whole truth?" Alam shouted.

" . . . She tried to," Unute said. He pointed at Shur.

"It was her who told you about your mission, wasn't it, Alam?" he said. "She told you what you are. She lied. You bring change. So did Vayn. And so do I. It's not life versus death, it's change versus entropy. Motion against the Thowless. You and me, we're of the first. Your grandmother and my father were the *same force.* Shur . . . she wants this because she's with the other. She wants to weaken change, I'm the strongest there's ever been, and she can't end me. No one can. Except maybe you. You're being played. You're being played," he said. "Brother."

Alam screamed. A double agent against himself, an enemy of everything except that utter rest which is no relief.

And he stopped screaming. And into the quiet, the tiny mimicry of that quiet that is entropy's endpoint and desire, came a new sound.

An ending. A shot.

Alam flew backward, arcing blood.

Shur stood with hate and misery on her face, her pistol out, smoking. "His inheritance was always dilute," she said to Unute at last. "If he won't end you, I'll end him. At least one of you'll be gone."

She aimed then at Diana. Unute leaped into the bullet's path.

He took the impact and braced himself for another. But she half-lowered her weapon hand.

"So many years," she said. She spoke the first language Unute had ever known. That echo below her voice was audible again, her lips not quite moving with the words emerging from the dark of her mouth. The dark of her eyes grew darker, and cold. "Looking out of whatever shrill meat I pressed my way into, disgusting as it was, riding the noise and motion of flesh, to find you. To find those who can stop you. To interrupt your fucking mission."

A noise of weapons and preparation came from the corner of the room. "Stonier!" Unute said. He gestured hard with his hands, trailing the stubs of the shackles. Hold, he indicated. Hold fire.

Shur raised her pistol abruptly. Unute leaped between her and Stonier. But she pointed her weapon up through her own chin.

Unute lunged for her, slammed his hand between the muzzle and her skin. She pulled the trigger anyway.

A muted roar. The bullet splintered his bones, passed through, searing, on up through the soft skin behind the smile that grew on her as Shur met Unute's eyes, her own eyes widening as the metal traveled her byways, opening the back of her head, and her thoughts and their container and her malevolence and mercy and the secret motivations that led her here rose out of her with the dregs of undying blood from Unute's hand.

Pure absence looked out at him through her eyes.

Shur exhaled smoke and blood that looked as dark as tar, and as she fell her eyes stayed on Unute, and from behind her ruined teeth, in that further voice, from beyond the darkness inside her, in that old language, he heard, Another time.

UNUTE TURNED AWAY FROM THE BODY OF THE CHAMPION OF THAT OLD trickster, silence.

From the floor, Alam stared at him. Fading.

Come back, Unute thought. He said, "Come back. Now's the time. Your mission isn't to kill me, it's to make change. I change things in my way, you in yours. Do it. Do your change! Change yourself. Kill your death."

Alam blinked, said nothing.

"Put your hands on yourself," Unute said. "You can. You know you can. Do it."

Did Alam smile? He strained. He gasped and lifted his arms. His lips moved.

"Kill your death," Unute said. Alam held his gaze, slowly put his hands down on the floor again. "No!" Unute said. He took hold of Alam's hands with his own and dropped them onto Alam's sopping chest, and Alam closed his eyes and let them fall.

Unute ran his hands across the floor. "Where is it?" he said. "Where's the caruncle?" He clasped Alam's hands. "Put it on your forehead!" When he released the hands, they fell again.

How long was he there? How long were any of them there, with Shur folded over and emptied, and Alam dying and dead?

After a time the door opened and Unute heard soldiers' boots come in.

"Stand easy, soldier," Unute heard Keever say, in a faltering voice. When he spoke again, it was stronger. "Everyone stand down. Give Unute space. Give him time. Give him whatever he needs."

. . .

WEEKS AND COUNTRIES THENCE.

A woman rose through the hot concrete of a stairwell and turned her key in her door and entered and closed it behind herself. Stood very still, listening.

She said, not loud but loud enough, and careful to control her voice, "Who's here?"

"Fadila." A voice from her front room.

It was full of light. A man sat on the sofa, stroking her tortoiseshell cat. She looked into his calm dark eyes. He nodded in greeting and stared across the room, to the shahada in vivid black upon pale gray, executed in fine Kufic script, hanging next to an etching of a sad figure interwoven with lines of Polish poetry.

"My mother," said Fadila. She pointed at the calligraphy.

"Yes," Unute said. "It's lovely. I wasn't sure if she was religious."

"I don't think she was," Fadila said. She lit a cigarette and spoke through the smoke. "But she loved the Quran."

"And that too," he said. Gestured at the poem. "I know whose that was." She inclined her head. He smiled and stood so that the cat leaped from him with graceful irritation. He walked to the frame and read aloud, translating from the Polish into his courtly Arabic.

"When I die ... bear my coffin, through a tunnel of horrors, to its far virgin noiseless soil ... Knowing no seasons, frozen in timelessness." He raised an eyebrow and glanced at Fadila and back at the words. "'The tale springs endlessly from itself, is thoroughly endless.' I don't know if I should be amused or flattered or insulted. Your great-great-grandfather never showed me this."

"You're no translator," Fadila said. "That was bullshit."

"I'm sure. You try doing justice to Leśmian. Still, I think we can agree on the gist. And the reference."

She took a drag.

"What is it? A virus? That someone who works with you gets infected with a little bit of your longevity? I had no business meeting my great-great-grandfather. Let alone talking about his favorite poetry with him."

"Generally, the people in my vicinity have their spans truncated more often than extended, Fadila."

"Why did you leave it with him?" she said. "The first time? It should have gone straight back to Warsaw, no? Wasn't that the whole method?"

"I thought he'd take it back there for me. But he'd met your great-great-grandmother by then. He liked it here. And I liked him. Methods come and go."

She looked at him in frank surprise. She stubbed out her smoke.

"You want the book," she said. "Where did you end and where did you restart this time?" She sighed. "What now? You don't need to patronize me with small talk . . ."

"Fadila." The way he spoke her name, she turned to face him.

"Listen," Unute said. The cat wound between his feet and he whispered a kiss at it. "What I came to say is thank you. I'll never come again. You're right. Your life's your own. You've honored your mother enough."

She was still and quiet a long moment. "You want the Book of Elsewhere yourself . . . ?" she said. "Have you got a new plan to figure it out . . . ?"

"I figured it out."

She gaped. She had never seen anyone look so sad.

"This'll sound like a fairy tale," he said. "It'll sound like something to tell children. I'm sorry about that—if I could persuade the universe to be less trite, I would. But I don't write the script. It turns out that figuring things out just pushes things back a step." He looked out her windows and down at the traffic.

"After a long time trying to understand, I know why I rise elsewhere, sometimes," he said. "When I lose my—" He paused. In English, he said, "Egg tooth." Continued in Arabic again: "When I lose that, from my body, which rarely happens—normally it just gets reabsorbed—when I little-die, whatever it is I am drifts to a new safe place, while I grow a new one. To split my way out at last. Occasionally the egg tooth comes off, and when it does, it grows again while I'm in the elsewhere. So. Mystery solved, right? Code cracked." He smiled. "Leaving, in its wake, the questions of why I grow an egg tooth, and why its loss untethers me. And what I am. And why. And when I will end, and everything."

"Your body," she said. "You may not like morals-of-the-story but it sounds like your body does. It's your body that's doing this, after all. When it needs to end a chapter."

He inclined his head, very slowly, in what could have been agreement or demurral.

"Anyway, you didn't get nothing out of all this," she said. "You can't tell me that didn't feel special."

"What?"

"How long has it been?" she said. "What a thrill to find words you don't know in all languages. What the fuck is an egg tooth?"

He actually laughed.

"The Book of Elsewhere's yours," he said after a silence. "Do what you want with it. Burn it for warmth. Wipe up shit with it. Sell it to an antiquity junkie and never work again—some of those early inserts should turn some heads. Thank you for keeping it. I know the answer, and, as ever, that's everything or nothing. Or neither."

"Or both," she said.

"Whatever it is," he said, "it's the truth, and it's all there is."

WINTER CAME IN STRONG. THE BIRDS FLEW QUICKLY. THE DAYS DARKENED.

Unute was looking into the forest when Diana came in.

"Welcome back," she said. "It is a wonderful view and it's wasted on you."

"You think because I've seen things before, I don't want to see them again?" B said.

"No," she said. She turned to face him. "It's wasted because you're barely ever here." He paced the big room. "You can't even sit behind the desk. You're like a cheetah in a zoo." He sat. "Stonier's gone," Diana said at last. "Broke out."

She would not look directly at B as he lowered his head to the desk, but she could make out in her peripheral vision that when he rose again, he gave an exaggerated laugh.

"Ultra-secure cell, huh?" he said.

"Malfunctions," she said. "You don't seem surprised."

"How did Shur know?" he said after a while. "That you knew something? When you went to see her."

"I don't know," she said. "Something I said, or how I said something. I don't know. I still don't even know what I knew. I turned, and . . . I don't know what she did to me."

"Derived from a poisonous beetle, apparently," Unute said. "Before she roughed you up."

"I thought it was some Thowless power at first," Diana said. "Lucky me."

Not with that body, Unute thought. That vehicle. "You OK now?" he said.

"I spent days puking, but I'm over the worst of it."

"Be glad she wasn't sure what you did know. You wouldn't be here."

"How's Keever?" she said.

"OK," he said slowly. "For a guy who came back from the dead."

"He knows?" she said.

"We could hardly keep it from him. He's . . ." He shrugged. "He actually seems like he's OK. He's exercising a lot."

"Taking his mind off it?" Diana's voice was incredulous.

"So?" B said. "Maybe that's part of the problem: everyone thinking it must be a big deal makes it a big deal. Maybe it doesn't have to be."

"You can show him the ropes," she said. "Now he's a new member of the smallest club in the world."

"Not as small as I'd thought," Unute said. "Not big, maybe, but not as small as I'd thought. Alam . . . I called him my brother, but technically he wasn't even my half brother, he was my however-many-times nephew. From my half sister's kid."

"Why did he do that to himself?" Diana said. "He could have . . ."

She placed her hands upon her chest.

"Spend centuries as a drifter," B said, "then get given a purpose then you find out that purpose was a lie? That'll mess you up."

Diana hesitated.

"What does this mean about the source?" she said, carefully.

"I'm its tool, I guess," Unute said. "And so was Vayn. She figured it out. And wanted nothing to do with it."

"You think she's still out there, don't you?" Diana said.

"Yes, I don't die. Why should she?"

"Alam died."

"He was dilute. Poor fool!"

Diana turned to look at him, at the tenor of his voice.

"She had a child," he said. "At least one."

"So?"

"So she's my sister. Why can't I?"

A vein of cold passed through the room.

"There's still a lot to learn," Diana said. She could have winced, but Unute was kind. He nodded as if what she had said was not an idiocy.

"Let's keep at it, I guess," he said. "You can still help me. I can still help you."

"And Caldwell?" Diana said. "You know not to trust him now. Him and his . . . cult."

"Maybe you can get some information from him," he said. "About that."

"Yeah, wish us luck with that," Diana said. "I know you've visited him."

There in his white robes, in his white hospital cell. Investigating the stab wounds that the jigsaw piece, that furious memento, had left. Which remained there still, only half-healed, and he still alive as he should not be. Making no sense at all. Whatever the state of Alam's powers when he'd exercised them on Caldwell, all they'd needed was his pass and the egg tooth.

"Maybe he'll come back a bit," Diana said. "Like I say, not that you can trust him."

"I don't trust any of you," he said.

"Maybe having been dead awhile will calm him down a bit," she said.

"I doubt it," Unute said. "It takes more than a little death to change people." He went toward the door. "I'll be back in a few days."

"Where are you going now?"

"To see a friend. To say goodbye."

"Shur," Diana said at last. "Who . . . what was she? We know she found Alam. We know she managed to spread rumors about herself in the right networks, put ideas in Keever's head, and he got this in motion. That's all we've got. We know she falsified her records when she got wind that we were recruiting, OK—"

"She must have thought her ship had come in," he said. "She's got to have been watching for any opportunity, ever since Alam found out from Thakka where we are. She had nothing to do with Ulafson, by the way. That was long before—Shur couldn't have persuaded him to do what he did. I wondered, at one moment. But." He set his face. "But his feelings were his feelings. If it hadn't been that, it would have been something else, she'd have found something else to get in on. But it was that."

"That's just it," Diana said. "How did she do what she did? People said she was great. She can't have really been a therapist. What, she trained up, fast? It's like a joke. About how easy it is to pretend to be one. Like they're all charlatans."

"You don't think that," he said. "Like you say, she was helping people. Some people, sometimes. You know you'll make a big deal out of the fact that I know how to do certain things that surprise you, and I'll just remind you that I've been around long enough to learn a lot of things. Well . . ." he said, and raised his eyebrows. Diana stared.

"You think she was like you?" she said.

"Clearly not," he said. "It's not like she got up again. But we don't know how long she'd been around. We know she knew how to do that. How to falsify records pretty flawlessly." He closed his eyes. Anyone else, you would have said he had remembered something. "Maybe she's not the point. She was a vessel. I used to hear things . . . You heard, at the end." He glanced at her and she could see he was uncertain.

"And if she was only around as long as it looked like—what, sixty years? Sixty-five?—we don't know what it was that was looking out from behind her eyes," he said. Diana stared at him.

"What was it she said to you?" she said. "What was that language? At the end?"

"She—it—expressed frustration," he said. "It told me it was intending to stop my mission. That was *its* mission."

"What does that mean?" Diana said.

"You heard," he said. "It was the opposite of change."

"And . . ." Diana steepled her fingers. "That means that you're change."

He inclined his head.

"Me, the pig, Vayn . . . You, too, though. Maybe not as powerful, not as much of a threat to what it pines for, but no less boisterous. And it really hates that."

"So, what? Kill you, end everything?"

"Hardly," he said. "But it's a classic tactic, isn't it? Take out your enemy's big guns first? It would be," he said, "a start."

Diana folded her arms. "Where do you think we stand with all this?" she said.

"On guard, would be my suggestion. It'll take some time to regroup, but time it has. Let me ask you something, Diana. Do you think," he said, "that change came first, or changelessness?"

"The latter," she said. "It had to be still for change to register."

"But without the change, it wasn't changelessness, it was just nothing."

"So you're saying change came first?" Diana said.

"No," he said. "I'm saying I don't know. But I'm saying they've both been around a very long time. And they both have agents. It thinks I'm one of them."

"Told you you were a tool," she said. "You going to get on with your mission? Or is 'do what you're for' maybe a better way to put it?"

"If I find out what that is, I'll decide," he said.

It was not silent while they did not speak. They listened to the birds.

"What happened with Stonier?" Unute said at last.

She shrugged apologetically. "He hadn't spoken for days. He hadn't opened his eyes for days. He kept whispering though—mics couldn't pick it up—and all the guards'll say was that his mouth looked full of shadows. And then one night…he's gone. The cameras all stopped working. By the time security got there, the room was empty. The window just…fell apart. As if it was thousands of years old. He stepped through and walked away. They checked the cameras: they were rusted and frozen and full of dust."

"Getting closer to the heat death," Unute said. "Everything getting cold and old. You can't be that surprised either. You don't think this is the end of this any more than I do."

MIDNIGHT. A WADI WITHOUT A NAME. A MAN TRUDGED OUT OF NOTHING and nowhere, weighed under a great pack. His feet sank into the sand, and he slid and slowed but did not stop. The moon came up and shone upon him and he arranged his cloak around himself.

Below the level of the sea, overlooked not by rock but by dense and jagged earth. He took the pack from his back and lowered it to the ground. Pulled out the great weight within with as much care as if it were a child. He laid it down. He ran his hand over the pulsing leather of its surface. He put his lips to it. He whispered to it, too quietly for anyone to hear. He watched. He was watching when the sun came up and his skin began to burn. He was watching when the sun was overhead and the shadows all bleached away. He watched when the moon returned.

Toward the second dawn, after hours of motionlessness, the egg twitched. The man watched. He held his breath. From within, a point like a spear pushed through it, stretched the fleshy membrane, splitting it, and out blurted a sopping pool of thick liquid. The rip grew wider, and out of the shade within spilled the raw pink body of a babirusa. Sharp bladed teeth. It lay wheezing.

"Welcome," Unute whispered.

The pig kicked, and staggered, and stood, and turned around and saw him. He sat still. A shudder passed all the way through its body.

"Not used to seeing me so quickly," Unute whispered.

The pig hunched. It stared at him.

"You don't have to," he whispered.

The pig spun. Found its footing.

"You don't have to," the man whispered.

It emitted its first sound, a horrid scream, into the desert night. It stamped, tusks shining, skin still growing upon it. The man put his hands out ready, and as it came for him, he turned it gently away.

The pig ran at him again, and he took hold of its tusks and shook his head. It stayed still. It watched him. He released it. The sun rose. The light grew strong and the pig slavered and ran at him once more and this time when he grabbed it he pulled it close, embraced it, rolled with it so they writhed in the dust, lay gasping in the sand.

After they had lain still awhile, taking back their breath, the man relaxed his grip and let the pig crawl free. It stood and turned. It looked at him. It tossed its head. Unute nodded.

He said, "I came to say hello. And goodbye. To set you on your way, brother."

The pig turned to face the sun. Looked right at it, full on, as you must not.

"Go well," the man said.

It waited, and watched him. He frowned, looked down. He rummaged for a while in the slurry below the egg. And smiled. Showed no surprise.

He raised in his fingertips the tiniest shard of keratin, fallen from a tusk. A protuberance the babirusa did not even need.

The pig threw its head down and back. It turned away, to face the sun again. The pig began to walk. The man watched it and it did not turn. So it did not see when he waved to it, though he waved to it for a long time, until it was gone from his sight.

The Doctor's Story

For one who holds himself to be an agent of, if not the Angel of, Death, my patient has always been a most gracious and thoughtful interlocutor.

One day at the end of our course of sessions, he told me a story. When it was done, he rose from the couch and turned and shook my hand, thanked me, told me I had been helpful to him, which I hope was not only politeness, expressed his own hope that he had been of help to me, as he had, though in ways that have disturbed me greatly, and informed me that I would not see him again.

I have thought of him often, and spoken of him to no one. Why would I give ammunition to those who believe me a charlatan? It has come as a surprise to me, in these my final days, that I am moved—driven—to write down the truth that there is at least one man who, repressed by death, always returns.

My patient had told me such baroque and freighted specificities of his endless life—eggs and pigs and blood and frenzy and the loss of the self like the oceanic release of the mystic. Were they stranger than his basic nature?

I remember once, perhaps the only time I ever saw him lost for words. While he lay there, alluding to some event that had happened before my great-great-great-grandmother was born, he said to me, "I do not forget anything, Herr Doktor. My memory is perfect."

This piqued me so greatly that I interrupted him—something I never do.

"Mr. ——," I said. "You have shown me enough that I do not doubt you when you say that. But I do not think that means what you seem to believe it does. You are a man, are you not?"

He was hesitant on that point. I am not.

"A most extraordinary man, as you could not but be," I said. "But what you feel and the fact that you feel at all place you within the range of the human. If you thought that was not the case you would not have come to me. And you came to me, I think, because you know something of the unconscious."

"And so?" he said.

"So you must know that there is a dark sea within you. That no memory is an exact recording. That to remember what you did cannot tell you why you did it. Do you not dream, Mr. ——? What are your dreams? Have you ever been unsure whether something you remembered was a memory or a dream?"

"No," he said.

I said, "How would you know?"

To that he had no answer. I believe he enjoyed this exchange.

The fact of him, the rising necessity within him, were crucial provocations, I have said. The final impetus to my intellectual revolution came from the story he told me on the last day of our acquaintance.

He told me of the babirusa that echoed his own life. That, he told me, might enter any room he was in, at any time, to try to kill him, again, for a final time.

"It must be very hard to live with so relentless and unchosen a drive," he said at last. "It did its best to end it another way, once." I waited for more. He continued, as I had hoped he would.

"Have you been to Gothenburg?" he said. "The truth is, I do not know if it could enter any room, anymore. Perhaps those days are over. Perhaps matters have changed. The last time I encountered it, I sought it, not the other way around."

"Why?" I said.

"This was more than two centuries ago. Go to Gothenburg. You'll see." I waited. "I had been seeking it for a long time. It had returned to the kinds of lands where it was born. I approached it as I always did, when I had to—guarded, careful, ready to do what was necessary.

"I was the only person on that little island," he said, and there was about his voice a sadness such as I had never heard. "And it was the only pig. I sought it in the interior. I found it. I heard it breathing. I smelled its strong smell. I saw a great body, lying down, wheezing, flanks rising. I came closer.

"The pig eyed me. It watched me come."

From his pocket my patient drew out a photograph. He passed it to me.

HJORTSVIN, I read, from a label on a display case. Above it was a skull in a vitrine, the fleshless remains of a pig head. Two lower tusks splayed out and back like the runners of a sled. Of the upper tusks, curling skyward from midway down the snout, the left was gone. Pre- or postmortem was impossible to say.

But it was the top right tooth that demanded attention. It arced back toward the forehead, the central line. The tooth tip came down right in the middle, above and between the eyes. Pushed through, made a hole therein. Ground it with the tusk itself. The tusk shoved into the dark inside the skull, centimeters deep into its own brainpan. To gnaw on its own thoughts.

"No one knows what they do with those tusks," my patient said, starting me back into the room. "But they constantly keep growing."

He gestured at the picture.

"I can't tell you what all this means. Only that if you ask me why it is that it was a babirusa that was born with something to it like whatever there is in me, why it is that it should be a deer-pig in particular that lives forever, I'll point you to that skull."

Weeks of pressure, a press against the skin, the shove of it, the split, the scratch and scrawling against the bone as the pig's jaw moved, self-scrimshanding with every bite. The grind. This was not the work of one tough grimace and the freedom of insight or death or both but long-drawn-out growth, a dreadful patience.

"This is an animal whose own teeth will try to kill it," he said.

"Or enlighten it," I said.

His brow furrowed. Which surprised me, because I had noted instantly the location where tusk punctured skull. At the spot of the ajna chakra. The pig had self-trepanned at the locus of mystical consciousness.

"Yes," he said. "Perhaps.

"All that fight," he said, "all that rage that I'd seen for lifetimes, was gone. What it looked at me with when I saw it that last time was tiredness. I came closer. It did nothing.

"It had not worn down its tusks on wood. The whole of this life—it must have taken years. It must have leaned on the tusk, as it grew, for hours every day, pushing it, curving it in toward the center of its head."

He touched his own forehead again.

"It must have been pushing thus for months. Through skin and bone.

"It tried to move. Not to fight. To raise its snout toward me. There was within its eye a terrible look of pain, and of determination. I sat with it, I put my hand upon it, I wished it peace. I still do.

"I waited with it, seeing in the deeps of its eye the pig thoughts scrambled by its own bone through that infected wound. I whispered to it, soothing it when I saw fear. It lay and breathed weakly, waiting to die. I sat with it. Its suicide took days. My poor brother's tooth grew steadily but slow."

He was silent awhile, and I was silent too.

When the man who would soon not be my patient anymore rose to leave, I thanked him for all he had told me, and he thanked me for my patience.

"Mr. ——," I said. He turned to look at me. "You've told me you don't wish to be a metaphor. But you do not get to choose. You have described to me the cocoon in which you return. Out of which you are reborn. Which encompasses your old body, or is constituted out of it. Mr. ——, I am sure, knowing everything that you do, that you know a great deal about butterflies. Perhaps more than do I. Yet our minds are perverse. Sometimes it is as if we write a message for ourselves and efface it in the very motion of writing. As if we strive to tell ourselves a truth and to obscure it at once. One thing seems not to have occurred to you.

"You came to me," I said, "asking if I could help you. And you have made it clear that this does not mean to die, but to become mortal. Now, what every child knows is that a grub enters a chrysalis and emerges as a butterfly. But that is not correct. A caterpillar in a cocoon, a grub in its case, a maggot in its pupa—they do not change form, but break down. They become a chemical Urschleim. Their body, their brain quite gone. They are nothing. And out of those chemicals of their destruction self-organizes quite another animal. The butterfly, the moth, is a newborn constituted of the dead flesh of another. A pupa is not a place for regeneration or revivification. It is an execution chamber and a birthing room, all at once.

"You came to me seeking to understand yourself, and mortality. You are mistaken. You seek to be able to die as if you have not died and died and died again. You are not immortal, sir, but mortal countless times. You are infinitely mortal."

We stood quite still, for a long time.

"Herr Doktor," he said at last. "I suppose I must ask you, in turn, whether there is any difference between those two."

"I believe there is," I said. "And I believe you know that now. And you will not forget knowing that, though you may no longer feel about it as you do now. Memory is a labyrinth. But that too you now know."

He held my eye and I saw surprise again upon his face.

I saw wonder.

ACKNOWLEDGMENTS

Our deepest thanks to: Celia Albers, Pam Alders, Laura Bonner, Ben Brusey, Season Butler, Mic Cheetham, Stephen Christy, Keith Clayton, Bill Crabtree, Cara DuBois, Richard Elman, Maya Fenter, Chris Fioto, Regina Flath, Matilda Forbes Watson, Matt Gagnon, Ron Garney, Rafael Grampá, Alexandra Grant, Ben Greenberg, Eric Harburn, Ashleigh Heaton, Tori Henson, Matt Kindt, Alex Larned, Julie Leung, Cheryl Maisel, Erin Malone, David Moench, Tricia Narwani, Jordan Pace, Mary Pender, Ramiro Portnoy, Sue Powell, Elizabeth Rendfleisch, Ross Richie, Clem Robins, Filip Sablik, Keith Sarkisian, Scott Shannon, Sabrina Shen, Scott Sims, Team BOOM!, Leila Tejani, Bonnie Thompson, Julien Thuan, Meredith Wechter, and Adam Yoelin.

As a remarkably eclectic actor, KEANU REEVES has made an indelible mark on the world of entertainment through the diverse roles he has played. He is best known for his starring roles in *The Matrix* and *John Wick* franchises. Reeves made his comic book writing debut in 2021 with *BRZRKR*, a twelve-issue and graphic-novel limited series distributed through BOOM! Studios, which quickly became the highest-selling original comic book series debut in more than twenty-five years. In 2023, he returned to the big screen in *John Wick: Chapter 4*, which became the highest-grossing film in the franchise. His other recent projects include *The Matrix Resurrections, John Wick: Chapter 3 – Parabellum, Always Be My Maybe, Toy Story 4*, and the video game *Cyberpunk 2077*. Raised in Toronto, Reeves performed in various local theater productions and on television before relocating to Los Angeles.

CHINA MIÉVILLE is a *New York Times* bestselling author of fiction and nonfiction. His novels include *The City & The City, Embassytown*, and *Perdido Street Station*. A recipient of the Guggenheim Fellowship for Fiction, Miéville has won the World Fantasy, the Hugo, and the Arthur C. Clarke Awards, among others. His nonfiction includes a study of international law and a history of the Russian Revolution.

chinamieville.net